SECOND SON

By Derek Blount

Happy Prince Media, LLC

For information, contact Happy Prince Media, LLC at info@happyprincemedia.com.

Visit us on the Web:
happyprincemedia.com
derekblount.com

FIRST EDITION

Print ISBN 978-0-9967006-2-7

E-book ISBN 978-0-9967006-3-4

For Bethany.

Always.

PROLOGUE
MAY 2

"THANK YOU FOR YOUR TIME, ma'am. Sorry for any inconven—"

The door slammed shut. Eric Johnson was just nimble enough to jump a half-step back, thus saving his nose from serious injury. He dropped the smile.

"The city of New York appreciates your cooperation," he said to the closed door loudly enough to elicit a colorful though muffled response from the other side.

"That's not actually possible for me to do to myself," Eric replied. "Basic human anatomy."

He turned and walked down the dingy corridor toward the front of the building. When it came to investigating crimes—or in this case, tracking down a very specific criminal—Eric had a nice arsenal when dealing with witnesses or persons of interest. Sometimes being friendly helped. The fact that he was young and handsome rarely hurt the situation. Sometimes having the same color skin as the individual he was interviewing was a benefit. But sometimes, the only color that mattered was the gold of his badge. He had not been welcome at address number six. Worse yet, it turned out there was nothing to be discovered at that location anyway. A waste of time and time was precious.

The sun shone on the other side of the glass door as he approached. George was already waiting in the car. Eric retrieved a pen from his jacket pocket and held up his notepad as he walked. Number six joined the first five as Eric scrawled a thick line of black ink across the address. Bust. Half the day spent and a big bag of nothing to show for it.

He looked to the next address. Brooklyn. He tucked the pen and pad back into one jacket pocket and removed his sunglasses from the other.

"On to lucky number seven." Spinning, he backed into the door, put on his sunglasses in a fluid motion, then strode into the light of day.

◇ ◇ ◇

The building stood among its brothers in the oldest part of Brooklyn. Dreary gray. Six stories high. Anonymous.

Putrid.

Maybe it was the heat. Nothing like the temperature breaching the nineties to really bring out the flavor of the stench. The garbage thrown from windows, beer bottles and fast food bags, dog feces on the sidewalk, dried vomit by the entrance and aged urine in the hall on the first floor. The building was a cornucopia of offensive odors.

Clive Quinn stood on the sidewalk and breathed deeply. One more smell he could identify. Death. Oh yes, death had been here. What he didn't know was how recently and whether it was his prey that was responsible.

He considered it possible, even likely, that the man he had come to find had killed someone here. Perhaps several someones. But this was not a good neighborhood. Death visited these buildings with great frequency. Sometimes as a victim of crime or drug overdose, other times simply dying of the flu from lack of access to decent health care.

Some would argue that the government should help the residents of this neighborhood more. Quinn would tell those people to kiss his ass. He had served his country, put his life on the line in hellholes all over the world. Had watched his buddies die. And these filthy low-lifes whine because the government doesn't give them enough money to pay for cheap liquor and premium cable. He didn't give a rat's ass what happened to the people living in this building on a daily basis. All he cared about was one. The one he was going to capture, dead or alive.

Quinn glanced to his right and left before leaving the sidewalk and walking up the steps leading to the building's front door. A white man in his late forties. Long brown hair to his shoulders with a handlebar mustache straight out of an old western. Black trench coat, black cowboy hat and mirrored sunglasses. There wasn't much danger of Quinn being mistaken for a resident of this building. Anyone who saw him going into the structure would guess he was there to cause some serious shit. And if anyone noticed the bulge of the twelve-gauge shotgun with the sawed-off barrel protruding from under his coat, their suspicions would be confirmed.

Quinn had been sitting in his car—an old Chevy Nova which looked as if it had been driven through a mine field—for the past twelve hours. He had seen his quarry walk into the building two hours ago with a hooker and a brown paper sack that had to have been holding a hefty bottle of whatever he enjoyed before or after sex. He felt sorry for the hooker. She looked young, couldn't be older than seventeen, with blonde hair, too much eye makeup and a scared look. Couldn't blame her. She had presumably only been hooking for a couple of months based on her appearance. Quinn figured she had probably never seen a guy as big as the one she was walking into the building with, much less been ridden by one.

Of course, by now she might be dead. Quinn felt kind of bad about that. Knowing as much as he did about the giant upstairs, he knew the hooker was probably in for the last ride of her life. But he wasn't in the hero business, and he sure as hell wasn't going to get paid for saving some teenage whore's life. He was here to catch the monster known as Silas Kane, and he wouldn't be able to do that without a little luck and a lot of patience.

Quinn had gone after hundreds of bad-asses during his twenty years as a bounty hunter. Once upon a time, he liked the challenge. He enjoyed finding his mark in a local bar and calling him out. It was particularly nice if the quarry in question thought himself a tough guy.

Especially if they were big. The bigger, the better. They'd have some words. The mark would throw the first punch, and Quinn would proceed to beat the living hell out of him. After two minutes, his target would be a quivering mass on the barroom floor.

The real fun came later. After having taken the mark to wherever he belonged, Quinn would return to the bar the next night and try to provoke a fight out of the local men, knowing that none of them would take him on. He'd have his pick of the women and usually enjoyed the company of one of them in the parking lot. That was what Quinn did in the old days.

Today, he was older, and he liked to think he was wiser too. The value of experience.

Quinn had never been a big man. He was, as his Drill Sergeant once described him, "scrappy". He had been trained as a lethal weapon, and he had learned his lessons well. Only a handful of men had ever given Quinn much of a fight. Most of his targets had only experienced barroom brawls and didn't know how to handle a man schooled in genuine combat. He began to view himself as unstoppable right up until the night he met Donovan Brady. Donny owed money to the wrong people. Mistake number one. Then he left Boston to start a new life without paying what he owed. Mistake number two.

At the time, Quinn had been in the bounty hunting field for a decade, and he had become well known as a dependable hire. He got probably eighty percent of his business from "unsavory" types with ten to fifteen percent under the table from local law enforcement when a suspect needed to be returned to proper jurisdiction without a lot of paperwork. The remainder of his work, like the job today, was culled from an advertisement he kept in *Soldier of Fortune* magazine.

Back then, one of the strong-arm types from Boston had called him with Donny's story. Wanted Quinn to track him down and bring him back to the city, preferably in one piece.

Quinn figured Donny for just another thug, a drunk Irish nobody. It would be the last time Quinn went after someone without doing a thorough background check first. Turned out ol' Donny had once been a weapons specialist for the Irish Republican Army in a previous life. Also turned out he was a bit paranoid, as Quinn learned when he set off the booby trap just inside Donny's back door. The scattershot from the homemade mine filled Quinn's left leg above and below the knee. When Donny walked in with an aluminum baseball bat, Quinn was lying on the floor in a spreading pool of his own blood, unable to defend himself.

Donny didn't kill him. He broke Quinn's jaw, three ribs and his right arm above the wrist. Donny left when he heard approaching sirens. Quinn learned two valuable lessons that afternoon: the practicality of good home security, and to never, ever underestimate your prey. Even today, every time he felt the weather about to change from the swelling in his leg, he remembered that second lesson. He wasn't about to forget it while going after Silas Kane.

Quinn opened the front door and stepped inside the building. He figured Kane would be good for at least an hour and a half of getting drunk and getting laid, and he hoped the additional half hour had given Kane a chance to nod off into post-sex slumber. Quinn didn't want his prey to be conscious when he came for him. If he was awake, that would mean combat, and that would mean one of the men would wind up dead. Quinn didn't relish the thought of the reduced bounty he'd receive if he didn't bring Kane in alive, and he also didn't care for the idea of being killed himself.

Quinn walked to the stairwell and cocked his head, listening. He reached into his coat and unfastened the leg-strap holding the shotgun in place. It now dangled by a single break-away strap over his shoulder. He didn't want to remove it just yet. The last thing he needed was some random resident opening her front door to see him with a gun. She'd surely scream and that would awaken his target, and then there would be hell to pay.

The bounty hunter wasn't sure what to make of the hooker's continued presence. He figured it whittled down to three options—she was dead, she had fallen asleep with Kane or she was one endurance-oriented fuck. The first two options didn't concern Quinn, but the third did. He had broken in on a few guys in the past while they were in the middle of humping a girl—or in one case, another guy—and he could've driven a dump truck up behind them without their noticing. But Kane was different. The normal rules changed when dealing with this guy.

Quinn had spent more time researching Silas Kane than any bounty he had ever gone after. Each fact he turned up led him to believe more research was required. He wasn't about to go after this man without understanding the nature of the beast.

Not many things scared Quinn. Kane did. But money was money.

He took another deep whiff of the hallway odors and climbed the stairs. Death was here. And he was moving toward it.

Quinn walked along the edge of each step to minimize possible creaks. It wasn't necessary. The building wasn't empty. There were a thousand different sounds of daily life happening all around him, but Quinn was working on instinct now.

When he reached the third floor landing, a young woman emerged from a doorway. She stopped for a moment and looked him over, the whiteness of her wide eyes a stark contrast to her dark skin. Quinn smiled a half-smile and tipped the front of his cowboy hat to her. The woman's expression did not change. She sidestepped and proceeded down the stairs at a fast pace.

Quinn attained the fifth floor landing without encountering anyone else. There were six apartments on the floor, three on each side with the hallway running the length of the building to a fire escape window on the opposite end. He knew his prey was in apartment 5B. Kane had only been staying there about a week, and Quinn was lucky to have made good on a tip he received about this building.

Quinn stepped to the side of the apartment's closed door, careful not to let his feet rest in front of the entry point lest they be visible as shadows at the crack between the floor and the door. He removed his hat and leaned his head close. No sounds. No snoring. No humping either. That was probably a good sign.

Quinn replaced his hat and made his way to the end of the hall. The window was fully open. This was no surprise since residents here couldn't afford air-conditioning. Ventilation was sought through any means possible, even in the hallways. The surprisingly hot spring was probably pissing off some of these folks, but that didn't concern Quinn. This worked in his favor.

He put one foot through the opening onto the fire escape landing and ducked his body through the window. Pausing on the landing, Quinn prepared himself. It was time. He was going to have to do this part quickly and hope for the best.

His intent was to sidestep along the ledge around the corner of the building and enter Kane's apartment from the window. Since the windows were open, this would give Quinn a silent entry as opposed to picking the lock on the front door and risking a booby trap. The greatest danger lay in Quinn having to pass three windows belonging to the apartment next door to Kane. Folks who live on the fifth floor tend to make a ruckus when they see someone walking outside their open windows. Quinn would have to move fast or risk Kane being alerted. And if the neighbors did raise an alarm, Quinn would have to make the split-second decision of whether to give up his mission or plunge into the lair of the awakened beast.

Quinn took a deep breath and threw his leg over the railing of the fire escape. He pressed his back against the wall for balance as he found a foothold on the ledge, then he swung his other leg over the rail. The ledge was eight inches wide, leaving the silver-tipped, narrow toes of Quinn's black boots dangling over the edge. Quinn took a series of quick breaths, wished he was fifteen years younger, and started side-stepping his way toward the corner.

◇ ◇ ◇

The unmarked police car, an older model white Crown Victoria, turned the corner fast. The older cop in the passenger seat lurched towards the door more than necessary and furrowed his eyebrows.

"Sweet Mary! Will you take it easy? This is the seventh building on the list, and we've got four more hours on our shift."

The young black man behind the wheel smiled at his partner, but his eyes remained serious, focused.

"It's why cars have seatbelts, George. So we can go fast and catch bad guys. And we're catching this guy. Today."

George O'Brien sighed, as if patience were a burden he had to bear often with the driver. "Eric, I know what he's done. He's the worst of the worst, but I've been doing this for thirty years and I'm telling you, sometimes you gotta take it easy. We've got a dozen suspect apartments on this list, and odds are all twelve will be misses. That's how the game goes. You gotta pace yourself. Treat this as a nine-to-five job. Don't put in the long hours and rush around all for nothing."

"More wisdom from the aged Jedi master," Eric Johnson laughed. "And maybe you're right, but I've got a hunch. You remember those, right? One of these leads is going to be hot, and I don't want to try and pace them until our shift ends. We're going to get this guy."

"Fine. Just try not to kill any pedestrians on your way to catch him," George said, clutching the door for support.

The car rounded another corner at the same fast pace. The building was only eight blocks away now. Not very far at all.

◊   ◊   ◊

Quinn made it from the fire escape to the corner of the building with no problems. The lack of windows on that side of the structure made it an easy trip. He maneuvered his left arm around the corner, feeling the indention of the first of the windows in the brick, it made a good handhold. As he eased his left heel around the corner, Quinn was thankful he wasn't any higher up. Oh, the fall would still kill him if he made a misstep, but at fifty feet off the ground, the wind was not a major factor. Anything higher than ten stories, the wind became a serious problem, especially on the corners.

Quinn kept his back straight and flat against the wall as he stepped around the corner. Not looking down, he risked a glance over his shoulder. Luck. The lights were out in the bedroom of the first apartment. Quinn pulled his right leg around the corner and breathed a sigh of relief. The worst part was still ahead, but at least he wouldn't have to take another corner.

He sidestepped past the bedroom window and looked over his shoulder into the second window. Lights out in the living room as well. He was in luck again. Kane's neighbors weren't home. He shuffled past the next living room window. All the windows in this apartment had been wide open for ventilation. A good sign.

Quinn put his left arm inside the last window to brace himself and swung his body, pivoting on his left foot so that his stomach was now pressed against the brick exterior of the building. He was aligned with the interior wall separating this apartment from the next. He knelt to lower his profile. His knee protested with a sharp pain that faded into a familiar ache. Keeping a tight grip on the window, Quinn leaned past the dividing wall and glanced into the bedroom of Silas Kane.

The light was off, but the window was open and let in ample light. The apartment was just as he had expected. Dank and gray with hardly any furniture, only a dirty mattress on the floor. The plaster on the walls was cracked and peeling. The door to the living room was open and the other two doors in the bedroom were closed. He assumed one was a closet and the other a bathroom. There was no light coming from underneath either door.

Quinn could see the young hooker lying on the mattress, but Kane was nowhere in sight. Two options, Kane was either in the living room or the bathroom. Either way, Quinn had to move. He was at his most vulnerable while clinging to the ledge, and his leg was beginning to cramp from supporting his crouched weight.

Quinn inched forward and ducked his head into the bedroom. Finding a grip on the sill with his hand, he eased himself inside. He took a step toward the girl on the mattress. She hadn't moved. Quinn wasn't sure if she was asleep or dead. She was lying on the mattress face up and spread-eagle. Nothing left to the imagination. She was not a natural blonde.

As Quinn stepped closer, he saw the girl's head lay at a disturbing angle. Her neck had been broken. Severely. He wondered whether Kane had killed her before or after the sex. Maybe it was during. Quinn knelt and cupped one of the girl's breasts. He squeezed it and grinned with nicotine-stained teeth.

His head snapped up toward the living room door. Contemplation of the dead hooker had taken only a couple of seconds, but that was still too long in this situation. Stupid.

No sounds came from the doorway. Quinn extracted the shotgun from his coat and gripped the walnut stock. Decision time.

If Quinn chose to look into the living room first, he would have to put his back against the bathroom door. If Kane was in the bathroom, he could notice Quinn's feet through the crack under the door. On the other hand, if Quinn chose to open the bathroom door first, he risked the almost certain noise of a creaking door alerting Kane in the living room.

Quinn's breathing had become short but remained quiet. His prey was an animal. Sometimes animals can sense when they are being stalked. They can prepare for it. On the other hand, Kane had always been the predator. Odds were that he had never known what it was to be stalked so he may not be in tune with it. It was likely that he got drunk after killing the whore and passed out in the living room. It was also possible that he was waiting for Quinn to make his move, commit himself, before attacking the bounty hunter.

Quinn took a shallow breath, gripped the shotgun until his knuckles were white, and eased toward the living room door, his back to the bathroom.

◇ ◇ ◇

The white Crown Vic parked in a space in front of the building. George pulled out his revolver to check it before getting out of the car. He glanced at Eric who was doing the same.

"Nice thing about the ghetto. There's always ample parking," George said.

"No one calls it the ghetto anymore," Eric replied. He opened the door and stood by the car, head tilted back, staring up at the face of the building. He looked over the top of the vehicle to his partner, who had just stepped out.

"Fifth floor. You up for it, old-timer?"

George half-smiled, "What are the odds they've got a working elevator?"

◇ ◇ ◇

Quinn stared into the living room, eyes wide. Silas Kane sat on the couch, head tilted back with an empty bottle of Jim Beam in his right hand. He was stark naked and deep in sleep. Quinn let out a quiet sigh of relief followed by a disbelieving shake of his head. For ninety-nine percent of the tough guys in the world, if you stripped them down to their birthday suits, you would no longer be intimidated. You'd realize they're only human. A little flab on the belly. The chest a bit deflated. And nine times out of ten they've got a pencil dick, probably explaining their unhealthy aggression.

Silas Kane, as usual, was the exception to this rule. Even sitting, Kane looked tall. Quinn's research told him Kane stood at six-and-a-half feet, but he was now certain the research was wrong. He looked closer to seven.

Kane was a physical specimen. No body fat was evident. Just mound upon hardened mound of muscle. He had to weigh in the three-hundreds. With each sleeping breath, Quinn could see Kane's abdominal muscles tighten and release. Belaying the animal-like appearance was the lack of hair on most of Kane's body. Except below the Mason-Dixon Line. Quinn shook his head again observing the large member springing from the pubic hair and lying on Kane's left leg.

Sumbitch is longer relaxed than mine is with a woody, Quinn thought. He again considered the dead hooker and wondered what went through her mind when Kane was going to work on her with that thing.

A cat screeched in the alley below and the sound of a trash can being knocked over filled the room from the open windows. Quinn held his breath.

Kane's head tilted from right to left, but never lifted from the back of the couch.

Quinn exhaled. That was too close. He crept around the sofa until he was behind Kane. He knelt and placed the shotgun on the floor then reached into the side pocket of the black trench coat and removed a brown bottle with no label. He pulled from the other pocket a white handkerchief attached to the center of a nine inch strip of duct tape.

Quinn slowly peeled the wax paper from the sides of the tape. He had found wax paper to be effective in preventing the tape from sticking to anything in his pocket while also eliminating the horrible sound associated with pulling a strip of tape directly off the roll. The bounty hunter couldn't afford that kind of noise at this point.

He twisted the cap off the bottle and held his breath as he upended the container into the handkerchief. With the cloth soaked, Quinn placed the bottle on the floor and grasped both sides of the duct tape. He moved into a crouch and leaned over, his face directly above Kane's head.

Just as Quinn poised the handkerchief over Kane's mouth, a pounding knock erupted at the door. Kane's eyes snapped open.

◇ ◇ ◇

"NYPD! Open up!"

Eric yelled at the door, his gun drawn. George stood across the hall, his revolver held at shoulder height. Eric banged on the door again.

"I repeat, this is NYPD! Open the door immediately."

From the other side, something struck the door with such force that Eric thought it would explode from the hinges and into the hallway. He and George backed up and looked at each other. Then Eric brought his foot up to kick in the door.

◇ ◇ ◇

As soon as Kane's eyes opened, Quinn brought the tape down hard. Kane's face met the tape as his head lifted from the back of the couch. Quinn's hands boxed Kane's ears, sealing the duct tape onto his cheeks. As the giant leapt to his feet, Quinn grabbed his shotgun off the floor.

The bounty hunter raised the weapon. He had expected Kane would immediately attempt to remove the tape, allowing Quinn the brief window of time to level his gun. But Kane instead lunged over the couch at Quinn, ignoring the tape. The giant hit Quinn in the chest with both hands hard enough to make him drop the gun and fall back against the wall. Kane grabbed him by the front of his trench coat and lifted him off the floor.

It was a surreal feeling. Although not a big man, Quinn had never been physically picked up before, much less by someone who made it seem to take almost no effort at all. Kane threw him forward. Quinn flew into the front door, the back of his head smashing into the wood. He heard a cracking noise that he hoped was a rib and not his skull or spine.

Before Quinn could slump to the dingy carpet, Kane crossed the floor and grabbed him again. This time he tossed Quinn across the room toward the open windows. By blind luck, Quinn angled his body in midflight and managed to strike the center partition between the windows. Glass shattered on either side of him as his elbows went through the window panes. Quinn was certain he had cut himself severely but had other things to worry about. He reached into his coat and tried to grasp the .45 semi-auto he kept for emergencies. He wasn't moving fast enough. His mind was in a fog. He glanced up to see the beast approaching. Was Kane slowing down?

The entire ordeal had lasted thirty seconds, and Kane had yet to remove the tape. Quinn realized the giant might be working in a fog, too. Probably the only reason he was still alive. Kane was four feet away from Quinn when the door exploded inward. Two men burst in with guns drawn and leveled at Kane. The titan spun to face them.

"Hands above your head!" yelled the younger, black cop.

Quinn managed to pull the gun from his coat and leveled it at Kane's back just as the giant dropped to one knee. Then, in slow motion, Kane's immense, naked body slumped forward onto the floor, the chloroform finally doing its job.

Quinn leaned his head back against the window sill and lowered the gun. He fought to keep his senses.

"You two are witnesses," he began, his words slurring as consciousness slipped away. "I had the suspect under control when you got here. I'm now officially relinquishing custody to NYPD. And I'm getting paid..."

CHAPTER 1
October 10
9:55 A.M.

G RANT ARMSTRONG'S DAY had just gone from bad to worse. Reaching London from Cameroon had required too many small planes and taken far too long. His flight from London to the States had then been delayed, forcing him to spend a less-than-pleasant six hours at Heathrow. This was followed by eight hours on the 747 during which he was unable to get any sleep. The family residing in the seats immediately in front of him had made certain of that. The three children were all less than ten years old, yet they shared a hive intelligence that was exceeded only by the evil inside of them. Grant somehow knew they had concocted an intricate plan to sleep in shifts, taking turns crying and creating enough general havoc to keep those passengers surrounding them awake the entire flight. He would have pitied the children's parents but the fact that they seemed oblivious to their offspring's malevolence and slumbered for most of the journey stopped that impulse.

The delay had caused him to miss his connecting flight from Philadelphia to New York. Going through customs in Philly just to catch that next flight had been a beating. He had only gone the Philadelphia route because the fare had been cheaper, but after all the delays, he realized flying direct to Kennedy would have been the smarter move. He had chosen...poorly.

Still, it wasn't the delays, the children of the corn, or Grant's current state of sleep deprivation that had set his nerves on edge—although those factors certainly didn't help—it was the circumstances behind his trip back to the States. He had planned on staying in Africa another four months, but the telegram from Uncle Phil had changed all that. It had changed everything.

Contrary to his normal personality, Phil had spared no expense to assure the message was relayed to Grant as quickly as possible. This feat had ultimately been accomplished by Ondobo, a young boy from Yaousté who had ridden the bus fifty miles to Grant's camp to hand deliver the telegram. Grant had tipped him well, not certain how much the telegraph office had given him already. Yes, Uncle Phil had certainly stepped out of character to make certain Grant got the message, and Grant appreciated it more than anything his uncle had ever done for him.

Within an hour of receiving the message, Grant had packed what few possessions he had and said his goodbyes. The staff of the medical station hated to see him go (he knew they assumed he wouldn't return), but they understood. They were good people doing a tough job, supplying medical care to the people of the Cameroon Mountains. The camp was supported in equal parts by the Peace Corps, the Sweezey International School of Medicine, and by a generous donation from Grant's grandfather which had swayed the Oxford Medical Program into allowing Grant to complete his second year of residency under the tutelage of the camp's senior physician.

Grant had made a difference over the past ten months. He had saved many lives, but he was leaving them behind to return to New York. Fortunately, the camp had reached a slower period of need among the local people. An outbreak of Lassa fever had been quelled and the infection rates for malaria wouldn't pose a challenge until the rainy season began. Grant should have finally had a chance to catch his breath and complete some ongoing projects for the camp before his replacement arrived in January. Instead, he was leaving Africa under the worst of circumstances.

Now, as Grant stood at the baggage claim conveyor belt at LaGuardia, he felt the weight of the straw that was about to break the proverbial camel's back. When he arrived, the luggage from his flight was already making its slow progression around the suitcase carousel. Standing amidst the other travel-weary passengers, his blue eyes bloodshot and brown hair unkempt from the hours on the plane, Grant waited for his single brown duffel to descend from the unloading belt and onto the oblong conveyor. It never came.

His fellow passengers had all departed ten minutes ago. There were still a couple of lonely suitcases riding the circle, but neither belonged to him.

Grant's bad day was continuing. His bag was either lost or stolen. Living in the mountains of Cameroon had taught him to simplify, and that duffel held what few personal treasures Grant had in the world.

Yep. The day just kept getting worse by the minute.

That's when the black man in the tan jacket twisted Grant's arm behind his shoulder blades and pushed him up against the wall.

CHAPTER 2
October 10
10:05 A.M.

"GRANT ARMSTRONG, you're under arrest."
The black man, somewhere in his late twenties, pulled Grant's other hand behind him and locked handcuffs onto his wrists.

"You have the right to remain silent. Anything you say will probably be held against you because you have a bad habit of making dumbass remarks when you're trying to be funny."

When the man spun him around, Grant's look of confusion transformed into surprised recognition.

"What's the charge?" Grant asked with the first hint of a grin his face had seen in two days.

"One count of being a selfish bastard. There's bound to be a phone somewhere in Africa. I was starting to wonder if you were still alive."

"Nearest phone was in a town on the other side of a snake-infested jungle. With bugs. Gigantic bugs. That's a long walk."

"You couldn't ride an elephant or swing on some vines? Think outside the box, man."

"Maybe if you were prettier, I would have risked it."

A winning smile broke out across Eric's face. He threw his arms around Grant and embraced him in a one-way hug. "Good to see you,

Grant. Can't believe these words are about to come out of my mouth, but I missed you, buddy."

"Then perhaps you can show how glad you are that I'm back by unlocking these Fifty Shades bracelets of yours." Grant jingled the cuffs behind him to emphasize the point.

At that moment, a pudgy, graying security guard came racing around the corner, gun drawn.

"What's going on here?!" His voice broke as he called out his question, sounding like he was not in the habit of running on a regular basis.

Eric raised his hands to shoulder level, palms up. "Take it easy, sir. I'm NYPD. Homicide. I'm going to reach into my coat and show you my badge."

Eric held open his jacket and extracted his badge and identification from the inside pocket. He held the badge up to the security guard for closer inspection.

"Sorry, Detective Johnson. Some lady just came screaming around the corner that a gang member was about to shoot someone." The security guard looked Grant over. "You need some help with this perp?"

"No thanks," Eric replied. "I should be able to handle this *perp* all on my own." Eric grabbed Grant by the shoulder and gave him a push toward the exit saying, "Get your ass moving."

The security guard walked off, looking dejected. Grant smiled at Eric, "Nice moves there, Shaft. You want to tell me why you didn't go with the truth?"

Eric found the key to the cuffs and unlocked Grant. "Did you hear that 'gang member' crack? It's hard enough for me to get respect without telling some fat-ass security guard that I'm using my job to jack with a buddy of mine."

"Yeah, well, you *are* using your job to jack with me. And speaking of your job, why don't you go find the guy who stole my luggage, detective?"

"Oh, don't worry about it. I picked it up earlier. It's over there." Eric directed Grant's gaze to the corner where, sure enough, his duffel bag rested on the floor. "You'd think a skilled physician who graduated from Oxford could afford something better than the same stupid bag he used for high school weekend trips. I recognized that piece of shit from the door, man."

The two walked over to retrieve the bag then headed toward the door leading outside.

"Yeah, yeah. So my taste in luggage doesn't run to the expensive. You know I'm not a big fan of that kind of thing. I was in Africa for a reason. I wouldn't have come back if it wasn't for..." As his thought trailed off, Grant's expression darkened.

Eric stopped and put a hand on his friend's shoulder. "Listen, I'm really sorry about your grandfather. You know how much I loved him. He was a great man. When we were growing up, he was the only person who didn't laugh at me when I talked about wanting to be a cop."

"Yeah, I know. I just can't believe he's dead. I had no idea his health was so poor. If I had known, I would never have left for as long as I did."

"You couldn't have known." As they walked out the door toward the parking garage, Eric's tone turned grim. "Besides, when we get to the car, there's something we need to talk about...and you're not going to like it."

CHAPTER 3
October 10
10:45 A.M.

ERIC SHIFTED HIS EYES from the road for a glance at the passenger seat. Grant's face was pure bewilderment.

"You've got to be kidding. Why would you want to have an autopsy performed on Granddad? I thought he died of a heart attack."

Eric tightened his grip on the wheel. He knew this couldn't be easy on his friend. He had worked a number of homicide cases in the two years he had been in the department, and most of them had been very cut-and-dried. Victim of a mugging decides to fight back and ends up victim of a murder. Wife-beating husband takes it too far one night and accidentally kills her. Wife notices a smudge on her husband's collar that isn't her shade of lipstick and goes off the deep end. In cases like those, you just had to be disciplined and follow the trail of the obvious.

Those cases were hard on the loved ones of the victim, but at least there was closure. It might not make sense *why* it happened, but you at least knew *what* happened...and who was to blame.

But then there were the mysteries. Murders that didn't make sense. Homicides that appeared random. Victims whose killers would never see justice. Eric hated those cases. They bore under his skin and remained there. Itching. His mind didn't allow for it.

He had sailed from the ranks of beat cop to homicide detective far earlier than standard not just because he was smart but because he was relentless. He *had* to solve each case. Scratch that itch. Know that if he couldn't give the victim's loved ones comfort, he could at least provide some kind of closure.

Driving to Still Pines with Grant, this was different. It wasn't just a puzzle to solve. Eric knew these people. He had grown up with Grant. He had played with him since they were in elementary school.

It had been an unusual relationship from the start. While Eric's family wasn't exactly poor (he preferred to think of their status as financially impaired), Grant came from money. Real money. Eric wasn't sure exactly how much wealth was stored in the Armstrong-family coffers, but he suspected the dollar amount started with a capital B.

Why Grant's grandfather, Abraham Armstrong, had chosen to settle his family in a predominantly blue collar, middle income town like Still Pines, New York, was always a mystery to the townspeople. After getting to know Grant and his grandfather, it made sense to Eric.

Even as a kid, Eric had always liked Abe Armstrong, and despite his gruff exterior, the old man seemed to have a soft spot for Eric in return. Eric never knew why. Maybe it was because Grant had needed a friend and Eric filled the role. Maybe it was something else. He'd never know. Abe was dead.

Eric avoided looking at his friend while he navigated through the traffic. "Look Grant, this isn't easy. Still Pines isn't even in my jurisdiction, and I'm not trying to make a case out of this. I just think that an autopsy is something to consider. Your grandfather was a very wealthy man."

"Bullshit. You know something you're not telling me. We're friends, Eric. If you think something happened to my grandfather, I deserve to know."

"Grant, don't do this to me. This is as straightforward as I can get. I'm being completely honest when I say that there is nothing concrete pointing toward murder. But look at the facts. You've got a very rich old guy who's dependent on others for his care. You've got a family tree full of people who have barely gotten a dime out of said very rich old guy and have made no secret as to their unhappiness about this fact…"

"Wait a minute," Grant interrupted. "Are you saying you think someone in my family killed him?"

"No. Look, I don't know what to tell you, Grant. I don't know what you want to hear. I loved your granddad. I did. I hate that he's dead, but I need to be sure he died of natural causes. If someone, anyone, did something to that old man, I want to know. I'd think you would too."

"Eric…" Grant looked at him in silence.

For the first time, Eric returned the look. His friend's expression was one of pain. Grant was a doctor, keenly aware of the ugly procedures required of an autopsy, and Eric had just asked his friend to consent to laying out his own grandfather on one of those cold, steel tables. Eric glanced back to the road and sighed.

"Fine. Look, I got a phone call two weeks ago from someone. I can't tell you who, but it was someone who was concerned about your grandfather. This someone was worried that he was in danger. He had been talking about rewriting his will. It kind of freaked everyone out."

"Rewrite his will? But I didn't think anyone even knew who was in the original will. That was always a closed subject for Granddad."

"Correct, but everyone assumed he would split the inheritance among the kids. If he started talking about rewriting it, that would introduce an unstable element to the situation. And unstable elements can be explosive."

"The money…" Grant was shaking his head in disbelief. "Always the damned money."

"Look, don't blame anyone yet. Just because someone is greedy, it doesn't make them evil. There's no sense in running a suspect list before we even know for sure how he died. Grant, all I'm asking for is permission to have the Still Pines medical examiner do a simple autopsy. Tox-screens, check for poisons, that sort of thing. It'll only take a day or two, and it'll be done before the funeral. Then we can worry about hating your relatives. Okay?"

"Who called?"

"What?" The question surprised Eric.

"You said someone called you to warn you. Who was it?"

"I'm sorry, Grant. I've already said that I can't tell you. I wish I could, but I made a promise."

They sat in silence as trees flashed by. They were drawing closer to the island on Still Pines Lake. Almost home.

Eric took his eyes off the road long enough to look at his friend. Grant was staring out the window at the familiar countryside. When he finally spoke, his voice was soft.

"Do the autopsy, Eric. I want to know."

CHAPTER 4
October 10
10:58 A.M.

MARTY SIMMONS was getting anxious. He had only been working at the prison for two months, but he was almost certain he was developing an ulcer. An ulcer at twenty-two was not something he wanted. His dad had an ulcer, and he saw how miserable it made him. No hard liquor, no jalapenos and no chili dogs. Marty liked chili dogs and the thought of living without them for the rest of his life—since he had never heard of an ulcer going away—made him even more anxious. He hated this job.

Wait. That wasn't true. He had liked this job for the first two weeks. The warden had given him an assignment in the solitary confinement unit. Marty's whole job was basically watching television. There were eight individual cells. No bars. Just an iron door with a four-by-twelve inch window for passing food trays through. The only time Marty actually saw a live convict was when the guards came to get each prisoner, once a day, for their allotted hour in the exercise yard. And that was only three times a day, since five of the cells currently sat empty.

All Marty had to do was watch television. Specifically, each cell had a small camera in the corner, protected by a sheet of plexiglass to keep out prying hands. Marty's job was to monitor the prisoners in their cells via the little black-and-white television screens on his console. Seemed like a dream job.

Until Silas Kane was sent to solitary.

Most prisoners were restricted to Marty's unit for only a few days at a time, usually for talking back to a guard or getting into a fight in the exercise yard or cafeteria. But two weeks ago, he was informed Kane would be staying for three weeks. Seemed there had been an incident in the showers. A prisoner was found on the tile floor with a broken spine. Very broken. Marty had heard the guy's heels were touching the back of his head. He was dead, of course. The injury had severed his spinal cord, and the shock had killed him.

Marty had heard he was one of the sisters. Maybe they had decided to test Kane. Maybe some of the initial fear of the giant's presence had worn down. Maybe the guy had actually touched Kane in the shower. Maybe it didn't matter because the guy was dead as dead got.

Of course, no one had actually seen Kane do it. The guard on duty was standing outside the door at that moment, and of the twenty prisoners in the shower during the incident, each one had somehow gotten soap in his eye and missed the whole thing. But it had to have been Kane. Despite all the weight-lifting and trash talking and overflowing testosterone found among the inmates, no one else in the prison had the sheer physical power necessary to perform such an act of brutality.

So Kane wound up in solitary for three weeks. A cheap price to pay for killing another human being.

Marty got his first face-to-face contact with Silas Kane when the guards brought him to his solitary cell. Marty had heard stories of the man's size (Kane had arrived at the prison over a month before Marty but he was still the main topic of discussion among the guards), but he had never bothered to actually go look at the man. This was a prison, not a zoo, and he knew that his coworkers were probably exaggerating for the new guy's benefit. But when Marty first laid eyes on Kane as the prisoner ducked under the caged entryway to the solitary hall, he could see there had been no exaggeration.

The guards had put Kane into the last cell on the left with no incident. Locked the door with no incident. And retrieved Kane once a day for his exercise, with never an incident.

So why did he bother Marty so much? It had taken him quite a bit of thinking before he could pinpoint exactly what caused his distress.

It was Kane's eyes.

Most men did fine with solitary for the first day, maybe even two. It got them out of work detail and away from any dangers of general population. They didn't have to share a cell or their toilet. They even had the exercise yard all to themselves when they were taken out. It seemed like a vacation. Most of the prisoners even laughed during that first day, all with Marty watching on the monitor.

Then the blurring began. No windows. Nothing but artificial light. No prisoners to talk to since the cells in the unit were more or less soundproof. They would eventually start to pace the length of the cell and back again. Start talking to themselves. Start talking to the camera. Marty had a sound switch he could activate for each cell and sometimes listened to the pleading of the prisoners to tell them what time it was.

But Kane did none of those things. He merely sat on the bed with his legs crossed and stared at the camera. Hours. Days. The only time Marty ever saw him move was to go to the toilet following breakfast and to do his push-ups after lunch.

The push-ups were impressive. No, they were beyond impressive. The push-ups were inhuman.

After passing the empty lunch tray through the door, Kane would turn and lie on his stomach in the middle of the cell's floor. He would make a fist with each hand and set his fists shoulder length apart. Then he would start doing push-ups. No waiting for his lunch to settle. Just push-ups. Slow and methodical. Each one taking exactly three seconds. He would do push-ups for one hour. Never stopping.

After witnessing this for the first two days, Marty decided he would count. He got to two hundred and fifty before he stopped counting. Kane was still going on the monitor as Marty did the math. He scratched the arithmetic on a piece of paper and estimated well over a thousand push-ups. Up. Down. Up. Down. Marty had never seen such an act of strength. And when Kane finished with his regimen—the last push-up as slow and methodical as the first—he sat his sweating body back on the bed and crossed his legs. Then he raised his eyes to the camera and stared.

There he would sit until supper was brought. Just staring.

It was hard to explain, but it wasn't even the act of staring in itself. Even in his short time at the post, Marty had seen men kind of "glaze over" and stare at the same spot on the wall for hours, like they had given up and slipped into a voluntary coma. Anything to make the time pass.

But Kane wasn't glazed over. He was alert. His eyes were sharp and focused. Staring at the camera. Staring at Marty. And Marty was getting an ulcer from it.

Thank God Kane only had another week in solitary. And later today, he would be taken from his cell for the first day of his appeal. In fact, Marty estimated that Kane would probably be there for only about half his usual shift this week.

Good. Let him spend his days at the courthouse. Let the guards worry about him there. Just keep him out of his cell and away from Marty's camera.

CHAPTER 5
October 10
11:42 A.M.

G RANT TOOK IN THE VIEW as Eric's Crown Vic crested the hill overlooking the expanse of water and the island estate. Still Pines Lake was one of the larger bodies of water in the State of New York, and Armstrong Island sat on the eastern side of it. Technically, the island sat in the middle of a sizeable cove. The lake was supplied by a large river which opened into the body of water at the mouth of the cove. The deepest channel of the river continued to flow between the island's south side and the mainland.

The island itself was impressive, over three-hundred acres of beautiful pine woods and two houses. Grant's grandfather's house would best be described as a mansion. It sat on the west side of the island for a better view of the sunset. Abraham Armstrong was a firm believer that a man ought to be working at sunrise so there was no sense in building a house overlooking the east side of the lake. Sunsets, on the other hand, were for relaxation and enjoyment. Hence, the house rested on the west bank of the island.

The second of the two houses was only a few hundred yards to the east of the mansion. The guest house was spacious by normal standards, but it seemed quite small when compared to the "big house" (as Abe liked to refer to it). Both houses were visible from the top of the rise. Grant's thoughts wandered as they approached the island.

The sole entry to the island was from the east side. Grant's grandfather had personally built a wooden covered bridge to connect the island to the mainland. It was, to Grant, an impressive accomplishment. The bridge spanned sixty feet across the flowing current of the lake. Its entrance was lined on either side by gargantuan pine trees, as large as any Grant had seen.

To some, it may have seemed inconvenient to place the bridge on the opposite side of the island from the house, but to Grant it made perfect sense. Abe Armstrong had purchased the island for a reason, and he wanted people to drive the entire winding road around the island to reach the house. He wanted them to appreciate the beauty of the trees and feel nature around them.

"You're awfully quiet over there," Eric ventured an attempt at conversation.

"Oh, sorry. Just thinking. You remember playing on the bridge when we were kids?"

"Sure. We used to climb up the sides and walk across the roof. We'd pretend it was a speeding train, and we were fighting the bad guys on top of the railcars."

Grant grinned. "Yeah, and I remember the time you almost fell off our speeding train and practically had a panic attack. Please tell me you stopped being so bullheaded and learned to swim since then."

"Cut me a break. I just don't like the water. Not then. Not now. You think it was easy growing up in Still Pines not knowing how to swim? That's why I work in the big city now, where no one expects you to swing off a rope into a lake."

"Oh man, I forgot about the rope..." Grant's thought trailed off as they approached the bridge. It had been almost a year since he'd last crossed the platform. Almost a year since he'd been home to see his grandfather.

Grant looked out the window as he spoke. "I remember after my dad died, right after the funeral, I came out to the bridge and cried. I just sat there and cried and wondered how God could let something like that happen. Having lost Mom when I was born, it seemed unfair that Dad had died, too. The bridge became my retreat for a while after that. Whenever I really missed Dad, when I'd feel sad or pissed off or empty inside, I'd go sit. Sometimes Granddad would come out and find me. He'd never ask what I was doing. He'd just gather up a bunch of pine cones and plop down beside me. We'd sit there, our legs hanging off the bridge, throwing pine cones into the lake and watching them float off. I guess that was his way of dealing with Dad's death, too."

"I wish I had known your dad better, Grant. He sounded like a great guy."

"He was. Granddad used to say I was a lot like him. I always took it as a compliment, and I think he always meant it as one. Sometimes I wonder how different my family would be if Dad had lived."

"Don't go there, Grant. People are people, and there's no sense in wondering 'what if' all your life. Besides, your family's not so bad." He paused. "Well, they could be worse."

"This is the same family you're considering as murder suspects, right?"

The Crown Vic passed over the bridge, the wooden roof blocking the sunlight and the tires making bumping sounds going over the beams of the wooden floor.

"Yeah, you know I'm just trying to be nice," Eric responded. "The only good thing about you being overseas in school was that I didn't have to see the rest of your family anymore. And I have to ask you a serious question, what did you plan to do anyway? I mean, I understand you going to Africa after med-school. You're a nice guy, relatively speaking, and I know you want to help people and I think that's great, but did you ever plan on coming back?"

"I don't know. The last time I came home to visit was suffocating. Granddad wasn't doing badly. He was in the wheelchair, but he seemed pretty alert. We talked for hours. But after he went to bed, the whole family closed in on me. Asking what I thought about his health. After all, I was a doctor. Did his breathing sound all right? Was there anything in particular they should *be ready for*? Like buzzards circling a dying animal. It made me sick. That's why I cut the trip short. Not a fun Christmas."

"I'm surprised you didn't stick around. Fend off the buzzards. That sort of thing."

"I thought about it, but Granddad really believed in what I was trying to accomplish in Africa. It seemed important to him that one of his kids—or at least his only grandkid—do something worthwhile. Besides, he had his healthcare worker so I assumed I'd get word if his health were to slip."

"Yeah, Julie, right?"

"Uh-huh," Grant replied as Eric negotiated the turns of the road. Grant tried to remember what Julie looked like. He had met her briefly during his last visit. She had been leaving to attend her mother's funeral. An even worse Christmas than his own. Grant chided himself for his lack of perspective.

But Julie had returned from the funeral to continue his grandfather's care. His grandfather had said a lot of nice things to Grant about her after she left the house last Christmas. He really liked her. Had said she was "good people"—one of his better and most all-encompassing compliments.

Grant glanced at his friend. "You know, I got so caught up in everything, I haven't had a chance to thank you."

"For what?"

"For picking me up at the airport. It's not like it's on your way. And for taking an interest in, well, all of this."

"Think nothing of it, amigo. I hate to admit this but picking you up and hauling your ass halfway across the state will be by far the best part of my day."

Grant realized this was the first time they had talked about Eric's life since getting in the car together at the airport. He felt guilty about not even asking his friend a few polite questions despite the other matters they had been discussing. "So what happens later today?"

"Afternoon court appointment. A guy I busted last spring is having the first day of his appeal. I want to be there."

"So let's have some details. What did this guy do?" Grant asked.

"He killed people," Eric replied, his voice quiet. "He killed a lot of people. And if we hadn't put him away, he would have killed a lot more. He didn't have much of a defense in the initial trial. I need to go and make sure he doesn't have one for the appeal."

"Anybody I would have heard of?"

"Probably not. Made some headlines around here, but I doubt it was big enough to make it to Africa. His name is Silas Kane."

Grant puzzled for a moment. "Kane. Sounds familiar."

Eric's gaze shifted to the horizon. "You remember that cult in New Mexico from a couple of years ago? All those people died?"

"Yeah. I remember. It made top headlines in England. People talked about it for weeks, even at Oxford, how a group of people could ever possibly get that way..."

"I'll tell you how. Marcus Kane." Eric spoke the name as if it left a bad taste in his mouth. "Let me fill you in on a little back story. Something that didn't make the papers at the time. Once upon a time back before there was such a thing as the internet, there was a man named Hiram Kane. The guy was brilliant but more than a few sandwiches short of a picnic. A dangerous kind of crazy. Hiram Kane was determined that the world was going to hell, and he wanted to be the one to hold open the door. He mailed a few bombs and was probably responsible for infecting a children's ward in Kansas with anthrax. The Feds investigated, and then the agent in charge of the investigation was found decapitated and the remains of his family were discovered in various pieces throughout the house. After that, Hiram Kane just disappeared. No one knows where. What we do know is that he took his three boys with him..."

"Wait a minute," Grant interrupted. "You're saying this Marcus Kane guy had parents? We all just kind of assumed he was raised by a pack of wolves or something."

Grant was joking, but Eric didn't laugh. "Picture a wolf with a graduate degree in philosophy from Berkeley and a degree in chemistry from MIT. Graduated magna cum laude. The guy was smart, and he knew how to elude the cops. It's possible that he just went out into the wilderness. Left society. Our best guess is that he spent the time after his disappearance 'educating' his sons."

"That sounds bad."

"Of course, as the years passed with no noticeable progress, interest in the Hiram Kane case waned and the authorities stopped actively searching. That is until Marcus Kane, the oldest of the three sons, turned up in New Mexico with a group of people who barely remembered how to be human and a pile of bodies in the desert."

Grant nodded. He remembered the story well. Who didn't?

Eric continued, "So anyway, a few months ago, a federal agent and a Texas Ranger appeared in NYPD's homicide department asking to review some open cases. Turns out they had been tracking down the second son—Silas Kane—and middle brother wasn't proving to be any better at fitting into society than older brother. Long story short, we caught Kane in an apartment with a dead hooker and put him away for life. I want to make sure that remains the case. So you can see why today isn't going to be a joy for me."

Grant looked at the seriousness in his friend's face. "Wow. Your job really sucks."

Eric cracked a humorless smile. "Yeah. It does."

CHAPTER 6
October 10
11:45 A.M.

MARTY SIMMONS almost felt good. The clock was about to strike noon. That meant two things: one, he was about to dig into the salami and pickle sandwich he had packed for lunch, and two, Silas Kane was about to be taken to the courthouse where he would stay for the rest of Marty's shift. Life wasn't so bad.

He had even decided this job wasn't quite as terrible as he thought. It was just nerves. He figured there were probably always prisoners that gave guards the creeps. Kane just happened to be really super creepy. And scary. Even when you were just looking at him through a video monitor.

Marty was feeling so good, he reached into the brown paper sack to grab his sandwich before the officially designated hour. Maybe if he finished it early, he'd have some extra time on his break to read the new issue of *Motor Trend*. His stomach had been a little upset all morning—maybe it was the ulcer—but he couldn't leave to go to the bathroom unless he called a replacement. But at break time, it was no worry. Spending the rest of the lunch hour in the bathroom with his magazine didn't sound too bad at all.

He looked up at Kane's monitor. He was still sitting there. Staring.

Marty suppressed a shiver and unwrapped the foil from his sandwich. A generous helping of mayo squeezed from between the slices of white bread as Marty took a big bite. Yep. He could handle this job.

A loud buzz came from overhead and Marty checked the entryway camera. The two guards had arrived to take Kane. A few minutes early, no less. Marty smiled and flipped the lever controlling the automatic door to let the men inside. He took another big bite of sandwich and walked to the door to greet them. "You know where he's at, guys." A small chunk of pickle flew from his mouth as he spoke. "Be careful."

The two men were professional, always following protocol when dealing with prisoners. Kane was not to be taken lightly, and security always made sure to handle him by the book.

Marty sank back in his chair and watched them proceed down the hall to Kane's cell. The taller guard rapped on the door and told Kane to stand next to the wall and place his hands in the yellow circles which were painted on the wall at shoulder height. Marty bit into his sandwich and watched on his monitor as Kane complied with the request. The guards saw this as well from the small window in the cell door.

Marty turned the knob that controlled the automatic door to Kane's cell and it opened. The guards went in together. One stood behind Kane with his wooden baton in one hand and a can of mace in the other. The second guard took care to place Kane in the arm and leg shackles. Kane offered no resistance and continued to stare straight ahead.

The guards walked Kane back down the hall, and Marty opened the gate at the end. He was going to get through this all right. It was just a case of misplaced nerves. He could handle it.

As Kane passed through the gate, he turned his head. He was looking straight at Marty.

Marty's knees went weak. He put his hand on the desk to brace himself, his stomach feeling much worse than it had a moment before.

Then, Kane did something Marty had not seen him do since he arrived at solitary over a month ago.

Kane smiled.

Only for a moment. And only for Marty to see. Then he faced forward and was led out of solitary by the two guards.

Marty dropped onto his chair. He was sweating. He twisted the lever again to shut the gate. He then reached beneath the desk and pulled the trashcan toward him, placed it between his knees and wondered if his sandwich was going to reenter the world.

CHAPTER 7
October 10
12:01 P.M.

ERIC PULLED UP to the front of the big house and switched off the ignition. "It's good to have you home, buddy."

Grant was looking out the passenger window at the house. "Thanks, man. Are you going to come inside?"

"Wish I could, but I've got to hustle if I'm going to make my court appointment. Here's my card. New number. Works for my cell or desk. Give me a call later if you need me. I'll be back for dinner, and I'll get back with you on...that thing we talked about."

Grant pocketed the card then reached into the back seat and pulled the worn, brown duffel bag into his lap. He noticed Eric take out his cell phone, grunt and return it to his jacket pocket.

"I guess not everything has changed since I left," Grant chuckled. "Does Still Pines continue to be the place where cell phones go to die?"

"I saw a preschooler with a smart phone in Central Park the other day, yet I still can't get one damn bar of signal out here. Epic technology fail. At least you'll be safe when the machines rise up against humanity."

Grant opened the passenger door then reached back to shake his friend's hand. "I take comfort in that. See you later."

He got out of the car, closed the door behind him and watched as Eric eased out of the circular driveway and back onto the road leading off the island. Then he was alone.

He inhaled deeply, the scent of the air so different from the smells of Africa, but so familiar from his youth. The temperature was cooling into fall crispness, jacket weather but not yet ready for winter coats. The breeze had picked up. Possibly a storm brewing?

He looked around at the home of his youth. Not much had changed. Not on the outside. But on the inside, something would be missing.

The thought of going into the house and not hearing his grandfather's voice calling out to him was hard. The idea that Eric had introduced, that someone in his family may have been responsible for his grandfather's death, made Grant's stomach clench. He felt queasy. He realized that he hadn't eaten anything since the previous day.

As he took his first steps toward the house, the front door opened. A young woman stood in the doorway, blonde hair pulled back in a ponytail. She wore a pale pink t-shirt and white shorts that accentuated her toned legs—her clothing courageously defying the onset of the fall weather.

Grant realized something else, he hadn't seen a woman this attractive in a very long time, and he was staring with his mouth open.

During the months he spent in Cameroon, he had only the villagers, an outdated copy of a *Sports Illustrated Swimsuit Issue* and Nurse Lorcet to provide him any sort of female company. And while Nurse Lorcet was nice, she was also in the later stages of fifty-something. A few of the women in the village were attractive, but Grant considered them all his patients and never entertained the thought of becoming romantic with them. That left only the ladies in a magazine and his left hand for romance. The girl in the doorway left them all in the dust.

"Hi, are you Grant?" Her question snapped him out of his reverie and into a state of embarrassment. He couldn't have been standing slack-jawed for more than a moment, but she had to have noticed. He hoisted his bag onto his shoulder and wiped his lower lip. One smooth motion. No drool. At least that was something.

"Yes. Are you Julie?" He walked to the door and extended his hand, grateful to be drool'less.

She returned his smile, nodded, and bypassed the proffered handshake, instead moving straight into a hug, her cheek pressed against his chest. "I am so sorry about your grandfather." Her words were muffled by his shirt.

Although taken aback, Grant returned the hug. It felt good, and it was nice to hear a genuine expression of concern. "Thanks. You didn't have to come get me. I was just soaking up the surroundings."

She pulled away. "Oh, I'm sorry. You probably wanted a few minutes to yourself. I heard the car pull up and then saw you standing out here alone..."

"It's okay. I was just on my way inside. I appreciate the effort." Grant couldn't resist another head-to-toe glance. Quick. Subtle. Hopefully. "I'm sorry for not recognizing you. The last time we met, you were on your way out the door."

Julie stepped inside and let Grant enter the house. "Well, we've both been through a lot since then," she replied. "I didn't recognize you right away either."

Grant stood in the entryway, looking around. So many memories. So long ago. "So is anyone else here?"

"Yes and no. Everyone is staying here for now, but no one's home." Julie walked toward the kitchen. "You must be starving, may I get you something to eat?"

Wow, and she reads minds, Grant thought as he followed her out of the foyer. His eyes drifted to her backside as she walked. He was chastising himself for behaving like a teenager—though that didn't diminish his appreciation of the view—when a thought struck him. "Wait a minute, everyone's staying here? I thought Phil and Loraine had an apartment in the city."

Julie stopped at the entry to the kitchen and turned to face him. Grant was thankful that his eyes were on her face at the time.

"They do have an apartment in the city, so do Brock and Mona, but I think they felt obligated to stay out here after your grandfather passed."

"Obligated why?"

"I guess to make sure I don't steal anything." Grant couldn't tell if the inflection in her voice was sarcasm or hurt. Either way, it was clear the subject bothered her.

"I'm sorry. I wish I could say something better, but that's my family." Grant felt embarrassed and even more so at the next question he felt compelled to ask. "Please don't take this the wrong way, because I'm glad you're here, but why are you still here?" Grant hoped he wasn't stepping onto shaky ground. He had known Julie for only a couple of minutes but already liked her.

"Funny. Your uncle asked the same question although he phrased it more along the lines of 'Pack up and leave, honey. Your job's finished.'" She proceeded into the kitchen while she spoke. "But then Abe's attorney called me out of the blue and told me I should stay in the house for at least the rest of the week. I'm glad. I want to attend the funeral, but I don't have anywhere else to stay."

Grant knew it had to have been Uncle Phil who confronted her. The man had the tact of a jackal, and as thankful as Grant was for the message Phil had sent about his grandfather's death, he couldn't help hating him just a little. "I'm glad you're here. It may not be my place to offer, but you're welcome to stay as long you'd like. I know you meant a lot to Granddad."

A bright smile lit Julie's face. Grant wondered if that was the first nice thing anyone in his family had said to her. She touched his arm and mouthed the words "thank you" then turned to the refrigerator.

"Well," she sniffed, "what would a man who's been on a plane all night like to eat?"

Grant set his bag on the floor and sat at the kitchen table. "If you have any leftover pizza in there, I may have to marry you."

"Then we may have to set a date, Dr. Armstrong." Julie emerged from the fridge holding a packet of foil. She unwrapped it to reveal three slices of pizza. "I hope sausage is okay."

Grant's mouth watered. He hadn't realized how hungry he was. He swallowed. "Sausage sounds great."

Julie put the slices on a plate and opened the microwave door.

"Don't you dare," Grant stopped her. "Cold is perfect."

"Gentleman's choice." Julie set the plate in front of Grant, then pulled two Cokes from the fridge.

He lowered his face to the plate, inhaled the aroma and dug in.

Julie smiled. "Goodness, you'd think the man hadn't eaten in a while. How's it feel to be back in the States?"

Grant chewed quickly and washed the bite down with a drink of soda. It was ambrosia. "Better now. It's the little things you miss, like pizza and indoor plumbing."

Julie laughed and sipped her Coke. She had a nice laugh.

Grant spoke between bites. "Julie, did you notice anything unusual about Granddad before he died? Anything to point toward heart trouble?"

"I never noticed anything unusual. We had skipped his quarterly check-up, but that was because Abe insisted he was doing fine. That he didn't like doctors and felt better when he was at home." Her face was serious as she looked him in the eye. "Grant, if I had had any idea there was something wrong with your grandfather I would have taken him to the doctor. I'm a healthcare worker, not a registered nurse, but I never saw anything to point toward heart trouble."

Grant nodded. He believed her, but he also didn't want to let her know why he was asking the questions. "It's okay. Heart attacks are common in men Granddad's age. It's impossible to predict and difficult to detect ahead of time. You didn't do anything wrong."

He realized how difficult the next day or two would be. Every time he spoke to someone in his family, he would be interrogating them. And what if his grandfather *had* died of a heart attack with nothing malicious associated? What if all of this was for nothing?

Grant was beginning to feel very tired. He finished the last slice of pizza, stood from the table and put the plate in the sink. "Thank you for the food. Just what I needed. I'm going to go upstairs and try to get a little sleep. Is my room still open?"

Julie nodded. "Yeah, Phil and Loraine are staying in the guest house and Mona and Brock are staying here in the downstairs suite."

Grant picked up his bag. All he wanted was to go upstairs, take off his shoes and sleep. He would speak to Julie more this afternoon. And his family.

Questions to ask. Answers to seek. He had never felt so alone.

CHAPTER 8
October 10
12:36 P.M.

ERIC SPED TOWARD THE CITY, his mind racing as fast as the
Crown Vic. He had just completed the call with the Still Pines
coroner's office. Eric had known Joe Stenson for most of his life and
considered him a friend. Joe had said he would bring in a Medical
Examiner to complete the autopsy later today or first thing in the
morning. Eric reiterated that he wanted this kept quiet, no sense in
stirring up rumors, and that he would still like everything ready for
Abe's funeral in three days. Joe understood. He was not only the
coroner, but also the town mortician. He could handle everything in
plenty of time. He was a good man. And discreet.

As Eric moved into the middle lane, he reflected on the morning. It
had been good to see Grant again. They had been an unusual pair in
their childhood, right up through graduating high school and
venturing their separate ways. Eric always suspected Grant's family—
besides Abe—had never particularly cared for him. He could sense they
felt Eric wasn't good enough to be hanging around the Armstrong
estate, shooting baskets in their driveway and eating their food. He
never thought it was a racial thing but more a matter of social standing.
Fact was, with the exception of Abraham Armstrong, Grant's relatives
seemed to think the whole town of Still Pines was beneath them.

But Grant was different. He never flaunted his money in school. He played sports alongside everyone else and drove an older model Jeep Wrangler. He even chilled at Eric's house and ate dinner with his parents on countless occasions. For the most part though, Eric and Grant spent their time on the island. Mainly because they could hang out by themselves. Abe was always understanding when it came to letting the boys have the run of the place after school. He would sit up in his room watching the news or stay in his study reading a book while Eric and Grant cranked up the stereo and shot baskets or played baseball in the field beside the lake.

Fortunately, Grant's aunts and uncles had all moved out of the house by the time high school rolled around. Although he never heard the full story, Eric knew Abe had pretty much put his foot down on how much longer he'd support his children without them earning something on their own. Of course, that pissed off the whole family except for Grant, who found the whole thing hilarious. Grant's Uncle Phil and his wife got an apartment in the city—supposedly supported by Phil's job as a consultant—while Grant's Aunt Mona moved in with whichever boyfriend she had at the time. The island had seemed like an entirely new place after that.

Eric hoped he was wrong about Abe's death. Though he had never been fond of Grant's relatives, he wouldn't have pegged any of them for murderers. And if one of them *had* killed Abe, Eric knew it would be devastating for the rest of the family. Especially Grant. He would drown in guilt pondering the array of 'if I hadn't been in Africa' *would've* and *could've* scenarios.

For as long as Eric had known him, Grant's nature had been to take the weight of the world on his shoulders. He felt responsible for everything and everybody.

When they were in school, Grant would buy the lunches for half-a-dozen of the poorest kids, and the thing was, Grant had never told anyone about it. Not even his best friend. It was pure coincidence that Eric happened to spot Grant slide some dollar bills into Virgil

Cromby's locker one day, casual as could be. Practically a magician's trick. A split second later and Eric would have missed it.

Eric thought that was peculiar so he started paying closer attention—the traits that would forge him into a detective already manifesting. Turned out Grant made several stops like that every day before lunch. Always with kids whose families were having a rough go of it. Eric decided to visit with Virgil Cromby one day, just to be sure Grant wasn't being coerced. Eric knew the idea was ridiculous. Grant was one of the most athletic guys in school and a pipsqueak like Virgil certainly couldn't muscle him, but he still had to know.

Virgil told Eric that he had a guardian angel watching out for him. Eric left it at that. He never told Virgil who his angel was and he never mentioned to Grant that he knew about his clandestine lunch charity.

Lunch. Eric could see the sign of an upcoming Arby's. His stomach grumbled in annoyance as he passed the exit, but a glance at the dashboard clock assured him there would be no lunch today, not unless he made better time than expected and could snag a hotdog from a vendor outside the courthouse. It didn't matter—regardless of the degree of protest from his empty stomach—it was worth it to see Grant and drive him home, but what kind of home was Grant walking into?

The Armstrong family was something else. Abraham Armstrong had three kids. Jack, Grant's dad, had been by far the oldest. Jack was apparently a surprise for the young Armstrongs at the time of his birth. They didn't have more kids until many years and many millions of dollars later. Maybe that was why Jack seemed so distinct from the rest of the family. He grew up in a different world. He was married and had a son while his younger siblings Phil and Mona were still navigating the waters of adolescence, which for them included having a nephew in Grant who was only a little over a decade younger than them.

Eric had few memories of Grant's dad—Jack had died not long after he and Grant had moved to the island on Still Pines Lake—but Eric did remember how things felt darker after that. He was an outsider to the Armstrong family but a brother to Grant, and even as a kid Eric could sense the impact of Jack's death on the family. Twenty years later, his absence could still be felt.

Things were different on Armstrong Island for the rest of Grant's— and Eric's—childhood. Abe became quieter. Phil and Mona became...more Phil and more Mona. And Grant grew into a man with Eric by his side.

Life goes on, right up until it doesn't.

Eric didn't know whether Abe Armstrong had been murdered, but what if he had? Who would do something like that?

He had warned Grant not to dwell on it unless the autopsy turned up some sort of confirmation. No sense in building a suspect list until you knew for sure. Just a waste of time.

Eric began to build the suspect list.

Five people in the house with Abe the night he died.

Julie Russell. Abe's live-in healthcare assistant. She seemed nice but Eric didn't know her well enough to build a profile. On the other hand, Eric could write a paper on Grant's family members.

Phil Armstrong. Grant's uncle. Somewhat smart and somewhat charming in an oily kind of way. Desire to be wealthy but only provided enough money from his father to be comfortable. Phil never seemed to think comfortable was comfortable enough. Resentment. An asshole to be certain, but a murderer?

Loraine Armstrong. Wed to Phil but didn't marry into wealth, only "almost wealth", and never seemed thrilled with that outcome. Eric had always been amazed that Phil had managed to marry someone even assholier than himself—that set the bar pretty high—but the universe is full of wonders. Loraine fit the category of "people who suck" and she'd certainly be pleased sharing Phil's inheritance earlier-than-expected, but could she have created that outcome with her own hands? It may be on the same road, but it's a long drive to get from *mean person* to *murderer*.

Mona Rutland. Grant's aunt. Youngest of the three Armstrong siblings. Hellraiser in her youth. Plenty of alcohol. Maybe drugs? Definitely men. A string of bad relationships including two failed marriages before she turned thirty. Perhaps the result of self-esteem issues. Leaving the island and moving to Manhattan probably didn't help things on that front. As long as Eric had known her, she had been in the gym or at the tanning salon or showing up with larger breasts after a vacation in California. It had to have been self-esteem problems for her to actually marry...

Brock Rutland. Mona's husband and everything a name like Brock would imply. She met him at a high-end fitness center in the city about three years ago. He was her personal trainer for two months, her traveling companion to Las Vegas for a weekend...and her husband by the time they boarded the return flight. Her future inheritance *may* have been a factor. Spontaneous marriages rarely sport prenuptial agreements. Eric remembered Grant coming home from Oxford on a break. After Grant had met Brock, he shared his impression of his new "uncle" with Eric: "Tan, handsome, terrible person." But Mona seemed to love him. Maybe the alcohol helped.

She had even sounded a bit tipsy when she called Eric two weeks ago, saying she thought her father was in danger. Well, that was an exaggeration. Mona had told Eric that she was *concerned* about her father. That Abe had mentioned possibly changing his will and asked her opinion on the matter. Mona took care of her father a couple of times a week while Julie had time off. Since Abe asked her about the will when Julie wasn't around, Mona assumed he was considering changing it for Julie's benefit.

She asked Eric if he would come out and try to talk some sense into Abe. Mona didn't know what the consequences would be if Abe included "that hussy nurse" in his will.

Eric assured Mona he would visit Abe as soon as he got the chance. Then he hung up the phone and laughed loud enough that his fellow detectives looked up from their desks in the precinct. Eric knew that if Mona was calling *him*, then she had to consider it a full-blown family emergency, but it was not the kind of emergency that got Eric's attention. The money was Abe's. He could do whatever he wanted with it, and if that meant sharing it with someone who was caring for him in his final years, then good for him.

So Eric didn't go to the island to visit Abe. He had been following up on the Silas Kane case. He figured Mona had overheard her husband or brother make a threatening remark about what they'd do if Abe changed his will and she panicked. She had probably indulged in too much chardonnay and decided to bring in the reserves. After all, calling him was a sure sign of near hysteria on her part.

But she *had* called him. And Eric didn't do anything. And now Abe was dead.

It was probably coincidence. Eric knew that. Old men die of heart attacks all the time. But *what if?* The thought haunted Eric. It made him itch. He hated the itch. So he had to ask Grant to authorize an autopsy.

Abe would never get a chance to include Julie in his will, if that was what he ever intended. Eric wondered if the whole thing was nothing more than a ruse on the old man's part to try and get some attention from his kids. Try to remind them that he was alive. Maybe he just wanted more company than Mona dropping by for a liquid lunch a couple times a week. And maybe his ploy alarmed someone enough to kill him before he had the chance to meet with his attorney.

If that was the case, if Abe had been murdered, then Eric would consider it his fault. He had let the old man down. Maybe if he had gone to see him when Mona had asked, he would have a better idea of what was going on out there. Maybe if Silas Kane hadn't still been on his mind, he would have made the time to visit. Maybe...

Eric was jerked out of his thoughts as an eighteen-wheeler cut across his lane to make an exit. Eric laid on his horn and held it as he passed the exiting truck. The driver of the truck gave him a one-finger wave. How friendly.

His thoughts left the *possible* murderer and turned to the *definite* murderer. Silas Kane would be back in court today. He had been caught, but there was still an itch on that file, too. Something didn't add up. The courts had convicted Kane on the murder of the hooker in the apartment where he was caught, but there were still more than a dozen open cases that had Kane's fingerprints all over them. Robbery and arson were the most common. All with no witnesses save a couple of people way down the street who just described a "really big guy— you know, pro wrestler kind of big."

In Eric's mind that was enough to pin Kane, but it wasn't sufficient for the District Attorney to proceed. The only other connection was the presence of a female at most of the crimes. Witnesses often reported a woman driving the getaway car. Unfortunately, three different witnesses at three different events described three different women.

Eric had spent many hours trying to figure out Kane's motives. Why had he burned down the bar on 83rd Street? Why had he killed the Korean man in the convenience store he robbed? Why had he murdered the old lady in the donut shop in the wee hours of the morning? As near as Eric could tell, he had no particular motive and there was nothing that linked any of the crimes. They all pointed strongly to Kane, but why he did any of them was a complete mystery. After almost a year of hard investigation, Eric had come to believe simply that Kane liked it, and that was the scariest motive of all.

Of course, the female driver aspect also bothered him. He and George had spent weeks mapping out the crimes, locations, dates and times, before reaching a chilling conclusion—Kane was using the hookers. Back checks on homicide files revealed that most times a Kane-linked crime was committed, a hooker turned up dead within a few blocks of the crime scene. Apparently, Kane would meet the hooker, talk her into joining him on whatever the day's crime was, then go back to her place once the job was complete. She would be found in her apartment within the next day or two, usually dead from a broken neck.

Eric later followed up with his witnesses by bringing them to the precinct and showing them photos of the dead girls. But again, no definitive results. Since the crimes had all taken place a few months before Eric had put the pieces together, by the time he showed the witnesses the photos, the reaction was typically some variation of "yeah, she could have been the one I saw driving. Probably. What happened to her?"

Since putting Kane in prison, Eric and George had come close to confirming ten deaths at the hands of Kane, seven of them prostitutes. Eric wondered once more how many others there had been. How many girls did they *not* know about? How many before Kane had shown up in New York a couple of years ago? What other places had Kane been?

Eric saw his exit approaching and signaled a lane change. There was something else that still bothered him. How had the bounty hunter found Kane before his own investigation? Eric and George had been studying the cases alongside the FBI, had been out on the street digging up leads. Eric had dedicated himself to finding and putting away Kane. So how had the bounty hunter tracked him down first?

He couldn't, wouldn't believe that Quinn was that phenomenal a "tracker"—which had been Quinn's response to Eric's question after he briefly regained consciousness in Kane's apartment. Something had led Quinn to Kane's hideout and Eric wanted to know what it was. It wasn't important to the case, wasn't important to Kane staying behind bars, but Quinn had beaten Eric to the target, and it pissed him off.

George wasn't much help. He did his usual "older-and-wiser" routine and told Eric not to sweat it. The bad guy had been caught and went to jail. What difference did it make who put him there? But to Eric, it made a lot of difference. It was an unsolved piece of the puzzle, and it was driving him crazy. He needed to know how Quinn got there before him, and he wanted to know who hired Quinn in the first place. Until he found out, he could not put the case to rest. It was just one of those things.

Eric glanced at the clock in the console and cursed at no one in particular. He was going to be late for court.

CHAPTER 9
October 10
12:58 P.M.

SILAS KANE SAT in the back of the police cruiser as the car wound its way through the streets of New York. He was, as usual, staring straight ahead, expressionless, but his mind was blazing. After six months of cooperation, his handlers were beginning to let their guard down. Where during the initial trial, they had kept Kane in the security van for all trips to court, generally with a cruiser and an extra pair of guards as an escort, they were now transporting him in a car, with no escort. This fit Kane's predictions to the letter.

He had spent his time of incarceration as a model prisoner, with the minor exception of killing the queer in the shower. That incident was unavoidable. The man had brushed his hand against Kane's ass while he was walking by and that was not to be tolerated. The man screamed when Kane lifted him over his head, implored that it had been an accident. His spine had snapped easily over Kane's knee. A satisfying crunch.

Kane regretted having to kill the man—not out of empathy for the fairy or any moral twangs of guilt—but he was afraid the incident might set his plan back a few months, and that was no good. He could not allow the trail to grow cold.

Kane had been concerned that if any of the prisoners informed on him to the guards, had pointed the finger for the queer's death, then security would continue to post a double guard on Kane's trips to the courthouse. Fortunately, all of the prisoners knew that Kane had been sentenced to life in the facility, and none wanted him for an enemy. Cons were smarter than most people assumed.

The recent weeks in solitary proved quite useful. No work detail and no jabbering inmates surrounding him. The silence was conducive to thinking. And that was what Kane had to do. Think.

He had weighed his options for escape from the beginning of his incarceration, but he knew it would not be feasible during the first few months. He had targeted his appeal as the first realistic opportunity. Law enforcement was a predictable beast. It was bound by rules and shackled by a minuscule budget. Kane knew they could not afford to continue assigning extra guards for his transportation. Sure, the initial trial had to have plenty of uniformed officers surrounding him, proving to the good citizens of New York that the boys in blue had the situation well in hand. But an appeal was never a newsworthy event, and Kane had doubted the same accommodations would be afforded to him the second time around. Particularly if he had never caused any problems while under custody.

He knew the guards considered him slow, even stupid. An animal. And that was fine with him.

Kane hadn't spent all of his time in solitary confinement pondering his escape. That was easy. It had taken him less than a week to develop a plan for freedom. Kane had never considered the New York Police Department to be a complex organization. If anything, it was the police officers who were slow, who were stupid. They were predictable and, more importantly, weak. He knew his escape would not be as difficult as his handlers would assume.

What concerned Kane more was what he would do after he escaped. Once he was loose, the clock would be ticking. He needed to proceed quickly once he was free if he was to find the men responsible for his capture. And when he found them. Oh yes...

Kane suppressed a smile. He couldn't risk the driver catching sight of a change in his demeanor in the rearview mirror. He wanted the officers to assume he was in his usual quiet, almost catatonic state.

Kane had spent his time in solitary thinking about the events leading up to his capture. He had mentally retraced almost six months prior to that day in the old apartment when the bounty hunter surprised him. He remembered people he had spoken to. Places he had been. Women he had slept with. Women he had killed. He kept coming up with dead ends.

It wasn't the policemen that concerned him. He had been to that apartment a couple of times in the past, and it was possible that someone in the building had called the cops with a tip. That had been his own mistake. But why was the damned bounty hunter there? The question occupied his mind during the endless hours in the cell. Who had hired a bounty hunter to track him down?

He traced back all the hookers he had killed, the businesses he had either robbed or burned down. There had been no prior connection to any of them. He didn't know any of those people. He just enjoyed killing. He liked hearing the screams of his victims. He liked the feeling of omnipotence that came when you held someone's neck in your hands and knew you held the power of life and death over that individual. That was what he had learned from his father all those years ago. That life is fragile. The weak live only at the indulgence of the strong.

Of course, he had never bought into any of that evil reckoning mumbo-jumbo his father had preached. Silas had never cultivated a spiritual side. He didn't believe in the supernatural. He believed in the strength of steel and the force of aggression. He believed in the thrill of blood being spilt for no reason other than to please him. He believed in the powerful aphrodisiac of grabbing a girl's neck while he was mounting her, and snapping it when he came. That's what he believed in. He would leave all the psychological and spiritual bullshit to his father and brothers. That was why he left the compound when he did.

He never liked the idea of being included in his older brother's plan in New Mexico so Silas left before he could be dragged into it. In retrospect, even sitting in a police car with a set of shackles on, he knew he had made the right choice. What a shit-storm that had been. He hadn't seen Marcus for over five years when he happened to see the aftermath of the whole cluster-fuck running nonstop on CNN.

Silas had deliberated tracking down the bastard responsible for the whole thing, that John Michaels guy, but then he reconsidered. The fact was, he didn't care about what had happened to his brother, they weren't exactly a close family, so he sure didn't see a need to change his lifestyle to find the guy and snuff him. He would leave that to his father.

The car slowed as the driver made a right turn. The two cops were yacking away about the previous night's football game. Who would have ever thought the Giants would be a playoff contender this year? Kane shifted in his seat. Very soon now.

His handlers were oblivious to the mistakes they were making. They were, after all, just doing their duty. Following the rules on prisoner transportation. Going by the book. But the book was never written with Silas Kane in mind. The trip to the courthouse would prove fatal for the two guards in the front seat based on three errors.

First, they were taking the same route to the courthouse that they had each previous journey during Kane's initial trial. Of course, that was the route they were supposed to take. It was all mapped out at the prison. This was the route that was least likely to lead to traffic problems and was the most efficient for time. Just following orders.

Second, they were taking Kane to the courthouse in a squad car rather than the security van. This was also standard procedure. The security van required more personnel to operate. It was typically used for problem prisoners or if there was a danger to that prisoner's safety during a trial. A chance at an enraged citizen trying to shoot the accused, for instance. The van was bulletproof and required the prisoner to sit on a bench in the back, in the secured area. The bench was equipped with metal rings which were designed for the arm and leg shackles to be attached. This would prevent the prisoner from lunging for the guard stationed in the back. But Kane had been a model prisoner, and his appeal was not generating enough media attention to garner additional protection. Consequently, he was being transported in a typical squad vehicle.

This, in turn, led to the final mistake of the guards. Kane's shackles had been removed from his feet. The standard shackles used for maximum security prisoners were in two parts. The first was more or less a typical pair of handcuffs, the primary difference being the thicker size of the cuffs for the shackles. The bands around Kane's wrists were over an inch wide. The second component of the shackles was a leg binding, essentially a longer version of the wrist cuffs designed to keep the prisoner's ankles bound, unable to run. The chain binding the ankle cuffs had an extension about three feet long designed to attach to the center of the wrist cuffs. When joined, this prevented the prisoner from being able to raise his arms above waist level.

On Silas Kane, the shackles were difficult. He was much taller than the average prisoner, and the chain connection between the ankles and wrists forced him to bend at the waist, becoming a gigantic, muscled hunchback. The guards had enforced the shackle rules for the initial trial because of the van. There were a set of steps which permitted entry into the back of the van, and Kane was able to traverse these steps and enter the van with the ankle shackles attached. Once inside, the van was equipped to accommodate a prisoner in the shackles as they could be attached to the metal rings on the bench, holding the captive in place.

But the squad car had a different set of regulations. It was very difficult for a prisoner of normal height to get into the back seat of a police car with the ankle shackles attached. The action required a great deal of maneuvering by the guards to assist the prisoner into position. For a man the size of Silas Kane, the act was almost impossible. Consequently, the leg shackles were routinely removed from prisoners when traveling in the squad car, and Kane was no exception. That was the biggest mistake of all.

The driver of the car signaled a left turn. Kane steadied himself. The route still mimicked the one he had observed from the single window in the back door of the security van so many months ago. Only a couple more blocks until the driver turned right. This would put them on the stretch of road Kane had been waiting for. The majority of the route to the courthouse was through residential or business areas. This street, however, was bordered on one side by an industrial site, and the other by a row of abandoned warehouses. Kane had taken careful notice of this area during his initial trial. He had watched for pedestrians, any faces in open windows, any sort of routine habitation of the area, and he hadn't noticed many at all. He didn't need it to be completely deserted, but the fewer eyes watching the better.

Not long now. Kane shifted his eyes without moving his head. The cops were still talking about a resurgence of their quarterback. Go Giants. Kane confirmed for a third time what he needed to see. The cage separating the rear seat from the front of the car was secured by four bolts, one at each corner. These bolts were secured through brackets on the cage and into the body of the car.

This was why the squad car had been a mistake. The cage was weak. Oh, it was steel, and Kane would not be able punch through the wire mesh even if his wrists were not shackled, but he wouldn't have to. The cage was weak because the car was weak. The bolts for the cage were imbedded in the vehicle's body. The body was comprised of thin sheet metal, not more than an eighth of an inch thick. The cage could withstand a beating, mind you, but it was designed to handle fits of rage by drug addicts trapped in the back seat. It would hold through that sort of unfocused tantrum. But it would not hold against Kane.

Since Kane's ankles were not shackled, his legs had full mobility. Police were so naïve, assuming that if you bound a man's hands then he was no longer a danger, but a man's real strength was in his legs and his back. That's where the power was.

Kane flexed the muscles in his legs. He was ready.

The driver slowed and signaled a right turn. The light was green. There were no other cars on the road. He joked to his partner that the NFC East was ripe for domination. The Giants were a team of destiny.

Kane struck.

CHAPTER 10
October 10
1:10 P.M.

G RANT ARMSTRONG was a young boy again.
He looked down at his reflection in the lake and estimated his age to be around twelve or thirteen. He recognized the poor choice of haircut from his days in middle school. The slight ripples in the water did nothing to diminish his youthful features, his lighter hair from spending summer days in the sun, or his thin, lanky body. Grant had hit a growth spurt in seventh grade, and his weight didn't catch up to his height until he was well into his university years. But the skinny body of his youth never impacted his love of sports, especially baseball, and he had been considered one of the best athletes in the local school system, right up there with his best friend.

He and Eric had always made quite a team. Grant was great at swinging a bat, the best hitter on the Still Pines Cougar baseball team, and Eric was the starting pitcher. They also played doubles tennis together. Eric had never even picked up a racket until Grant introduced the sport to him on the family's court on Armstrong Island. Within a couple of months, Eric was pushing Grant to new levels. Football, soccer, wrestling. Anything but swimming.

Grant had spent an entire summer one year trying to get Eric to swim, had even offered to teach him, but Eric would just shake his head. Some people didn't like the water.

Grant noticed a small rock between his feet and tossed it into his reflection in the lake. His youthful face dispersed in rippling waves. He stood, backed away from the water and looked around. He saw the big house rising above the trees at the top of the slight hill. He realized he was back in the field.

The field was the one area on the island not covered in pine trees. It was bordered on three sides by pine groves and on the fourth, opposite the trail leading to the house, was the lake. The shore was actually a steep ledge, with a drop of five feet to the water below.

The water was deep in this section of the lake. Once you hit the water from the drop-off, you'd have to go down another twenty feet to reach the bottom. The ledge was too tall and steep for boats to comfortably access the island, but it was a perfect place for diving and for...Grant turned his head to see it and smiled. The tree was there. In the big field, there was only one tree that rested at the edge of the lake. A massive oak, beautiful and towering. One large limb jutted out over the water at a forty-five degree angle from the shore. It was there that Grant's dad had hung the rope.

The rope was twenty feet long and made from a thick grade of nylon, as big as the handle of a tennis racket. It hung straight down from the branch about four feet beyond the shore ledge and dangled above the water. Some of Grant's best memories of his dad were the times they spent by that tree, swinging from the rope way out above the water and letting go. Looking back, Grant could hardly believe his dad would let him do something that seemed so dangerous at that early an age—he had installed the rope when Grant was still in elementary school—but they were both strong swimmers and only one would swing at a time, with the other always spotting for safety. His dad had even constructed a rope ladder which hung from the base of the tree over the edge, making it possible to climb back onto shore from the water.

Sometimes Grant's grandfather would join him and his dad by the tree. He would sit in a lawn chair and laugh at the antics of his adult son acting like a kid alongside his own wide-eyed boy who screamed from terror and fun each time he swung out over the water. Those were good times.

After Grant's father died, the rope had never been the same. Some of Aunt Mona's college friends had come to the island for a weekend once. Grant hid in the woods and watched them drink beer, smoke what he would later learn to be pot, and use his rope to swing into the cold lake water. He had been furious. He wanted to storm out of his hiding place and tell them to leave it alone, but he was only a child and feared the group of boys who were much larger than him. And, of course, when one of Mona's girlfriends took off her top to sunbathe, Grant decided he would let the incident slide.

Grant stared at the rope and wondered, if he was dreaming, why couldn't he be dreaming of Mona's topless college friend? Or perhaps a topless Julie, sunbathing by the tree.

Instead, Eric Johnson stepped from the trail between the pine trees, but it was not the Eric of Grant's youth. This was the adult police detective who had picked up Grant at the airport, well over twice the age of the young boy next to the big oak tree. He waved to Grant and made the motion of swinging a bat.

Only then did Grant recognize the utter silence surrounding him. The thought hadn't occurred to him until his friend had declined to speak, choosing instead the rudimentary sign language. There were no birds singing, no crickets chirping, no wind whispering through the pines. Even the lapping of the lake against the shore made no sound.

Eric again mimed swinging a bat while he walked across the field toward the lake. Grant looked down at the oak tree again. There, at the base, was the large wooden box that Grant's grandfather had given him. It resembled, more or less, a child's toy box, with a lid which swung on hinges. Inside the box, Grant and Eric had kept all of their sports equipment—baseballs, gloves, footballs, a Frisbee—anything they could use to entertain themselves in the field.

The summer of their seventh grade year, Eric found a Penthouse magazine in the trash can outside a convenience store. The boys marveled at their luck, and they kept it hidden under the sports equipment all summer, pulling it out and gazing with wonder at the models on the pages, always checking the path to make sure no one was coming from the house. The oak box was a treasure chest of his youth. There was even a slight notch cut beneath the lid of the box for the handle of the hickory baseball bat, a Louisville Slugger, to protrude.

Grant walked over and opened the lid. He reached in and grabbed a baseball with one hand and the bat with his other. He noticed the Penthouse wasn't in the box. The dream wasn't so accurate after all. He turned and threw the ball to Eric who caught it barehanded without a grimace. Just as when he was a kid, Grant knocked the dust off his nonexistent spikes with the end of the bat. Then, he set up his swinging stance in front of the oak tree.

It was a ritual the two had been through a thousand times. Without a catcher, it was a difficult game. But Grant was confident in his batting skills, and Eric was equally confident in his pitching abilities. The game was simple. Eric would pitch the baseball at the tree, immediately above the box. A solid hit would result in Eric running into the trees to chase the ball. If Grant swung and missed, the ball would bounce off the tree and be considered a strike. On the other hand, if the pitch missed the tree and flew into the lake behind it, it would be considered a "ball."

Of course, the event of a ball was a tremendous pain in the ass. The two had rigged up a long pole with a butterfly net attached to the end to retrieve these. They kept it tied against the trunk of the tree using an extra-long bungee cord they found in the garage. Still, a pitch into the water ground the game to a halt and left the ball soggy for the rest of the game. Fortunately, Eric rarely made a bad pitch as the pocked and dented bark of the oak's trunk could attest.

As the young Grant ground his foot into the dirt, preparing his swing, the adult Eric wound up his pitch. Eric released the ball, and Grant waited until the perfect moment to swing. The bat connected with the same silence that permeated the field. A foul tip. The ball traveled straight above Grant's head, into the big oak tree. It silently bounced off the branches, knocking leaves loose, then fell. The odds were in favor of it landing on the shore, near Grant, but as it made its descent, it bounced off one final branch and ricocheted into the lake.

Young Grant uttered a swear word only adult Grant would know, but no sound emanated from his mouth. He looked back at Eric, who shook his head and shrugged his shoulders, it wasn't his fault. Grant grabbed the pole with the butterfly net and unsnapped the bungee cord, freeing it from the oak tree. He walked to the edge and peered into the water. The ball was nowhere to be found. This was unusual. A baseball will always float for several minutes. Plenty of time to grab the pole and retrieve it.

Grant set the pole on the ground, aligning it with the ledge, and got onto his hands and knees to peer closer into the water. He rested his chest on the ground and hung his head entirely over the edge. He was again struck by his youthful appearance in the water's reflection, but something didn't look right. Something was distorted.

Grant leaned closer to the water. Peering through his own reflection, he saw his grandfather beneath the surface. Abraham Armstrong was staring straight up at Grant, a foot under the water, eyes wide and gray hair floating around his head. Grant pushed himself back from the ledge, yelping a soundless scream.

He took a breath, then lowered himself back to the edge. His grandfather was alive, mouth moving though no air bubbles were breaking the surface. At first, it looked to Grant as if his grandfather was standing underneath the lake's surface. As he looked closer, Grant realized his grandfather had been bound, his hands tied behind his back and his feet weighted. He was drowning.

Grant had to save him. He reached down from the ledge, but his arm stopped well short of the water's surface. Grant saw his own hand and remembered that he was still just a child. He pushed himself up and spun around to find Eric. He was a man. He would be able to help. But Eric had vanished. He was no longer in the field.

Grant looked back at the water, his grandfather was still struggling, looking to his grandson for help. Grant did the only thing he could think of, he turned and dove off the ledge and into the water.

When Grant broke the plane of the lake, it was not the shock of the icy water, but the sounds which overwhelmed him. It was as if the surface of the lake had been containing all the noise of the world. Where the air was silent, the water was pulsating with screams and sounds of all sort. He spun himself under the water to face his grandfather. Here, Abraham Armstrong was no longer silent. He was yelling, pleading with Grant to free him, to not let them kill him. Never questioning the impossibility of voices traveling so clearly underwater, Grant swam toward Abe.

He was terrified. He could not let his grandfather die again. He maneuvered behind his grandfather to try and free the ropes binding his hands. Grant could hear the old man yelling, and the panicked sound of his voice frightened him even more. He had never heard his grandfather panic.

"Never mind my hands, boy, get 'em off my legs!"

Grant assumed his grandfather meant the ropes tied to his feet so he kicked his legs up over his head and swam lower. His lungs were starting to burn from holding his breath.

That was when Grant saw "them." There, deep under the water and holding the ropes binding his grandfather's feet, was Grant's family. Phil and Loraine were holding one rope while Mona and Brock held another. All four of them were wearing diver's masks with oxygen tanks, breathing comfortably while his grandfather's lungs filled with the freezing lake water. Although he couldn't see their mouths, Grant knew they were smiling.

Grant's lungs were on fire. He was sure his grandfather couldn't last, but when he looked up he noticed his grandfather's hands were now somehow free. Abe reached down and grabbed the young Grant's t-shirt, pulling him up to face him. Grant wanted to scream, but knew the icy water would fill his lungs. His grandfather's expression had gone from fear to rage. An expression Grant had never seen Abe

Armstrong wear. But then, the thing holding the young boy under the water was no longer Abraham Armstrong. The thing's eyes had turned completely black as if coated in oil. It screamed. "You're too late, boy! You couldn't save me, and now Julie gets everything!"

The black-eyed creature that once was Grant's grandfather began laughing. Grant tried to kick to the surface, he knew he was about to black out, but the old man's grip was tight. He kicked the thing in the groin but his skinny young legs had no strength. He stretched one hand up and it broke the surface. His fingertips could feel the air he needed but could not quite reach. He looked from the surface back to the figure holding him. Its teeth had turned black and become sharpened fangs. When it closed its mouth, the fangs sank into the thing's blue lips.

The freezing water seeped into Grant's nose as his breath gave out. The grandfather-creature pulled Grant's face close to its own. It stopped laughing and looked at the boy intensely, its black eyes burning into him.

It opened its mouth and spoke using a voice completely alien from his grandfather's soft tone, "What are you going to do now, boy?"

Grant could contain it no longer. He opened his mouth to scream and the water poured in, freezing his throat and lungs as it filled him.

He bolted upright in bed, gasping for breath. Grant clenched his teeth to stop the scream. He was sweating through his clothes, beads of perspiration trickled down his forehead and into his eyes.

It took him a moment to get his bearings. He looked around with hazy vision and remembered he was in his old room. He had laid down on the bed, fully dressed, and had fallen straight into the first real sleep he had experienced since getting word his grandfather had passed away. How long had he been lying there? Grant checked the clock by the bed. He had slept less than hour.

He sat in bed, breathing hard and sweating as his senses gradually returned, and realized that he smelled like someone who hadn't showered in far too long. He swung his legs over the side of the bed and got up. At last, a problem he could solve.

CHAPTER 11
October 10
1:15 P.M.

T HE TIME was now.

Kane raised his arms above his head and braced them against the ceiling of the squad car. He leaned back, his butt stretching to the edge of the seat with his shoulders firmly planted into the back padding. He drew his knees to his chin and drove his legs forward.

Kane's feet struck the cage above the head of the guard in the passenger seat. A loud clang filled the car as the cage bent outward and struck the man hard. The driver jumped as if he had been shot. Kane saw him look to his partner in the passenger seat—leaning forward with hands protectively covering the back of this head—then saw the driver's eyes flash to him in the rearview mirror. Kane drew his knees to his chin again.

Kane pistoned his legs out striking the cage at the same point. He had hoped the bolt would come free after the first kick. It had not, but he had felt it loosen. He figured he had another three seconds before one of the guards recovered his senses and pointed a gun at him.

The second kick forced the cage out further, the bolt was now bent, but had not given way. The guard in the passenger seat was regaining his composure. If his head had been resting against the cage, he would surely have been knocked unconscious from the initial blow.

The driver hit the brakes. Hard.

Kane felt the brakes and smiled, even as he drew his legs back again. Had the cop accelerated and tried to clear the industrial area, he may have reached a populated street. Although that would not have stopped Kane, it would have hindered his escape. Someone would see what was going on and a massive police movement would be underway in the area within minutes. Kane didn't want that. He needed at least five minute's worth of head start.

The guard in the passenger seat was reaching to unholster his revolver. Kane struck his legs out once more. The side of the cage exploded outward just as the guard was leaning back, his gun free. The cage smacked the back of his head with a thud. The guard fell forward, forehead bouncing off the glove compartment. The cage was bent in half and resting between the unconscious passenger and the driver, the bolts securing the cage behind the driver still attached.

The car had almost stopped. Kane moved fast. If the driver got out of the door, he would be able to draw his gun before Kane could work his way into the front seat. Both the driver's hands were off the steering wheel now. His left hand was on the door handle while his right was reaching for his revolver. Kane leaned over the front seat through the opening in the cage and grabbed the guard's arm at the wrist, halting his efforts to remove the gun. Kane wrenched his own hand upward and felt the driver's wrist snap. The man howled in pain and pulled on the door handle, his thoughts clearly turning to escape.

Kane leaned far over the seat and braced his knee against the bent cage by the driver's head. He grabbed the driver's wrist with both hands and pulled it toward the passenger door, above his partner's limp body. The driver's shoulder slid under the cage so that only his head was pressed against the unforgiving steel mesh. Kane pulled the arm further, as if he was forcing the driver to touch the passenger window.

The driver screamed as he tried to lower his head, slip it under the cage, but the pressure was too great. Kane pulled harder, exertion mixed with glee on his face. He felt the driver's shoulder separate as the arm pulled out an additional two inches without the guard's head moving. Kane was careful to keep constant pressure, he didn't want to tear the man's arm off and risk the driver making it out of the car onto the street, screaming and waving a bloody stump around. That would attract attention even in this part of the city.

The driver's ear filled with blood as the steel mesh drove deeper and formed crisscross lacerations into his flesh. His screaming paused to take a breath, and in that instant when his neck had to relax ever-so-slightly in order to inhale, Kane pulled harder.

The driver's neck cracked and his head flopped to his left shoulder. The resistance abruptly gone, his body was dragged fully under the cage before Kane could stop the momentum. The driver's right ear, already bloody from the pressure, snagged on the bottom of the steel mesh and separated from the head.

Kane released his grip on the now limp arm and righted himself. The whole episode had taken less than a minute. The car had almost come to a stop but remained in gear and traveled along the center of the road at the speed of a slow walk. Kane saw the driver's ear hanging from a catch in the mesh of the cage. He considered putting it in his pocket as a keepsake.

He leaned forward and reached into the passenger guard's front pocket. Kane had seen him put the keys to the shackles in there. He felt around and found a pocketknife, some lip balm, and...jackpot. Kane removed the keys and freed himself from the wrist cuffs.

He opened the front passenger door and slid out of the moving car. He looked around and couldn't believe what he saw. No one. Not a single witness to what had just occurred. The noise of the city was all around him, but there wasn't a single person in sight who might have seen what happened and called the cops.

Fucking-A.

He walked to the other side of the slowly moving vehicle, opened the driver's door and maneuvered himself onto the seat next to the dead body. He stopped the car and scanned the area again. Next step was to hide the vehicle and disable the GPS. It wouldn't take long for someone to figure out something had gone wrong, he was due in court in twenty minutes, but if there was no car then no one would know where along the way he had escaped. That bought him some time.

Kane stepped on the accelerator and drove toward the open garage door of one of the abandoned warehouses. He was free.

Time to find the bounty hunter.

CHAPTER 12

October 10
1:45 P.M.

G RANT BENT his head forward and let the hot water cascade onto the back of his neck. He was still stiff from so much quality time in an airplane seat, and his nap hadn't done much in the way of relaxing him. He couldn't shake the image of the oily-eyed grandfather-creature under the water. Or his scream.

What are you going to do now, boy?

Grant looked at the bar of soap. It was held in the full-sized hands of a man, not a kid.

The nightmare bothered him. Not so much that he had had a nightmare—bad dreams were common for people under stress, and Grant felt his current situation certainly qualified as stressful—but he was concerned about the nightmare's nature. He had never experienced a dream like that before. His nightmares usually consisted of being surrounded by snakes or of falling from an airplane, what he considered pretty normal stuff, but this had been different. This had been his grandfather.

From an analytical standpoint, Grant believed he understood the underlying cause of the dream. Eric had told him that his grandfather may have been murdered. A murder, unlike a heart attack, may have been preventable. If Grant had been home instead of venturing out saving the planet, perhaps Abraham Armstrong would be alive today.

But what about his aunts and uncles holding the ropes? Had he really bought into the idea of murder so quickly? Was he already subconsciously classifying his entire family as a bunch of blood-thirsty monsters? He couldn't believe that. He couldn't let himself think anything like that, at least until Eric had something concrete for confirmation.

What really bothered Grant was the transformation his grandfather had undergone while drowning. His grandfather had been gruff, yes, but still had been one of the kindest men Grant had ever known. It didn't make any sense for him to mutate into something hideous and then try to drown Grant in the process. And what in the world was the remark about Julie? Did Grant really care about the money? Deep down, was he concerned that his grandfather had been thinking of including her in the will?

Grant had always prided himself on not caring about the money. Sure, he was appreciative of the opportunities his grandfather's wealth had brought, he never would have been able to afford college at Oxford without it, but he had worked hard all his life. He had always believed himself to be above what he considered the petty greed of the rest of his family, but dreams often open the doors left closed and locked when awake. Maybe Grant really did care about the money.

He raised his face and let the spray from the shower hit him on the forehead. It was a moot point anyway. Murder or heart attack, his grandfather had died before he had a chance to rewrite anything.

Grant vowed to himself that he would make sure Julie was well-compensated regardless of the feelings of the rest of his family. If money was so important to everyone, let them watch what he planned to do with it. Grant knew he would be included in the will. In truth, he suspected there was a strong possibility he would inherit the majority of the estate, and if he wanted to reward Julie for taking care of his grandfather, that was his prerogative.

He tried to imagine what his grandfather's last days were like. Was he happy? Did Julie push his wheelchair outside so he could smell the fragrance of the pine trees? Did he get a chance to read the last letter Grant had sent?

Grant stepped back so the water cascaded against his chest. When was his last letter mailed? He routinely wrote to his grandfather every Tuesday. International mail typically took about a week to ten days which meant his last correspondence wouldn't have arrived yet. Grant shook his head. It had been a good letter. He had written about the little girl he had saved from gangrene. She had been bitten on the leg by a cobra and instead of taking her to the clinic, the girl's parents had taken her to a local shaman. The butcher had used a ceremonial bone knife to cut off the portion of her calf that had been bitten.

To an extent, the old witch doctor succeeded in saving the girl. She had not died from the snake venom, but by the time they brought her to Grant, a full week later, her calf was rotted with gangrene. Grant had used a new technique in infection therapy and had been able to save the girl's leg. She would have a limp for the rest of her life, but she would be able to walk without a prosthetic limb.

Grant knew his grandfather would have been proud. He wondered if Abe's sight had been strong enough to read the letters himself or if Julie had read them for him. The last time he had been home, his grandfather's glasses were looking like coke bottles, but the old man loved those letters.

Grant knew the correspondence had always been special to his grandfather. It started the summer after his father had died. Grant went away to camp for three weeks, and his grandfather had given him a wrapped box with instructions not to open it until he got to his cabin. When Grant tore open the paper, he found a box of stationary with a stack of blue envelopes and a note from his grandfather. The note requested that Grant write at least twice a week so his grandfather would know he was doing okay. He said the envelopes were blue so he could spot Grant's letter in the mailbox and be sure to open that one first.

Knowing his grandfather would be lonely without him, Grant had written him every day that first summer. It was a tradition he had maintained. Every summer camp, he would equip his bag with stationary and blue envelopes. Grant continued the correspondence throughout his years in college. Granted, Abe never wrote him back, but he had never expected it. That wasn't what the letters were for. When his grandfather saw the blue envelope in that day's mail, he would know Grant was thinking about him. Thus the blue envelopes had eventually made weekly trips across the Atlantic, first from England and later from Africa.

Looking back, Grant wished that he had called at least once during the past few months in Africa, but people are creatures of habit. He had written his letters and stamped his blue envelopes and had never even thought about going into the city to place a phone call, but he wished he could have heard his grandfather's voice just one last time. Now, all he could hear was the raspy voice from the thing in his nightmare. It wasn't fair.

Grant dressed in clean clothes, khaki pants and a white shirt, and looked around his room. It was amazing how little had changed. His dresser still had the trophies reflecting his two high school loves, baseball and science. He picked up the trophy from the New York State Science Fair from his junior year. Second place. Not first but not bad.

He picked up a photo of himself, his father and his granddad. They were standing in front of the big oak tree by the lake, all of them smiling with their arms around each other. Grant remembered the day. It had been the first summer after Grant and his father had moved in with Abe on the island, the summer his dad had tied the rope to the tree.

He put the picture back on the dresser and walked to the window. He could see the distant roof of the guest house over the trees. He wondered if Phil and Loraine were there. He had hoped to speak with them before he saw Mona and Brock. Partly because Grant still needed to thank his uncle for the message, more so because he wasn't up to enduring the Brock Rutland experience quite yet.

Grant left his bedroom and started down the hall. He stopped in front of Julie's room and peeked in the half open door. Her room was empty. On the dresser next to her bed were some basic medical tools—a blood pressure strap plus a few odds and ends—and a picture.

Indulging his curiosity, Grant stepped into the door and picked up the small silver frame. It was a photograph of Julie's family on a picnic. There were four people in the picture. A mother and father and two young girls, both blonde but only one smiling. No one looked especially happy, and only the one little girl was making an attempt to smile. The picture reminded Grant of the old black-and-white photographs from the late eighteen-hundreds when everyone felt obligated to look solemn and wouldn't dare smile for a picture. Grant wondered if the smiling little girl was Julie, or if the woman who had been kind enough to feed him pizza this morning was the somber child in the photograph. The girls were too young and similar in age to discern one from the other.

Grant realized he knew very little about the person who had spent the most time with his grandfather before his death. Granted, he had liked Julie immediately, but he knew that was at least partly influenced by a physical attraction. Not that he didn't trust her. She had, in fact, already displayed more genuine grief for Abe Armstrong than Grant suspected the rest of his family had felt combined. She had even seemed to feel guilty about his grandfather's death given her role as his healthcare worker.

In a way, that made Grant trust her more. In his brief time since graduating medical school, he had seen more death than most doctors his age. And with each death, even though there may have been nothing he or anyone else could have done to save the individual dying, Grant felt pangs of guilt. He cared about his patients. Julie cared for his grandfather. That much was evident. And if Abe's death was the result of a heart attack, Grant couldn't fault Julie for not being able to save him.

She had mentioned that she was not a Registered Nurse. That hadn't surprised Grant at all. Most in-home healthcare workers he had known were young women with Associates degrees in nursing, specializing in simply being there for patients who needed minor physical therapy and, more than anything, someone to talk to. Healthcare workers of that category never worked for those with any serious medical needs. After his grandfather had broken his hip with the fall in the backyard a year and a half ago (Grant had been serving the first half of his residency in England), Grant had recommended he get a list of qualified healthcare workers from the hospital. He knew Abe had interviewed several candidates before deciding on the one he enjoyed being around the most. And based on their brief time together, Grant could understand why his grandfather had chosen as he did.

Grant studied the picture in his hand. The somber family out for a picnic on a sunny summer afternoon. He wondered what Julie's father and sister were doing since her mom died last Christmas. It had taken Grant a long time to recover from his own father's death, and having a friend like Eric was a large part of that recovery process. He wondered if Julie kept in touch with her family since the funeral. He would ask once they had spent more time together.

He placed the frame back in its original position on the dresser and left the room. He felt guilty being there without Julie present. She may have been an employee of the house, but she still deserved privacy.

As Grant proceeded down the hall toward the master suite, the back of his neck began to tickle. The hairs there were standing up.

The last overhead light in the hallway, the one closest to his grandfather's room, was not burning. With no windows in the hallway to provide illumination and with the doors to the rooms aligning either side of the hallway closed, the end of the corridor was dark. Grant remembered as a child asking his father why they had built the house so big. He didn't like having to walk down the hall by himself at night. The fear of a child, but one that perhaps never went away, particularly not after the dream.

What are you going to do now, boy?

Grant realized he had stopped in the middle of the hallway. He shook his head. Ridiculous. He was a grown man who had endured the hardships of Africa for the past year, he wasn't about to let one bad dream affect his ability to walk through life, much less walk down an empty hallway. And yet, Grant paused, hesitant to pass into the darkness towards the room of his deceased grandfather.

Instead, he turned toward the door closest to him. His father's old room. The door was open a crack. Grant touched his fingertips to the door and it eased open. He remained in the hallway rather than entering.

The room was as it had been since Jack Armstrong died. Same furniture. Arranged the same way. Grant doubted anyone had ever spent a night in this room after the accident. His gaze stopped on the desk. The desk was an antique. A roll top. Big and old. Its cubby holes and drawers and various compartments had harbored his father's keepsakes. Pictures of Grant and his mother. Work files. Cards and letters of personal significance. Even an old revolver once owned by General George Patton purchased at a charity auction. With the exception of once showing it to his son, Grant didn't think Jack Armstrong had ever removed the gun from its cloth-lined wooden box. It stayed in the bottom drawer of the desk. The locked drawer. Forbidden treasure in the mind of a young Grant.

But something about the desk *had* changed since Grant was last here. It wasn't clean. There were books and papers scattered on the surface. The desk was actually being utilized. That was good. It shouldn't just sit unused and collecting dust.

He pulled the door shut. The sight of his father's room had calmed him. He felt more in control. He could face the ghost at the end of the hall. Even if it was dark.

Grant reached the entry to the master suite. As he grasped the knob and opened the door, it creaked. The effect was disconcerting. The memory of the creature from his nightmare remained fresh, and the little boy from the dream expected the opening door to reveal a monster awaiting him in his grandfather's room.

The room was empty. The curtains had been drawn and the room was dark, but it was vacant. Grant walked to the nearest window and threw open the curtains. Afternoon sunlight filled the room. He opened the curtains of the remaining windows until the room was bright.

Grant glanced around the room. A glass of water was on the nightstand by the large oak-framed bed. He wondered how long the glass had been sitting there. Had his grandfather been drinking it the night he died? He started to pick it up and changed his mind. Eric had made him paranoid. If his grandfather had been murdered, then this room would become a crime scene.

Grant knew his friend was doing his best to keep this quiet. If Abe had died of natural causes, the public implication of murder would leave harsh scars on a family that was already dysfunctional at best. The autopsy was a litmus test. If the results came back as a confirmed heart attack, then no one would ever know of Eric's suspicions except Grant. But if the autopsy results pointed toward murder, then things would get intense. As they should.

Grant walked into the master suite's bathroom and turned on the light. Tile and porcelain and marble shone. Everything was spotless. This was how Grant remembered his grandfather. Always running a tight ship. Making sure the cleaning lady always did a good job on his bathroom when she came to the house on Fridays. Grant wondered if Mrs. Gonzalez still managed the cleaning duties. She was a sweet woman who always whistled softly while she cleaned and had been coming to the house since Grant was a boy. Grant never knew how much his grandfather paid her, but he knew it had to be significantly more than she made on her other jobs because she was always so happy to see Abraham Armstrong.

Grant wondered if Mrs. Gonzalez had heard about his grandfather's death. Surely she had. Still Pines was a small town and this was big news. Would she come by on Friday anyway?

He saw his reflection in the mirror. How much of his grandfather could he see in himself? Ever since his father had died, Grant anticipated seeing Jack Armstrong's features develop on his own face as he grew older. He had gotten some. His blue eyes were undoubtedly his father's. And his hair had begun to recede above his temples, much as his father's had. But now he could see the family resemblance through three generations. He had Abraham Armstrong's chin.

Grant pulled open the mirrored door to the medicine cabinet. He wasn't sure what he was looking for. Clues, perhaps? Is this what Eric did for a living? Grant perused the contents of the cabinet. There was all the usual stuff, toothpaste and mouthwash, deodorant and shaving cream, and an assortment of pills not unusual for someone his grandfather's age.

He started inspecting the bottles of prescription medication. Hydrochlorothiazide for a diuretic. Triazolam for insomnia. Cholestyramine for cholesterol. And some Advil. Nothing unusual and nothing which could have triggered a heart attack, although any one of them could have been used for a fatal overdose if given in high enough quantities. Grant doubted that possibility. Deaths from an overdose were messy. The movies sterilized overdose deaths by showing the victim slumping over and quietly passing on. In the real world, the body attempts to save itself and overdose victims almost always vomited or defecated themselves as their bodies tried to express whatever was poisoning the system. The description of Abraham Armstrong's death matched that of someone suffering a massive coronary infarction, not a victim of poisoning.

Grant put the bottles back in the medicine cabinet and turned to leave the bathroom when something caught his eye. He took a step toward the clear glass door of the shower, not believing what he was seeing. His grandfather had always abhorred baths and hadn't even bothered having a tub put into his own bathroom when the house was built. He was a shower man. Quick. Efficient.

The shower itself was as it had always been, a large tile and glass facility equipped with a handicapped seat which had been installed after Abe had suffered the broken hip and was confined to the wheelchair. What was inside the shower gave Grant pause. He opened the door to get a better look and couldn't help smiling. There, hanging from the shampoo rack beneath the showerhead, was a mesh puff bathing sponge. A pink one. The kind you used with bath gel to work a lather.

Grant shook his head. It was something small yet monumental. For as long as Grant could remember, Abraham Armstrong had always been a man's man. He would refer to any severe cut as "just a scratch" and would turn up his nose to any meal that involved quiche. That was just the way he was. And Grant was sure he had always used a simple "washrag" whenever he would take a shower. He knew because that was what his father had used and what he used himself. Now, to see something so frilly as a shower pouf and, wait, it couldn't be, but it was. There, resting on the shower rack above the pouf, was a bottle of raspberry scented bath gel.

Grant closed the door to the shower, still smiling. He was struck by the realization at how little time he had spent with his grandfather in the year before he died. On reflection, over the past several years. Once he started medical school, he had stopped coming home during semester breaks. And the past few years, with the exception of brief holiday visits, he had not seen his grandfather at all. The shower pouf represented a different Abe Armstrong than he knew, a changed man. It wasn't a big change, a minor adjustment in hygiene attitude, but it altered Grant's image of the static, rock of a man he had always imagined his grandfather to be.

The immensity of his lack of communication during the past year struck home. After he had left from his Christmas visit, he had not even called. He had written his letters regularly, but had not even considered trying to dig into what was happening in his grandfather's life. He had assumed it was business as usual in the Armstrong household unless someone contacted him and informed him otherwise.

He was selfish.

The thought hit him like a punch in the face. He had patted himself on the back for writing so regularly, but it didn't mean anything. He had not bothered to call his grandfather once. Had not made the effort.

Internal rationalization kicked in as Grant left the bathroom and switched off the light. Perhaps he was being too hard on himself. It was just a shower pouf. Even if he had called, it's not as if his grandfather would have said, "Guess what, Grant. I'm using raspberry bath gel these days." It was probably a gift from someone, and perhaps Abe used it once or twice to be nice.

It was a small thing to change, but sometimes the little things matter. And no matter what Grant said to make himself feel better, he couldn't erase the feeling of guilt.

Grant started to leave the room but stopped by the door. There sat his grandfather's stainless steel wheelchair. After the fall and the broken hip, Grant had never heard Abe complain once about his accident. Had never said a discouraging word about having to be confined to the wheelchair. Shit happened. It was part of life. But it's what you do with the rest of your life that matters. That's what Abraham Armstrong believed. But that life was over.

What are you going to do now, boy?

Grant knelt in front of the chair and placed his hands on the armrests. Abraham Armstrong was really gone. The chair would never be sat in again. Grant dropped his head, squeezed his eyes shut against the onset of tears and whispered, "I'm sorry, Granddad."

The sound of a car door slamming outside interrupted him. The rest of the family was home. Grant lifted his head, wiped his eyes with the backs of his hands and walked out the door.

A reunion awaited.

CHAPTER 13
October 10
2:05 P.M.

"**H**OW COULD he have escaped?!" The question was more than loud enough to be heard over the ringing phones and dull roar of cop talk.

"Take it easy, Eric. We don't know for sure that he escaped." George O'Brien was doing his best to calm his partner down. He had a good guess that he would not succeed.

"What other explanation is there? We haven't been able to contact the officers in the car, and why the hell use a squad car? And why isn't the GPS registering? And did I mention why the hell weren't they using the van in the first place?! I mean, what...the...fuck?!"

George slumped his shoulders and hiked up one leg to half-sit on top of the desk. He felt old. Although he tried to prevent Eric from jumping to the worst of conclusions, he had already made that same jump himself. Silas Kane had escaped, and no one knew what to do about it.

Sitting on the desk was a type of compromise for the older detective. Eric was pacing up and down the squad room, a young lion ready to pounce. George had been on his feet all morning and even the adrenaline of an escaped lunatic didn't give him the energy to stalk the desks of the precinct, but dropping into his well-worn desk chair didn't seem appropriate given the circumstances. So he had cleared the pencils and forms off a section of his desk and perched himself there as he talked to his agitated partner. He felt old indeed.

"Has the captain said anything yet?" George hoped to redirect Eric to a useful topic, to keep his partner on track.

"Yeah, he called a minute ago. Said he wanted to see me at two-fifteen."

George glanced at his watch. "Looks like you've only got a couple minutes." The words didn't appear to register on his partner so George continued to sit, pretending to be deep in thought about Silas Kane, but truthfully just watching Eric pace. He knew that Eric's mind was racing through a thousand different scenarios of how Kane had escaped, and a thousand different possibilities on how to recapture him. George was proud of him. Proud of the cop he had become.

Eric Johnson had joined the NYPD homicide team as the youngest detective ever accepted to the department. He had gotten where he was through hard work, intelligence and impressive street psychology. Eric had a way with people. When he joined the department, all he really needed was some guidance, someone to show him the ropes. That someone was George O'Brien, and the arrangement had worked out very well. For the last three years, George had watched Eric develop into one of the best homicide detectives in New York. He was quick, mentally and physically, and nine times out of ten, it was the mental quickness that was the most important in their job. Speaking to people. Asking the right questions to find the answers that led to the truth. These were the things Eric had proven adept at, and the truth was, he was now better at it than George.

George shook his head as he watched his partner look over the large map of New York City tacked to the wall. Eric was tracing the route from the prison to the courthouse with his finger.

George didn't mind how fast his partner had developed. He knew his place in the food chain. He was a decent cop who was pushing retirement and was never going to be promoted again. He could accept those facts with dignity. He knew he wasn't as smart as his partner. He knew he wasn't as good when it came to working with witnesses and suspects as Eric even though he had been patrolling the streets when his partner was in diapers. Eric had a gift, and George could recognize and appreciate that gift without feeling slighted at his own abilities.

Eric pulled his finger away from the map and straightened. He stared at the paper with an intensity that should have burned a hole through it. George didn't expect the map would tell them much, but Eric stood entranced. George could tell his partner just *knew* the answer to the escape was buried within the street names and multi-colored zip-code sections which served to mark jurisdiction lines.

George could remember when he felt the same as Eric. When he was on fire to catch criminals and protect the good people of New York. Of course, George had been in his mid-forties by the time he joined the homicide division. He had spent the first two decades of his career as a beat cop, patrolling the streets, but he had always wanted to work in the big leagues. Solving murder cases, just like the guys on television.

Unfortunately, George's strong suit had never been his intellectual prowess, but he worked hard, and he had gotten to know a lot of people on the street. It was these connections that had finally gotten him into the homicide department. It was worthwhile to have a guy on board who was familiar with the street and with the city's players, and that had been George's ticket in, but he had never been instrumental in solving a case. He had never "cracked a big one" during his career. He was more of a catalyst. He used his connections to help other cops in the department solve the case. But he didn't mind. He had come to accept his role and was proud of the job he did. He was important.

And he had taught Eric a lot since they had been together. His partner's skills were evident when he first came into the department. Homicide rarely took cops under the age of thirty. It wasn't a written policy, but the job took a lot of maturity, a lot of patience. Eric had been the exception, joining the team in his mid-twenties. George knew that Eric had been assigned as his partner for a very simple reason, they complimented each other. Eric's strong suits were his intuitiveness and his drive, George's were his street connections and his patience.

They had made a great team, and Eric had turned into a hell of a detective. But his partner was obviously still learning when it came to patience.

"Son of a bitch!" Eric's exclamation caught a number of officers off guard and activity in the room ceased. Eric was still staring at the map, transfixed. He addressed George without taking his eyes from the wall. "I think we got him, George. It had to be here." He was pointing to a street. "That's where he had to do it. We would have gotten a call if it had been anywhere else. Someone would have seen something. It had to be there."

George pushed himself off the desk and walked to the wall to look at the spot Eric was pointing to on the map. He knew the place. "Yeah, industrial section. Just some old warehouses. Not much foot traffic. Could be..." He glanced at the white clock on the squad room wall. "Get your ass into the captain's office. You're late. We'll hit this once you get out."

"Yeah...that's the place." Eric was in his own world as he walked out.

George was left staring at the map. The kid could be right. If the guards had taken the required route from the prison to the courthouse that would have been the only spot where no one would recognize something big go down. George walked to his desk and flopped into his comfortable chair. It creaked beneath his weight. The kid was good. George just hoped his partner was right.

Eric stepped out of the captain's office after ten minutes. It had been a short meeting, and he was still in shock. Captain Foley had put him in charge of the recovery operation. Had said that although there was no confirmation that Kane had escaped, the department assumption would be that he had. The captain had told Eric that the first step in the operation was to issue an all-points-bulletin for Kane. After that, it was up to him. He said that Eric knew more about Kane than anyone else, and that he would have the best chance of bringing him back in.

Eric was reluctant to accept the command, but he knew Foley was right.

He had then told the captain about the warehouse district and his suspicion that it had to have been the point of escape. Foley had nodded, told him good luck and opened the door.

Now Eric stood outside the door with a sheen of sweat on his face. He had never been directly in charge of a major operation. He and George had worked on their share of cases where they had some level of autonomy to call the shots, but nothing like this.

George.

Eric hoped he wouldn't be upset about this. George would never say anything, of course. He'd never say it was unfair for a cop half his age with a fraction of his experience in the department to be running an operation recovering a criminal he had helped put away, but still...

George was his friend. Eric knew what other people in the department thought of him. Had heard their conversations. Not the sharpest crayon in the box. Not the brightest bulb in the chandelier. But everyone knew him to be a good, honest cop, and it pissed Eric off when he overheard George's "friends" saying those things about him.

But then here he was, about to take command of a man old enough to be his father. About to head an operation spanning multiple departments and giving orders to a lot of men who were working the street when he was still in junior high. But the only one whose opinion mattered was George.

Eric walked to the water fountain and bent down to take a drink of the semi-cool water. It tasted of copper. What was he doing? He could handle this. He knew he could. He *did* know Silas Kane better than anyone else, including George. And he was the best chance the force had of bringing him back into custody.

Eric lowered his head and let the water run over his face, washing away the sweat. He straightened and shook his head from side to side, most of the water flying onto the tiled floor of the hallway in small droplets. He put both palms to his face and pushed them back over his ears, forcing the remaining water off.

All that mattered was Silas Kane. He was a killer. He was on the streets. He would kill again if he wasn't caught. And Eric wasn't about to let that happen. He turned and marched down the hall to the squad room. Eric was going to bring Kane back in, even if it killed him.

George took his seat in the conference room along with about twenty police officers, some homicide detectives plus several street cops assigned to the operation. It had been less than fifteen minutes since the captain had assigned Eric command of the recovery force, and George was impressed with how quickly the officers responded to the impromptu meeting. Eric looked around the room from his place by the white-screen on the front wall. No smiles among the attendees and not a donut in the room. This was serious.

"All right, people." The murmurs of the officers quieted as Eric began to speak. "Although we don't have confirmation, our working assumption is that Silas Kane escaped en route to the courthouse approximately an hour ago."

Eric placed the transparency with the highlighted map onto the overhead projector and flipped the switch. Some precincts actually had laptops with projectors for this sort of thing. The budget hadn't allowed that here yet. The white screen behind Eric became a black and white city map with a red line tracing the path from the prison to the courthouse. A green circle stood out as the only other color on the screen.

"Our priority here is getting Kane back under wraps fast. Every hour he's on the street is going to make it exponentially more difficult to find him. This man is dangerous and smarter than you think. Most of you know the facts behind this guy. We cannot give him the opportunity to disappear on us again. We've got to bring him in as quickly as possible."

Eric stood to one side of the white screen and traced his hand along the red line. "This represents the assigned route for the prison transportation unit. They were driving a standard vehicle, not the van, so be sure you know what you're looking for."

George sat on the far end of one of the tables, watching his partner. He could hear the disgust in Eric's voice when he mentioned the van. That was a stupid mistake for the prison to make.

"Odds are Kane escaped in this area here." Eric's hand traced the green circle several times as he spoke. "It's an industrial area. A lot of warehouses, some of them abandoned, not much traffic. Since we haven't received reports from any witnesses yet, we're going to assume that's our best bet. We've already got three cars patrolling the area looking for Kane. It's doubtful he would have stayed in the cruiser so the vehicle is probably dumped in one of these warehouses. Blue squad and green squad will canvass these warehouses immediately. No time for warrants. Look through any broken windows, walk through any open doors. If there are no broken windows or open doors, put your shoulder into it, one may miraculously appear. Just be sure to check any space big enough for a car."

George smiled. Eric had already broken up those attending the meeting into four groups and assigned color names for their squads. You would have thought he was running a military reconnaissance mission into Afghanistan, but if it worked, no place for an old fogey like him to argue.

"Red squad and yellow squad, George will provide you with a list of our contacts used in Kane's initial apprehension. We will not let him go to ground. Our weaknesses: Kane has more than an hour head start, and he knows the city. He knows how to disappear. Our strengths: Kane likely hasn't reached a safe house yet. It's daylight, and if he's still on the street, it's not easy for a guy his size to hide. I want him found, ladies and gentlemen, before nightfall, or we may not find him."

The group of cops knew the meeting was coming to a close, and they were gathering up their things. Ready to get started. George was glad no one had made any smart-ass remarks to his partner. Kane was a major hitter, and no one was giving Eric any grief for being put in charge of the operation.

Eric was wrapping up. He turned off the overhead projector and took a step forward, standing in front of the first table and moving his eyes to look at each officer individually. He lowered his voice, making the room go silent so everyone would listen. "This guy is serious, people. No one moves on him alone. If he's taken out the prison detail, that means he's armed. Last thing, everyone partners with Deputy Kevlar. We're all wearing vests on this one. No exceptions. Keep me updated...go get him."

The room erupted in motion and was cleared within ten seconds, only George remained in his seat. Eric looked tired. He looked as if, for the first time, the realization of just how difficult this recovery was going to be had struck him. As if relaying orders to the team of officers had broken through the adrenaline and brought the harsh touch of reality to him.

"You did good, kid." George braced his hands on the armrests of his chair and pushed himself to a standing position. "All the right moves. We're gonna get this guy."

Eric nodded. His gaze somewhere past his partner. "Yeah, I hope so."

CHAPTER 14
October 10
2:23 P.M.

GRANT STOPPED at the top of the stairs, collecting himself and listening to his family enter the house. Loraine's voice was the first he heard.

"I told you it was a waste of time, Phil. What made you think he'd tell us something in person but not over the phone? Driving downtown and back. I've wasted a whole day."

"Oh for Pete's sake, Loraine." Phil's voice, exasperated. This same conversation must have taken place on the ride in from the city. "Sometimes people will talk to you in person about things they wouldn't mention on the phone. You just have to schmooze them a little. That's what you learn in business."

"Yes, you're a regular Dale Carnegie with the way you influenced Lister. He was practically falling over himself telling you all that nothing."

"Drop it, Loraine. It didn't work out, but that's no reason to give up."

"No, it didn't work out, did it? Remind me, when's the last time something did work out?"

"Oh, will you two please give it a rest?!" A new voice. Mona. "I've spent the past two hours listening to you two bitch and moan about that lawyer. I'm starting to wish I had gone with Brock."

"Really? Your husband actually invited you to accompany him?" Loraine's tone was acid. She knew how to throw a verbal punch.

The house was silent for several seconds. Finally, Mona spoke. "I need a drink. Anyone else?"

Grant started down the stairs. He knew where this was going to lead, and he wanted to catch Mona before she embarked on her journey to Happyland. The trio was passing the base of the stairway when Grant spoke.

"Greetings," he said. Three sets of eyes glanced upwards, but Mona was the first to respond.

"Grant! Come down here and hug your aunt right now!" Grant descended the final few steps and put his arms around Mona. She hugged him tightly. "Oh, we missed you."

"Put her there, partner." Phil extended his right hand and Grant broke the hug with Mona to shake it. "When did you get back?"

"This morning. Eric picked me up from the airport. Hi, Loraine." Grant moved to hug Phil's wife, and she returned the hug in a cursory fashion. The same ritual as always: Grant bound by politeness and respect for family, Loraine enduring some horrid tradition.

When he stepped away, Mona put one arm around him, as if to temper the cool reception he had received from Loraine, and walked with him. When they reached the living room, she stopped, as if just remembering something, and turned to him.

"Sweetheart, I'm sorry about Dad. I know you two were close, but it's good to see you again." She hugged him once more.

"Thanks. It's still hard to believe he's gone." Grant was grateful she said something. Mona had always been more in tune with people's emotional needs than the rest of the family.

He faced his uncle, who was walking into the room with Loraine. "By the way, thank you for getting me the message so quickly, Uncle

Phil. If you hadn't bypassed the normal channels, I never would have made it home in time for the funeral."

"No problem, my boy." Phil shouldered Mona aside and put his arm around Grant. "No cost is too great to get my favorite nephew back here."

Grant didn't know how to respond. Who was this guy? Phil had always treated him with a mix of tolerance and disdain. Never anything like this. He felt the victim of a schmooze job, but why the effort from Phil?

Grant stopped himself. He needed to cease analyzing everything. Perhaps his uncle was emotional after Abe's death. Grant felt a tug of anger at Eric for introducing the possibility of murder to him before he even had a chance to see his family. Loraine interrupted his thoughts.

"So tell us, Grant, how was life among the jungle-dwellers? Cure any horrible diseases?"

"As a matter of fact, I did, Loraine. But I don't want to bore you with details about helping people. You wouldn't be interested in that kind of thing." The response was harsher than he intended, but that was how things seemed to work. No matter how much Grant viewed himself on a higher moral plane than his family, he was just as easily sucked into petty confrontations as the rest of them. He regretted his words, but Loraine seemed unaffected.

"Yes, perhaps you can save those stories for later," she replied in her normal cool voice.

Phil stepped into the conversation as Mona went to the bar to pour herself a drink. "So is the place like you remember it? Loraine and I haven't been out here much this year." He sounded proud of the fact, and Grant had to hold down a sense of anger at him.

"Yeah. Things are mostly how I remember them. A few changes here and there. So where have you guys been today?"

Phil responded quickly, "Oh, we were just downtown working on some matters related to Dad. You know, there's a lot of papers to be signed and all."

Loraine cut in. "Your uncle was trying to get Abe's lawyer to give us a copy of the will. With very little luck, I might add."

Phil shot his wife a cold look. How had these two managed to live with each other for this long? Phil turned back to Grant with a pleasant expression.

"Just a matter of time, Grant. Lister said we'd have to wait until after the funeral for the reading of the will. I just thought it would be good for the family to know ahead of time what the estate looked like. You know how Dad was always so secretive about everything. And I'm sure you're anxious to find out what you'll be getting."

"Actually, I haven't given it much thought. I have everything I need already."

Mona set her now-empty glass on the table hard enough to make the ice cubes jump. She opened the decanter and poured another. "Good for you, Grant. At least someone in this house is content. Dad's death isn't a damned winning lottery ticket."

Phil cast a hard gaze at his sister. "Oh please, don't try to come off as holier-than-thou in front of Grant. You need it just as much as the rest of us. We've spent a long time waiting for that money."

Grant sighed. Ten minutes. Only ten minutes for the conversation to turn to this. All about the money. Phil. Loraine. Mona. Brock. Nothing ever changed.

"So where's Brock?" Grant directed the question to Mona even though he really didn't care. There was plenty of fun in the room without Brock, but he knew the question would at least redirect the conversation.

"He had to work. A personal training session downtown. He'll be in later tonight," Mona responded.

"Hard at work," Phil weighed in. "Somebody has to lift those barbells off the floor and put them down again."

"Well at least he has a job! Not floating around trying to sell worthless investment opportunities!" Mona emptied her glass in two gulps. Grant didn't judge. Given the turns of the conversation thus far, drinking didn't seem like such a bad idea.

It felt as if he had never left. These were the same exchanges he heard every time he came home to visit. No one had suddenly turned warm in his absence. It was all just one big game of insulting each other and talking about how rich they all were going to be.

Grant felt another pang of guilt. He had gone to Europe to escape this. Then to Africa. But he had left his grandfather here with it. Even less than this. If Phil and Loraine hadn't been coming out much this year, then that meant that his grandfather had almost no company. Only Julie.

Grant had spent a whole ten minutes with his family. Time to retreat.

"So, has anyone seen Julie?" Grant asked.

Phil turned from the exchange with his sister. "No, was she here this morning? There's nothing missing is there?"

"What? No." Grant was taken aback. Why was everyone so hostile towards her? "She was here this morning when I got in, but I went upstairs to take a nap and haven't seen her since. Why would you think something is missing?"

Loraine, now nursing a glass of wine, responded, "Because, Grant, her job here is over. She wanted the big money, but now that she's not getting it, she might try to take something of value from the house instead."

Grant was shocked to hear the accusation stated so bluntly. Grant knew his family wouldn't appreciate anyone growing close with Abe. The thought of an "outsider" getting her hands on part of the Armstrong fortune was intolerable. No one in the room even wanted to share with any other family members much less someone outside the family.

Still, to hear such a strong accusation made toward Julie, a woman who had devoted her time to helping Abe and giving him companionship, made Grant ashamed of his family. Julie was beginning to represent something new to him. He was going to protect her. He was going to make sure the people standing in this room were not going to hurt her.

"You know, she seemed quite nice when we talked this morning. And I know Granddad liked her."

Loraine cut him off, choking on her drink. "Of course he liked her. Have you seen her? She could make any man like her."

"She was here as a healthcare worker. She was doing a job. You can't fault her for the way she looks. And so what if Granddad wanted to include her in the will? Is sharing that painful?"

Phil leaned against the fireplace, the back of his head almost touching the shotgun mounted above the mantle, and smirked. "Moot point now. No sharing necessary." The comment was made under his breath but still audible.

Grant wanted to punch Phil in the jaw. To scream at him, *He was your father! He's dead! Can't you feel anything?!* But he held his tongue. He looked at Mona. She was staring out the window to the lake.

He couldn't stand it any longer. "I'm going for a walk." He turned and left the room. The feeling of being a little kid again hit Grant hard. This was the same thing he used to do to get out of the house when he was young. He would go for a walk. Sometimes for hours. He would walk all over the island. Not caring where he was, so long as he was out of the argument. Not having to hear his family fight. Was it like that before his father had died? His recollection was vague. In dim memory, it seemed as if his father was able to quell the fights. To step in with a voice of authority and reason. Grant wished he could be more like that, but he wasn't. Not today.

Grant opened the front door and stepped into the afternoon light. He noticed the clouds were building as he made his way down the front steps. A cool breeze blew, and he inhaled deeply. The air had the kiss of moisture. It was going to rain later. The pre-rain breeze had a different taste in Still Pines than it had in the jungle. The air was so much heavier in Africa, winter and summer. The air there was thick and pungent with the smells of the village. Strong odors long banished from most of Western society. On Still Pines Lake, there was no scent of open sewers, no odor of animal dung, no mildew smell from the jungle. Here at his grandfather's home, there was only the sweet smell of pines and rain to come.

Grant walked down the path toward the lake, hands in his pants pockets, wishing he had grabbed a jacket on his way out the door.

Things were so beautiful here, and he could never have appreciated it at this level without experiencing what he had in the jungle. He didn't deserve this place. None of them did.

He wished everyone in the house could spend one month with him in Africa. Could see how good they already had it, just by virtue of living in the United States. Could see how selfish they were and maybe, just maybe, gain a little clearer understanding of life's priorities. He smiled at the thought of Loraine having to use an outhouse. There were often spiders there.

Grant leaned over and plucked a pine cone from the path. He inspected it and shifted it from hand to hand as he walked. He knew he was kidding himself. No one was going to change. Somehow, somewhere along the line, his relatives had lost sight of the priorities his grandfather had set. He wondered whether it had to do with his own father's death. After his dad had died, Abe had become harsher with the rest of the family. Had seemed to feel that no one else was living up to the same standard. Grant, as Jack's only child, had probably been treated better than the rest of the kids. Perhaps that was why the family's focus became more and more centered around riches. About having more than anyone else. What a miserable life.

The trees ended and Grant stepped into the field. He stopped where he was and looked toward the lake. There was the big oak tree. The rope was still intact and hanging over the water. Grant took a step forward then stopped again.

What are you going to do now, boy?

The nightmare was still strong in his mind, and he decided that he didn't need to go down to the water just yet. Instead, he walked along the edge of the tree line, across the field and parallel to the water's edge. After seeing his family again, he understood the dream more. It was no wonder he had pictured the family trying to drag his grandfather under the water. It was probably subconscious memories from his childhood about the fighting, but it had seemed so real.

Grant's thoughts turned toward his conversation with Eric in the car. Someone had called Eric and warned him that Abe may have been in danger. That he was thinking about rewriting the will. But then there was that a-hole remark by Uncle Phil a few minutes ago about that being a moot point. How did Phil know Abe hadn't already rewritten the will if the attorney, Lister, hadn't shown it to them? And who was in the will to begin with? Had someone seen a copy of it?

Questions burned through his mind. He wished Eric would get in touch with him and let him know about the autopsy. Maybe he'd have some information by this evening. Eric had said he would come to the house and eat dinner with him. Save him from spending too much time alone with his family. Though Grant also planned to spend some time with Julie. Hopefully, she'd be back at the house tonight. He wanted to speak more about his grandfather, learn more about the night he died. He was anxious to get her take on what had been happening out here the past few months.

Grant reached the corner of the field and turned, moving along the border of trees on that side toward the water. As he walked alongside the field, a flood of memories hit him. He and Eric had spent so many afternoons here. Not just with baseball, but playing football and Frisbee and once even golf. Grant had found his dad's old set of golf clubs in the garage, and he and Eric went to the field to hit golf balls into the lake. They were doing pretty well, it was the first time either had ever swung a club, when Abe Armstrong walked up behind them. He had told them to stop wasting golf balls, those things weren't cheap and money didn't grow on trees. They had stopped, of course, but Grant wasn't sure if his grandfather was really upset about the golf balls or about Grant playing with his deceased father's clubs. Grant had never played golf again.

He reached the water's edge and paused. It was just a dream. Just a subconscious flurry of memories and stress. He was not going to let a stupid dream beat him. Grant walked along the water's edge toward the big tree. The water had risen since he had last been home, it was only about three feet down the little embankment rather than the five he remembered. The area must have experienced more rain than usual this fall. The water also looked cold.

He reached the tree and there, as always, was the big wooden box. The handle of his hickory bat still sticking out of the notch cut beneath the top. The lid creaked as he lifted it. The rain and lack of use had taken a toll on the rusty hinges. Within the box were the same items Grant had remembered. A football, the bat, a couple of baseballs and...he reached in and withdrew his glove. It had grown stiff with lack of use and water damage. Grant peered closer into the box, sure enough, there was a small pool of water at one end. Once upon a time, the box had been more waterproof, and Grant and Eric had no problem keeping their prized sports equipment in it. But time had apparently weakened it.

He reached down and gripped the football. Flat but not entirely deflated. He tossed it into the air, just below the lowest branch of the tree, and caught it as it fell. It smelled wonderfully of old leather. He returned it to the box and closed the lid.

He looked at the rope and wondered when the last time someone had swung out over the water and dropped in. Grant was sorry that his aunts and uncles had never had any kids. He would have enjoyed having cousins, even if they would have been much younger than him. The island was a great place to spend the latter part of his childhood, and he imagined it would be an even better place for younger kids to romp and swim and play, but would the kids really be happy? Would he have been happy with Phil and Loraine as parents? Much less Brock? Maybe it was for the best that there were no other grandkids.

Grant dropped his stare from the rope to the water below. The longer he spent in this place, the further away the nightmare seemed. He took a step closer to the water's edge and peered in. Nothing. Just the deep blue of the lake. He was anxious for Eric to arrive at the island for supper. He needed to know the results of the autopsy soon. He needed to confirm that a killer did not reside within his family. He needed to put the dream to rest.

He wondered what Eric was doing now. Probably still sitting in the courthouse. He felt sorry for his friend. As exciting as the movies made police work seem, he knew a lot of it was paperwork and tedium. On the other hand, his friend had apparently put away Silas Kane, and that guy sounded dangerous. The courthouse thing might not be so bad after all. It sure seemed to Grant that it would be better than chasing a killer like Kane.

CHAPTER 15
October 10
2:35 P.M.

SILAS KANE was getting closer to his goal. He stood between two dumpsters in an alley with his hands on his knees. He was breathing heavily and sweat poured off him despite the chill afternoon temperatures. The six months in prison had taken a toll on him in terms of physical activity. He had done plenty of push-ups and lifted weights in the yard when he was permitted, but the prison yard was too confined for running. He had now covered over eight miles at a fast clip. He could feel it.

His options had been limited once he disabled the cops in the prison transport. He briefly considered driving the damaged cruiser to his destination, but decided it would draw too much dangerous attention. People watched police cars. Law abiding citizens doing nothing more than walking down the street still found a reason to watch a police car driving by until it was completely out of sight, and the car from which he had escaped had too much visible damage to risk driving it around the city.

After stashing the vehicle in one of the warehouses, Kane had debated stealing a car. If he knew how to hotwire a vehicle, he would most certainly have taken one from a parking lot somewhere, but that was a skill he had never acquired. In order to procure a vehicle, he would have to steal one that was already running. He had done it a few times before, but there was too much uncertainty in carjacking. You never knew when the driver might have a gun, or when a passerby might decide to be a hero. He wasn't overly concerned about the personal risk, but he could not afford to have some imbecile taking a shot at him and alerting the neighborhood. He had too much to do, and this was too important.

So Kane stayed with his original plan. He dragged the larger of the two guards outside the car and stripped him from the waist up. Kane was far too large to fit in either cop's pants, or the rest of their uniforms for that matter, but that was not his goal. He didn't want to look like a cop. He took the guard's undershirt, and using a folding knife he found in the man's pocket, cut the sleeves and collar off the white shirt.

Kane removed the bright orange prison uniform shirt he was wearing and replaced it with the makeshift tank-top. Even with the sleeves and collar gone, the shirt strained to contain Kane's mass and it stretched taut across his immense chest and back. But it reached his waist and that was the important thing.

Kane then used the knife to cut off the legs of his orange prison-issue pants from about four inches below his crotch. He had stripped the legs off and stood, looking down at himself. A decent pair of shorts. A tight tank top. He was already wearing white socks and prison issue white tennis shoes. He would pass as a jogger, and he would get to his destination the old-fashioned way, he would run.

Even in the cool temperatures, the running felt good to Kane as he weaved his way down alleys and unpopulated side streets. Three blocks from the warehouse district, he came upon a young boy in an alley listening to his iPod through a pair of oversized headphones. Perfect. The boy willingly gave Kane the iPod and headphones and ran away.

Kane loved kids. Their instinct for self-preservation was always in full force. No bickering over possession. Only one priority – survival. Oh sure, the runt would run tell his mommy that some man had stolen his iPod, but he hadn't even had to hit the kid to get it. That was perfect because the police weren't about to respond to a call like that—if it was even reported—in a neighborhood like this. More importantly, no one would ever connect him to the crime once the cops realized he had escaped. Different departments for different crimes. Kane loved the police force, too.

With the headphones on, listening to the first music he had heard in six months, Kane now looked fully like an athlete in the midst of a brisk afternoon run. Naturally, heads turned and people stared when he came across a populated street. But the looks were not of fear, they were of envy from the men and appreciation from the women. He ignored the looks as mundane. He knew that his image would linger in their minds for a few moments and then fade away. Even if his face was flashed on the television screen as an escaped murderer, he doubted a single person would make the mental connection to the large runner they had seen earlier, and if they did, so what? It would be too late by then.

Another advantage to running was that it provided a quicker means to his destination. Even hours before the evening traffic congestion, the streets of New York were not a friendly place to automobiles, and it was never quick to drive anywhere in this town. By running, Kane was able to take a more direct route and bypass many delays that would have been unavoidable in a vehicle. Besides, with his long stride and quick pace, Kane would be beyond the initial search perimeter before the cops even realized he had escaped.

He had traveled eight of the eleven miles to his destination when the stitch first struck his side. He tried to walk it off for a couple of blocks, but it was getting progressively worse. So he had stopped between the dumpsters to catch his breath and let the pain subside. He had been running for an hour, and the time in prison had taken a toll on his stamina.

He allowed his thoughts to wander and remembered his childhood in the woods of Arkansas. He and his older brother would run for hours, chasing each other, sometimes chasing others. Jonas, the youngest of the three boys, would never join them. His legs were too short to keep up, and he was always a bit of a sissy. Always preferred reading their father's books to going out and doing things the way Silas and Marcus did.

Silas recalled the time he and Marcus had found the old hobo by the train tracks deep in the woods. They spotted him in the distance and ran to where he had stationed himself to await another train. He was sitting by the tracks, and laughed as he told the two boys that he had gotten so drunk the previous night, he must have accidentally fallen out of the boxcar he was riding. He hadn't even woken up till that morning, and it turned out he had cut his arm something fierce. He pulled the ragged sleeve of his jacket up to show the boys a nasty gash running up his forearm. The cut was long and quite deep. It had stopped bleeding but should still be stitched.

The man wondered if maybe the boys had something he could wrap his arm in, or maybe if they had anything he could eat, or drink, while he waited for another train. He licked his lips as he mentioned something "to drink," perhaps hoping two underage boys could procure him some alcoholic beverage. Silas found the man pathetic.

The two boys had listened closely. They hardly ever saw people out this far in the woods, and their father never let them make the journey into town. They were both young, Marcus barely into his teens and Silas closing in, but both were large for their ages. Marcus moved closer to the hobo and asked if he could see that cut again. The old man obliged and pulled up the sleeve once more. He had a smile on his face. Perhaps he was so accustomed to people wanting to keep their distance, he appreciated the boy expressing interest in him.

Marcus knelt and gently put his hands on the man's forearm, one thumb on either side of the wound. Silas stood a couple of feet back from his brother, curious as to what he was up to. Marcus looked into the hobo's face and smiled as he pushed his thumbs into the cut and pulled them apart. The man screamed as the flesh and muscle of his arm parted to reveal bone. He jerked his arm from Marcus's red-covered hands and scrambled to his feet.

Marcus stood where he was, watching as the hobo ran away down the middle of the tracks, glancing fearfully over his shoulder every few steps. Silas stood behind his brother, excited by what had just occurred, but unsure of what to do now. After the hobo was about two hundred yards away from them, Marcus looked at his brother and grinned, then he took off down the track after the old man. Silas raced after him, anticipating what might happen next.

When the old man caught sight of the boys bearing down on him, he emitted a terrified yelp. He was limping on his left side. Marcus and Silas drew to within forty yards of the man, and Marcus stopped, holding his arm out to halt his brother. He knelt and selected a smooth rock from between the wooden railroad ties, about the size of a baseball. Silas picked up a similar rock of his own. This one had fresh blood on it. He smiled at the thought that the hobo's forearm must be pouring.

Marcus threw his rock and overshot the old man, the rock whizzing just above his head. Silas threw his a moment later and gauged the distance better than his brother. The rock struck the hobo on his ass, and they heard the old man squeal at the contact, but he did not fall. He continued to run down the tracks, sensing now that he was running for his life. The two brothers erupted into fits of laughter and waited there, laughing and giving the old man time to go farther down the tracks. There was really nowhere he could run. The boys knew there wasn't a settlement for miles around. The old man would find no sanctuary from the brothers.

The boys ran after and soon pulled to within thirty yards of the old man. He was moving slower now, bleeding arm clutched in front of him and limping more severely. Silas guessed the old alcoholic hadn't run this far in a very long time. The two boys again picked up smooth rocks and Marcus again sailed his first. This time the rock found its mark and the old man was struck hard on the left shoulder. He swayed toward the left side of the tracks and at first, Silas thought he would catch his foot and fall over, ending their game, but the man straightened and continued his limping run. Silas threw his rock and pumped his fist in the air as the projectile struck the vagrant in the lower back, just above where his first rock struck. This time he fell. He stretched out his good arm to break his fall as the injured arm remained clutched to his chest. He screamed again but retained consciousness.

The two boys stood on the tracks and waited for the old man to get to his feet. He started moving farther down tracks, weeping softly. His limp was now pronounced and his speed was wavering, but the hobo pressed on, desperate to live. The boys remained still, transfixed by the sight of the bleeding, haggard man moving slowly away from them. Silas was breathing heavily, not from exertion but from excitement. He realized he was hard.

Marcus was in a world of his own, staring at the old man. Silas knew his brother was pondering how to kill the hobo. Silas racked his brain for suggestions. He wanted to impress his older sibling.

Silas ventured forth an idea, "You know, we could tie him to the tracks and wait for a train to run him over."

Marcus turned to him. "What are you, stupid? The brakeman would stop the train, and the guy wouldn't get killed. Then he'd tell the cops about us. Daddy'd skin us."

Silas looked at his feet. It was a stupid idea. He then raised his head to watch the departing man. His limp was bad, but he was moving steadily. Not quickly, but surely putting distance between himself and his tormentors.

Marcus spoke again. "Hey, that does give me an idea though. You got your pocket knife with you?" Silas nodded, the knife had been a gift from his father when he had turned ten, a good-sized Swiss Army model, and he was never without it. Marcus smiled. "Then why don't *we* skin *him*?"

Silas furrowed his brow. He considered the deer they killed and how they field-dressed them in the woods. The hobo wasn't much bigger than a buck deer. It was a good plan.

He looked back to the old man, now about eighty yards away from them. Apparently, the hobo had excellent hearing because he seemed to gain new life. The old man's legs started pumping, limp gone. He veered away from the tracks and headed into the woods.

Marcus broke into a run. "Shit!"

Silas bolted after him, legs pumping to keep up with his brother. The two boys split from the tracks where they had been standing, hoping their path would intersect with their prey. Silas marveled at his brother, he moved like an animal, leaping bushes and swinging around trees, using their trunks as leverage to gain speed. Silas followed at a slight distance, not as agile as his brother. He caught sight of the old man moving through the brush about fifty yards away. They had overshot him. Marcus saw him too and altered his route.

Within ten seconds, Marcus was upon the old man. He leapt from the brush and caught the hobo's head with one outstretched arm, clotheslining him at full speed. The man's feet flew from underneath him as his forward progress was brought to a violent halt, and he crashed hard onto his back. Silas burst out of the bushes, only a moment behind his brother, and at first assumed Marcus had killed the old fart, broken his neck, but the man's legs were moving as he lay whimpering in the dirt. They were still going to be able to have their fun.

Marcus stood over the old man's body, hands resting on his knees with sweat pouring off his forehead and onto the hobo's shirt. His mouth upturned in a grin. Standing there in the woods, Silas thought that all his brother needed was fangs to complete the look of a wild animal. He had never been so proud.

Silas stood now in the alley, hands resting on his knees and looking at the small pool of sweat forming between his feet as it dripped from his face. He wondered how much he resembled his brother. Did he too look like a wild animal?

But Marcus Kane was dead. So fuck him. Silas Kane was very much alive.

Silas took a deep breath. The air stank from the garbage in the dumpster, but the action alleviated some of the sting from the cramp beneath his ribs. It had been a long time indeed since he spent hours running without feeling any effect. But he was still strong, and cunning, and he would get his revenge on the people responsible for putting him in prison. One of his safe places was only three miles away. Once there, he would shower and change into some real clothes. Then he would go see Frank Colletti and get the information he needed for the next step in his mission. He would make them pay.

Silas Kane straightened and began running once more, the pain in his side now gone.

CHAPTER 16
October 10
3:04 P.M.

GRANT HAD LEFT the water's edge and was making his way through the pines to the guest house. He had no particular reason for moving in that direction, but it had been a while since he had taken time to explore the island, and despite the chill in the air, he didn't feel like returning to the main house yet. When he was within sight of the guest house, he heard the sound of a car approaching. He stopped and leaned against the nearest tree.

Phil Armstrong's Mercedes crept up the driveway toward the house. It was less than a ten minute walk to the guest house from the main house, but Grant wasn't surprised Phil was opting to drive rather than risk dirty shoes trekking the path through the woods.

A gust of brisk wind blew through the trees past Grant and reminded him that rain was approaching. Perhaps Phil had a legitimate reason for driving. Grant mused that maybe he shouldn't be so quick to judge others when it looked like he was going to be the one to get wet if he stayed out here much longer. He began navigating the path toward Phil's car.

The Mercedes had come to a stop, and Grant could hear the radio through the vehicle's open windows. He was approaching from behind the car on the passenger side so he doubted his uncle had seen him yet.

"Another sports update, bad news for UCLA as quarterback Zach Hancock injured his knee in practice today. A MRI is scheduled tomorrow morning to assess the damage, but an anonymous team source says Hancock is likely out for the season with a torn ACL."

Grant was ten feet from the vehicle, about to emerge from the trees, when he heard his uncle erupt at the news. "You worthless piece of shit! I already locked the odds for UCLA and you pull this pansy-ass bullshit?! I hope they amputate your leg, you cocksucker!" Phil was pounding the steering wheel hard enough to make the car shake.

Grant stopped with one foot still suspended in the air. He had never heard Phil lose it like this. He had heard him yelling before, numerous times, but nothing like this. He sounded furious. His words strung together in such a wave of obscenities that Grant worried his uncle may be the next family member to have a heart attack, and soon. All because some college football player got hurt?

He knew there had to be money involved. The only time anyone in his family ever severely lost their cool was when money came into play, but this was ridiculous. Grant debated whether or not to continue his progress toward the vehicle. He returned his foot to the ground and stood with his hands in his pockets. He considered staying where he was in the trees, unmoving, and hoping his uncle wouldn't notice him standing there when he got out of the car. That seemed like a reasonable plan for at least the next couple of minutes.

The sports announcer gave way to regular news briefs. North Korea was upset about US involvement in another Asian country. The Fed was considering lowering interest rates. A family of four died in an apartment fire earlier that day in the city. The two children weren't even old enough to start school yet. Grant listened intently, but his uncle had stopped his tirade. Figures. Some twenty-year-old in California hurts his knee and Phil goes ballistic over the loss, but the news of two small children burning to death in an apartment fire garners no reaction.

A minute later, the news gave way to the weather. Rain was expected tonight while severe thunderstorms were making their way up the coast and would hit the state tomorrow. The cool wind blowing by Grant confirmed the meteorologist's prediction. That did it, he didn't want to stand out here all day.

Just as Grant took a step toward the car, Phil opened the door and stepped out. The look on his face was one of disgust until his eye registered movement in the trees. Grant called out, hoping to alleviate any embarrassment. "Hey, Uncle Phil. I was just walking around and saw the car pull up so I came over."

Phil's face broke into a big grin, if the man was insincere, he sure didn't think anyone else could recognize it. "Grant, my boy. Glad you're here. There's something I've been wanting to talk to you about, you know, in private."

Apparently, Phil either didn't suspect Grant had heard his tirade over the UCLA quarterback injury or he didn't care about it. Grant was just glad his uncle had pulled back from whatever emotional meltdown he had been having. "Okay, sure. Where's Loraine? I thought both of you were staying out here."

Phil closed the car door and walked toward Grant. "Oh she is, but she's still at the main house. I just wanted to come over here and make some phone calls. There's still a few hours left in the business day, right?" Phil threw a play punch at Grant's shoulder, and Grant instinctively pulled back. Phil's smile grew larger. "But I guess you wouldn't know much about the business world. And why should you? You, you don't need all the headaches of business and investments and such. It's a cutthroat world out there, and I, for one, have to say I'm glad you're not in it. You're too good for that kind of stuff, Grant. You're doing exactly what you should be doing. Working to help others. That's the kind of thing that would have made Jack proud. And Dad, too. That's the kind of thing I've always wanted to do..."

His thought trailed off, and Grant knew he was supposed to feel obligated to jumpstart him. Phil had left the question primed to be asked, practically choreographed, but Grant didn't feel like playing the game right now. Besides, he was confident he would hear about this again at some point.

Phil was in the process of putting his arm around Grant's shoulders, about to launch into whatever monologue he had prepared regarding using the Armstrong fortunes to help humanity through whichever deal he was working on when Grant blurted out the question.

"Uncle Phil, what happened the night Granddad died?"

Phil's arm stopped six inches from Grant's back, and he stood for a moment with a puzzled look on his face, his arm suspended in midair. The question voiced was not the one he had expected, and it took him a moment to respond. "What do you mean?"

"I mean, what happened the night Granddad died? Your message only said that he had passed away from a heart attack, but I haven't spoken to anyone about it." Grant purposely left out his conversation with Eric for obvious reasons. "That night. Who was there? Did anyone try and help him? What happened?"

Phil let his arm drop to his side. "We were all there. The whole family. Me, Loraine, Mona, Brock. Everybody. Dad had asked if we could all come out for dinner that night. Said he had something he wanted to talk to us about, but we never got the chance to hear what it was. Julie went up to get Dad for dinner and when she found him in his room, he was dead. She tried giving him CPR and everything, but he was already gone. I would have helped, but I never took a class in any of that stuff."

Grant nodded. He wanted to learn more, but he was afraid Phil might sense an interrogation. He had hoped to get more information of that night from Mona, but he knew she would be too drunk to provide any coherent details by this point. Besides, if the autopsy did turn up something unusual, alibis would be forthcoming. This was a perfect time for him to ask some innocent questions, and these were also things he really wanted to know. "Did you get to see him that evening, before he died?"

"No. I went in to have a drink with everyone, then I stepped outside to smoke a cigar. I had had quite a bit of luck with some of my investments that day, and I thought I'd take a little time to celebrate.

It was a good cigar. Cuban. A business associate of mine had been to Miami earlier this month and had brought me a box. I had almost finished it when I heard Julie yelling for someone to call an ambulance. By the time I got inside to see what was going on, Dad was already gone." Phil was gazing into the trees. Grant wondered if this was hard on his uncle.

"So how was Granddad doing before he died? Julie said his health didn't seem bad. Was he under any kind of stress or anything?" Normal questions for a grandson, who also happened to be a doctor, to be asking.

"To be honest, I really don't know. I've been pretty busy the past few months and hadn't had much time to spend on the island. Mona used to come out a lot. She would eat lunch with Dad. My schedule never allowed for that sort of personal indulgence. But I do think Dad was happy, if that's what you're asking. Hell, when I'm his age, I plan on getting a nurse like Julie to keep me happy too." Phil raised his eyebrows in a conspiratorial gesture between guys, but Grant didn't respond to it. He didn't care for the implication.

"So what do you think Granddad wanted to talk to everyone about?"

Phil hesitated. "I'm not sure. Probably just wanted to get everybody together. You know Dad, he liked having the family around."

Sure, thought Grant, *too bad he had to be stuck with this family.* He decided to get straight to the point. "Do you think Granddad was thinking about changing his will? Maybe wanting to include Julie in it?"

Phil looked surprised. "Oh Grant, don't you worry about that. I'm sure Dad didn't change his will. We won't have to worry about Julie for much longer."

Grant was taken aback. "That's not what I'm saying. What does everyone in this family have against Julie?" He hadn't planned to ask that particular question, but it was out of his mouth before he even considered it.

"I've got nothing against her, now. She's a good-looking woman with a tight ass and a nice rack. Dad was old, not dead, and it was pretty obvious she was trying to weasel her way into the will using whatever methods were necessary. Not that it matters now, but I sure as hell didn't appreciate it at the time. Mona came out here early one day and saw her swimming in the pool...topless." Phil's mouth curled up in one corner as he spoke the last word.

"She was topless? Was Granddad out there?"

"No, but he might have been watching. She was probably just teasing him. I confronted him about it one day, but he said I was crazy. Said that she was a special girl, and it was none of my business anyway. That pretty much answered my question. I'll be honest with you. I was surprised by it, but it didn't bother me. Dad was old. He needed some companionship, and Mom's been gone a long time. I'm not heartless. But if that little bitch was trying to get to my, *to our*, money...well, like I said, it's not a consideration anymore."

Grant was in shock. What his uncle was describing didn't seem possible. First, Grant could never believe his grandfather capable of having an affair with a woman young enough to be his granddaughter. He was too decent a man to do something like that. Second, Julie didn't seem the type of person to instigate something so...sleazy. She had seemed so genuinely nice when he had met her earlier, nothing at all like the gold-digging tramp his uncle was painting her to be. Besides, when he had last spoken to his grandfather at Christmas, he had gotten a clear impression that he looked at Julie more as a granddaughter type of figure, someone who worked for him but that he cared for, not at all as someone he was interested in sexually.

Of course, that conversation had taken place almost a year ago, and, much like most people viewed their own parents and grandparents, Grant had never thought of his grandfather and sex in the same sentence. But he now had to face the possibility that Phil's insinuations brought to light. Abe Armstrong was still a man. And it was common for men his age to continue to be interested in sex, or at least the idea of it. And Julie Russell was certainly an attractive woman and Grant didn't know her very well. As difficult to accept as the idea may be, he had to consider it.

Grant noticed his uncle looking at him with a peculiar expression, as if he was trying to dissect his thoughts. "You like her, don't you?" The question was more of a statement, and Grant chided himself for allowing his feelings to show. The next few days were too important to risk wearing his emotions on his sleeve.

"I hardly know her." He again felt like a little kid with an adult questioning whether a girl he had mentioned was his girlfriend. "I just don't think that now is the time to point any fingers, given the circumstances."

Phil looked hurt. "Hey, like I said, I've got nothing against her. She's a fine piece, and you've been away from civilization for far too long. Give it your best shot," he paused, again conspiratorially, "and let me know how it turns out."

Grant was tired of the conversation and decided he would chance the rain after all. "I'm going to walk back to the big house before the rain starts, Uncle Phil. We can visit more later." He turned and started back for the tree line.

Phil called after him, "Grant, we never got a chance to have our conversation. I still want to talk to you about an opportunity that's perfect for you." Phil had taken a few steps after Grant when the first big drop of rain hit him on the forehead. He glanced up at the darkening skies.

Grant had made it to the tree line and hadn't noticed the rain yet. He called back, "We can talk later. I still want to do some walking." With that, he started into a light jog heading down the path and into the trees. Behind him, Phil shook his head and walked into the guest house.

Grant was fifty feet into the woods when the rain started to penetrate the canopy of pine needles and land on the path. The clouds had thickened and the rays of sunshine penetrating them were now gone. A large drop landed on his cheek and ran down the side of his neck. The rain was cold on an already cool day, and Grant knew he would be soaked and freezing by the time he reached the house. He accelerated to a brisk jog.

Fortunately, he was wearing a pair of tennis shoes—the only acceptable footwear for a doctor in Africa on his feet all day—so he could run comfortably down the path toward the house. With any luck, he would beat the worst of the rain.

As he ran along the path, Grant considered the conversation with his uncle. Had he learned anything useful in investigating his grandfather's murder? The thought had a frightful impact on Grant. At what point had it made the progression from *possible murder* to *murder*? Ever since his conversation with Eric, he had told himself repeatedly that he wouldn't consider the possibility of homicide to be real until Eric had received the medical examiner's report. But here he was, only a few hours after the subject had first been brought up by his longtime friend, certain that his grandfather had been murdered.

Was it something said during the conversation with his uncle? Was it the nightmare? Grant had taken several psychology courses at Oxford and knew the power a dream could have on a person's perceptions of reality. Of course, he also knew that more often than not, it was the reverse of the equation that proved to be true—a person's perceptions often revealed themselves through the subconscious in the form of dreams. That would mean that Grant had been convinced of foul play in his grandfather's death before he went to sleep earlier that day. But how could he have been sure? Eric hadn't exactly painted a certain picture of murder. He had, in fact, admonished Grant to not jump to any conclusions until the autopsy report was completed.

The rain grew heavier. He was going to get very wet, but Grant gave it little consideration. Why did he have this strange, sure feeling in the pit of his stomach? Why was he certain his grandfather had been murdered? And, more importantly, was his gut feeling the right one? He couldn't stand it any longer. He couldn't wait for his friend to come to dinner. As soon as he got to the house, he would call Eric.

The wind picked up as the rain started to pour, the pine canopy now affording little protection from the onslaught. Grant bolted into a dead run for the main house.

CHAPTER 17
October 10
3:15 P.M.

ERIC JOHNSON STOOD by the open door of the warehouse watching the rain fall outside. The storm had hit twenty minutes ago, right after he and George had entered the abandoned warehouse where the police cruiser had been found. Although he was by no means a superstitious man, it was hard not to take the weather as a bad omen.

"Give me a timeline." He spoke to the rain, but Lieutenant Richards was behind him, listening.

"This vehicle was discovered approximately forty minutes ago. If Kane escaped en route from the prison, that would give him around a two hour head start on us." Lieutenant Richards was the officer in charge of the homicide scene. He was calm and collected, and he had not questioned Eric's authority on the recapture mission for Silas Kane, and for that Eric was grateful. When a fellow officer was killed, the revenge instinct was strong.

In the movies, the death of a fellow policeman made it okay for the star of the film to take off his badge and play by his own rules to ensure justice was swiftly dealt out to the bad guys. In real life, when a cop went down, plenty of officers felt the same way. They wanted justice both swift and brutal, but it was never that simple. Contrary to how the movies made it appear, New York was a big city, and it would take the cooperation of the entire department to bring a man like Kane to justice. They couldn't afford to have rogue cops trying to catch him on their own. In a city this size, even a man of Kane's enormous mass could get lost easily, and with a two hour head start, the window for finding him was closing fast. The rain wasn't going to help.

He turned from the door and walked toward the cruiser where George was inspecting the interior. He was leaning inside the passenger door being careful not to touch anything.

"What do you think, George?" Eric asked.

George spoke from inside the car. "I think that guy is one strong mother. I've never seen anything like it. No one could have planned for something like this." He was shaking his head as he studied the iron barrier that had been bent back upon itself.

Eric leaned against one of the building supports next to the car. The body of one of the officers was still lying a few feet from the opposite side of the vehicle. The dead man's service revolver was still in its holster. The photographer was nearly finished with his work and the black coroner's body bag was nearby, its attendants awaiting the green light. No one wanted to leave the body at the scene any longer than necessary. George moved out of the car and looked at his partner, then glanced over at the body as a camera flash lit the room.

Eric walked around the back of the vehicle and squatted down, assessing the scene from a lower view. The other cop was still alive when the car had been discovered and had immediately been taken to a hospital. He was unconscious after having suffered a severe blow to the head. He was lucky to be alive. His gun was still in its holster as well, making absolutely no sense to Eric. There was no telling when the guard would regain consciousness and even if he did, it was doubtful he would be able to remember much of the incident preceding such an injury. Things weren't looking good.

"Got something, Lieutenant!" The shout came from a room in the office portion of the warehouse. Eric, George and Lieutenant Richards walked toward the voice. They entered a small office with one tiny window, set just underneath the ceiling and providing very little light, and found the officer who had given the call. He was standing over a rusty desk with one drawer open, his flashlight beam directed into it.

The three men walked to the desk and peered inside. Eric removed a ball point pen from his jacket pocket and, leaving the cap on, speared a piece of cloth and pulled it from the drawer. It was bright orange, prison issue. Eric laid it on top of the bare desk.

"It's a pants leg," George observed.

Eric reached back into the drawer and removed Kane's orange prison shirt, also laying it on the desk. His third trip into the drawer with the pen yielded a sheet of white cotton, not prison issue.

The officers all stared at the cloth, trying to make sense of it. Eric was the first to speak, addressing the officer who had found the cache in the desk. "Go check outside and also call the hospital, find out if either of our boys is missing an undershirt."

"Yes, sir." The young officer turned to leave.

Eric called after him, "Hey, good work in here. This was a nice find." The officer nodded, and left the room to check the body of the dead cop in the warehouse. The three other men stayed in the office, contemplating the contents of the drawer.

"Why the hell would he cut the legs off his pants?" George asked. "It's cold outside. And why take a guard's undershirt? If he's going to go to all the trouble, why not just take his uniform?"

"Because people notice cops," Eric was speaking to himself, gaining more respect for Silas Kane with each new thought, "and he figured they'd *really* notice one with a shirt three sizes too small. But cut the sleeves and collar off an undershirt, and you've got a tank top that will work for just about any size guy. Same token, if you go out in prison issue orange pants, people might notice. But if you go for a run wearing bright orange shorts and a white tank top, odds are no one will think twice, even in weather like this. I see guys running in nothing but a pair of shorts in the middle of winter. I think they're nuts, but they pretty much slip right out of my memory in a matter of seconds. Son of a bitch. That explains why he didn't take either man's gun. Would have been too conspicuous."

That was it. Eric knew it. Kane was literally running. That meant he could have gone in any direction. He wasn't bound by any road construction or detours. And a man like Kane could probably run a long way in a short amount of time.

Eric continued, still speaking to himself as much as his partner, eyes half-glazed as he worked out the problem. "So the real question is, where was he going? He couldn't have planned on running all the way out of the city. He would have to get a car at some point, requiring a friend—of which we're pretty sure he had none—or stealing a car or getting one of his own that he had left somewhere."

"Of course," Eric paused, "maybe he isn't planning on leaving the city. Kane has made a home for himself here. He's not exactly afraid of cops. But he had to be going somewhere. After all, why didn't he take the time to kill the other officer? He must have either been in a hurry or considered him inconsequential. Now since he took the time to take an undershirt, he wasn't in too much of a hurry, but he must have some sort of priority if he let the other cop live. We just need to know what that priority is..." Eric dropped his voice to a whisper. "Where the hell are you going, Silas?"

Knowing how Kane left the scene wasn't going to make finding him any easier. The only people to have seen him jogging would have been outside at the time, and the rain had surely driven all of those people indoors by this point. Things were not looking good for an immediate recapture.

Eric stared at the wall and tapped his fingers lightly on the desk top, the rhythm matched that of the William Tell Overture.

The conversation apparently over, Lieutenant Richards moved for the door. "I'm going to check on things out here. You guys let me know if you need anything."

George looked at his partner and frowned. Eric was still tapping out the music, mouth slightly open and brow furrowed. "I'm thinking our net may be set too tight," George said.

Eric was pulled out of his reverie. "Yeah. I think you're right. We've got our check points too close to the scene. Wherever Kane went, you can bet he's farther out than we thought. We have to go public."

"You sure? It may be smart to keep a lid on this while we can. Once it's out there..."

"I know where you're coming from, but I can't believe the lid has stayed on this long. Besides, I don't think we can catch him on our own. Every minute puts him farther out of our reach. And once people know, well, it's hard to mistake a guy like Silas Kane. With the exception of a few pissed off professional wrestlers and maybe a linebacker or two, we shouldn't get too many false alarms on this one. At least we can manage the information flow."

"Good plan, boss." George said the remark in an off-handed way as they walked out of the room and back to the warehousing area, but it unsettled Eric. George had never called him "boss" before. Not that he really meant anything by it now. Eric had heard George use that expression a hundred times in the past addressing many different people in the department, but never him. The effect added to the nervousness Eric felt building in his stomach.

Silas Kane was his responsibility. He had put him behind bars once, and now it was his job to do it again. Everyone was looking to him for direction. Kane was no longer just a maniac who killed hookers. He was now a cop killer as well. He had to be brought to justice.

If only Eric could figure out where he was going next.

CHAPTER 18
October 10
3:29 P.M.

THE CLOUDS BURST just as Grant came within view of the main house. He could see its facade through the trees even as his surroundings grew dark with the blackening clouds. The rain pierced the canopy of the pines and poured onto him, soaking his shirt. His pants clung to his legs and slapped against his ankles as he ran toward the driveway. He emerged from the trees in a dead run, hunched over from the storm and thinking to himself how purposeless the rush was—he was already soaked—but with only about fifty yards of distance left to cover, he ran anyway.

When his first step hit the driveway, he heard the sound of tires screeching and turned to see a pair of headlights bearing down on him. His first instinct should have been to dive out of the way, but he was frozen in place by the sight. Grant saw the vehicle's front tires turn, but the car did not follow the new direction dictated by the wheels. The vehicle was hydroplaning on the wet cement. He was about to be hit by a car.

He regained his senses the moment before impact and leapt into the air, hoping to avoid his shins being struck by the bumper and potentially being dragged under the vehicle. Grant pulled his knees up as he jumped, the front of the car moving beneath him as he landed tail first on the hood. He rolled toward the windshield and thrust out a hand to cushion the impact, envisioning the windshield shattering and his hand being mauled beyond repair, his medical career tragically cut short from not paying attention to his surroundings. But the windshield did not break. Instead, Grant's hand struck the glass and his wrist bent back. He continued rolling forward until his shoulder struck the windshield resulting in an abrupt halt to his momentum.

The car came to a stop as well, thirty yards from the garage, and Grant's course was reversed as he rolled backward away from the windshield and over the hood. His feet hit the ground in front of the vehicle, stopping his fall. His arms were stretched to either side, elbows partly supporting his weight, making him look like he was doing the limbo while resting his shoulders on the front of the hood. His wrist throbbed with pain and his hand lay limp. The cold rain hit him directly in the face as he stared up into the dark clouds.

He heard a car door open and a woman screaming, "Ohshitohshitohshit, are you okay?" The voice was Julie's. Grant took a moment to collect himself as he lay on the hood looking at the heavens. He eased himself forward and sat on the front bumper. He pushed his elbows off the hood and leaned forward, forearms on his knees.

Taking a quick physical inventory, Grant realized he was okay. His wrist hurt like hell, but when he moved his fingers and rotated his hand, everything seemed to be functional. He would watch it for swelling, in case there was a fracture, but everything appeared in working order.

Julie's voice was louder now. She was kneeling on the ground in front of him. She put her hands on his shoulders, lightly, as if she was afraid she might break him. He realized that he hadn't yet responded to her. "Yeah, I'm okay. Are you all right?"

The question was stupid. Of course she was all right. She had been driving, he had been the one hit, but it just came out of his mouth. Courtesy mixed with stupidity and a dash of shock. Julie shook her head and Grant noticed tears in her eyes, mixing with the rain droplets running down her cheeks.

"No, I'm not okay. I almost killed you. I was trying to get to the garage and I was driving too fast and then you ran out of the trees and I tried to turn but the car didn't turn and I was afraid you were dead and..." Her words ceased as she took a deep gasping breath. Grant put his arms around her, pulling her into him. She rested her head on his chest, still kneeling between his outstretched legs as he sat on the bumper.

"Hey, it's okay. The car hydroplaned. Not your fault. I'm in one piece. Just banged up my wrist a little." Grant flexed his hand again and assured himself that it wasn't too serious. The pain *was* serious, but he tried to ignore it out of respect for his masculinity. "I should have been watching where I was running. It's just a good thing you weren't going any faster, or I may have joined you right through the windshield." He tried a smile.

As the adrenaline subsided, Grant decided it could have been much worse. She hadn't been going that fast—he had just popped out of the trees very close to the car—but if the vehicle had been going any faster, he probably wouldn't have been able to jump in time and he would have had a pair of broken legs...or worse. He hugged Julie tighter in the rain and reflected on how isolated the island really was. If he had broken his legs, it was a long way to the nearest hospital. Still Pines County had a medical center that would work for most cases, but if the breaks had been severe, as he was pretty sure would have been the case, he would have had to go to a hospital in the city. That would have meant a long car ride in a lot of pain or a surprise trip in a helicopter.

The thought made him shiver. Doctors don't fare well as patients.

Julie pulled back to look at him, the tears less prominent now. She sniffed and used one wrist to wipe her eyes with a sleeve already soaked by the rain. Mascara smeared onto her cheeks. She swallowed loudly, gaining control of herself, and looking into Grant's eyes from only a few inches away. "You're okay?"

He nodded. Smeared make-up. Puffy eyes from tears. Blonde hair dripping and hanging in front of her face. She was beautiful. He felt the urge to kiss her. Right there. In the pouring rain. In front of the car that had almost run him over.

Instead he slid his hands from her back to grip her shoulders, the injured hand doing a weak job of it. "We're soaked. Let's get inside." She nodded, eyes still wide, and they both got to their feet. She turned and started walking toward the open garage, forgetting about the running car behind her.

Grant walked to the open driver's door. Rain had soaked the seat and the door panel. He wondered if that sort of thing hurt the controls for the locks and windows. He closed the door and put the car in gear, his wrist flaring with pain at working the gear shift, and leaned back in the wet seat. He drove slowly and stayed behind Julie. When she was ten feet from the garage, she turned and saw Grant piloting the vehicle behind her. Her face broke into a goofy smile as she realized that she had forgotten it. It was the best thing Grant had seen all day.

He turned the wheel to direct the car into the garage and his wrist was momentarily assaulted with agony. The sprain was severe. It was going to be tender for a while. He would need to ice it and keep it wrapped for a couple of days.

Grant stopped the car and stepped out. Julie was standing by the entry to the house. She was wearing the same outfit that she had greeted Grant in earlier that day, but the pink t-shirt was soaked through. Her curves beneath the shirt were evident, and the chill in the air was having quite the effect. He shifted his gaze to her eyes and for the second time that day, he hoped she hadn't noticed his glances.

If she had, she didn't say anything. "I saw you behind me and hoped you weren't out for revenge." She was smiling and looking embarrassed. "I'm really sorry. I've never hit anyone with a car before."

"It's a first for both of us. I've never been hit with a car before." He returned her smile and opened the door leading to the kitchen. He held it open for her, careful to use his uninjured hand, and she took two steps inside before turning around.

"Shit. I forgot the food." She turned bright red and put a hand to her mouth. "Shit, I'm sorry. Wait…dammit. Sorry, that just slipped out. Each time."

It took Grant a moment to realize she was apologizing for swearing. It was endearing. "No worries, I've heard worse. I'll grab the food. What is it?" He returned to the car and opened the back door. Inside were two large brown grocery bags.

Julie walked beside him and reached inside, grabbing both bags before he had a chance. "Back off. I already broke your arm. I'm not going to make you carry my bags in with it." She waited for Grant to close the car door then proceeded into the kitchen, her arms full. "Tonight we have lasagna and garlic bread. I'll make a salad to go with it. I was going to prepare something special for your first night back, but with the rest of your family staying on the island, I figured I'd just pick up something easy. This way everyone can eat when they want to."

Grant followed her into the kitchen as she set the bags on the counter and began removing their contents. "Lasagna sounds great," he said. "One of my favorites. You know, you don't have to cook for the whole family." Julie extracted a large silver pan covered with foil from one bag and two loaves of garlic bread from the other. She opened the refrigerator and began clearing a shelf for the lasagna.

As she bent forward into the fridge, Grant noticed her white shorts had turned rather transparent in the rain. He could distinctly see her panties. They were pale pink, a shade matching her t-shirt. He swallowed. Hard. She continued the conversation, speaking into the refrigerator while she worked. "Oh, I don't mind. Somebody needs to do it, and I used to cook for your grandfather."

She turned, and Grant looked intently at the lasagna pan as he handed it to her, as if it was the most interesting thing in the room. "Well, that's really nice of you. So everyone doesn't eat together then?"

"Nope. Everyone dines at different times. I usually eat early and try to stay out of the way. I have a TV in my room so I spend most evenings up there." She put the bread into the bread box under the counter and opened the fridge once more, retrieving a head of lettuce from within.

She reached across Grant to get a knife, and he felt a warm flutter in his stomach as her wet arm brushed his on the return trip.

He felt the need to say something, anything. "Really." It came out not as a question, but more of a statement. Brilliant.

Julie removed a cutting board from a cabinet, not seeming to notice the comment, for which Grant was thankful.

She placed the lettuce on the cutting board, and as she looked down at it, she started laughing. Light and beautiful. Grant couldn't help smiling. "What's so funny?"

"Look at me." She still had the lettuce in one hand and waved the knife with the other as she spoke. "I'm soaking wet and probably look terrible. And here I am cutting up a salad and keeping you from getting into dry clothes. I'm so sorry."

"I wouldn't go with 'terrible' as an adjective of choice, but you're right. We both should put on some dry clothes." He started to walk out of the kitchen, taking the exchange as his cue to leave.

"Grant," Julie spoke his name softly, and he turned around. The knife and lettuce were on the counter and her hands were clasped at her waist, resting on the countertop. Her shirt still clung to her and her hair was dripping onto the tiled floor. "I really am sorry for what happened out there. I'm glad you're okay."

He took a quick breath. "I'm fine. Don't worry about it." He turned and left the kitchen, finding it quite difficult to tear his eyes away from her.

Grant removed his underwear and threw them onto the pile of wet clothes in the corner of the bathroom. They had been soaked, but considering he had just been hit by a car, he felt it a victory that it was only rainwater soaking them. He grabbed the towel he had used earlier off the rack and wiped himself down with it. His wrist still hurt, but there had been minimal swelling, indicating it likely wasn't fractured. He wiggled his fingers in front of his face, assuring that he could still pursue surgery one day if the urge ever struck him.

He assessed himself in the mirror. He was dry now and his hair was a mess, but he looked fine. He had lost weight over the past year—the cost of being not only a doctor but also a plumber, ditch-digger, builder and water-carrier. And there had been neither occasion nor resources to overindulge at meal times. As a result, he was lean. His body had retained most of the muscle he had developed as a teenager, but his chest and shoulders were no longer as broad as his college days. He impulsively flexed in the mirror and his muscles responded. He held the pose for about three seconds before he dropped his arms and chuckled. How long had it been since he had done that?

He heard the sound of a door closing down the hall. Julie. She had waited a few minutes before following Grant upstairs, for which he was grateful. As excited as he had been in the kitchen, it would have felt awkward for the two of them to walk upstairs together, each knowing the other was about to get undressed in a room not far away. He felt like he was in high school again.

Despite the chill of the rain and the wind—and despite being struck by a car—when Grant undressed, he was partially erect. He ignored it, something that he wouldn't have done in high school, so perhaps he had matured after all. Still, he found himself thinking of Julie. The way she had looked in the kitchen, shirt clinging to her perfect breasts. And she was getting undressed right now, just across the hall.

Grant turned on the cold water in the sink. He cupped his hands under the stream and splashed water onto his face. This was ridiculous. With all of the circumstances of the week, with what Eric had told him, with what Phil had said about Julie, with the nightmare, he didn't have time for this sort of thing. And it was just wrong.

Could Phil have been right about Julie? She was a beautiful woman, but certainly didn't seem the type for what Phil had described. Maybe Phil had jumped to the sleazy conclusion based on her looks and the mention of Abe changing his will. Or perhaps he was outright lying to Grant now, it certainly wouldn't have been the first time, but why would he lie?

Grant stepped out of the bathroom and removed a fresh pair of underwear from his duffel bag. He pulled them on and grabbed a clean pair of pants from the bag as well. The pants were wrinkled from the trip and, although clean, Grant could still smell the aroma of Africa on the cloth. The scent sparked a brief longing for the life he had started there, where things were simple. Simple felt a great distance behind him now.

He pulled the pants on and walked to the closet. There were still several of his shirts there, none of which had been worn in years. He selected a navy tennis shirt and put it on. The short sleeves would be chilly outdoors, but given the weather, he didn't plan on leaving the house.

He returned to the bathroom and retrieved the wet pair of pants, fishing around in the front pocket until he removed a soggy piece of paper. It was time to get this over with. He picked up the phone off the nightstand next to the bed and dialed the number on the card. The digits were smudged but still legible.

Eric's voice answered. "You've reached the voicemail for Eric Johnson with NYPD Homicide division. Please leave a message and I'll return your call as soon as possible. If you have an emergency, please dial 9-1-1. Thanks."

A harsh beep followed, and Grant spoke. "Eric, this is Grant. I know you said that we'd continue our earlier discussion over dinner tonight, but I'd appreciate it if you'd call and fill me in on any news you may have received." Grant wasn't sure why he was trying to be so discreet, but he didn't like the thought of leaving a recorded message discussing his grandfather's possible murder. "I know there may not have been time to get any results yet, but I'd appreciate an update. You know the number. I'll see you tonight."

He placed the handset back in the phone's cradle and wondered how often Eric checked his voicemail.

Grant felt like he was going crazy. Each thought led back to the possibility of murder. Phil, Loraine, Brock, maybe even Mona. He was looking at his own family as if they were criminals, killers. He didn't have any concrete reason to believe it, but whatever had happened that night, Grant was growing more certain that Abe Armstrong had not died of a heart attack.

What are you going to do now, boy?

He hoped Eric checked his messages soon. Maybe he had already received the report from the medical examiner. Maybe he was on his way out to the island now. After all, it sounded like all he had to do that day was go to the appeal of that Kane guy.

Grant stared out the window at the rain and wished his friend would get back to him.

CHAPTER 19
October 10
4:31 P.M.

SILAS KANE LOOKED across the street to confirm the address of the building. It was an address he had memorized when he first came to New York but had yet to call upon it during his time in the city. The building was nondescript, a two-story brick structure with a dry-cleaners in front. The green awning stretching over the sidewalk read *NY Cleaners – Shirts only $1.79*. The dry-cleaning operation ostensibly continued through to the back of the building, with the equipment and racks requiring a great deal of room, but if his father's description had been accurate so many years ago, the laundry at this particular venture was sent out each day to be serviced at another facility. And the area where the large equipment should have been would be occupied by a series of offices. The largest and most prominent of which would serve as the business home of Mr. Frank Colletti.

Kane crossed the street. Two oncoming vehicles braked hard to avoid him. No horns honked. New York drivers were rude but not crazy. Following a brief stop at one of his older safe houses, Kane now wore a pair of blue jeans with a black leather jacket. The wardrobe did nothing to conceal his size and even the bravest of cabbies would not likely risk a confrontation with the man by using his horn. Kane sidestepped between two parked cars on the other side of the street to reach the sidewalk. He stood in front of the cleaners and peered into the large plate glass window. Inside were two women working behind a counter, placing laundry into a large red bag. The customer who dropped off the clothes opened the door and passed by the immense man standing under the awning without even looking up. Kane caught the door before it closed and stepped inside.

One of the women behind the counter, the younger of the two, glanced up and her eyes momentarily widened before she smiled and said, "Yes sir, may I help you?"

"I need to see Mr. Colletti." His statement was blunt. His face unsmiling.

The girl put a puzzled expression on her face. "I'm sorry, I don't know a Mr. Colletti."

That was almost real-looking, thought Silas, but he had no desire to continue the game. He stepped to the side of the counter and walked past the two women toward the back of the store. Neither tried to stop him. The younger woman snatched up a phone from beneath the counter and hit the red button on the base. "You have company coming. One man. One really large man. No identification. I don't think he's blue." She then replaced the handset on the cradle and moved to the opposite end of the counter, much closer to the front door.

Passing the strategically placed racks of clothing and assorted pressing machines, none of which were being used, Kane opened the door leading to the offices. His father's description had been remarkably accurate. The hallway proceeded straight for twenty feet, then made a ninety degree turn to the right. As Kane stepped around the turn, he was confronted by two men. Both large, both ugly. The one on the right had a pink scar running down his cheek from beneath his eye to just under his chin. The man on the left was younger than Scarface and sported a short-cropped flat-top for his blond hair and a three-day growth of beard. Both men kept their arms at their sides, hands free and ready for action. They had done this type of thing before.

Kane looked past the two men and saw a door at the end of the hallway. The door was plain, but the doorknob was gilded brass, looking out of place in a dry cleaners. He knew the inside of the office was probably decorated more ornately than the grays and greens of the hallway. He stopped three feet in front of the two guards. Despite the size of the two men, Kane stood taller than either and looked down at them. He noticed Flat-top had an ugly brown birth mark on the top of his scalp.

"This is private property. I'm gonna have to ask you to leave." There was no politeness in Scarface's statement. A poor choice.

"I need to see Frank Colletti. Step aside." Kane was curt. He did not have time for courtesy, and these men deserved none. He was going to get in that office one way or the other.

Scarface was clearly unaccustomed to anyone speaking to him in such a manner. He had the look of a lifelong tough-guy, and Kane's dismissal was an insult to years of respect. Still, men in his profession required a certain level of discretion. No violence unless it was absolutely necessary. When he spoke, his tone was hard. "Mr. Colletti ain't here. Please take your business outside."

Flat-top clenched his fists. He could sense where this was going.

Kane glanced from one man to the other, then focused his attention on Scarface. "Mr. Colletti will want to see me. Step aside."

"Sorry, buddy. Mr. Colletti don't see nobody without an appointment. And let me check his appointment book." Scarface raised his palm and perused an imaginary book, then looked up at Kane once more. "Nope. You ain't on it. Now get your ass outside, or we'll take it outside."

Kane looked past the men at the door. This wasn't getting him anywhere. Time for the direct route. He took a step forward between the two men and toward the door. Flat-top reacted first, making an instinctual move to stop Kane's progress by putting his hand on Kane's chest. Exactly as Kane had anticipated.

In one fluid motion, Kane turned—moving with the light force of Flat-top's touch—and advanced a step so he was facing him, then drove his palms forward, catching Flat-top on either side of his rib cage. The force stunned the bodyguard as he was propelled into the wall. Two ribs cracked as Kane's hands continued their forward motion after the wall had stopped Flat-top's momentum.

As soon as Flat-top hit the wall, Kane drew up his right leg and drove his foot backward, the heel of his boot connecting solidly with Scarface's knee. There was a loud crack as the knee buckled and the upper part of Scarface's shin broke through the skin and split the fabric of his pants. As the man fell to the floor screaming, Kane reversed his motion and pulled Flat-top violently away from the wall and toward him. He drove his forehead hard into Flat-top's nose before the man could react and Kane felt the guard's cartilage crush into his sinuses.

He pushed the guard back against the wall and smiled at the expression on Flat-top's face. His eyes were wide and protruded from their sockets, an interesting contrast to the now sunken mass of pulp where the man's nose used to be. He let Flat-top fall to the floor and turned to Scarface. The tough guy was out of commission, lying on the floor in a widening pool of blood and gripping his leg on either side of the protruding bone. He was deep in shock and posed no further danger. Kane began walking to the end of the hall.

The door opened and an older man, somewhere in his fifties and wearing a gray suit, pointed a revolver squarely at Kane. "That's far enough, son." Kane stopped, still ten feet from the door. He could see the office inside was indeed lavishly decorated. The interior was all wood with what looked to be a very nice rug on the floor. The older man with the gun continued, "State your business."

"I need to see Frank Colletti. My name is Silas Kane."

The man with the gun gave no reaction, but a voice came from behind him. "Let him in, Joey. Let him in."

Joey stepped aside and lowered the gun, but did not place it back within his jacket. The revolver stayed in his hand at his side. Just in case.

As Kane stepped into the office, Joey looked back down the hall at the two guards, both still conscious but writhing in pain on the tiled floor. "I think we may need to get the boys some medical attention."

The comment was addressed to the man sitting behind the large mahogany desk at the end of the office, out of view from the door. Kane noted that there were no windows in the room. Just bookshelves lining the wood-paneled walls and a couple of leather sofas. Two chairs covered in red velvet sat in front of the desk. Kane walked behind one of the chairs and assessed Frank Colletti.

The man behind the desk looked to be about sixty years old. His hair was gray, but traces of black were still noticeable. He wore a dark gray suit with a black tie that complemented his looks. His face was wrinkled, but not excessively. At one point he had been a handsome man.

Colletti addressed Joey first. "Call Dr. Litto. Have him come out here immediately. We don't want to take them to a hospital unless it's absolutely necessary. And call Claire in from the store. Have her bring a mop. There's no sense in letting the blood set into the tile, is there?"

Joey walked to the other end of the office and, gun still in hand and still facing Kane, used his free hand to pick up the receiver and dial. He spoke softly into the phone as Frank Colletti addressed Kane.

"So you are Silas Kane." He pulled a white handkerchief from his jacket pocket and offered it to him. "You seem to have gotten one of my men's blood on your forehead. Please, use this." Kane reached across the chair and desk and accepted it. "I read about you in the paper, Mr. Kane. I thought you were in prison."

Kane wiped off his forehead, then tucked the bloody handkerchief into his leather jacket. He leaned forward and placed his hands on the back of the chair in front of him, gripping the wood framing. "I wasn't followed. I need your...help." It was not an easy thing for him to say.

"Your father told you about me."

Kane nodded.

"He and I knew each other many years ago. He is an interesting man, your father. He has interesting...plans. For the future." He let the sentence hang in the air, but Silas Kane did not speak. "What is it that you require?"

"I need to learn the location of a bounty hunter. A man named Clive Quinn. I've been unable to track him down, and I need to...ask him some questions."

Colletti put his hand to his chin and rubbed it between his thumb and forefinger. "I'm afraid I do not know this man, but I may be able to help you. I have certain connections that may be able to locate a reliable source for the information. Once I locate the source, obtaining the information will be up to you."

Kane nodded. He hadn't been sure what to expect, but this would have to do. "That's fine. I'd like the information as quickly as possible."

"You can expect it within the hour. Do you have a phone?" Kane shook his head. "Joey, please provide Mr. Kane with a cellular phone."

Joey had completed his calls and was listening to the exchange. He opened a drawer on a credenza and extracted a small, handheld phone. He walked to Kane and handed it to him. "Please dispose of this after we have called." Kane nodded again.

Frank Colletti continued. "We will contact you with the source soon. Joey will escort you through the back door as you will undoubtedly soon become a man of much notoriety once again, as soon as the evening news airs I would imagine."

Kane turned and started out the door. He was stopped by a comment from Colletti.

"You do realize, of course, that this information comes with a price."

Kane turned to face the man behind the desk.

"You have already cost me a great deal of money by disabling two of my better bodyguards. You have placed my office, one which I have kept wholly discreet for a great many years, into danger by coming here. The information you have requested will not be easy to obtain. And yet, the price I ask is quite small."

Kane narrowed his eyes, unsure of what to expect next but not trusting Frank Colletti.

"The next time you see your father, tell him that I have assisted you. I am not a superstitious man, Mr. Kane, but I am a cautious man. Should your father succeed in his plans, I wish to be...remembered. Tell your father that the debt you now owe me also applies to him. Tell him that for me, Mr. Kane."

Kane nodded and followed Joey out the door. He was led through a side door in the hall, turning before reaching the two bleeding bodyguards on the floor. Within moments, Joey opened a door leading into an alley. The rain was coming down hard now, and some splashed into the building. Kane put the phone inside his jacket to keep it dry, and stepped into the damp. The door closed behind him without a word, and Kane heard the clank of a lock being slammed into place.

As he walked down the alley and turned onto the sidewalk, he smiled. Within an hour he would have the information to complete the next step of his revenge. He would find the bounty hunter, then he would find out who had hired him. Then he would kill them, slowly. And all it took was a promise to tell his father about a favor from a New York mobster. Not a bad trade considering he hadn't seen his father in years and didn't plan on seeing him again for a long time, if the old man was even still alive. He was surprised that a man of Colletti's status would even concern himself with Hiram Kane's plans, but hey, whatever. All that mattered now was the information.

All that mattered was finding Clive Quinn.

CHAPTER 20
October 10
5:16 P.M.

G RANT LEFT HIS ROOM and ventured into the hallway. He glanced toward his grandfather's door. The dream no longer frightened him. It had been several hours since he had awoken with the dying scream in his throat, and the impact of the nightmare had dissipated leaving only a thirst for answers.

He had spent his first few hours on the island bouncing from place to place. Ever since his conversation with Eric that morning, he couldn't bear a conversation longer than five minutes with anyone. Since his arrival, he had spent a few minutes speaking with Julie, had the briefest of conversations with Mona and Loraine, spent half the afternoon walking around by himself, and then abandoned a conversation with his uncle that may have led to a better understanding of the family climate since he had left for college.

That had been a mistake. He fled that discussion because he hadn't liked the insinuations that Phil had made regarding Julie's relationship with Abe. Grant didn't like the implications toward Julie or toward his grandfather, but instead of facing them and continuing the conversation, he had taken off for the main house and been hit by a car for his efforts.

He looked towards Julie's room. Her door was closed. He was spending too much time thinking about her. His rational mind recognized the infatuation as a likely byproduct of his months away from modern civilization and the maelstrom of emotions he'd experienced since his grandfather's death. Rational. Reasonable. But not practical. He needed to focus.

Grant turned from her door and headed for the stairs. He paused before descending and studied the stainless steel contraption bolted to the railing along the main wall. His grandfather had the wheelchair lift installed after he had broken his hip. The doctor had advised him to just move into a room on the ground floor, that stairs were not going to be a part of his life anymore. Abe disagreed with that assessment and the lift was in place by the end of that week. He was stubborn but inventive.

He had died upstairs in his bedroom so the plate was resting at the top of the stairs. Grant's stomach lurched at the thought that it would never be used again. Whoever took over the house would just have it removed. Probably consider it an eyesore. The memory of Abe Armstrong would become an inconvenience.

Grant started down the steps, taking them two at a time without grasping the handrail. He had avoided confrontation long enough. Had chosen not to pursue questioning his family until he had confirmation from the autopsy that Eric was having done. But he no longer needed that confirmation. He was certain his grandfather had been murdered. As sure as any feeling he had ever had. Maybe it was the nightmare. Maybe it was something else. But he knew.

Now he had to find out who did it. Surprise was on his side. No mention of murder had been made to anyone in Grant's family. That meant whoever was responsible may have let down his or her guard by now. His relatives were bright people, but Grant considered himself pretty smart too, and he had the advantage of having been away for a long time. He could ask just about any question, and no one would be suspicious. He just needed to focus. Plan his attack. He had already spoken with Phil in a limited way so he would hold off and catch him when he came back to the main house. Brock was still off the island, which was okay with Grant. That left Mona and Loraine. And Julie.

Grant immediately ruled out speaking to Julie next. Although he suspected she could provide him with information regarding his grandfather's relationship to the rest of the family, he couldn't trust himself to stay on track. He would proceed with either Loraine or Mona. He decided to let fate decide.

Reaching the base of the stairs, he could hear the sound of a newscast emanating from the living room. That would be it then. He briefly debated going into the kitchen to get some ice for his wrist, but it had already started to feel better. It was still stiff and sore, but the throbbing pain had gone away, and Grant was positive the bone was not fractured. Besides, he was anxious to get on with it.

He walked into the living room and saw Loraine sitting on the couch with a brandy cradled in one hand and a cigarette in the other. A small plate from the kitchen sat on the coffee table serving as a makeshift ashtray. The local news was playing loudly on the big-screen television, flashing colors and shadows across Loraine's face.

Grant lowered himself into a chair near the couch and ventured a conversation. "I didn't think anyone ever smoked inside the house."

Loraine shot him a quick glance and turned back toward the television. The reporter was delivering a story about a crisis in South America. "In case you hadn't noticed," Loraine began, "It's raining outside. Besides, that was Abe's rule. Not mine. It no longer applies."

Grant took the remark in stride. Loraine knew that Grant had been close to his grandfather. The comment, casually designed to remind him that Abe Armstrong was no longer here, was a low blow. Phil's wife had always gone straight for the jugular in most conversations.

Grant wondered if she just disliked all people. He had seen her use insensitive remarks to cut conversations short with many people since he had known her. Neither gender nor race nor religion nor political leanings mattered. Everyone was fair game. Making others as miserable as her was a sport at which Loraine excelled.

"Well," he began, "I'm not going into any new territory that hasn't been covered by a thousand doctors before me, but smoking's not exactly good for your health. Direct or secondhand."

"My health is really none of your business, *Doctor* Armstrong, but it's nice to see you learned something in medical school. As for the secondhand smoke, if you don't like it, there are plenty of other rooms in the house, all of which are smoke free."

"But those rooms lack the sparkling repartee." Too sarcastic. Stupid. Grant chided himself for playing this game instead of focusing on the task at hand. He redirected his approach. "So what have you and Uncle Phil been up to lately?"

Loraine's eyes remained on the newscast. "Same as always. I spend my days waiting for my brilliant husband to do something wonderful, to take me away from all of this, and he spends his days playing grab-ass with his bookie."

Grant leaned back in the chair. The self-righteous part of him wanted to strike out at Loraine and ask what "all of this" was that she was trying to get away from. He wanted to ask if she understood that she was living a life far richer than ninety-nine percent of the world's population, but he held his tongue. It was a battle he would not win.

Grant knew that even if Loraine and Phil had access to the entire Armstrong estate, even if she spent the rest of her life cruising warm seas on a luxury yacht, she would still be unhappy. No wonder Phil preferred time with his bookie. Which also explained the eruption he witnessed when his uncle heard about the football injury in the car. Grant decided to pursue this track a bit further. "So Uncle Phil does a little gambling? I used to go to the dog track with some buddies in England. Those greyhounds are incredible. Do you two ever go to the track?"

A commercial for aluminum siding came onto the television, and Loraine turned to face Grant as she answered. "No. I don't go to the track. I prefer to spend my days doing more productive things. I volunteer for a local soup kitchen. I teach blind people how to read. I knit. I'm also working on a new fuel system that will allow cars to run on saltwater instead of gasoline. Further questions?" She raised one eyebrow.

Grant's only reaction was an upturned eyebrow of his own. His aunt had grown even more sarcastic since he had left for school. Impressive. "I'm sorry. I wasn't meaning to pry. It's just that, well, with Granddad gone now, I don't have much family left. I thought maybe I could try to get to know everyone a little better. I've been gone a long time." He hoped that such a statement would soothe the beast.

Loraine's expression softened. Maybe it had worked. "I understand, Grant, but the thing is, I don't really want to get to know you any better. I've spent my life married to your uncle, waiting for the promise of things to come. Waiting for the fabulous riches and wealth he wooed me with when I was younger. And you know what? I'm sick of waiting for them. I've already waited so long. Then, at last, the old man dies, and his bastard lawyer tells us we have to wait till after the funeral before he can read the will."

Her expression was grim, but she hadn't raised her voice. "I want what's rightfully mine, Grant. I've given up the best years of my life, and I deserve something back for it. So forgive me if I don't want to get all sentimental for you now that you've come home. If you wanted to get to know me better, maybe you should have tried to do it before now." She turned to the television, eyes narrowed, and used the remote to increase the volume. The commercial break was over and the meteorologist was about to give the forecast.

Grant let out a deep breath. That was more than he had expected. He had never seen Loraine so on edge. Based on his first encounter with the three of them when they got back from the attorney's office, and based on Phil's explosion and Loraine's cold outburst, Grant was struck with how distant his family had really become. They had been greedy before his grandfather had passed away, angry and resentful that the wealth hadn't already been distributed, but that seemed to have multiplied tenfold since he had left for school. Had things really become so cold since he had last lived on the island, or was it just the culmination of emotions due to his grandfather's death?

The meteorologist, an attractive woman with dark hair and a red dress, stood in front of the green screen to give the forecast. Her voice was melodic, but far too loud with Loraine's earlier manipulation of the television's volume. "We'll have continuous showers tonight through tomorrow morning, and tomorrow midday will see the arrival of the *big one*. That storm system moved up the coast from Florida and headed out to sea, but it will come back into New York tomorrow bringing powerful rains, flooding and electrical storms to much of the state." The green screen behind the woman showed a massive swirl of red off the east coast of the United States, and it jerkily moved toward New York State in a time-lapse radar, then leapt back to its original position to repeat the process as she spoke. "There is a possibility that the storm will dissipate, but if it doesn't, plan on being off the streets and in some form of shelter tomorrow. This will be a severe storm and dangerous."

"Thank you, Cathy." The picture cut to the anchorman who had taken on a serious expression. He lowered his chin as he read the teleprompter. "Speaking of dangerous, authorities report that convicted killer Silas Kane has escaped from custody and is currently at large." Grant turned his full attention to the report and leaned forward in his chair.

A menacing picture of Kane posed with a prison number appeared above the anchorman's left shoulder as he continued the report. "Silas Kane was responsible for the brutal slaying of a young woman in New York City and remains under suspicion for several other murders. Police are requesting cooperation in finding this man but ask that no one approach him. He is considered very dangerous. Authorities ask that anyone with information on his location contact them at the number below." A phone number appeared on the screen beneath the anchorman. "We'll update you with more information on this developing story."

Grant didn't hear the rest of the newscast. His first thoughts went to his friend. Eric was supposed to see Kane today. Was he okay? Had something happened to him?

He rose from the chair without giving Loraine a glance and walked out of the room. He had left Eric's phone number back in his room. He needed to call his friend.

CHAPTER 21
October 10
5:45 P.M.

ERIC PACED the sterile white hallway on the fourth floor of the hospital. He was frustrated. At George's suggestion, they had come to the hospital to check on the officer who had survived Kane's attack. If the man did wake up, George reasoned, it was possible that he would have some insight on where Kane was headed. Perhaps there had been a conversation before the prisoner had kicked the dividing cage into his head.

Eric seriously doubted it. According to the floor warden at the prison, Kane hadn't spoken a word to anyone in six months. Eric found it hard to believe Kane would have suddenly opened up to the two officers transporting him. But it was not impossible. Besides, it was the first suggestion his partner had made since the operation began. Eric didn't want to damage his relationship with George by dismissing the thought—particularly when he had no further ideas himself—and he could make phone calls and be reached just as easily at the hospital as at the station.

He looked out the window. The rain was coming down harder now. Not violent, but steady. It struck the glass and ran in thin streams. Close to the bottom of the window, many of the tiny streams combined to form a larger one. Eric stopped pacing and leaned down, inspecting the running water. All the minuscule imperfections in the pane of glass, so small you couldn't see them with the naked eye, forcing the water to bend and flow as gravity pulled it earthward.

Eric straightened but his eyes remained on the water. He thought he knew Silas Kane. Thought he knew him inside and out. But now that he had escaped and had a whole city—a whole world—to hide in, Eric found he didn't know him well at all. He didn't know where to turn. Didn't know where to look. And the rain kept pouring down.

He turned and rededicated himself to pacing the hallway. George stayed where he was, leaning against the doorframe of the officer's room. When they arrived, they had been politely informed by a nurse that the patient had not regained consciousness yet, and that it may be quite a long time before he did. In the meantime, she would appreciate them not entering his room, but they were welcome to stay in the hallway.

George's eyebrows furrowed as he contemplated what to do next. He rubbed the gold cross which hung from the long chain around his neck between his thumb and forefinger. It calmed him.

The hospital had been a waste. He shouldn't have suggested it, but neither of them knew what else to do. The hope had been that after the news broke regarding Kane's escape, someone would spot him and phone the information in. But the rain was hindering that likelihood on two counts: both limiting the number of people outside and diminishing the accuracy of what they saw. The department had received only two calls so far. One turned out to be an exceptionally tall homeless man, the other was the well-muscled owner of a nutrition supplements shop walking home from work in the rain.

George looked to his young partner. Eric was pacing the hallway. Walking from the nurse's desk to the window and back again. As George watched him, all he could think was—doesn't he ever get tired? With the exception of their time riding in the car, Eric had been pacing all day. George couldn't help but wonder if all the steps were helping his partner make any mental progress towards Kane's whereabouts.

Eric paused at the nurse's desk and put his hands on the counter, slightly leaning over the top. The nurse, a pretty young woman, looked up and smiled as she addressed him. "You know, the doctor said it may be a day or two before your friend wakes up, are you sure you want to stick around?"

The question was a polite and subtle way to let Eric know their presence was not entirely welcome. He couldn't blame her. She was probably accustomed to seeing only concerned family members on her shift, not men with guns pacing her hallway. He offered her his best smile, the first he had given since he'd received news of Kane's escape. "I think we're about to take off then. Would you mind if I borrowed your phone for a moment first?" He gestured his thumb at the *No Cell Phone Use on This Floor* sign adhered to the wall. The nurse nodded. She was obviously pleased the two would be leaving in a few minutes. Soon it would be business as usual.

Eric picked up the phone and dialed the department's voicemail system. After entering his access code, Eric's voicemail responded. Four new messages.

The first message was from a woman who had been a witness in a case Eric was working prior to Kane's escape. She had called to let him know she could remember more details about that night. She had just woken up from a nap and could suddenly remember more. Could he call her as soon as possible?

Sorry, lady, thought Eric, *but we've got some more pressing matters to attend to right now*. He saved the message with the woman's number for later.

The next message was from Grant. He was asking if Eric had heard from the medical examiner yet, and whether or not he was still coming to the island for dinner. Eric shook his head. In all the excitement, he had completely forgotten about both, but there was no way he would be able to make dinner.

The third message was coincidentally from Joe Stenson. The county medical examiner had finished the autopsy, and Joe wanted

Eric to call him when he got the chance. He would be in the office late tonight, so Eric should call regardless of the time. Eric wrote down the number.

The final message was again from Grant, wanting to know if Eric was all right. He had seen the news and learned of Kane's escape. The message had been sent only a few minutes ago. Eric deleted it and hung the phone up using his index finger, leaving the handset nestled between his shoulder and ear. He started to dial Grant's number but stopped midway through. He would call Stenson first. If Joe had results of the autopsy, Eric wanted to be able to deliver it when he next spoke with his friend.

Stenson picked up on the first ring. "Still Pines Coroner's office. Joe Stenson speaking."

"Joe, this is Eric. I got your message."

"Hey, glad you called. Just heard the news that Kane escaped. That was one of yours, wasn't it?" Joe had real concern in his voice.

"Yeah, and I'm working on bringing him back in."

"Watch your back. That guy sounds like bad news. You want to make sure he's not out for revenge against you or anything."

Eric hadn't even considered the notion, and didn't care for the thought, but he brushed it aside in favor of the business at hand. "I'll be careful, Mom. You said you had something on Abe Armstrong's autopsy?"

"Yeah, M.E. finished it a couple of hours ago. Looks like Mr. Armstrong did die of congestive heart failure, but it may or may not have been from natural causes."

"What do you mean? Drug induced?"

"No. Tox-screen came back clean. Nothing in the blood that wasn't normal for a man his age."

Eric rested his forehead in his hand as he spoke, "So what caused it?"

"Well, there weren't any drugs in his system, but both the M.E. and I did notice a recent puncture mark in the skin of his left forearm. Penetrated to the vein. Someone poked Mr. Armstrong with a needle."

"I don't get it. I thought you said there weren't any drugs in his system."

"There weren't, but drugs aren't the only way to kill a man. If someone knew what they were doing, they could insert an empty syringe into a vein, and push an air bubble through. The bubble travels to the heart resulting in a gas embolism. In layman's terms, the heart seizes, and in a man Abe's age, it's not likely to get going again. Unlike drugs, an air bubble leaves no trace to be found in an autopsy. So as a practical matter, I tell you he was an old man who died of a heart attack. It happens all the time. Plausible, and even likely, that the expiration date on Abraham Armstrong's ticker was simply reached. But seeing as how I'm speaking to a homicide detective, I'm also comfortable telling you that the presence of a needle puncture—when the subject was not taking any intravenous medication or giving blood samples—is a legitimate cause for concern."

Eric gripped the phone harder. "What do you mean, *cause for concern*? We're talking about a potential homicide case here. I need to know, Joe, was Abe Armstrong murdered?"

Joe Stenson sighed on the other end of the phone. "I can't say for sure, Eric. I'm sorry. All I can give you here are possibilities, not facts. Whether it's enough to launch an investigation...well, that's your field. Perhaps an investigation would lead to more solid evidence. Perhaps not. I can tell you this though, if a gas embolism did spark the heart attack, know that this sort of death is quick. So whoever did it was right there the night he died. Also, the syringe had to be inserted directly into the vein. So he was probably asleep when it happened. If he struggled, the odds are very low that a vein would have been hit."

Eric placed his thumb and forefinger to the bridge of his nose and rubbed hard. This was not the news he wanted to give Grant. "Thanks, Joe. Listen, call me if you get anything else. I appreciate the help."

"No problem, Eric. Remember what I said. And keep your eyes open."

Eric placed the handset back on the phone's base and stared at it. He didn't want to call his friend. Didn't want to tell Grant that his grandfather's death had gone from *maybe-possibly* a murder to *really-possibly* a murder. As bad as Eric's day had been with Kane's escape, Grant's was about to be even worse.

Eric looked up at his partner. George was sitting on a folding chair near the window, watching the rain hit the glass the same as Eric had been doing only a few minutes before. He was still absently rubbing the gold cross which hung from his neck.

He no longer looked contemplative. He looked tired. Eric wondered how long it had been since George had spoken to his daughter. Eric had met Trish a few times. She seemed like a good kid. She lived with her mom. The cross had been a gift for Trish, a "sweet sixteen" present two years ago. George was supposed to take her to dinner to celebrate. He had gotten hung up in an investigation. When he tried to give it to her later, she handed it back to him, so the cross went around his own neck. George had kept the incident to himself, up until a night of whiskey made him excessively honest with Eric.

"Sir, are you done with the phone?" The pretty nurse pulled Eric out of his reverie.

"Just one more," Eric said as he picked the receiver up again. He was delaying what had to be done. He wished fervently that Kane hadn't escaped. That he could be on Armstrong Island to share this news with his friend personally. Instead, Grant would have to deal with this alone. He dialed the number.

"Hello?"

"Hi...Grant?"

"Eric? It's me. Man, I saw the news. What happened?"

"Kane escaped from the prison transport on the way to the courthouse. Killed one guard, the other still hasn't regained consciousness."

"How'd he get away?"

"Son of a bitch kicked his way out of the back seat. Never seen anything like it. We're on his trail. Speaking of which, I'm not going to be able to make it to dinner tonight."

"Yeah, I kind of figured. Totally understand. Wish you could be out here though. I could use some Poirot-style thinking. Any word on the autopsy?" Grant's voice lowered as he asked the question.

"Yeah, I just got off the phone with him. Here's what we know." Eric took a deep breath. "There was no trace of drugs from the tox-screen, but there was a puncture mark on his left arm from a syringe. It's possible that someone injected an air bubble into your grandfather's bloodstream. That would..."

Grant interrupted. "Cause a gas embolism triggering a heart attack, yet not have a residual trace in an autopsy." There was a pause on the phone. "Any sign of a struggle?"

"No, the M.E. didn't find any. He said that—*if* the trigger was a gas embolism—Abe was probably asleep when it happened."

"Maybe, but a needle in the arm has a tendency to wake someone up. Whoever did it would have to be awfully quick to insert the needle and plunge the syringe before he fought back or cried out for help. The whole family was here at the time, somebody would have heard something. It doesn't make sense."

"I know. Look, Grant, as soon as I get Kane back under custody, I'm going to meet with the Still Pines Sheriff. You may remember Mike Puckett. He and I go way back. I'm sure he won't mind a little help on the case. We'll find out what happened."

"Thanks, Eric, but I don't plan on waiting that long. I'm going to feel around here. See if I can dig something up."

"Be careful, Grant. If it happened like that, well, whoever did it will be on guard. There's no telling what they're capable of. Listen to your gut. If you get uncomfortable, back off and wait for me."

"You know it. You be careful, too. From what you told me about this Kane guy...oh hell, it's your job. You know what you're doing. Just don't get yourself killed before you get a chance to pitch me another one of your sissy fast balls."

"Tough talk there, Slim. You've always been jealous of my balls."

"Dream on, buddy. I'll talk to you later." Grant paused. "Take care of yourself."

"You too." Eric hung up the phone and walked to the window. His partner looked up from his seat. "Let's head back to the station, George. We've got a long night ahead of us."

CHAPTER 22
October 10
6:07 P.M.

GRANT HUNG UP the phone on his nightstand. He was glad he had waited in his room for a few minutes to see if Eric would return his call. If there was ever a conversation that needed to be private, this was it.

Puncture mark but no drugs. Abe Armstrong had been murdered.

Grant sat on the bed. The room had grown dark and the light from the small lamp by the bed cast shadows on the wall. The reality of what Eric had told him was sinking in. Five minutes ago, Grant had felt certain that his grandfather had been murdered but he now realized the extent of how much he had hoped the autopsy would prove him wrong. Now, faced with the blunt reality of the needle puncture, there was no turning back.

This wasn't the first time in Grant's life that he had been angry. When his father had died, Grant had been filled with anger, with emptiness, with the same sort of loss he felt now, but his father's death was not premeditated. The drunk behind the wheel had apologized. He had been devastated with guilt. And while Grant hated the man for what he had done, he knew it had been an accident.

This was different. His grandfather had been murdered. *Murdered.* Someone walked into his room, looked down at him, and pushed a syringe into his arm. Someone watched as the air bubble hit his heart and the first streaks of pain shot through his body. Someone stood there and observed the man Grant had loved for a lifetime take his last breath. Not a peaceful one, but a pain and panic-filled gasp as his life was wrenched from him.

Grant felt more than anger. He clenched his fists, his injured wrist throbbing with a pain he ignored, his fingernails cutting half-moons into his palms. It was rage. He squeezed his eyes shut but hot tears forced their way through his eyelids and ran down his cheeks. He pounded his fist into the bed, the mattress sinking beneath each punch, denying him any satisfaction. What hurt before ached ferociously within him now. If the killer had been in front of him at that moment, he would have grasped the person's throat and choked until he heard their dying breath.

Grant tried to get ahold of himself. He tilted his head back and looked at the ceiling. Tears trickled past his earlobes onto his neck. He was hot. His wrist throbbed. His stomach hurt and his nose was running. He leaned forward, forearms on his thighs, and took a series of deep breaths.

The rage was still there but becoming contained. It would do him no good to lose his cool. He had to use the anger, not allow himself to be a slave to it. He had much to do.

Grant headed toward the lounge holding an ice-packed towel to his right wrist as he walked. The episode in his room had aggravated the injury, and he decided that a cold compress might not be such a bad idea after all. He opened the door to find Mona stretched out on the couch, staring into the warm glow of the fireplace, glass of white wine in hand. She looked up and saw him framed in the doorway.

"You know what the problem is with this fireplace, Grant?" Her words slurred. She didn't wait for a reply. "It never changes. Ceramic logs. You push a button to turn on the gas, and you have a fire. It's easy. But it never changes. You never have a crackling log or a smoking log or a log that burns really hot. You just have the same old fire every night."

Grant moved to the chair closest to the fireplace and sat. "If you didn't have the ceramic logs, you'd have to keep firewood by the hearth and build the fire and use a poker and keep adding wood as it burned. It's a trade-off. The logs may be ceramic, but it's still a lovely fire. Maybe there's something to be said for consistency, that it may not change, but it will be a nice fire every time you turn it on."

"You know what? You're right. I love this fireplace." Mona sipped from her glass. She was drunk but seemed coherent enough to carry on a conversation. "That's what's wrong with people. Not enough consistency. People change. They want change. They need change. They don't want to be stuck with the same old boring unchanging person."

Grant studied his aunt. Perhaps it was the shadows cast by the fire, but she looked different than he remembered. He had noticed it this afternoon, but it was even more apparent now. She looked...hopeless. "Aunt Mona, are you all right?"

Mona blew her lips out at her nephew. It was supposed to be a dismissive gesture but came out more as a child's raspberry. "Oh, I'm fine. Just too consistent. Men need variety. Bastards. Not you, dear, no offense."

The conversation made sense now. Brock was apparently still out. And apparently with someone else. "Why do you say that?"

"Because it's true." She was looking into the fire now. "I'm not stupid. It's just life. It's not his fault really. He trains all these beautiful women. Of course they're going to come on to him. He has to make a living. He has to support us. But he won't anymore. He won't have to work anymore. We'll have enough money that he can just stay home with me." She trailed off as she watched the flames dance.

"So I guess you're looking forward to getting your inheritance."

"Of course I am, silly." She turned to Grant. "Oh honey, I know you're upset about Dad, but people die. It happens. I'm sorry about it too, but that doesn't mean we can't find happiness. We have to allow ourselves to move on. Just be glad he didn't suffer through an illness or something."

"Mona, would you mind if we talked about him? I feel like I missed out on a lot this past year."

"Sure, hon, we can talk about whatever you'd like. I know you've been gone a long time, and I know you missed seeing Dad, but we were all glad you were doing something important."

Grant somehow doubted anyone had given him much thought—much less considered what he was doing in Africa—but perhaps he was wrong. "How was Granddad doing before he died? I mean, was he happy? Uncle Phil told me you came to the island more than anyone else."

"I used to come out once or twice a week. Whenever Julie would have afternoons off. I didn't mind. I wanted to spend more time with Dad, but he kept growing more distant."

"What do you mean?" Grant interrupted. "Was he becoming less coherent or..."

"No, no. It just got to where, well, he didn't seem to want to spend as much time with me. Most days, he would just go to his study even while I was here at the house. So I spent most of my time at the pool or in here."

"Why do you think he got that way? More distant, I mean."

"Oh, who knows? His hearing was getting worse so maybe he didn't like trying to carry on a conversation. Or maybe he was just mad. There were a few arguments the past year. Phil started giving Dad a really hard time about the money, and I guess I may have mentioned it a few times, too. I mean, come on, it's ridiculous to have all that money sitting there doing nothing. Dad wasn't using it. We just thought that it would make more sense for Dad to be able to see us enjoying it instead of waiting until after he died to give it to us. I guess it doesn't matter now."

"I guess not."

Mona glanced up at the comment but her gaze soon returned to the flames. "But it's not like it was all our fault. I'm sure Miss D-Cup Delight had something to do with it."

"You mean Julie?"

"Of course I mean Julie. It was ridiculous. I'm sure she was telling Dad all sorts of bad things about us. *That's* why he grew so distant. And the lawyer may have said she could stay until the funeral, but as soon as it's over, I plan on seeing her out the door myself."

Grant shook his head. "Mona, are you sure Julie would do something like that? Granddad said very nice things about her at Christmas, and she just doesn't seem like that kind of person."

"Let me guess." She stood and walked to the bar to refill her glass. "She's been oh-so-nice to you since you got here? Perhaps wearing tight clothes or short-shorts?"

"She hit me with a car."

Mona paid no attention. She returned the wine bottle to the chiller and continued. "She's being nice to you because she lost her chance at Dad's money. Now she's after you. Mark my words. She's a gold-digger, Grant. Trust me."

"Just because she's attractive doesn't make her a gold-digger. She was recommended by the hospital as a caregiver so she had to have a solid resume. It's not like Granddad picked her up at a bar or something. She's a healthcare worker."

Mona returned to the couch and leaned forward conspiratorially. "Grant, listen to me. Dad introduced Julie to me when she started working here and she seemed pleasant and Dad liked her. She didn't know her place at first. Kept trying to talk to the rest of us instead of just doing her job with Dad, but that didn't last long. After a while, she stopped trying to intrude. Learned to be more like what's-her-name...the maid."

"Mrs. Gonzalez. She's worked here for twenty years."

"Right, Gonzaga. Lovely woman, I'm sure. But people change, Grant. If you're around money enough, you get a taste for it. Julie may have blended in to the background but that was all part of her plan. More alone time with Dad. Being awfully friendly toward him."

"Wait a minute, did you ever actually see Julie being...more than friendly...to Granddad?"

"No, but that doesn't mean she wasn't. Grant, it's just like that fire. People aren't consistent. I'm sure Julie seems nice, and I'm sure at one point she was, but then she decided she wanted the money. She still wants the money." Mona let the last comment hang in the air as the flames danced in front of her.

Grant joined her gaze. Mona may have had too much to drink, but she was making a lot of sense. Hadn't he noticed a change in his own family over the years? Hadn't he observed them grow steadily more greedy and hateful after his father died? If they were not immune to it, how could he expect someone like Julie to be? She had probably grown up in a much less financially secure family. To suddenly be surrounded by so much wealth, it had to have an impact. Couple that with her mother passing away last Christmas, she was sure to have gone through an emotional gauntlet. Trauma can be a catalyst to change. Would it really be so surprising if she decided to try to gain access to the Armstrong fortune? And she *had* seemed to be flirting with him over the course of the day. Moreover, she outright admitted to consciously avoiding the rest of the family.

Grant reclined into the leather of the chair. But then, if he had the choice, wouldn't he avoid his family as well? And hadn't he been flirting with Julie since he first saw her at the front door?

He didn't know what to think about Julie, but it was a secondary issue. His love life could wait. He had more important matters to look into.

"Mona, there's something I've been wondering..." He paused, waiting for a prompt from the woman on the couch. None came. Grant stood and approached the sofa. Mona's eyes were closed. Her breathing was steady. *Still the same Mona*, thought Grant.

Grant extracted the wine glass from Mona's hand and placed it on the coffee table then returned the ice-packed towel to his wrist. He stopped on his way out the door to look at the fire once more. Consistency. But people changed. Had Mona changed enough from the girl she once was to have actually committed murder? Was getting Brock out of the arms of other women enough to make her kill her own father?

Grant pulled the towel away from his arm. His wrist had grown numb from the ice during his conversation with Mona. He walked to the kitchen to dispose of the towel. Maybe he would have a brilliant insight over a plate of lasagna.

CHAPTER 23
October 10
6:32 P.M.

MICKEY LITTLE walked down the hall to his apartment door whistling softly. He twirled his keys around his finger, never even glancing down as he passed by a large pair of black boots sitting in the hallway. People left crap in the hall all the time.

He unlocked and opened the door to his apartment and tossed his coat on a nearby chair. He closed the door, relocking the main bolt and securing the six interior locks one by one. He knelt and removed his shoes and socks, setting them by the door. They were dripping wet, and he didn't want to leave tracks on his carpet.

Mickey had just had new carpet installed in the two-bedroom apartment. It was white. Stark white, some would say. It was the kind that was specially treated so if you spilled anything, you could just wipe it up with no stains. But Mickey hadn't spilled anything on the beautiful white surface yet, and he didn't want to start now. Things were finally starting to pay off for him, enough to where he could afford the luxuries in life, like new carpet. He had never lived anywhere with carpet, much less fancy stuff like this.

He had built his contacts over the last few years to include every pimp and hood in a ten mile radius. Nothing happened in this part of the city that he didn't know about. And there was nothing he knew that couldn't be bought, for a price.

He had come a long way since he had been busted on his second offense seven years ago. Had come a long way since first agreeing to sell small bits of information to the police in exchange for his freedom. In time, he came to realize that what he sold for peanuts to the cops could be worth gold on the open market. If handled discreetly. Eventually, he established an underground corporation of information exchange and Mickey Little became Mickey The Mouth.

Once the statute of limitations ran out on his second offense, the police no longer had any leverage on him, and the price of his information soon went up. He decided that it was only fair for the citizens of New York to be charged the same amount for information as bounty hunters and the occasional pissed off mobster. After all, it was a capitalist economy.

He ran his little empire in virtual anonymity. None of his sources knew any of his other sources. None suspected that they were a part of a snitching pyramid scheme. That was the only reason Mickey had not been discovered and terminated by the organized crime families he dealt with. And he fully intended to keep his enterprise a secret. All it took was caution.

Mickey's bare feet sank into the carpet with each step. It felt good. He scrunched the material underneath his toes and grinned. Life was good. Except for the fact that he had been pinching off a wicked need to piss for the last hour and a half. A situation that would soon be remedied.

He switched the bathroom light on and stepped inside, checking himself out in the mirror. Not bad. Just a little primping and he'd be back on the scene for dinner. There was a smoking brunette working the corner near his apartment building, and he felt like he could use some TLC that evening. Ever since the waitress at the diner that afternoon had told him she only liked "tall" guys, he had been ready for action.

Mickey unzipped, freed his member from his pants and started pissing. The urine made a loud sound as it struck the water, the evening's pressure finally relieved. He looked down at himself, smiling. The waitress didn't know what she was missing.

As Mickey appraised himself, he didn't see the large hand emerge from behind the edge of the shower curtain. The noise of the water splashing in the bowl masked the sound of the curtain being pulled back, revealing the giant of a man standing in the shower behind him.

Silas Kane stepped out of the tub and stood behind Mickey in the cramped bathroom. He was standing in his bare feet as well.

In a fluid motion, Kane wrapped his left arm around the smaller man's chest, pinning both his elbows to his sides while Kane's right hand clamped over Mickey's mouth, his palm covering well over half Mickey's face, and pulled his head back.

Mickey screamed, barely audible through Kane's muffling hand. He shook violently, trying to free himself as the last of the urine stream showered his legs and the back of the commode and the wall. Kane pulled his left arm tighter, hugging Mickey's back to his torso, allowing only his legs to flay and kick. When he spoke, he whispered into Mickey's ear, spittle flying onto the smaller man's cheek and neck.

"Listen carefully you little prick. If you kick me in the shin again, I will tear your fucking head off and leave it in the toilet. Do you understand me?"

Mickey's legs ceased movement. He dropped limp in Kane's arms in full compliance. Kane kept him pulled close, Mickey's arms trapped in a vise grip and his toes fully a foot off the floor, and carried him out of the bathroom. Kane proceeded into Mickey's office and stood him in front of the desk. His address book sitting open in the middle of it. Kane whispered again in his ear.

"I'm glad you showed up when you did. I've spent a little time going through your address book. Now your life depends on how you answer this next question. It's real easy. All it requires is a yes or no. Since I don't want you alerting your neighbors, I'm going to keep my hand over your mouth. You will nod for yes, and you will shake for no. Am I clear?"

Mickey tried to nod his head for yes but found that he could not move. The monster's grip prevented it. The giant was going to kill him. He wouldn't be able to nod to answer his questions because the man's grip was too tight, and he was going to die for it. It wasn't fair. Tears welled in Mickey's eyes. He couldn't breathe well through his nose with his mouth covered. He didn't want to die.

But Kane could feel Mickey's effort at nodding. He understood. "Good. Now here's the question. Your address book there is opened to a man named Clive Quinn. A bounty hunter if I'm not mistaken. I need to get in touch with this man. The question that your life depends on is this – is this the correct address for Clive Quinn?"

Mickey was flushed but suddenly relieved. *That was the question?* Perspiration from his forehead ran down his face and collected where the giant's fingers were mashed against his cheek. He knew the answer to this. It was the right address. He had sent some information to that address less than a year ago. He was going to live. He attempted to nod vigorously, but his head again remained motionless.

Kane leaned forward. "Good, Mickey. You did good." Kane released his grip, allowing the shocked man to fall out of his arms. He put his hands on Mickey's shoulders, turning his body to face him. The top of the smaller man's head came to the bottom of Kane's immense chest.

Mickey was still in shock, so much so he hadn't even considered screaming. He had come so close to death, but he had answered the question correctly. After all these years of dispensing information, all it took was confirming an address to save his life. He raised his gaze to his attacker's face. What he saw there scared him. The man was grinning, but there was no joy in that expression. The giant leaned toward him and spoke once more, a deep growl.

"Put your dick back in your pants. It's fucking embarrassing."

Mickey realized for the first time that his penis was still hanging out of the open zipper. His face flushed. As Mickey bent forward to push his member back into its home, Kane pulled the letter opener from his own back pocket. He had removed it from Mickey's desk while searching for Quinn's address. He swung his arm hard and plunged the letter opener into the side of Mickey's neck, piercing all the way through to the other side, the tip emerging covered in red.

Mickey was still leaning forward, one hand on his penis and the other on the zipper. The abrupt sting in his neck shocked him, then the pain spread throughout his body. He dropped to his knees, unable to take a breath. The blade of the letter opener had pierced his windpipe. He fell on his side, the protruding tip of the letter opener hitting the floor and forcing the handle slightly out of the other side his neck.

Kane bent forward and spoke to the dying man in a casual voice. "Thanks for the information. If you had said that wasn't the right address. Well, I would have had to let you live. But I would have tortured the correct address out of you anyway, so this is probably easier on both of us. Definitely faster. Now if you'll excuse me, I've gotta go see an old friend."

Kane ripped the page out of the address book, stepped out of the office and walked out the front door of the apartment, closing the door behind him. Frank Colletti's tip on this guy had been dead-on.

Mickey Little lay on the floor, eyes open and blood pouring from the two openings in his neck. He watched his beautiful white carpet turn crimson. His last thoughts were spent wondering if the treated carpet repelled blood as well.

CHAPTER 24
October 10
7:05 P.M.

GRANT PUT THE LAST FORKFUL of lasagna into his mouth and chewed slowly, savoring the taste. The food in the village had not been terrible, but it was more about sustenance than enjoyment. After so much of the land had been stripped over the years, the villagers had become dependent on the supplies flown in from government agencies and charitable organizations. Typical fare consisted of a grayish, millet-based gruel and bread.

Grant had taken his meals with the villagers. The clinic had provided decent rations for the medical personnel, but Grant often gave away his food to the children and shared their gruel. He had grown accustomed to the meals, and his taste buds had grown numb over the months. It was no wonder he had shed weight in his time away.

He dropped his fork onto the plate with a clink, feeling spoiled for having enjoyed his repast to such an extent.

Grant pushed his chair back and stood, gathered his plate and silverware, rinsed them in the sink and placed them into the dishwasher. As he closed the dishwasher door, he saw Phil standing in the doorway, watching him.

"Good to see you're eating. You look like you may have lost a few pounds." Phil walked into the kitchen and pulled out a chair on the opposite side of the table. He sat and spread his hands on the table. "Sit with me, Grant. We didn't get a chance to finish our conversation earlier."

Grant took a seat across from his uncle. "Which conversation was that?"

"Our conversation about you, Grant. I want to talk about where you're going. You're a young man with a lot on the ball. Degree from Oxford. A doctor, no less. Where do you plan to be in five years? Ten?"

"I hadn't given it much thought. I devoted myself to the clinic while I was away. I'm not sure what comes next."

Phil nodded. "The clinic, yes, very important. Noble even. I'm sure it does a lot of good. But we need to be thinking about your life here, in the good old U-S-of-A. Grant, listen to me carefully, you won't always be this young. I know that right now, money may not seem all that important, but one of these days, you're going to have a wife and kids and a lot of responsibility. It's critical to have financial security overseen by someone you trust."

"I understand what you're saying, Uncle Phil, but money won't ever keep me up at night. It doesn't take much to make me happy, and I'm pretty sure I'll always be able to earn a living. I like to think I'm a good doctor. I should be okay."

"But that's the whole point, Grant. Everything you said is true, but it's all uncertain. It depends on you being able to function and *work*. To be able to provide for your family."

"Are you selling me insurance?"

Phil narrowed his eyes, the joke unappreciated. "What I'm trying to make you understand is that you stand to inherit a portion of Dad's estate. We're going to meet with his attorney after the funeral, and he's going to read the will. I want you to be prepared for whatever happens."

"Still not following you."

"Grant, you're a doctor. You're good at helping people. It's what you enjoy. I'm good with money. I know how to invest it, make it grow. What I'm offering you is the chance to continue doing what you do best—the doctor stuff—and let me do what I do best, invest money. Once the estate is distributed, I'd like you to grant me power of attorney to handle your monetary affairs. After all, you don't want to spend your valuable time worrying about finances. You need someone who knows what he's doing to take that load off your shoulders. And the last thing you want is to give it to some heartless shark at a big bank who doesn't have your best interests at heart."

Grant sat with a blank expression on his face. Had his uncle just asked him to sign over legal control of his inheritance before the will had even been read? The reason Phil had gone to so much trouble to get Grant to New York before the funeral was becoming clearer.

Phil continued. "You want to keep the wealth in the family. That's what I'm here for, to look out for you. I've always tried to do that, ever since Jack died. Right?"

Grant gathered his thoughts before saying anything. It was only money, and Phil was only being greedy, a trait not exactly out of character for his uncle. It bothered Grant that the man sitting across the table still considered his nephew the mental equivalent of a ten-year-old. That Phil was low enough to invoke Grant's father in the conversation was even more bothersome, but there were more important things to be concerned with at the moment, and Grant had to maintain his focus.

"Right. So...when's the will-reading scheduled?" An innocent question.

"Day after the funeral." Grant knew the funeral would be in two days. "I just wanted to discuss this with you now before all the pressures of the will-reading and the documents and all that stuff."

"I see. Well, it's a very generous offer, Uncle Phil. I'll think about it."

A broad smile spread across Phil's face. He smacked his palms on the table. "Great. If you have any questions, just let me know. Oh, and one more thing..." Phil's voice dropped into a conspiratorial whisper as he leaned across the table towards Grant, "...don't tell anyone about this. I'm not offering this arrangement to Mona and Brock." His eyebrows raised as he finished the sentence, seeking a response.

"Sure thing. This is just between us." Phil started to get up from his chair, but Grant reached across the table and grabbed his uncle's wrist. "Wait a minute. Would you mind if we talked a bit longer?"

Phil's smile lingered as he took his seat and leaned back. "Of course, my boy, what's on your mind?"

"Well, I was talking to Mona a few minutes ago, and I was wondering...oh, never mind. I don't want to pry..." Grant left the verbal bait hanging. Phil pounced on it.

"Go on, Grant. What do you want to know?" Talking about other members of the family was a sport at which all Grant's relatives excelled.

"Well, it's just that she doesn't seem very happy. Are she and Brock...is their marriage having difficulties?"

"Difficulties? The Titanic had difficulties. Mona and Brock's marriage is a fucking catastrophe. Mona is my little sister so you know I love her, but she's always been set to self-destruct. The party boys in high school, the drugs in college...marrying Brock was just one more bad decision in a long line. Loraine and I didn't think it would last a year, but give her credit, Mona has stuck it out. Funny thing is, I used to think she married Brock just to spite Dad—Dad always hated him—but she's been with him long enough now that I almost believe she actually loves him."

"Is he cheating on her? I got that impression when we talked."

"Constantly. Brock will bang anything with boobs and a heartbeat. He's worthless. But don't tell him I said that. I'm trying to be civil, mind you. Keep the family peace."

Grant suspected it had less to do with peace and more to do with Phil never wanting a physical confrontation with Brock. Grant didn't really blame him.

"What did Brock think of Granddad?"

"I think Brock hated Dad as much as Dad hated Brock. He married Mona for the money, we all knew that, but there was no money to be had. I'd say that's why he started cheating on her, but that's not true. A dog is a dog, and you can't expect it to behave like anything else."

"But you said Mona still loves him. Do you think she'd do anything to keep him?"

"What do you mean 'keep him'? They're still married. He just spends his days screwing his clients. Not a bad job really. I wonder if he gets a Christmas bonus."

Grant was walking on dangerous ground here. He decided to redirect the conversation. "Let me ask you something else. You told me that Granddad had called everyone out to the house the night he died to talk to the family, but he never got a chance. If Granddad hadn't had a heart attack, what do you think would have happened?"

Phil's eyes narrowed. "I suppose we would have eaten supper and he would have talked to us about whatever it was."

"That's what I'm asking. What was it?"

"I think we've covered this before, Grant. I don't know. And it doesn't really make a difference. Why are you so interested in that night anyway?"

"It just sounded like Granddad had something important to talk about. I'd like to know what it was." He tried to sound as innocent as possible. Phil had given a stronger reaction to his question than he had anticipated, but he didn't know if it was due to not wanting to speak about the night his father died or something else.

"I told you before. It was probably just business. Dad and I sometimes talked about his business."

"Did he ever talk to Mona or Loraine about his business? Or Brock?"

Phil stood and pushed back his chair. "No. He didn't. Grant, I'm tired. I'm going to get a drink and watch some television. Think about my offer. I'm serious."

Grant directed his final question toward his uncle's back as Phil left the room. "Do you think Granddad was going to change the will?"

Phil stopped but didn't turn around. He was silent. Grant tried again. "What do you think? Would he have changed his will if he hadn't passed away that night?"

Five seconds ticked away before Phil responded. He walked out of the kitchen muttering his answer, just loud enough for Grant to hear. "Maybe."

CHAPTER 25
October 10
11:15 P.M.

ERIC AGAIN STOOD his vigil four feet from the oversized map on the station wall. He had been staring at it for half an hour. His eyes focused on the red tack marking Kane's escape point, then followed a set of roads into the compacted mass of the cityscape. From there, his eyes would return to the tack and begin again. He was frustrated. All these months studying Silas Kane and he had no idea where the man was going. Eric's team had checked every location on file regarding Kane's former haunts with zero leads to show for it.

Eric moved his eyes in a sweeping circle around the twelve mile perimeter he had mentally drawn. He didn't think Kane would run farther than six or eight miles, but he had underestimated the man so far. Better to err on the side of caution.

He had to assume Kane's first goal was to either change clothes or find a method of transportation. Jogging away from the scene extricated him from a reasonable search area but wouldn't have fulfilled either of those priorities. The clothes would be a dilemma. Given his size, Kane wouldn't likely steal clothes off some man on the street. Having no means of payment, purchasing clothing at a store wasn't an option.

That meant he was going to a safe-house. Either a girlfriend—assuming he hadn't killed them all—or someplace he had kept for himself. Somewhere he had left clothes or a vehicle. But the city was immense. The possibilities were endless. With no reports of any sightings or activity fitting Kane's M.O., Eric was losing hope. He was close to accepting that the department may be in for another several months of hunting...waiting for Kane to make the first move. To show himself. But how many people would die in the meantime?

George sat at his desk, shoulders slumped. The long day was turning into a longer night. His years of experience cried out for him to go home. To go to bed and get some sleep. They would not catch Kane tonight. When a man wanted to disappear in New York City, he could do so. And even though he was an animal, Kane was quite capable of the disappearing act. But George was stuck here thanks to his aggressive young partner.

He wanted to tell Eric to knock off for the night, but he couldn't. Not because Eric was more or less his superior during the manhunt, but because his partner was so intent on catching Kane. Even if George mentioned how smart it would be to get some rest and try for a fresh start tomorrow morning, he knew what the response would be. "You go on ahead," Eric would say. "I'm going to stick around here for a little while." Then George would return in the morning to find Eric in the same clothes as the night before. So George didn't leave, and he didn't mention it. Yet.

He watched his partner. The kid was something else. One minute, George wanted to nail Eric's feet to the floor to stop his pacing. The next minute, he wanted to poke him with a ruler to make sure he was alive. George wondered what it was like to get lost in your own mind like that. It was something he had never experienced, except for maybe watching the Super Bowl.

The phone rang on George's desk, and his eyes snapped open. He hadn't realized they had been closed. He grabbed the receiver and spoke into it. After a sixty-second conversation, George hung up. His partner had shifted his gaze from the map to him.

"What's the word?" Eric asked.

"That was Rybeck. They haven't had any luck with our street contacts. Those guys are hard to track down, most of them aren't even home yet."

"Did you give them a full list of the contacts we used on the Kane case? Comprehensive?"

"Yeah, straight out of our files. I even dispensed a few extra just in case somebody else knows something, but like I said, these things take time. It may be a couple of days before we get a chance to talk to all the people on the list."

"That's two days too long. Kane's out there. Is your computer on?" George nodded. "Pull up tonight's multi-precinct activity report. Let's see if anything sounds like the work of our guy."

George turned the monitor toward his partner. "I've kept the board open all night. We've got two deaths. A drunk woman ran over a teenager in Queens, and a guy shot his roommate while cleaning his gun. Maybe accidental, maybe not, but neither of those is what we're looking for."

Eric shook his head and sighed.

George returned his monitor to its earlier position. "Look, partner, I know you want to find Kane, but the guy's not gonna poke his head up out of the grass. Not tonight. He just broke out of prison. A life sentence. What would he have to gain by going out and killing someone tonight? I'm not saying he's not going to kill again. We both know he will. It's in his blood. But not tonight. He's too smart for that."

Eric nodded, his expression one of weariness. "Maybe you're right."

"What do you say we call it a night, huh? Let's take another crack at this in the morning. A fresh start." George looked at his partner, eyebrows raised. Giving it a shot.

"You go ahead, George. I think I'll stick around here a bit longer. I'll catch up with you in the morning." Eric's eyes went back to the map on the wall.

Shot missed. George pushed himself out of his chair and went to the coat rack. Donning his jacket and hat, he walked out the door, wishing he were younger.

CHAPTER 26
October 10
11:47 P.M.

GRANT STARED at the ceiling in his room. His bed was comfortable, a whole different league from the thin mat upon which he had slept the past several months. His pillow was soft, and his head sunk deep into its center. The blankets were warm, and the sheets had the crisp scent of laundered freshness, but sleep refused to come.

He glanced at the clock on his nightstand. Almost midnight. He had gone to bed well over an hour ago, his will to continue the investigation of his family drained for the night. Not that he had much of an option. Mona had remained passed out on the couch. Grant had brought her a blanket, tucking it behind her shoulders. Phil and Loraine had returned to the guest house. Brock hadn't come to the island yet. And Grant hadn't seen Julie since their incident with the car earlier that afternoon. The door to her room had been closed all night though Grant could still hear her television from across the hall.

When he went to bed, he had pictured himself falling into a quick slumber. His body was exhausted, still feeling the effects of jet lag despite his earlier nap, but his mind was reeling.

Being back in his old room should have been comforting, but it was not. It was just odd. When Grant had first seen his room earlier today, he had been struck by how it had not changed since his youth. He had been abroad, had experienced life and death, and he had grown into a man. But in that bed, surrounded by trophies and pictures from high school, he could have been sixteen again, lying between the sheets, thinking about the baseball game he would play that weekend or fantasizing about one of the cheerleaders.

He was again reminded of just how long he had been away. Not just since last visiting at Christmas, but the years in Europe, rarely returning home. Losing almost all contact with his aunts and uncles, keeping in touch with his grandfather through one-way letters. Despite the familiar surroundings, he had become an outsider. His only real connection lay dead in the coroner's office.

Grant had caught Phil once more before he left for the guest house to ask who was handling the funeral arrangements. Phil told him he had given the Still Pines Funeral Home a generous budget and informed them to make any and all decisions.

Apparently none of the family members wanted to be bothered with the details of the funeral.

Grant felt like an outsider indeed. The feeling intensified as he considered the events of the day, replaying the conversations in his mind.

After spending time with each member of his family, the sad truth was that he felt closer to Julie than any of his relatives. Even considering the accusations leveled at her from Phil and Mona, she had been the only person that day to display any apparent sadness over the death of Abe Armstrong. Grant didn't think that had been faked, nor did he think the feelings between them were the result of her trying to seduce him. It seemed more and more that Julie was a sweet girl who had been sucked into the same lust for money that had gripped Grant's family for years. Perhaps greed was contagious. Grant couldn't hate Julie for that, only pity her.

Grant wondered if Eric had known anything about Julie, or more to the point, just how much his friend knew about what was going on period. Eric had said that someone called him to warn him, that the caller feared for Abe's life. If not for that call, Grant doubted any suspicions would have been aroused. A full autopsy certainly wouldn't have been performed, and everyone would have peacefully believed that his grandfather had died of a heart attack.

Had the phone call been made by someone who knew something was going to happen, or just someone fretting over an offhand remark? Did one of Grant's relatives know who the killer was? Or even recognize that it was murder?

With the exception of Eric and Julie, no one he had spoken with that day had shown what Grant would consider genuine grief. A new thought struck Grant. Had the call been placed by Julie? Up until now, he had assumed that his aunt or uncle had gotten in touch with Eric. After all, he wasn't sure if Eric and Julie knew each other. But if she was really after the estate, and if Abe was close to changing his will, then Julie stood out as the one with the most to lose if Abe was put in danger. Grant sighed. If true, that meant every member of his family remained a suspect.

He closed his eyes again, taking deep breaths as he tried to slip into unconsciousness. He allowed his mind to grow still as his body relaxed. At last, he could feel himself drifting. Images flashed through the darkness.

Mona on the couch.

Phil pounding the steering wheel in his car.

Julie hugging him in the rain as he sat on the car bumper.

His point of view altered, as if he was being pulled to the heavens in an out-of-body experience, the image of Julie and the car now far below his feet. The rain ceased.

His ethereal flight yielded a bird's eye view of the entire Armstrong estate. The island was beautiful and green despite the time of year. His grandfather had loved evergreens. He said they made him feel as if it was always springtime.

From his vantage, Grant tracked the winding road that proceeded from the main house, turning back on itself and lengthening the drive that could have been reduced to half if the road had been cut straight through the trees. He could see the old covered bridge on the far end of the island. A car was entering it from the other side. It was Eric's white Crown Victoria.

Grant focused on the bridge. It swayed under the weight of Eric's vehicle, shuddering more than normal. In the blink of an eye, Grant was yanked down in his dream-flight until he was alongside the bridge, so close he could almost touch it. He was floating over the river running beneath the structure.

Something wasn't right. The bridge bucked and swayed beneath Eric's car, but the air was still. The storm had ceased and there was no wind. Nevertheless, Grant could hear the old timbers of the bridge creaking and cracking. He needed to warn Eric, tell him to speed up, to get off the bridge. Grant looked to the island. How much farther until the Crown Vic reached safety?

Then he saw it, an immense figure cloaked in darkness. Apelike in size and appearance, it was hanging by one arm from a girder beneath the bridge. In its free hand was a jagged saw. It was cutting into a support beam. Although the swipes of the saw were slow, it was shearing the wood impossibly fast. Grant realized many of the other beams supporting the bridge had been sliced through as well, explaining the instability of the structure.

Grant was in motion but still not in control of his surreal flight. He was pulled beneath the bridge, flowing under it in pace with Eric's cruiser, hearing the rhythmic bumps of the tires as they rolled over the planks and the cracking of the weakened wood girders, ever closer to the dark troll sabotaging the final beam. Grant wanted to stop—or fly away in any other direction—but he was somehow bound to the car above, unable to divert his path from a certain encounter with the shadowy assassin at the end of the bridge, growing larger with each passing second.

The sawing stopped. The dark figure pulled the saw from the beam, held it up, as if showing it off for Grant, then opened its long fingers and let it fall. Grant watched the saw plummet. The water—in the real world only a few feet from the bottom of the bridge—was hundreds of feet below in this nightmare. The saw fell until it was barely discernible as it struck the water's surface.

Grant pulled his gaze up. The thing under the bridge was still hanging there by one arm. Grant could see now that it was wearing a black cloak with a hood, a makeshift executioner's guise. Grant had a revelation. The beast under the bridge was Silas Kane. The hood masked the troll's features, but he was certain that it was Kane, there to kill Eric.

He wanted to shout to Eric, to warn him, but the dream rendered him mute. Mere feet away from the final severed beam, Grant focused on the Kane-creature that hung from it. From the darkness under the hood, its eyes glowed red. A smile spread under those flaming crimson orbs, the bright white teeth of a fanged Cheshire Cat.

Grant tried to scream but the breath caught in his throat. The only audible sound was the beam cracking. The Crown Vic had reached the final mark of sabotage. The weight of the vehicle split the beam and the car crashed through the bottom of the bridge, planks shattering and flying to either side.

Grant plunged toward the water, falling in time with the car above him. His mind raced, knowing the vehicle would crush him if the impact from striking the water did not.

As he plummeted, he vaguely recalled that if you fall in your dreams, you always wake up before hitting the earth. Within the dream, he closed his eyes, willing himself to awaken.

He struck the water. The cold shock forced his eyes open. He was completely submersed. Instinctively, he ducked his head and raised his arms, shielding himself from the immense weight of the car about to strike, but no impact came. After a moment, Grant kicked his way to daylight. He broke the water's surface and took a deep breath. Eric's car was gone. Grant looked to his right and left, knowing that his friend could not swim, knowing that he would need his help. But neither the car nor Eric were anywhere in sight.

Grant looked straight up. The bridge was gone as well. And there was no sight of the hooded creature that had tried to kill his friend. He turned and focused on land, only twenty yards away. What he saw made his stomach clench. There, on the shore, stood the big oak tree with the rope swing. He had emerged from the water on the opposite side of the island.

He didn't want to swim for it. Didn't want to go to the shore. He had been here before. He knew what lay in wait beneath the surface of the water in front of the tree. He turned, preparing to swim for the opposite bank, away from the island. But there was no opposite bank. The lake went on forever. Grant could have been treading water in the Atlantic. There was no land in sight.

For the briefest of moments, he considered staying where he was, preferring to tread water forever then to go back to that place, but the water was too cold to endure for any length of time. Even in a dream.

He turned toward the oak tree, braced himself and swam toward the shore. Slow, even overhand strokes, legs rhythmically kicking. He kept his head above the water. He couldn't bear to place his face down in the typical swimmer's position. He didn't want to see what was below the surface.

Closer now. Fifteen yards away. He kept his pace. Only ten yards to the shore. Five yards.

A cold hand clamped onto his ankle beneath the water, interrupting his kick. He sucked in a quick breath as the hand effortlessly reversed Grant's direction and pulled him beneath the surface. Beneath him, as before, he saw the same divers deep in the murky depths of the lake. His family—Phil and Loraine and Mona and Brock—holding onto the bindings of the struggling creature gripping Grant's ankle.

Grant didn't want to face it. Could not bear to again look into the face of the black-eyed monster that used to be his grandfather. The hand on his ankle swung him around in the water, forcing him to face it even as it released its grip on him. But the creature was not there. In its place was Julie. She was wearing a white gown, billowing in the water around her, and her ankles were bound by ropes below. Unlike the black-eyed creature, Julie could not speak underwater. She was holding her breath, eyes wide and panicked as her blonde hair floated about her thrashing head.

Grant had to save her. He tried to kick his way down to her ankles to free her. But his legs would not move. He tried to use his arms, to swim deeper to face the villains holding the ropes, to fight them into releasing her. But his arms were paralyzed. Julie was looking at him, terrified and confused. Grant wanted to shout, "I'm trying!" But his lips would not form the words. He was a prisoner within his own body.

Julie's eyes grew wider as the final air bubbles trailed from her mouth. Even surrounded by the cold water of the lake, Grant thought he could see tears escape her eyes, blending with the darkness. As the expression of fear left Julie's face, turning into one of blank death, the paralysis left Grant's body. His lungs transformed into burning pits. He needed air. He used his newfound strength and kicked his way upward. Away from the woman he had failed to save.

Grant broke the surface of the water and sat up straight in bed. The sheets and blankets had entangled themselves around him as he mimicked the swimming movements. Half awake, he shook himself free of the bedding with flustered, jerky motions. He looked about, trying to get his bearings. He heard rain outside his window. The sound returned him to reality.

He was breathing hard and covered in sweat. He looked at his clock. The glowing numbers indicated he had been asleep less than twenty minutes.

Grant flung his legs out of bed, and his feet hit the floor. There would be no more sleep for a long while.

Lightning flashed in the distance, illuminating the outline of the hills surrounding the lake. A distant crack of thunder reverberated through the air several moments later. Grant lifted a can of soda to his lips, drank deeply then placed it on the small metal table by the porch swing.

After his nightmare, the notion of closing his eyes again was unthinkable so he had decided to stop by the kitchen to make a snack then ventured to the covered porch at the rear of the house. He had devoured the peanut butter and jelly sandwich in four bites, his taste buds ecstatic after so long without this simple pleasure. The sandwich reduced to crumbs in a paper towel, Grant was now enjoying the soda and the lightshow the storm was creating.

The wind was blowing hard, and the rain was coming down in sheets. Grant found it hard to believe the storm was going to get even worse the next day. Another gust of wind howled through the trees, and Grant was thankful the back porch faced west. The storm was blowing in from the ocean, and if the porch had faced into the wind, each new gust would have pushed the rain under the roof and onto the deck, making it impossible to sit out and enjoy the storm. As it was, the back porch was dry but Grant was grateful to find a blanket on the swing and used it to shield his body from the cold. His sweat pants and t-shirt wouldn't have been adequate.

As another burst of lightning illuminated the night sky, Grant considered his most recent dream and wondered if he would ever get a good night's sleep again. The logical adult doctor rationalized that the nightmares were a result of the overwhelming emotions he was feeling about the circumstances of his grandfather's death, but the little boy who had returned home was simply frightened by the dreams, searching for meaning in the terrifying images they represented. Looking out into the darkness, waiting for the next flash of light, Grant hated the world.

A crack of distant thunder was joined by the creaking of the back door. Grant looked up and saw Julie standing there, half inside the house and half out. She was wearing a loose-fitting pajama top and a pair of matching shorts. "Grant? Are you okay?"

Grant smiled. "Yeah, I'm fine." He returned his gaze toward the horizon. He couldn't allow himself to look at her that way. Not anymore. Not if what everyone said was true.

Julie bit her lower lip. "I just wanted to make sure your arm wasn't hurting, keeping you up."

Beneath the blanket, Grant flexed the fingers on his right hand. Still sore, but not bad. "It's okay. The wrist hasn't swelled at all. Should be good as new in a few days." He turned to her again. "Why are you still up?"

She looked at the floor and moved her bare feet against each other. "I haven't slept much since Abe died. I thought I heard somebody moving around down here, and I just wanted to make sure you were okay."

"Would you like to come out? Watch the lightning?" The words were out of Grant's mouth before he thought to stop them.

Julie considered for a moment, her hand still resting on the doorknob. "Okay. Just for a minute." She allowed the door to close behind her, walked past Grant to the vacant spot on the porch swing and sat down, pulling her feet onto the front edge of the seat. She wrapped her arms around her bare legs and pulled them tight, resting her chin on her knees.

Grant couldn't help a half-smile. "Yes, I am willing to share." He lifted the side of the blanket toward her.

Julie shook her head and pushed his hand down. "No. You'll get cold. You've already been on a plane for two days and been hit by a car after getting soaked in a rain shower. You'll be lucky if you don't catch pneumonia. I'm not about to be any more responsible for it."

Grant slid closer to Julie and threw half the blanket over her. As it descended, the edge of the blanket landed on the front of her head and pulled her hair down over her face. She turned to Grant, poked out her bottom lip, and blew a puff of air from her mouth. The errant strands of hair lifted from her face and came to rest alongside her ear. Grant's half-smile turned full.

Julie's lip continued to protrude in an affected pout. "Leave me alone. I need to get it cut. I just haven't had time in a while."

"Sorry. I thought it was cute. No offense intended." Grant paused. "So you've been busy lately?"

"Yeah. You know, work and all."

"You seem to do a lot around the house. More than just as a healthcare worker." Grant waited to see how she would respond. This wasn't ground he had planned on covering tonight, but it was eating at him.

"Well, Mrs. Gonzalez only comes out once a week. There's plenty of stuff to do around the house that can't be completed in just one day. Laundry and cooking are daily events. I've just been busy."

"So you did housework and cooking as well? Granddad was quite lucky to find you."

"No. I was lucky to find him. I wouldn't trade this past year and a half for anything. It's been the best time of my life."

Her candidness caught Grant off guard. "Really? That surprises me. I loved Granddad, but I know he could be a bit of a bear to work for..."

"Oh, he just has that tough surface, but underneath, he was so sweet. He would always say such nice things. He even got me to..." Julie glanced at Grant. She had been talking into her knees, remembering Abe, but had been pulled out of her contemplation. "Never mind."

"No, please," Grant said. "Julie, I didn't get to spend much time with Granddad these past few years. I'd really like to hear any stories you have."

Julie nodded. "Okay, but please don't tell anyone about this. It's embarrassing." Grant returned her nod. "Abe talked me into going back to college."

"What?" Grant didn't know what to expect, but this hadn't been it.

"I got my associates degree a couple of years ago, but never got a bachelor's. Your grandfather told me how silly that was. That I was just as smart as any of those kids graduating, and that I ought to go back to get my full degree. That's the real truth about why I've been so busy. I've been studying and taking online courses. Going to the library a couple days a week. You know, to get back in the swing of things."

Grant sat in stunned silence. What she had said sounded just like something his grandfather would have done, not at all like the lustful old man Grant had been picturing after his conversations with Phil and

Mona. He remembered seeing books and papers scattered across the roll top desk in father's room. "You've been studying in Dad's old room."

"On the big desk...it's perfect. I hope that's okay."

"Of course! That's great, and I'm glad you're going back to school. A bachelor's degree will open a lot of doors for you."

"I can't tell you how important this is to me. You know, your grandfather is the only man who ever believed in me, who ever said anything encouraging to me. Certainly the only man who ever called me smart."

"I find that hard to believe, but yeah, that's Granddad."

"I see a lot of him in you, Grant. You've been so nice since you got here. Nicer than you needed to be. You didn't even get mad when I hit you with the car." The corners of her mouth turned up as she spoke. "A lot of people take that kind of thing for granted, but I don't. You're so much like Abe." Grant was surprised to see tears welling in Julie's eyes as she spoke. "I miss him."

Grant put his arm around her. A cool, damp breeze washed over them as she leaned onto his shoulder. When she spoke, her voice caught in her throat. "I'm sorry. I don't mean to be blubbery. You probably think I'm a head case and maybe I am. It's just that, well, Abe was all I had. The only friend, the only family I had left."

"Shhh, it's okay. I don't think you're a head case. I've broken down a couple of times today, too. Perfectly normal. And I can't believe you don't have any friends or family. What about your dad or maybe a sister?"

Julie pulled away from Grant's shoulder, sitting straight. She sniffed and wiped her eyes with the back of her hand. "I don't have any family, Grant. Everyone's dead. They've been dead all my life."

Grant's mind flashed to the picture he had seen earlier that day. The somber man and woman. The two little blonde girls, one smiling, the other with the same stoic expression as her parents. "All your life? I thought your mother passed away last Christmas."

"You wouldn't understand. Look, it's not easy to talk about, and I doubt you want to hear it." Lightning flashed across the sky and lit her face as she spoke.

"Wrong. I do want to hear about it. Really. I'd like to know more about you."

"Fine," Julie exhaled. "My mother did pass away last Christmas, but she was dead long before that. You might not understand, but do you think it's possible to die in spirit before your body passes on?"

Grant's thoughts went to some of his patients who had given up when they received the diagnosis of a serious disease, who didn't bother to fight for their own lives. "No doubt. When someone loses hope, it's a kind of death in itself."

"Exactly. My mother had given up hope a long time ago. Back when I was still a kid."

"But why? You seem like you were probably a great kid..."

Julie's expression turned intense. "Grant, this isn't easy for me." She sighed. "I'm going to tell you something, and when I'm done, if you don't see me the same way anymore, I'll understand."

Grant furrowed his eyebrows. "I'll take that bet. Try me."

The response caused Julie's reddened eyes to light up with the barest hint of a smile. "Thank you. It's just that, when I was growing up, my father...he wasn't a good man. He wasn't anything like you or Abe. He...did things to my sister and me when we were growing up. Bad things. My mom never tried to stop him. I think she loved us, but it was like she gave up without a fight. I hated her for that, for never even trying. When I was thirteen, my father shot himself and died. It sounds terrible, but it wasn't. That was the happiest day of my life. How messed up is that? I thought things would get better after that. I thought that maybe we could be a normal family, but my sister ran away a few weeks later. I haven't seen her since. My mom sort of lost it after she ran away. She went to a special hospital, and I went to live in a foster home. And that was that, no more contact, not until the hospital called here to tell me she had died. I used my savings to pay for a funeral. I guess I owed her that much for having me. I thought I had everything under control, but when I got back here after Christmas, I kind of lost it. Abe was worried about me, and I broke down and told him everything. I've spent my entire life hiding my past and hating men. All men. I've never even had a boyfriend. But Abe told me everything would be okay. Said that I was like a daughter to him and he'd never let anything happen to me again. I believed him, and I loved him. I spent so many nights wishing I could have been you, Grant. Growing up here, with Abe as my grandfather. It would have been so perfect."

Grant cleared his throat of the lump that had formed during Julie's story. He felt for her, and he hated himself for his misled thoughts about her relationship with his grandfather. She was resting her cheek on her knees now, her face turned toward him. Grant brushed a tear from her face. "Julie, I'm so sorry."

She interrupted. "Don't be. Look, all that stuff happened in the past. There's nothing that you, or anyone else, could have done about it. I probably shouldn't have said anything. I just wanted you to understand how I felt about Abe."

"That's what I'm talking about. I owe you an apology. Some things were said, and I believed them without even getting to know you. I should have known better, about Granddad if not you. I'm ashamed of myself."

"What are you talking about? What things were said?"

"Things about your relationship with Granddad."

Dawning realization came upon her face. "They didn't say I was sleeping with him, did they?" Grant nodded, embarrassed. "How could they say something like that? I knew they were angry with me, but..."

Grant stopped her. "Angry about what?"

"Well, one weekend this summer, Abe had invited the family to the island. No one had been out to visit him in weeks, and he wanted to see his kids. Brock and Phil found me in the kitchen. I was making Abe a sandwich. Anyway, Brock pinched my ass, and I stabbed his hand with a fork." Grant grinned but Julie chided him. "It wasn't funny at the time. He got really angry. I was scared. He told me to get off the island.

That I was fired. I told Brock that he couldn't fire me. So Phil said that *he* was firing me. That I should 'get my gold-digging ass away from his father.' That they would hire a real healthcare worker for him. Anyway, Abe overheard the whole thing. He had been rolling into the kitchen to ask for some chips. He told Phil and Brock to get out, and he didn't speak much with the family after that. No one came to see him, and he didn't ask them back to the island. At least until the night he died."

Things were starting to become clearer. "What about Mona? I thought she came out once or twice a week."

"Your Aunt Mona's a different story. I think Abe always had a soft spot for her. I was glad she would come. It gave me time to run errands and study at the library in town."

Grant nodded, still feeling like an idiot. He cursed himself again for jumping to conclusions.

"Grant, I have to ask. What exactly did they say about me?"

"Well, one day when Mona came to the island, she said she saw you in the pool." He paused. "You were swimming *sans top*."

"Shut up! Someone saw me?" Julie exclaimed. "I didn't think anyone was watching."

"Well, she didn't say that Granddad was out there, just that anyone could have seen you."

"I cannot believe this. Abe was asleep. He had a headache so he went down for a nap. His bedroom window is on the opposite side of the house from the pool so I figured it would be okay. I went out for a few laps. It was a beautiful day. I have *one* 'what-the-hell-live-dangerously' moment and *this* happens? My life is so messed up."

Grant laughed. The expression on Julie's face was so comical, one of utter embarrassment and horror, that he couldn't help himself.

Julie punched his leg under the blanket. "It's not funny. How could someone say something so horrible about your grandfather and me?"

Grant shook his head. "You said you fantasized about being part of the Armstrong family...welcome to it."

Julie smiled back at him.

A large bolt of lightning struck somewhere over the hill. The crash of thunder was followed by a voice in the darkness. "Damn it!" A moment later, a large figure raced around the corner of the house and sprinted up the steps onto the back porch, a string of profanity spewing from his mouth.

Brock Rutland was soaked. He shook his head in a doglike manner, water spraying from his hair, then assessed Grant and Julie.

"Huh. Look who's back from the Amazon."

Brock stood just inside the porch, the rain cascading behind him. His clothes clung tightly to his well-muscled form. His pectorals flexed under the tight material of his shirt. Grant didn't know if it was conscious or if Brock was a routine chest flexer.

"The Amazon is in South America," Grant began. "I was in…"

Brock shook his head once more, hair flying back and forth, droplets of water landed on the blanket covering the pair on the swing.

"…never mind," Grant finished. He felt Julie slide closer to him under the blanket.

Brock shifted his gaze from Grant to her and back again. "Am I interrupting something?"

"Just watching the storm," Grant answered.

"The storm…yeah, it's a real fuck-gusher. Didn't think I'd ever get here, and when I finally pull in, my garage door opener is dead." He glanced over his shoulder toward the rain. "Coming down hard. Real hard and very wet. You think it's wet, Julie?"

Julie gripped Grant's arm under the blanket. He responded for her. "Rough storm. Hey, Brock, why don't we spend some time together…tomorrow? It's been a while. We can catch up."

Brock raised an eyebrow. "Oh yeah, our lack of quality time has been keeping me up at night. Why don't you meet me for a workout? We'll hit the weights. Put some hair on your chest. But for now, I'm heading to bed. Anyone not named Grant is welcome to join me…" Julie kept her gaze directed to the rain and away from Brock.

"Mona's asleep on the sofa in the lounge," Grant ventured. "Maybe you could help her into bed."

"She'll be fine. She sleeps on the couch all the time." Brock walked toward the back door, lightly punching Grant's shoulder as he passed the swing. "Catch you in the morning, doc." The door slammed shut in the wind behind him.

Julie released Grant's arm and leaned back. Her eyes remained on the back door, as if expecting Brock to reemerge. "Okay, I kinda hate that guy. He really creeps me out."

Grant rubbed his shoulder. It ached from the punch. Brock had made it harder than necessary. "Yeah, I don't care much for 'Uncle Brock' either."

Julie lifted the blanket and put her bare feet on the floor. "Grant, would you do me a big favor?" He nodded. "I know this sounds stupid, but would you walk me to my room? I'm just not comfortable with him here."

Grant grabbed his empty soda can with one hand and scooped up the blanket with the other as he stood. "It doesn't sound stupid at all. I should head back to bed myself."

They entered the house and proceeded upstairs without encountering Brock. Julie opened her bedroom door and faced Grant. "I hope I didn't freak you out earlier with all the stuff we talked about."

Grant lowered his eyes and shook his head. "You didn't freak me out." He realized he was looking at Julie's chest. Her oversized pajama top was hanging open at the collar, and he could see braless cleavage there. He returned his gaze to Julie's face, half-lit by the glow from behind her open door. "I'm glad you told me."

"I trust you, Grant. It's nice. Thanks for walking me up here." She stood on her tip-toes and leaned forward, hands pressed against his chest, and gently kissed him on the cheek. "Goodnight," she said, stepping inside and closing the door.

"Goodnight," Grant said to the closed door. He pulled the blanket away from his waist, no longer afraid of Julie noticing his visible excitement that had made a surprise appearance.

He walked the few steps to his room, hopeful that if sleep did return to him, the nightmare might be replaced by a dream considerably more enjoyable.

CHAPTER 27
October 11
5:38 A.M.

CLIVE QUINN'S EYES moved rapidly beneath his eyelids. He was in the throes of a wild and convoluted dream. It happened every time he took the pills the doctor prescribed, but he could not sleep without them. Could not live without them.

Not when it rained.

The doctors had informed him it would get better. That each passing day would push the memories farther away, and that eventually, he would be able to sleep through the night regardless of the weather outside. But that had been many years ago, and it had never gotten better.

Quinn had tried to block out the noise of the falling rain before. Had shoved tiny foam plugs deep into his ear canals. Had slept in sound-proofed rooms. It didn't matter.

The nightmares never came when the wind blew or when it snowed or when the night was peaceful. But on nights such as this, when the heavens wept, the nightmares would come. The sleeping pills were Quinn's only hope for peace.

Most of the time the pills worked. Quinn had learned years ago that doubling the prescribed dosage would do the trick. Most of the time. Not all.

Doubling the dosage made something in his brain shut down. The nightmare synapses would no longer fire. Granted, he would be incapacitated for six or eight hours, an uncomfortably vulnerable state, but he would sleep. And the demons would not torment him.

But some nights, when the rain pounded the roof like machine gun fire, the pills failed him. This was one of those nights.

Quinn slept, but he did not rest. He drifted in and out of consciousness. In and out of reality. He closed his eyes within his dreams and opened them into new worlds. And in each of the worlds, it rained.

He opened his eyes and saw Frankie, lying in the dark jungle mud, his leg missing. Quinn had been here many times before, and he knew the script. Frankie would scream at him and beg for help, but the cries would be muted by the rain. The rain was everywhere. Flowing down his friend's face, collecting in his twisted mouth, mingling with the blood pouring from the mangled stump of leg.

Quinn closed his eyes tight, knowing it was over for Frankie. He would die in that dream jungle just as he had in the real world. Quinn reopened his eyes and found himself in the whorehouse in Bolivia. A large woman was tying his arms and legs to the bedposts with colorful silk scarves as the rain fell outside the open windows. Quinn glanced down and realized he was naked. And growing. Quinn had never been into large women, but perhaps there was something special about sizeable Bolivian ladies.

She was much larger than the type of woman he normally paid for, but she was attractive. And this dream sure as hell beat the jungle. The woman laughed as a rumble of thunder shook the walls. Quinn shifted his eyes to the open windows as the lightning flashed to reveal two guerilla soldiers standing outside, AK-47's trained on his naked form.

Quinn jerked to roll off the bed but the silk scarves were taut. He was paralyzed. The trigger fingers of the soldiers tightened, and Quinn squeezed his eyes shut as the retort of the guns was drowned out by another crash of thunder.

When he opened his eyes, he was lying on his stomach. Water and mud pushing against his mouth and nostrils as he kept his face pressed to the earth.

This dream. Shit.

This was the worst. The nightmare he would give anything to avoid. It was too real.

He could hear the rebel soldiers walking all around him, boots splashing and squishing in the jungle mud, speaking to each other in a language of which Quinn wished he knew more than ten words. He had been sent to scout the territory and stumbled upon a moving band of the fighters. His only option had been to slide to the ground beneath a large growth of vegetation. It was a good temporary hiding place. Unfortunately, the soldiers had decided to pitch camp there. Quinn was forced to lie in the mud, rain pouring over him, for thirty-six hours. Afraid to breath. Afraid to sneeze. Unable to risk detection to even pull off the leeches that squirmed their way up the legs of his pants. Feeling them burrow into the warm folds between his scrotum and his thigh. Nursing themselves on his blood. Unable to stretch to relieve the cramping in his back. Drinking mud, trying to strain the dirt between his teeth as he fought for enough water to survive. Praying every minute that the sound of the rain would continue to prevent the soldiers from hearing the growl of his stomach from the searing hunger pains that wracked his body. Knowing that if he gave himself away, he would suffer before he was killed. Choosing instead to suffer now. Listening as the men talked and patrolled. And the snake. The snake that had slithered by his face, forked tongue flicking into his eye. Unable to even blink against the tiny slapping on his eyeball knowing that it may provoke a deadly and venomous strike. And the rain. The never ending rain.

Quinn closed his eyes once more, against the water and against the mud, begging God to let him find another world when he reopened them. Moments passed. He could no longer feel the numbing sting of the cold mud against his face. He slowly opened one eye and through blurry vision, he saw his bedroom. He could still hear the smattering sound of the rain bouncing off the roof. Quinn opened his other eye. And there, at the foot of the bed with his gargantuan arms crossed, stood Silas Kane.

Quinn assumed it was another dream, an odd one, but one that had the potential for true terror if he gave it time. He closed his eyes again and reopened them, hoping to transport himself into another world. He shook his head and his vision cleared. Kane still stood at Quinn's feet, looking at him with a curious expression. When he spoke, Quinn knew it was no longer a dream.

"It's about time." Kane held up the prescription bottle. "How many of these fucking things did you take anyway?"

Quinn blinked and looked to his left. His pistol had been removed from the nightstand. So had his phone. Kane smiled. "Oh, I didn't want us to be interrupted. No phones. And thanks for the gun." He placed his hands on the wrought-iron foot railing of Quinn's bed.

Quinn tried to jerk his knees up to his chest, to roll off the bed and put as much distance as he could between himself and the psychopath that had found him, but his legs wouldn't move. His ankles were secured. As he fought off the effects of his drug-induced slumber, he realized that his hands were immobile as well, arms raised over his head.

The smile on Kane's face remained. "Oh, you're trying to get away. Sorry, but we can't have that." Kane grabbed the sheet covering Quinn and pulled it from the bed, like a magician jerking a tablecloth from underneath a set of fine china.

Quinn assessed the situation. He was naked. His legs were spread with each ankle bound by heavy wrappings of duct tape secured to the iron foot railing. His wrists had similar gray tape shackles attached to the iron headboard. The dream of the Bolivian hooker drifted through his mind.

Quinn jerked hard, testing the strength of his bindings. He didn't gain a centimeter. He was afraid he wouldn't. He had used duct tape many times before for this sort of thing. Nothing worked better.

Kane watched as Quinn struggled. "Not to get weird, but you got a stiffy when I was tying you up. I don't even want to know." He tossed the prescription bottle onto the nightstand. "So tell me, Mr. Quinn, how did you find this place? I spent some time poking around, waiting for you to wake up. I have to say I like it. Did you buy or do you rent?"

Quinn narrowed his gaze at Kane. This was going to be bad. This was going to be real bad.

Kane continued. "Don't feel like talking? Come on, Quinn. That was an easy question. I'd think you would want to try and make friends with me. Don't you want to be friends?" Kane slapped the bottom of Quinn's bare foot, hard. Quinn winced and glared at his captor. "Now where were we? Oh yeah, your place. I like it. Great for a man who likes his space, and his privacy. Took me forever to find it once I got the address. All these empty buildings around here. Not many lights. And what did this place used to be, a factory? What did they make here, Quinn?"

Quinn remained silent. Kane again put his hands on the foot railing and leaned forward, coming to a stop over the top of Quinn's legs and peering directly into his face. "I suggest you open that mouth of yours, or this is going to get bad fast," he growled.

"Textiles," Quinn muttered. "They used to make textiles."

"Textiles," Kane repeated. "There, that wasn't so hard. You know, I found your play room back there. The one with the chair bolted to the floor and all those neat tools. You like to bring people out here, don't you, Quinn?" The bounty hunter didn't answer. "Yeah, your line of work, sometimes you need questions answered, and the person just won't cooperate. You blindfold them, gag them, throw them in the trunk of that shitty car you drive and bring them out here. You take them to your little room and you *influence* them. Out here all alone. No one around to hear any screams. I bet they answer your questions, don't they, Quinn? And the lowlifes you deal with wouldn't dare go to the cops, would they? Not a bad little business you're running."

Quinn glared at the giant as he spoke. He didn't know how Kane had escaped prison, but it didn't really matter. It had taken Quinn over two months to recover from the injuries Kane had inflicted when he was captured, but the payday had seemed worth it.

Right up until now.

Quinn sensed where Kane was going with his speech, and he steeled himself against the fear gnawing at his belly. He had already been through hell in the jungle. He could handle this. It was now a matter of survival, of finding a way out.

"What do you want, Kane?"

Kane walked to the side of the bed. He sat down and Quinn felt Kane's hip pressed against his own as the bed sank under the giant's weight. "Oh, don't worry, Quinn. We'll get to what I want soon enough. I want to spend a bit of quality time with you first. Get to know each other. Develop a mutual understanding. I want to make sure you're really in the mood to talk before I start asking questions."

Kane leaned close and whispered, his breath hot in Quinn's ear. "I know you're tough, Quinn. But I'm going let you in on a little secret. It doesn't matter how tough you think you are. You will tell me what I want to know. It's not going to be worth it to protect the information." He paused. "You never should have come after me in the first place."

Quinn spit in Kane's face and watched it run down his unshaven cheek. "Go to hell, you fucking mutant."

Kane gently brushed the spittle off his cheek with one hand. "You're going to beg me, Quinn. You're going to beg for me to kill you. But first you're going to tell me everything I want to know. Every. Single. Thing."

Quinn closed his eyes and wished he could open them and be back in the mud in the jungle.

CHAPTER 28
October 11
9:18 A.M.

GRANT ARMSTRONG rolled onto his side and peered at the clock on the nightstand. The numbers indicated the sun should have risen long before but his room remained dark. As his senses cleared, he discerned the sound of rain. The storm was still underway. He rolled the opposite direction to look at the window. The clouds beyond the open curtains were dark and ominous and the rain coursed down the glass in rivulets.

Grant laid back and stared at the ceiling. He had slept more than eight hours. A deep and peaceful sleep untouched by dreams of any kind. For the first time since he embarked on his trip to return to the island, his body felt refreshed. The good feeling was short lived, however, as his mind returned to the lingering questions of Abraham Armstrong's death.

He lay there for several minutes, observing the slow rotations of the ceiling fan as he considered the events of the previous day. A doctor by training, but for now, he was a detective. Eric was the professional. He should be the one doing this, but Eric had his hands full at the moment. In a way, Grant was glad. Professional or not, Grant wanted to be the one to bring Abe's killer to justice. He felt he owed it to his grandfather.

If one thing stood out to Grant through all of his interactions with the family yesterday, it was that Abraham Armstrong had been left horribly alone. In the twilight of his life, when he should have been enjoying the company of his children, and watching his grandchildren romping in the yard and playing in the pool, Abe Armstrong was spending his days alone in his study.

Besides the occasional visit from his alcoholic daughter, Abe was left to die in solitude. Only an outsider, an abused girl hired to assist him with his exercises and physical therapy, showed him any sign of warmth. Only Julie offered him the love of a daughter for which his own children seemed incapable. All this while his only grandson, the man whom he had devoted so much time and energy into raising, spent his days far away from his family working half a planet away. The only communication from Grant had been a weekly blue envelope with a letter detailing Grant's own life while rarely inquiring into the life of his grandfather.

Grant was just as guilty as everyone else.

Lying in bed, Grant wondered if things would have turned out differently had he been home. Would the family have been so overcome by greed and distrust? Would the killer have struck anyway? Would there have been a reason?

Grant sat up and scooted back in the bed until he was leaning against the headboard. He took a mental inventory of his facts. Since he had visited last Christmas, the family had grown increasingly aggressive regarding Abe's fortune, to the point of threatening anyone who got too close. Abe had become disgusted with their greed—possibly triggered by the incident with Brock, Phil and Julie in the kitchen—and essentially shut himself off from everyone except Mona. Then, months later, he had asked his kids and their spouses to come to the island for dinner. The invitation would result in his death.

Abe had been killed with everyone present at the house, eliminating geographical alibis for the entire family. The only motive Grant had uncovered so far was the will. And why not? Things always seemed to go back to money in the Armstrong household. Everyone assumed Abe was planning on telling the family he had decided to, or at least was considering, changing his will, presumably to include Julie, thus lessening the wealth for the rest of the beneficiaries.

The murderer used a syringe to inject an air bubble directly into the vein. That would have taken steady hands and practical knowledge, but the mechanics of injecting into a vein was not difficult for a person to learn. Another question lay in why there was no apparent struggle. Either Abe was held down—a feat requiring some strength, even to subdue an old man—or he didn't offer a struggle, perhaps sleeping through the ordeal.

Julie found the body and tried to revive him. And based on the conversation with Phil, none of the family had assisted her. Nice. By the time the ambulance arrived, there was nothing to be done. Now Grant and his family stood to inherit a great fortune, though none knew how large. And Abe's attorney, Ronald Lister, refused to divulge any information until the will-reading after the funeral.

Upon review, everything Grant knew served to confirm only that his relatives were assholes, but nothing singled any individual out as a murderer.

Perhaps he was going about this all wrong. He was assuming, along with everyone else, that his grandfather had invited everyone for dinner that night to discuss the will. But why? Grant understood his aunt's and uncle's assumption, since they seemed to believe the world revolved around the will, but why had Grant been so quick to assume they were right? His grandfather had never been as obsessed with wealth as his children. Maybe the dinner was an attempt to mend fences. Perhaps Mona, or even Julie, had convinced Abe that the fighting wasn't worth it.

Grant shuddered. If that had been the case, if Abe hadn't been planning on changing his will and just wanted to see his kids again, that would mean he had been killed for nothing.

Grant swung his legs over the side of the bed. He had spent enough time dancing in conversation with his family the previous day. It was time he took a more direct approach. He needed to know why Abe had made the dinner invitation. He needed to know if there was substance to the theory of Abe changing the will. And if so, which dinner guest was so confident in the news that he or she was willing to commit murder.

Grant decided he would shower and spend the morning in his grandfather's study. Perhaps he would find some information of value in there.

As he made his way to the bathroom, his thoughts flitted to Eric. He wondered if the police had had any luck recapturing Silas Kane. The name brought a sudden and frightening image to Grant's mind, the hooded giant from his dream sabotaging the covered bridge in an attempt to murder his friend. Goosebumps rose on the back of Grant's neck. He reached into the shower and turned on the hot water, pushing the nightmarish vision from his mind.

CHAPTER 29

October 11
10:45 A.M.

ERIC JOHNSON pulled the rough white towel to and fro over his back, drying the last of the wetness from his shower. He walked across the slick tiled floor of the station's locker room in his bare feet and sat on the narrow wooden bench in front of his locker. He hadn't left his desk all night, sleeping intermittently while leaned back in his chair with his feet propped on the open drawer of a filing cabinet. George had stopped by Eric's apartment on the way in and brought him a fresh change of clothes. Partners know each other well.

The evening had been long but uneventful. Since most homicide detectives worked day shifts, Eric had called into service several of the beat cops that night. They had worked diligently and had managed to find almost half of the informants on the list. Unfortunately, none of those individuals knew anything about Silas Kane.

Eric had watched the board intently. It had been a quiet night in the city. The storm was bad enough to severely limit the number of people going out for the evening. Street crime was nearly nonexistent. And no reports had registered across the screen of any crime fitting the profile of a man on the run, much less Kane.

Eric opened the door to his locker and began dressing. Earlier that morning, much earlier, he had pulled the Kane file and reread its contents for the hundredth time since his initial capture. He reviewed the locations of his crimes, studied the pictures of his known victims, and deliberated the timeline they had created of his killings during the trial. Although nothing in the file pointed to where Kane was heading next, the review bitterly reminded Eric of the importance of stopping him.

Half-dressed, Eric removed from his locker the Ruger LCR snub-nosed revolver. It had a short barrel and a five-shot cylinder, and the gun fit entirely in the palm of his hand.

"Looking good, Habanero Pete." He flicked his wrist and checked to ensure the pistol was loaded. The reverse movement brought the cylinder back into the gun with a metallic snap. Eric wasn't in the habit of naming his firearms. Just this one. A feisty little weapon that packed a .357 magnum punch.

He put his foot on the bench, pulled up his pants leg and strapped on the discreet ankle holster. He slid Habanero Pete inside and secured the snap. He hardly ever carried a backup weapon. "Times change," he said to the empty locker room.

He checked to ensure the bulge at his ankle wasn't obvious. Then he grabbed his undershirt from the locker and continued getting dressed.

"Donuts beget donuts. We are such a cliché," Eric spoke to himself. The break room was empty. He tore off a paper towel and grabbed both a glazed and a chocolate covered donut from the box. With a coffee cup in his other hand, Eric pushed open the door with his backside.

George was walking down the hall on his way back from the men's room, newspaper folded beneath one arm. "Hey, Eric. I knew you'd come around to the donut way of thinking eventually."

Eric rolled his eyes. "Have you seen the average pants size in this department? We really ought to switch to fruit."

George laughed as they made their way to their desks. "Cops are cops, my friend. So what's up now?"

Eric set the coffee on his desk and took a large bite of the chocolate covered donut. "Just met with the captain." His words were distorted as he talked with his mouth full. "I got the distinct impression he would have liked to have Kane back in custody by now."

George opened the top drawer of his desk and slid the newspaper into it lest someone else on their way to the can decided to snatch it. "He's not riding you too hard is he?"

Eric could hear the concern in his partner's voice. He appreciated it.

"No. Not too bad. You hear anything?"

"Nothing new. We've gotten in touch with a few more of our sources than I would have expected. That's pretty fast. The weather may be helping us out. If it's keeping them inside, maybe Kane hasn't been out much either."

"I wouldn't count on that. I just hope he's still in the city." Eric took a drink of the coffee. It was terrible. He took a bite of the glazed donut to remove the taste. "Have we heard anything out of The Mouth? It was his lead that landed Kane in the first place."

"Mickey? Not yet. We've called a few times and sent a black and white by his place twice. But no one's been home."

Eric nodded. He realized he was probably expecting too much out of the informants anyway. The odds of Kane falling back into old habits this soon were slim. He was smarter than that.

George's phone rang and he grabbed it before the first ring finished. The conversation lasted all of twenty seconds. When George hung up the receiver, Eric's eyebrows were raised, expectant.

"Speak of the devil," George began. "Switchboard just received a call. Lady found her apartment's superintendent. Dead. Guy's neck was broken so severely his head nearly came off."

Eric sat up straight.

George continued. "The building address is the same as Mickey's apartment."

Eric leapt from his chair and grabbed his jacket. He looked at Sarah, the office assistant, and shouted, "Call the switchboard supervisor to get the details, but I need a search warrant from the D.A. for Mickey Little's apartment before I get there. Twenty minutes!"

Not giving her time to ask any questions, Eric strode out the door with George following immediately behind.

CHAPTER 30
October 11
11:46 A.M.

EVERYTHING HAD GONE BLACK, but the deep voice pierced the darkness.

"Don't you fucking think of passing out on me."

A sharp smell shot through Quinn's nose, spreading into his sinuses and burning his nasal passages with a fierce intensity. His eyes opened. Silas Kane was leaning over him, waving smelling salts under his nose.

Quinn turned his head, pushing his face away from the acrid odor. Kane nodded. He withdrew the smelling salts and set them on the bedside table next to the tweezers, the sandpaper and the wire cutters. He then picked up the hand towel he had retrieved from the bathroom and wiped his palms with it.

"Sweaty work, isn't it, Quinn?"

Quinn averted his eyes. As he had before he lost consciousness, he looked past his tormentor and focused his attention on the spider web hanging in the corner of his bedroom, spun between the ceiling and the joining of the two walls.

"Of course, it's sweaty." Kane continued. "Why, your bed is already soaked, and we haven't even gotten to the good part yet."

Quinn concentrated intensely on the silky strands of the web, a pain management technique he had learned from a Buddhist in Asia in a different lifetime. He had used the method to survive broken bones and mangled flesh in the past. The secret was to focus your energies on an outside place. To focus so intensely on an object that you became one with it. Leaving your body, and the pain, behind you.

He tried to control his breathing, inhaling deeply. The dry air burned his nostrils, still sensitive from the harsh effect of the smelling salts. Even his nose...

Quinn had never endured suffering like this, and he knew it was going to get worse.

The spider's web was complex and glistening. He drew in a slower breath. Redirect away from the body. Focus the mind. Become one with the web. Don't think about the pain.

"I was looking through some of your tools in the other room. Half of them didn't look like they'd ever been used. You probably got those over the internet. In fact, I'll bet you don't even know what a lot of them are for. You keep them out on the table to scare the shit out of whoever you've got tied to the chair." Kane's tone was casual. Friendly even.

Quinn looked at each connecting point of the web. Focused on the nucleus of the structure. Traced the path of each strand as it made its way from the center to the wall.

"Truth is, you're an amateur. Your version of torture probably consists of punching a guy in the mouth a few times or cutting his arm and rubbing some salt into it. Right?" Kane raised his eyebrows but received no response.

"Yeah, they don't teach you army pussies anything worth knowing. Not that I haven't been trying to make you feel at home." Kane reached to the end table and snatched the blue cardboard cylinder with the little girl in the rain storm on the label.

Quinn's focus on the web wavered. As hard as he tried to ignore his captor, he could still see Kane in his peripheral vision. He witnessed the slow stream of fine white salt pouring into Kane's cupped palm, and Quinn knew what would be coming next. New beads of sweat appeared on Quinn's already glistening forehead as he redirected his efforts on the silken latticework.

Kane had been meticulous in extracting strands of hair from Quinn's armpit with a pair of medical tweezers. A hundred? A thousand? It was slow work. Kane didn't seem to mind. The pain centers by the lymph nodes were phenomenally sensitive. The hairs that remained were removed by the sandpaper. The raw, swollen skin bled. Kane had already worked salt into the left armpit quite vigorously, causing Quinn's initial blackout, but the pink, blotchy skin under Quinn's right arm was still available.

"This may sting a little." Kane let the salt slowly pour from his palm onto the exposed wound. He formed tight circles in the air with his hand to ensure an even spreading across the reddened area.

Quinn jerked his arms forward, but the duct tape held tight. He clenched his teeth, willing himself to contain the scream. Through the fire igniting his body, he renewed his focus on the web. He saw tiny specs of water on one of the strands, looking almost like dew.

Kane pushed his fingertips into the soft flesh under Quinn's arm. He massaged the salt into the wound, individual grains wedging deep into the exposed follicles. "Come on, Quinn. Who hired you? Who hired you to track me down?"

Sweat poured from Quinn's forehead. It ran into his eyes and caused them to burn as he continued concentrating on the web. He would not talk. It wasn't a question of allegiance. He didn't give two shits about the people who hired him. It was a matter of pride. Kane may torture him, may even kill him, but he would not talk.

Kane pulled his hand back and sighed deeply.

"How much longer, Quinn?" He retrieved a pair of wire cutters from the table and held them three inches from Quinn's nose. "Is it time to lose another one? How many have you got left? Let's count."

Kane looked down to Quinn's chest and began collecting the bloody, amputated toes that rested there. He set the wire cutters next to Quinn's neck and used his free hand to pluck the toes from his open palm. "One little piggy. Two. Three. Four. That's four little piggies that'll never get home, Quinn! That means you've only got six left. Do you really want to make it five?"

Quinn squeezed his eyes shut. The vision of his dismembered toes was blocking his view of the spider's web. The pain from under his arms spread into his chest. Flames of salty agony compressed his heart. He felt Kane's weight move off the bed. Heard footsteps.

"Open your eyes, Quinn. No more roast beef for this little guy unless you talk." Not wanting to, but unable to resist the command, Quinn opened his eyes to see Kane standing in front of him, the blades of the wire cutters open and surrounding the middle toe of his right foot. The two stumps toward the outside of his foot bled slowly, the hot liquid trickling down the top of his foot, running through the dark hair there, and pooling on the sheet beneath his ankles. He looked away, towards the web.

Kane's face grew red. "Fine by me!" The blades closed and Quinn heard a loud cracking sound. The toe bounced off his ankle as it fell onto the bed. The suffering was intense. White-hot streaks of agony snaked their way up his leg, coming to rest in his pelvis. He let out an involuntary grunt, grimacing with teeth clamped tightly together, the enamel grinding off his molars.

Kane was enraged. He threw the instrument across the room. The bloody cutters made a loud clanging noise as they bounced off an exposed pipe. Kane wrapped both his powerful hands around the iron railing of the footboard and began shaking it, making the headboard smash into the wall with each violent thrust. Quinn was jostled against his bindings as he moved with the rhythm of the bed. Each shake brought his tortured feet into contact with the iron railing, each jolt a fresh wave of mind-numbing pain.

Kane stopped and took a deep breath. He looked at Quinn, who was staring into the corner, tears of pain running down the side of his face. Kane sighed again. His voice was calm, almost serene. "No, no, no. Not going to happen. I'm not going to kill you, Quinn. Not until you've told me what I need to know."

Kane walked around the corner of the bed and stopped in the center of the bounty hunter's vision, again blocking his view of the web. Quinn had no choice but to look into the eyes of his executioner. There was an eerie stillness in those eyes that frightened Quinn more than the earlier rage.

"I wonder, Quinn, how much you know about me. You're a professional. That means you probably studied your target before coming after me. Tell me, did you read anything about my family?"

Quinn maintained silence.

"No answer. Shocking. That's okay," Kane continued. "I'll give you just a brief family history. My brothers and I were raised by my father. He was a very, very smart man. He was also a psychopath. Don't get me wrong, I've got nothing against the old man, he is my father, but that doesn't change the fact that he's more than a little fucked upstairs. He studied all sorts of weird shit about demons and the occult. About blood sacrifices and," Kane leaned close to Quinn's face, whispering, "and here comes the good part...torture. Now I'm probably not as smart as my father or my brothers, but I picked up quite a few things in my youth. For instance, do you know what being 'gut-shot' is?"

Quinn's stomach churned as Kane continued. "Of course you do. You're an army guy. Here's the thing with being gut-shot. You get shot in the stomach or a grenade goes off and shrapnel slices your belly, and your insides spill out. Now there's a lot of pain there, but those organs can continue to function for quite a while even in the fresh air. Oh yeah, there's a lot of pain, but pain's not enough to kill. Is it?" Kane was smiling now.

"All your military experience, you may have even seen people gut-shot. Heard them screaming for hours, and the best you could do was put a bullet in their brain to stop the suffering." Kane paused. "But the problem, Quinn, *my* problem lies in how to gut-shot someone without accidentally killing him. I mean, there are a lot of ways for a man to die when you start messing around with his internal organs. The bullet could go into a lung, or ricochet off a rib and hit the heart. And we wouldn't want *that*, now would we?" Kane raised his eyebrows at

Quinn as he asked the question. "No. That's not any good. But my father found a way around all that. He took the theory and transformed it into a more exact science."

Kane straightened his back and stretched then wiped his hands on his pants. The blood and salt left speckled dark streaks on his thighs. "Now if I remember right, I think I saw a scalpel and some forceps in your play room down the hall. When I get back, I'm going to show you something really cool."

Suddenly, brutally, Kane pushed his hand against Quinn's cheek, forcing the side of his face deep into the mattress. He leaned forward, his lips grazing Quinn's ear as he spoke a barely audible whisper, "And before I'm done, you're going to tell me everything. Everything."

Kane stood and walked out of the room, leaving Quinn lying on the bed.

Sweating profusely, bleeding from his feet and his armpits, Quinn resumed his focus on the spider's web. Through tear-blurred vision, he spotted the spider in the upper portion of the web. He concentrated to free himself from the pain, to put his mind as far away from what was about to take place as possible.

The spider was fiercely moving its forelegs, engaged in some activity. Quinn focused his vision, fighting through the salty tears to see what the spider was doing.

There, wrapped in the silky web, was a struggling fly. Quinn watched as the spider bobbed up and down, feasting on the blood of the helpless creature, consuming it alive.

Quinn began to scream.

CHAPTER 31
October 11
2:42 P.M.

G RANT ARMSTRONG slumped back into the large leather chair behind his grandfather's teak wood desk and sighed. He rubbed his temples, trying to push away the headache he had been battling for hours. He had spent the entire day rummaging through Abraham Armstrong's study, not sure of what he was looking for. He had examined the contents of filing cabinets, rifled through papers on the desk, and even removed the large-print books from the shelves. So far, nothing he had discovered provided any clue regarding his grandfather's will or his frame of mind at the time of the murder.

What he had uncovered consisted of the past five years of utility bills for the island and a collection of cards from his eightieth birthday. The entire office yielded nothing of insight. No business contracts. No personal journal. Nothing.

Grant leaned forward and flipped open the copy of *The Old Man and the Sea* sitting on the corner of the desk. It had been his grandfather's favorite book. The extra-large print made the edition much thicker than Hemingway's actual story. As he gently turned the pages of the well-worn book, Grant could hear the voice of his grandfather reading the words.

It had been the first non-illustrated book of Grant's childhood. Abe had read the book aloud in thirty minute snippets at bedtime over a handful of nights during a summer vacation. Grant in his Spiderman pajamas. Abe sitting in the chair next to Grant's bed, glasses low on his nose.

When Abe finished the story and closed the book that last night, Grant scolded him. He had spent a week listening to the story of the old man's battle with the great fish, rooting for him as only a child can. Upon hearing that the fish had been devoured by the sharks and rendered worthless by the time the old man brought it home—and that the story just *ended* that way—Grant had told his grandfather that he had read it wrong. That the old man was supposed to bring the fish back in one piece and the village would celebrate. Abe sighed, adjusted his glasses, and advised Grant to consider it more, and that he would read it again to him another time.

The next summer brought a retelling of the same story, but it no longer seemed so sad. The old man had fought to overcome his hardship, and Grant could see nobility in that, but he was still angry the fish did not arrive to the village in one piece. The old man had fought but had ultimately lost in the end.

And so it went through Grant's childhood. Abe Armstrong reading the story to his grandson, never telling him his own opinion of the meaning of the fable but allowing the boy to figure it out for himself. It was after Grant's father had died, and long after anyone sat by his bedside to read him a story, that Grant picked up a copy of the book and read the tale once more. He had cried when he finished it, understanding for the first time that the victory was not in winning the race, but in running it. The fish didn't matter. The old man had fought, and because he had fought, he had won. Grant never told his grandfather about the revelation, but in the years following Jack Armstrong's untimely accident, the story eased some of the pain of his father's death.

Grant closed the cover of the book and slid it back across the desk. So many things he never told Abraham Armstrong.

The calendar on the corner of the desk caught Grant's attention. It was a single day, tear-away model which sat upright and had large, bold print. Grant wondered again how bad his grandfather's eyesight had become in the past year. He reached forward and snatched the calendar. The date was October 8th. The pages had not been torn since his grandfather's death. There was a space on the calendar for writing appointments or reminders, but the lines were empty.

Grant tore off the top pages to display the current date. There was something written in the notes section of the page with a bold, black marker. The handwriting was neat and loopy, certainly not Abe's shaky scrawl.

Lister – 5:00 P.M.

Grant set the calendar on the middle of the desk and rested his chin on the desktop, staring at the note mere inches from his nose.

Abe had an appointment this afternoon with his attorney. And someone else knew about it. Was the appointment regarding the will? Who had written the meeting on the calendar? Who else knew about the appointment?

He picked up the phone, determined to call Ronald Lister, then placed it back in its cradle. Phil and the others had apparently had little luck with the attorney the previous day. He would need to be cautious with the call. He had met Mr. Lister several times in the past. He would occasionally come to the island for barbecues. Phil and Mona had rarely attended. That could possibly give Grant an edge with the lawyer, but he didn't want to risk an unscheduled call that could lead to a hasty brush-off.

Grant decided to wait until five o'clock to place the call. He doubted that Lister had scheduled another meeting for that slot, and the timing could put the lawyer in the proper frame of mind to discuss private matters with him. At least that's what Grant hoped.

In the meantime, Grant needed to rid himself of the headache raging at his temples. He pushed the chair away from the desk and stood.

Exercise might do the trick, both in counteracting the headache and working out some of the kinks that still lingered from his time on the plane the previous day. The house had an excellent home gym, and it was possible that Brock would be there. Grant still hadn't spent any time questioning Mona's husband since he arrived the night before, and there was a good chance he would be working out.

Somehow, the thought made Grant's headache worse.

The rain had slowed to a drizzle. Grant stood at the back door and watched the dark clouds drift beyond the hills overlooking the lake. He wondered how long the respite from the storm would last. A quick check of the local TV news while he was getting dressed had indicated the violent weather was far from over. The worst of the storm was yet to come, but would not arrive for another few hours.

He had changed into a pair of gray sweatpants and a blue sweatshirt with *Still Pines Cougars* emblazoned across the front in faded white lettering.

He turned and headed toward the exercise room. It was located behind the garage and accessible through a small hallway from the kitchen. As Grant walked through the kitchen, he wondered if the room had seen much use since he and Eric had graduated from high school. Growing nearer, the pulsing bass of a song playing from behind the closed door assured him that the gym was at least being used today.

Grant opened the door and was greeted by louder music than before. The room was framed on one side entirely by windows and a glass door, offering an excellent view of the subsiding storm, and was equipped with a stair-climbing machine, a treadmill, a stationary bike and various weight lifting equipment. Brock was sitting on a stool in the corner of the room facing away from the door. Mona was using the stair-climber, legs pumping as she gripped the handrails to maintain her balance. She wore a pair of headphones attached by long cord to a television hanging from the ceiling in the corner. Some sort of home renovation reality show was playing.

Grant watched Brock for a moment. He was wearing a small black tank top that did little to contain his bulging back muscles. Brock's tight black shorts left even less to the imagination. He was digging through a small black duffel bag, removing gloves and towels and setting them to one side. Finally, he secured what he was looking for.

Still facing the wall, Brock removed a black leather pouch resembling a large wallet and unzipped the side. He removed a stainless steel syringe and inserted a hypodermic needle, screwing it into place at the base of the instrument. He pulled a small glass bottle of clear liquid from the wallet and inserted the needle into the rubber covering the top. Securing his thumb into the loop at the top of the plunger, Brock filled the syringe with a calculated amount of the steroid and removed the needle. With the quick and steady hand of a man familiar with this drill, he inserted the needle into his forearm. His thumb pressed the plunger down and the drug left the syringe as it flowed into Brock's arm. He withdrew the needle, placed it on the floor next to his bag, and pressed a small ball of cotton against the puncture. He took a deep breath and exhaled loudly.

Grant pressed the "stop" button on the stereo. The silence made Brock jump. He spun and faced the doorway, thumb still pressing the cotton against his forearm, eyes flashing anger. Mona continued climbing stairs, her headphones rendering her oblivious to the silence as the couple on television began demolition of an outdated kitchen.

"It's not information restricted to medical schools," Grant began, "but that stuff isn't exactly good for you. There's a reason it's illegal."

Brock snorted. "It ain't illegal. Not like its heroin. Doctors prescribe this shit all the time."

Grant walked over and held his hand out to Brock, palm up and eyebrows raised. Brock passed him the glass bottle, and Grant studied it.

"Doctors prescribe this for patients with serious muscle damage," Grant said. "It's a short-term aid for rebuilding muscle tissue. It's not designed for long-term use and certainly not for getting pumped up."

Brock snatched the bottle from Grant's hand and shoved it back in his bag. "Thanks for the insight. The fact is, if you know what you're doing, this stuff won't hurt you. Plenty of pros use it."

"The fact is," Grant interrupted, "this stuff will shrivel your nuts. It'll give you violent mood swings, and eventually, it'll rot your body."

"It'll put hair on your sack," said Brock. "Now if you'll excuse me, these weights don't lift themselves." He dropped the duffel bag on the floor and walked to the weight bench.

Grant stepped back to allow him passage. He turned, deciding he wasn't in the mood for a workout after all when he caught sight of her. Julie stood in the doorway. She was wearing a pair of blue Lycra shorts and a white sports bra. Her bare midriff was taught and her belly button was pierced with a small gold hoop.

"I was just coming in for a workout," she said to Grant. "I didn't realize it would be so crowded."

Before Grant could speak, Brock stood from the bench and whistled. "That's more like it! Did you come down for some training tips from ol' Brock? I accept payment other than cash."

Julie's face suggested nausea, and Grant was reminded of her fear of Brock from the previous night. He started to say something, but then Brock slapped him hard across the back, catching him by surprise. Grant took an involuntary step forward, regaining his balance before falling to the floor.

"Now you see, Grant, *that's* what you've been missing living in the jungle! I remember when Mona used to have an ass that tight. Kind of."

A sound not unlike a whimper came from across the room. Grant turned to see Mona, off the stair-climber with headphones in hand, staring at her husband. A look of humiliation on her face. She dropped her headphones and ran from the room, Julie stepping to the side to avoid being run over.

Brock showed little remorse. "What? It's true." With that, he lay back on the bench and pushed the barbell off the rack.

Julie spoke. "I don't need to work out after all. Excuse me." She turned and walked back down the hall.

Grant shot Brock a look of disgust and jogged out the door. He caught her in the kitchen. "Julie!" She stopped. "I had planned on going for a run on the treadmill, but I think the rain may hold off for a while longer. Care to join me?"

A small smile formed on her lips. "Okay," she said. "Let me run upstairs and grab a sweatshirt."

Grant leaned against the kitchen counter and let out a deep breath. His headache was gone.

CHAPTER 32
October 11
2:50 P.M.

THE FORENSICS OFFICER pulled the zipper on the black bag, sealing it over Mickey Little's pale face. Grabbing the handle sewn to the head of the bag, the officer lifted it in conjunction with his partner stationed at the opposite end. They placed the heavy canvass onto the gurney and wheeled it out the front door of the apartment.

Eric Johnson stood behind the desk in the makeshift office in the apartment's second bedroom. His fists clenched as he stared at the immense maroon stain on the white carpet a few feet away.

Kane.

The forensics team speculated that Mickey had been dead at least twelve hours, but it was difficult to say beyond that. Questioning the apartment tenants had revealed the building superintendent was still alive at lunch the previous day. He had worked on a garbage disposal for the resident in apartment 5A.

Piecing together the details as best he could, Eric deduced the superintendent had been murdered sometime in the late afternoon. Kane had taken his keys and let himself into Mickey's apartment. The Mouth was known to be extremely paranoid, which was not surprising given his business, and had excellent security in the form of very expensive door locks and interior bars on the windows. If Mickey returned home to find his door damaged, he would have turned and run the other direction. That explained why Kane needed to kill the super.

After doing so, he let himself into Mickey's apartment and waited for The Mouth to return home. Then, he stuck a letter opener in his throat. At least, that was the way Eric envisioned it, but the scenario still left too many questions. The most important of which – why Mickey?

George returned from the bathroom, scratching his head. "It doesn't make sense, Eric," George said. "What the hell is Kane's connection to Mickey? I didn't even think they knew each other."

"They didn't," Eric confirmed. "The only connection is that Mickey is the one who provided us the information that led to Kane's arrest, but that was kept confidential during the trial. And Mickey had never even met Kane."

"Right. He specifically told me that the Kane information he sold us was secondhand. He reminded me of the benefits of 'working with The Mouth'—sources that no one else had—the usual talk. Said that he got it through the Concubine Grapevine."

Eric nodded. The "Concubine Grapevine" was slang for prostitutes and their pimps. Eric wondered whether half the people who used the phrase even knew what a concubine was. Still, it made sense. Based on his research during the first capture, Kane's primary human contact seemed to be with ladies of the night. And he didn't always kill them. There were a few the police had come across that had seemed shocked that Kane was a killer, but most were not surprised. Seemed he put the fear of God into most of the hookers with which he dealt. And the most unfortunate ones, he sent to meet Him.

"So how did Kane find out about Mickey?" George asked. "Did one of his sources rat him out?"

Eric had turned his attention again to the desk, poking at the papers with his latex-gloved hand. "Hard to say, but why come after Mickey at all? If Kane was out for revenge, why hit the middle man? Why not go after the judge? Or us?" Eric's question was casual, but hearing his own words made the hair on the back of his neck rise. He noticed George loosen his collar, releasing the second button of his shirt.

Neither man spoke for the next few minutes. Eric continued to shuffle through the files on Mickey's desk as George wandered from bathroom to office, reconstructing the murder scene.

Finally, Eric walked to the uniformed officer standing by the door to the office and spoke in a low voice. "Hey Jackson, get on the phone with the department and have them alert Judge Alvarez about this. I don't know if he's in town, but if he is, have a couple of officers stationed as protection for his family. Use my numbers for the board."

The officer left the room, and Eric circled the maroon stain. He squatted and studied the carpet. Kane had dragged The Mouth into the study for a reason. He could have just killed him in the bathroom judging by the stench of urine that had coated the walls. Mickey didn't look like he had been tortured, just killed. But what could Kane want from a police informant?

A soft clicking noise. Eric cocked his head to one side, listening intently. The sound of a small motor whirring was coming from somewhere in the room. George took a step from the hallway toward the door, but Eric motioned for him to stop. "Hang on. Can you hear that?"

George stopped where he was, head poking just inside the office. He paused, then nodded.

Eric paced the room, circling its perimeter, trying to pinpoint the sound. He stopped in the corner and looked directly overhead. The noise was emanating from the air conditioning grate in the ceiling.

Eric grabbed the desk chair and positioned it beneath the grate. George held the chair steady as Eric climbed, bracing himself against the wall. He reached his fingers toward the white metal.

"Careful," George said.

The word, spoken just loud enough to startle him, made Eric reflexively draw his hand back. He shook his head and returned his fingers to the vent. Eric forced his fingernails beneath one side of the grate and pulled lightly. The lattice moved forward. The screws designed to secure the thin metal bars were missing. The grate had only been pushed into place.

The whirring ceased. Eric removed the grate and saw a small video camera. He reached into the duct, grasped it with one hand and stepped off the chair.

"Mickey was definitely old school. This isn't digital," Eric stated as he studied the camera in his hands. "Looks like the tape ended. It must have been rewinding itself. The camera has a motion sensor. It would have only recorded when there was activity in the room."

George nodded. "So Mickey was just as paranoid as people said. He must have left this running while he was out of the apartment. Make sure nobody was spying on his files." He glanced at Eric. George said what both of them were thinking. "You think this tape's got the murder on it?"

Eric nodded. "Let's get this thing hooked up to a television and see."

Eric and George stood in the living room of the apartment, the video recorder connected to the television by RCA cables they had discovered in a drawer. Eric hit the "play" button.

The recording began with The Mouth's face in extreme close-up. He eased away from the camera, his features becoming more in focus, and returned the grate back into place. The metal lattice obscured fully a fourth of the remaining picture, with broad stripes darkening the video.

Mickey could be seen walking across the room and replacing the desk chair he had been standing on. He made a brief phone call, scratched himself, and left. The phone conversation was muffled. Eric increased the volume on the television. The air-conditioning duct was clearly not an ideal place for capturing sound in the room. There was then about five minutes of empty room footage before the camera's automatic shut-off activated.

The next picture consisted of Silas Kane entering the office. The face was unclear, but there was no mistaking the gargantuan body. He spent several minutes rummaging through the desk and assorted files. He pulled a book from a drawer and flipped through the pages before apparently finding what he was looking for. He placed the open book in the center of the desk and left the room.

Eric fast-forwarded through another five minutes of non-activity in the office, a quick slide of darkness indicating the automatic shut-off, then Kane roughly carrying a struggling Mickey into the office. Eric stopped his fast-forward and increased the volume to maximum. There was a tremendous amount of white-noise on the tape, and Eric and George strained to make out the words of the conversation. Kane was holding Mickey in front of the desk and speaking to him. After several seconds, he released the man and set him on the floor. George flinched as Kane drove the letter opener into the side of Mickey's neck.

Kane appeared to say something else to the dying owner of the apartment. Then he tore a page from the book and walked out of the room.

Eric didn't wait to see what happened after that. He knew the remainder of the tape would consist of footage of Mickey dying and the NYPD's entrance onto the scene the next day. He raced back into the office and snatched the book off the desk. George followed closely behind.

"It's an address book," Eric said as he inspected the evidence. "He's missing the pages for P and Q. Well, that narrows it down. Why wasn't the sound better on that tape?!"

Eric pounded his fist onto the top of the desk. If life was like television, he could simply call the hyper-advanced computer team at the precinct and they would clean up the sound before he could finish stating his request, but that scenario wasn't close to reality. Even if he could get priority status on the request, it would be hours—if not days—before he would get results. Eric had no hours to spare.

He carried the book back into the living room and rewound the tape. The stain on the carpet became smaller as the blood returned into

Mickey's neck. Kane reappeared, walking backward into the room and reassembling the address book. Mickey magically returned to his feet as the letter opener popped out of his neck and back into Kane's hand. Mickey then jumped into Kane's arms as the giant marched himself and his captive backwards from the room.

Eric hit play once more and kneeled in front of the television. He pressed his ear against the speaker and concentrated on the conversation. George stood behind him, hands resting on his knees as he leaned toward the picture. The words were mumbled, running together.

"I think I heard 'county.' Did you hear county?" George asked.

Eric nodded. "Yeah, something like that." The rest of the conversation was too garbled. It would be worthless no matter how many times they listened to it here.

He stood and walked to the window. The rain had let up, but the clouds were still dark over the city. He muttered to himself, "county...county...county." What the hell had Kane been talking to Mickey about? Why was he here? Why would he take revenge on a nobody police informant when there were so many more deserving targets?

Eric's eyes widened. *Deserving targets.* So effing obvious.

"George, the day we arrested Kane, the man in the apartment, the bounty hunter, did you ever follow up with him?"

George shook his head. "No, once he got out of the hospital, he disappeared."

"I hope he disappeared well because Clive Quinn is our missing 'Q' in this address book."

Realization dawned on George's face. "Oh hell, Eric, that explains why Quinn was there that day. He must have bought the same information from Mickey that we did. Son of a bitch."

Eric pulled his cell phone from his pocket and started dialing. He needed an address on Quinn, fast.

CHAPTER 33
October 11
3:37 P.M.

THE BREEZE BLEW through Grant's hair as he jogged down the winding road. He closed his eyes and inhaled deeply. The air smelled of pine and rain. He could hear the distinct rhythmic slapping of his steps along the wet pavement, echoed by Julie's lighter footfalls.

"You still with me?" Julie asked, slightly out of breath but still able to carry on a conversation.

Grant opened his eyes and glanced to his right. She was keeping pace next to him, blonde ponytail bobbing with each step. He tried to sound normal as he spoke, even though he was out of breath as well. "Yeah, I'm great. Running was about the only exercise I got in Africa."

"That must have been incredible. Living a whole continent away. When I was a little girl, all I wanted to do was move to an island somewhere, some place with a beach. Just get away from my family. But I never went anywhere." She smiled as she made the confession. "Have you ever wanted to do that? Spend your life on an island?"

"Living the island life. Oh yeah. But Africa was great, too. Not in terms of standard of living, of course, it was nothing like this, but the people there were incredible. They were so happy with what little they had. So...appreciative. It was refreshing. I was just like you, always wanting to get away. So I did. Just what the doctor ordered...so to speak."

Julie pulled up the sleeves of her sweatshirt as she ran, trying to keep the cuffs at her elbows. "But Grant, I have to ask...why? Why would you want to get away from here? This is not a bad lifestyle."

Grant laughed. "You're right. I know it has to be difficult to understand. I probably sound really selfish, especially to someone who had to grow up the way you did..." Grant paused, hoping he hadn't offended Julie, but she showed no reaction as she continued running next to him. "It was never the place. It was the people. I just couldn't stand their attitudes any more. Everyone was so centered on money all the time. I just wanted to get away."

"But what about your grandfather? Did you two have a fight or something?"

"No, that's the worst of it. I got so caught up in not wanting to be around the rest of my family that I ended up sacrificing my last days with Granddad. If I had any idea that this was going to happen, I would have come home after medical school, done my residency in the city."

"I'm sorry I asked. I didn't mean to drudge up anything..." Julie's apology drifted into silence, replaced by her steady breathing.

Grant stole glances at her as he ran. Watched as a trickle of sweat ran down her forehead onto the tip of her nose. Julie repeated her trick from the previous night as she poked out her bottom lip and blew. The water droplet flew from the end of her nose. He smiled. "Don't worry about it. I won't judge your drudge."

He turned his attention to the sky, measuring the dark clouds above them. The two had run farther than he had intended, and he knew the rain would be returning soon, but he didn't want to be the first to recommend turning around, partly due to masculine pride but mostly because he was enjoying himself.

They rounded a bend in the road, and Grant slowed. The covered bridge leading to the mainland was a hundred yards away. Queasiness crept into his stomach. He reduced his pace to a trot, then to a walk.

Julie had moved ahead of him by several steps before turning to check on him. "Come on. We can turn around at the bridge and go back to the house."

The sight of the bridge summoned vivid images into Grant's mind from the previous night's dream. He pushed away the irrational thought that the hooded giant could be lurking beneath the structure, serrated saw in hand. This time, his masculinity served to push him forward, moving his legs once more into a dogtrot. He forced a smile. "Sounds good."

As they approached the bridge, the nightmare lost substance with each step. This was not the ridiculously long covered bridge from his nightmare. It didn't stand hundreds of feet above the water. It was the simple wood structure from his youth. The one that he and Eric had played on as kids, Eric always a little more cautious than Grant when it came to falling in the water.

Julie reached the bridge first and stepped onto the planks that composed the floor. Grant followed behind, bending over to grab a couple of pine cones from the side of the road before walking onto the platform.

Julie was resting her forearms on the railing along one side, head stretched over it so she could peer into the water six feet below. Grant set the pine cones on the railing and leaned over as well. The lake was deceptively deep here. The channel that fed Still Pines Lake from the river ran directly beneath them. From this vantage point, this portion of the lake appeared to be a mere continuation of the river, running between the island and the mainland. The mouth of the river to the island's north split and fed the lake—the same as to the island's south— but the main course of the river continued through this thin stretch beneath the bridge.

The lake had risen in the last twenty four hours and the channel was moving quickly. Whenever there was a great deal of rain, the river would expel the excess directly into Still Pines Lake. Once, when Grant was in high school, the water beneath the bridge had risen to within three feet of the supporting beams.

Grant picked up one of the pine cones with his left hand and threw it a few feet from the bridge. The current snatched it and brought it back underneath the structure. He and Julie each took the few steps to the other side of the bridge and watched the pine cone emerge from beneath them and continue its journey past the island.

They both smiled at the nautical trek of the pine cone. It felt childish. Grant didn't care. The fear from the nightmare was gone. This was his bridge, and he was sharing the beauty of it with an incredible woman.

Julie stepped to the opposite side of the structure and grabbed the other pine cone. She grinned at Grant and threw the brown prickly thing overhand into the channel, the pinecone landing farther away than Grant's effort. It repeated the course of its predecessor, and Julie rejoined Grant by the other railing to watch its triumphant float down the current until it was out of sight.

Julie raised her ankle onto the railing and leaned forward, grasping her uplifted foot with both hands as she stretched her hamstrings. The Lycra shorts were flattering. Grant realized he wasn't blinking.

He decided that stretching was an excellent idea. It would diminish the likelihood of both developing a cramp on the run home and of Julie glancing up to catch him ogling her buttocks. He leaned forward and wrapped his hands around his ankles as he tried to touch his forehead to his knees. He was not very successful, but it felt good in his tight muscles.

"Julie, can I ask you a question?" He spoke the words through his knees as he stretched.

"Sure." She pulled her leg off the railing and switched ankles.

"The night Granddad died. Do you remember where Brock was?"

Julie straightened from her stretch, a puzzled expression on her face. "No. I was in my room most of the night. Like I said earlier, I didn't spend a lot of time with the rest of your family. Why would you want to know where Brock was?"

For a brief moment, Grant wanted to tell Julie the whole story. Maybe she could help him. Maybe between the two of them, they would be able to track down the killer. He straightened his spine and reached forward, grasping the railing.

He leaned back, pulling against the board as he stretched his shoulders. His aching right wrist forced him to use mainly his left hand for the effort.

In truth, he wanted to tell her so he wouldn't feel so alone any more. With Eric unable to come to the island, Grant had felt isolated as he struggled with the truth behind his grandfather's death. Revealing everything to Julie would give him a partner, a friend. He drew in a breath, about to speak but unsure of how he could break the news to her.

His train of thought was interrupted by a loud cracking sound. Before he could relax the tension he was creating from pulling on the railing, the board broke and Grant fell backward. He landed hard on his rear and grunted as Julie emitted a startled shriek.

He winced at the splinters gouging his left palm and looked at the railing broken in three places and sticking out toward him. "Wow. Guess I don't know my own strength."

Julie squatted next to him. "Are you okay?" She took his hand in both of hers and held it up for inspection.

Grant smiled. "Yeah, I'm fine. You should see the other guy." Julie released his hand as he stood. He inspected the broken board. "Rotted through." He moved his gaze to the underside of the bridge's roof. The weathered, gray wood appeared weak. He kneeled to inspect the flooring. The wood there appeared to be in better shape.

"What happened?" Julie asked.

"Looks like the lumber Granddad used when he built this thing wasn't weather-proofed very well...or maybe it's just old. The roof and railings are practically rotten. The floor looks better. I guess since the roof kept the rain off of it for the most part. Still, we need to get this looked at pretty soon." The bridge had begun to again give Grant a distinct feeling of unease. He walked toward the road.

"You still didn't answer my question about Brock." Julie stopped him with the observation.

Grant reached a painful decision. He couldn't talk about it with her. Not yet. "No real reason. I just..." he waited, offering a reasonable sounding pause, "I just wanted to know what happened the night Granddad died. I don't like the thought of him dying alone."

It was a cover-up. What Grant really hated was the thought of his grandfather *not* dying alone. The thought of him dying *because* someone else was there, pushing the needle into his vein. He didn't expect the reaction he got from Julie.

She steadied her gaze on Grant for several moments. The only sound interrupting the peacefulness was the running current beneath them and the water dripping from the branches of the pines all around. Her eyes were misty as she walked to him. She wrapped her arms around his back and rested her head against his wet *Cougars* sweatshirt. She stayed in that same position until Grant returned the hug. It was then that Grant realized how profound her feelings for Abe were, and how the thought of a man she considered a father dying alone must have haunted her as well. After all, Grant had been a world away, but she had been just down the hall. And both had been equally helpless.

He was overwhelmed with emotion. Guilt at having spoken a lie that affected Julie so much. Desire for the woman resting her head against his chest. Confusion over the rush of feelings he was experiencing.

The only thing of which Grant could be certain, if even at a subconscious level, was that at some point in the past two days, he had begun to fall in love with Julie Russell.

He gently pushed her away from him, until she was staring up at his face. He lowered his lips to hers, offering the first gentle kiss, hoping it would be returned.

In the cool breeze that blew through the opening of the covered bridge, Julie returned his kiss with a gradual intensity. Their arms tightened around each other.

Grant raised his head and their lips parted. Julie opened her eyes. They were still red but alight with joy rather than sadness. She smiled as she whispered, "Let's get back to the house. I'll get those splinters out of your hand." She released Grant, turned, and ran down the road.

Standing at the edge of the bridge, Grant Armstrong felt alive. He took a couple of wobbly steps, lightheaded from the kiss, then quickened his pace to catch up with the blonde ponytail bobbing along ahead of him.

The first cool raindrops of the rebuilding storm fell against his face and the ominous presence of the bridge was left behind.

CHAPTER 34
October 11
3:56 P.M.

ERIC PEERED around the corner of the alley for what felt like the hundredth time. No activity anywhere around the factory. The front door remained closed. He walked back to the Crown Victoria—backed far enough in the alley to remain concealed from anyone in the building across the street—and sat behind the steering wheel. He closed the door with caution. No noise.

"Talk to me, George. Where's SWAT? They should be here."

George still held the microphone of the vehicle's two-way radio. "Out of luck. A-Team encountered resistance during a raid on the docks. No telling how long they'll be tied up. It'll be at least thirty minutes—maybe an hour—before we can get a secondary ESS unit instead."

Eric clenched his hand on the steering wheel. "Damn it. Too long. Kane could slip out by then." He took a deep breath. "We've got six men here now?"

"Yeah, Ramirez and Stewart are stationed at the back entrance and Miggins and Cruz are watching the loading docks. But that shouldn't matter because the Captain said to wait for SWAT. Right?"

"Yeah, right," Eric said under his breath. He was weighing his options. He didn't like any of them. "George, I need your advice. If

Kane is in there, then if Quinn isn't dead already, he probably will be very soon. We've got the exits covered, but Kane is...Kane. If we give him time, he'll find a way out. We may not get this close again..."

George sighed. "You're asking if I think we should go in without SWAT. My answer is no, backed up with hell no. Not just because it's dangerous but because we'd be going against orders. It's lose-lose, Eric. If we take Kane down, you still get your ass busted for disobeying the Captain. If he gets away, you're in even worse shape."

Eric stared at the factory across the street, wishing he knew what was happening within those walls. "I get what you're saying, George, but I don't know if any of that matters. Not when I'm trying to sleep at night. We both know what Kane is capable of, and we both know this is our best chance of catching him. Right here. Right now. If we don't strike while we can, and if Kane gets away because of it, how could I live with myself the next time he kills someone? This is my responsibility."

George was staring out the windshield too. The rain had begun falling again. The face of the factory grew blurry as the water gathered on the glass. George spoke. "Your call, boss. Smart or not. I'll have your back."

Despite their time working together, Eric hadn't been sure how George would respond. He made up his mind. "Roger that. I'm making the call."

"Listen, Eric. I've never said this before, but if we hit trouble in there, shoot to kill. Then shoot a couple more times for good measure. Let's not screw around with this guy."

Eric nodded. They had fallen back into the same pattern they had grown accustomed to over so many years. Although Eric was technically in charge of the operation, he knew George couldn't help but give advice gleaned from his experience. It was what Eric needed to hear.

"Alert the others, then call for some back-up," he said.

George lifted the handset for the two-way radio. "Will do, chief. And right after I do, we'll make a hasty exit from the car to conveniently not hear the shit-storm that'll come through that speaker."

George pressed the red button on the side of the handset and notified the other officers of their plan.

Eric stood to one side of the factory's front door, his revolver clasped in both hands in the ready position. George stood on the other side of the door, gun held in the same pose. The rain was falling with more consistency now, and George's thinning hair was matted against his scalp.

Eric nodded. George lifted his hand to the gold cross around his neck, touched it with his thumb, then reached for the handle and turned. Unlocked. As George pushed the door open, Eric stepped inside with pistol leveled. George followed and moved to the opposite side of the door, not allowing himself to be framed in the light from the doorway. Both men swung their guns to the right and left, searching. The entry room was empty.

Eric took a couple of steps then glanced back toward the door. He froze. Eric motioned for George to remain in place as he returned to the side of the doorway. There was a two-by-four bolted to a spring hinge to one side of the doorframe. The board was filled with exposed nails, designed to swing into the legs of anyone who entered beyond a foot into the room.

Eric pulled on the two wires which had been yanked from the motion-sensing device serving as the trigger mechanism for the booby trap. It had already been disabled.

Eric dropped the wires and heard a relieved sigh from George. "Lucky that thing's not operational," George whispered. "You would have been in a wheelchair."

Eric looked around the room. "It's not luck," he whispered in reply. "Kane's here. He must have used this door. Disarmed the booby trap." His expression changed as a thought struck him. "If this was at the front door...we've got to stop the others from forcing entry."

The loud retort of a shotgun echoed through the building, followed by screams of pain. Eric and George bolted toward the sound, abandoning caution as they ran down hallways and past offices. They emerged at the back door where Officer Stewart lay on the floor, writhing in pain. Both his legs were filled with buckshot from the twelve-gauge resting at knee height just inside the doorway. The blood seeping through his black pants made them appear shiny in the half-light of the door.

A loud clanging noise sounded from somewhere above. "Go. I'll radio officer down," Ramirez said as he knelt next to his partner.

Eric spun and returned deeper into the factory through a different hallway with George close behind. Gun drawn, he advanced through the corridor more cautiously than before, checking each room, a series of unused offices. The first two were empty. The third was vacant save for a large chair bolted to the floor with various tools on a tray table next to it. The chair was equipped with straps on the armrests and legs, resembling an old-fashioned electric chair. Eric looked at George and was met with upraised eyebrows. Eric didn't care to think what Quinn used that setup for. The next room was empty as well, but the desk and file cabinets seemed to serve as the bounty hunter's office.

Approaching the end of the hallway, Eric noticed more light emanating from the remaining open doorway than the other rooms. He signaled to George for cover then spun into the room, both men repeating the drill they had performed at the front door.

Both of their guns were trained on the bed. Eric couldn't believe what they were seeing.

Clive Quinn lay spread eagle, wrists and ankles bound to the iron bed railings. Trailing from a small incision in his abdomen, roughly fifteen feet of small intestine lay looped about his body, some falling to the floor in wet coils. Blood seeped from the wound as well as from the toe-stumps at the end of his feet. His throat had been cut, and crimson liquid still pumped from the jugular vein.

Eric fought to maintain control. Shock, nausea and anger overwhelmed him, but he knew the force of blood flowing from Quinn's neck meant the fatal gash had been made only moments before. Kane was here. Close.

Eric spun and ran from the room, passing a slack-jawed George, as realization of the earlier sound dawned on him.

He shouted over his shoulder as he ran. "The roof! He went to the roof!" He raced down the hall, caution abandoned. He glanced to his right and left, looking for a set of stairs as he ran.

He threw open a door that led to the factory floor. The large space was filled with dusty equipment. Running along one wall was a stair case leading to the roof.

Eric bolted towards it, ignoring the calls of his partner to wait. George was twenty yards behind him, outpaced by his younger partner. Eric raced up the stairs two at a time, reaching the door in moments. He gripped the handle and shoved his shoulder against the metal door. It flew open and smacked against the sheet metal siding of the building, echoing the sound Eric had heard moments earlier.

The skies had grown dark and the rain was falling harder now, making it difficult to discern detail in the grays and blacks of the factory rooftop. He scanned for any sign of Silas Kane, seeing nothing.

Eric stood in front of the open door, trying to peer through the falling sheets of water. He saw movement. His vision focused on the massive shape standing next to a large vent fan, black jacket blending in to the tar sealant covering the piping.

Kane looked as if he was pointing at Eric.

Gun.

In an instant, Eric saw a flash in Kane's hand and felt the pressure of a pair of hands against his shoulders. He bent forward under the weight of his partner's lunge as he heard the retort of Kane's pistol. He felt no impact. No pain. The shot had missed.

Eric crashed onto the wet roof, his face smacking against the dingy tar surface and water splashing as George's weight dropped on top of him. He heard a commotion as Miggins appeared at the doorway, gun drawn, firing shots toward Kane. Cruz was right behind him on the steps.

The giant ducked behind the piping and ran toward the edge of the roof, leaping the chasm of the alley below and splashing onto the roof of the neighboring factory.

Eric tried to roll over, but George refused to budge. "Let me up, George," Eric said as he rolled to one side, pushing his partner off his back. "Shit, that was too close."

George collapsed onto the tar roof. Eric turned to look at his partner and cried out. The left half of George's neck was a gaping hole, the bullet from Kane's gun having torn through flesh and arteries. Blood poured from the wound, the gold cross awash in a flow of red.

Eric screamed into the door, "Get an ambulance!" His voice sounded odd to him, as if it was coming from another world. Cruz raced back down the stairs.

Eric ripped his jacket off, cradling George against him and holding the material against the flood of blood. It wasn't enough. George's mouth moved, but no words came. His eyes stared into space, unfocused. Tears ran down Eric's face as he held his partner, repeating the same word, "No, George. Please no. No, George."

Miggins stood at the edge of the roof, looking into the pouring rain across the expanse of rooftops in the sea of abandoned buildings. "There's no sign of him!" he shouted.

Eric didn't hear him. He was holding his partner, clutching George's head to his chest, rocking his lifeless body in the driving storm.

CHAPTER 35

October 11
4:00 P.M.

GRANT AND JULIE were within sight of the front porch when the skies opened and the drizzling rain became a downpour. They sprinted the last hundred yards, but by the time they reached the covered entryway to the main house, they were both soaked.

They stood under the protection of the front porch, watching the rain fall and hearing the distant rumble of thunder. The weather forecast Grant had seen earlier had predicted the second wave of the storm to be more powerful than the first, but it was expected to pass over by late evening.

Grant's eyes left the storm to glance at his running partner. The sweatshirt was plastered against her body, heavy from the rain. The elastic waistband no longer held the bottom of the shirt at her hips. The weight of the wet material forced the shirt to hang straight down, making it look too big for the woman wearing it. Julie's blonde ponytail hung wet onto the back of her neck. Portions of her hair had escaped their bindings during the run, and they clung against the side of her wet face. She was the most breathtaking woman Grant had ever seen.

Julie turned from the rain and noticed him staring at her. She glanced down at herself and laughed. "I'm a drowned rat."

Grant joined her laughter. "But you pull off the drowned rat look remarkably well."

"You're sweet," she replied. "Let's get your hand fixed up." She opened the front door and they stepped inside.

Through unspoken agreement, they moved quickly through the house to the stairs, not speaking. Neither of them wanted another encounter with Brock or Mona. Jogging by the guest house on the return trip, Grant had noticed that Phil and Loraine's car was still parked in the driveway. He supposed they hadn't wanted to risk going into the city with the threatening weather or even risk coming to the main house for that matter. That was fine with Grant. At the moment, he didn't want to be with anyone but the woman making her way up the stairs in front of him.

As Julie climbed, her buttocks flashed in brief appearances from underneath the sweatshirt. Right at Grant's eye level. The feeling of being a sixteen year old trapped in a grown man's body again suffused him.

They reached the top of the staircase, and Julie led him into her room. She closed the door and fell back against it. "Why do I feel like a teenager sneaking a boy up to my room?" she asked.

Grant chuckled. "I was thinking the exact same thing...except reversing the gender."

Julie walked around her bed, turned on the light in her bathroom and extracted a pair of tweezers from the medicine cabinet. "Give me your hand," she instructed.

Grant stepped into the bright light offered by the bulbs lining the bathroom mirror and held his left hand out to her with his palm up. As Julie lowered the tweezers, Grant deftly plucked them from her grasp with his other hand. "Please allow me," he said. "Not questioning your skills whatsoever and not that I'm a baby when it comes to pain—I'm a manly man—but I do have a knack for tweezing. You know, doctor training and all."

Julie smiled and stepped back, relinquishing her hold of his hand. Grant adjusted his grip on the instrument and bent his right hand forward to achieve the proper angle. Pain flared up his sprained wrist, and he dropped the tweezers to the tiled floor with a light clink. "Ouch!"

Surprise etched Julie's face. "Are you okay? What happened?"

Grant was embarrassed more than hurt. The pain from bending his wrist was already abating. "I'm fine. So much for manly man."

Julie knelt to retrieve the tweezers. "Your wrist is still sore from yesterday isn't it?"

Grant nodded. "Just a little."

"I am *so* sorry. I know I said it before, but...I apologize for running over you with the car." He smiled and she returned it. "Here, let me get this. It's the least I can do."

Grant offered his hand, and she held it close to her face as she went to work, gently extracting two inch-long pieces of wood from his palm.

"You're good," he said.

"You trained eight years to be a doctor. I trained my whole life as a woman. We have a very rigorous curriculum in tweezing."

She attempted to grasp the final splinter. It was smaller and burrowed into the side of Grant's left index finger. He flinched as she worked the tips of the instrument around the invader.

She pulled her hand back and sighed. "Sorry, Dr. Armstrong, but this may require surgery." She set the tweezers on the bathroom counter and walked into her bedroom. Grant raised his hand to inspect the buried piece of wood. It had worked itself deep into the fleshy part of his finger.

Julie returned to the bathroom holding a sewing needle. She extracted a small pack of matches from the medicine cabinet and struck one, then held the needle over the flame. The matchstick went into the toilet. It made a *pish* sound when the flame extinguished upon hitting the water. Julie held the point of the sterilized needle under the faucet.

Grant again offered his hand to her, three of his fingers closed to allow easy access to the index finger. She grasped the digit and worked the needle around the splinter. After a few moments, the tip of the intruding piece of wood was maneuvered out of the skin.

Julie set the needle on the counter and picked up the tweezers. She pinched the splinter from Grant's finger and held it up for inspection. "A successful surgery, Doctor."

Grant smiled. "That's great, but will I be able to play the piano?"

Julie placed the tweezers onto the counter and moved in close to Grant, their wet, heavy sweatshirts touching. "Of course," she replied.

"Good," he began, "I always wanted to play the—" Julie pressed her lips against Grant's, interrupting the punchline of the old joke. He wrapped his arms around her and slid one hand up until he was cradling the back of her head, her ponytail between his fingers.

The kiss was hard at first, then softened as their lips parted, experiencing the full sensations of the deep kiss. They explored each other for several minutes in the embrace until she broke the kiss. Her eyes remained closed as she spoke. "Grant, I don't...we barely know each other but...I don't want to sound...it's just that I feel so..."

Grant lifted one hand to her cheek, caressing the water droplets that had fallen from her wet hair. "Shhh...Julie, you've lived here more than a year. You knew my grandfather. You know me."

"But you don't know me," she said her eyes opening.

"I know everything I need to know about you," he whispered. "You're sweet and kind and beautiful. And my grandfather loved you. That's all I need to know." He meant every word.

Grant thought he felt a shiver go through Julie's body. He pulled her close for another kiss which she returned with a silent passion. She reached down and pulled off her sweatshirt, separating the kiss as the heavy cloth passed between their faces. The wet material dropped to the floor in a soggy heap. Grant removed his own shirt and let it fall next to hers.

They embraced, smooth wet bodies molded against one another. Grant could feel the press of her breasts against his chest, the pinpoints of her nipples straining against the sports bra. The kiss was more aggressive than any of their previous. Their hands roamed freely, exploring backs and buttocks, caressing and grasping, stroking and tugging. Grant reached between them and massaged her breasts through the tight material.

Julie backed away and slowly pulled the sports bra over her head, freeing her breasts from their spandex bindings. She grabbed Grant by the arm, pulling him into the bedroom.

They lay in bed as the sounds of the storm raged outside her window. The sheet was pulled up, shielding their naked bodies from the cool air of the bedroom. Julie's head rested on Grant's chest. Her blonde hair, free from the ponytail but still damp, lay across his shoulder and neck. Her eyes were closed as she pushed her leg up and draped it over him. He could feel her warmth against his thigh.

Grant rested his head on the pillow as he stroked the smoothness of her back. He inhaled deeply, savoring her feminine scent. For the first time in what seemed like years, he felt happiness. Amidst all the pain and grief and turmoil of his grandfather's death, he had found a serenity.

For a long time, Grant Armstrong lay unmoving, his body intertwined with Julie's. Content. Happy. He had no way of knowing the woman in his arms would be dead before the night ended.

CHAPTER 36
October 11
4:31 P.M.

Eric WATCHED the ambulance pull away. The siren was silent, and the bar of lights on the roof remained dark. The man inside was dead, and nothing Eric or the paramedics inside the white vehicle could do would change that fact.

He heard Ramirez speak from behind him. "You okay?"

Eric shook his head. The rain stung his cheeks and ran down his face. The wind bit into his soaked clothes. A blue windbreaker with a bold yellow "NYPD" emblazoned across the back had replaced Eric's blood-soaked tan jacket. It offered little protection from the elements, but he felt no cold.

"I'm nowhere near okay." A rumble of thunder punctuated the remark as he turned and stepped past Ramirez into the open door of the factory.

His soaked clothes left a trail of water down the hallway as he proceeded to the room where Quinn had kept his files. He yanked out the top drawer of the desk and turned it upside down over the desk's surface. Pencils and bankbooks, address books and paperclips poured forth. Eric sorted through the mess, throwing any items he deemed useless across the room into a corner.

Captain Foley stepped into the doorway, Ramirez close behind. "Detective Johnson...Eric, what the hell are you doing?"

Eric didn't look up. He continued flipping through papers, discarding them onto the floor after he reviewed them. "Going through Quinn's files, sir. Kane wasn't just here to kill him. He needed information, just like he did with Mickey Little."

"I ordered you to go home, Eric," Foley said. "And I meant it."

Eric looked up, eyes wide, distraught. "He's going after whoever paid the bounty. Kane wanted to know who hired Quinn. Why else go to all the trouble of that kind of torture?"

"Kane's a psychopath, he doesn't need a reason. Now go home. We can handle it from here."

"I can't, sir. Kane killed George. I've got—"

"That's *exactly* why you will leave, Eric," Foley interrupted. "You're not thinking with a clear head anymore. You're off the case."

Eric slammed his fist onto the desk. "No! Kane's mine!"

Foley responded with his own raised voice. "You were in charge of this operation, Johnson! You disobeyed a direct order and not only let Kane get away but put one cop in the hospital and another in the morgue!"

The Captain took a deep breath. "I'm sorry about George, Eric. He was a good man. He was a friend. But this is it for you on this case. If you can't accept that, then you'll be facing suspension. Now go home. We'll discuss this later."

Eric stood unmoving, glaring at the Captain. He swept his hand across the surface of the desk. Foley and Ramirez watched as the swirl of papers flew across the room.

Without saying a word, Eric marched around the desk and walked past them. He proceeded out the door and into the driving storm.

Eric pulled the Crown Victoria into an open parking spot on the side of the road. He had driven ten blocks from the factory to a point where he was sure there would be no more police activity. He flicked on the interior lights of the vehicle then reached into his jacket pocket and removed Clive Quinn's bankbook.

Sweeping the papers off the desk before leaving had been a melodramatic diversion allowing him to pocket the pad-sized book. He knew the theft, coupled with the fiasco earlier, could result in his removal from the force, but he had no choice. His mentor, his dear friend, lay dead as a direct result of Eric's arrogance. He thought they could take Kane on their own. He was wrong. And George had paid the price for it.

Kane would not get away with it. Eric knew, he *knew*, that Kane was going after whoever hired Quinn. It was the only thing that made sense. Vengeance. Eric had spent the past year trying to get inside Silas Kane's head, trying to understand the motives behind his actions. Now, it was crystallizing.

In Kane's mind, it was the police department's job to arrest him. But the bounty hunter. That was personal. That's why Kane hadn't come after George or Eric or the judge. That explained why he hunted down and murdered Mickey and Quinn.

Once Kane completed his quest for vengeance, Eric had no idea where he would go. He might head west, or go to Canada, or swim to Australia, but wherever he went, he would kill. Eric couldn't stand the thought of more innocent people dying when he may have had the power to stop it.

Vengeance.

Kane was no longer the only one with a score to settle.

It was simple. Eric would track down whoever hired Quinn, and would intercept Kane in the process. It was the only option left.

He flipped through the bankbook, hoping to find an entry along the time of Kane's initial capture, when the bounty would have been paid. The book only had four entries. The first was dated August. It was a new book.

"Son of a bitch!" Eric pounded his fist against the steering wheel.

He stopped his fist before it could strike the wheel a third time and inhaled deeply. He had to regain his composure. It would be the only way he could take down Kane.

He looked at the small black book in his hand. It didn't have the information he needed, but it wasn't over yet. Opening the front cover of the book, he found the phone number for Quinn's bank. He grabbed his cell phone and dialed. Checked his watch as it rang. Almost closing time.

A pleasant young woman's voice answered after the second ring. "First Bank of New York. How may I direct your call?"

Eric attempted to sound equally pleasant. He was surprised to hear his tone sounded almost natural. "Yes, this is Detective Eric Johnson with the New York City Police Department. I need to make an inquiry about one of your accounts please."

"One moment," the pleasant woman replied.

There was a click then Eric was listening to a recording on how easy it would be to consolidate his debt with the bank's new one-stop loan shop. He was learning about exciting low interest rates when another woman picked up the call. She sounded older than the first but just as pleasant.

"This is Debra, may I help you?"

"I hope so, Debra. This is Detective Eric Johnson with the New York City Police Department, Homicide Division. I need to research activity on the account for Mr. Clive Quinn. Specifically, I need to know about any large deposits made during the first part of May of this year. Can you help me?" Eric closed his eyes, hoping this would be easier than expected.

There was a pause on the other end before Debra answered. "I'm sorry, Detective Johnson. I'd like to help, but we have a strict policy about client privacy. I'm not allowed to discuss any of our customers' personal financial information. I believe the proper procedure requires a warrant before we're allowed to release any of our records."

"Debra, I understand your policy, and please realize I don't want to get you in trouble, but Debra," he paused, looking for the words, "I need your help. Clive Quinn has been murdered, and I'm afraid the killer is after someone who would have deposited a large sum of money into his account last May. I need to know who that was. Today. That person's life may depend on it. There's no time for the usual procedure."

There was a long stretch of silence on the phone before Debra responded. "Look, I'm sorry, but I don't know who you are, and I could lose my job." Despite her words, she sounded unsure, wavering.

Hope.

Eric pushed harder. "Debra, I know you don't have any reason in the world to believe me, but you have to trust me when I say that this information is critical. I know you're not supposed to do this, I know you could lose your job, but someone's life is at stake. If you believe there's even a *possibility* that I'm telling the truth, then please help me. Help me save that person."

It was a full minute before Debra responded. Eric was afraid the call may have been disconnected when she finally spoke. "Can you give me your badge number?"

Eric opened his eyes and leaned back in his seat, a wave of relief crashing over him. He spoke his badge number and gave her time to write it down.

In the amount of time it likely took her to enter the number into an internet search engine and at least verify that there was, indeed, a cop on the NYPD with that badge number by the name of Eric Johnson, she again spoke. "Okay," she said, whispering into the phone. "What do you want to know?"

"His name is Clive Quinn. I've got the account number." He read the digits from the bankbook. "I'm looking for any large deposits made into his account in the first weeks of May."

Eric could hear the clicking of the keys on a keyboard over the phone as Debra entered the information into the computer. "It looks like Mr. Quinn only has one account with us." She paused a moment as she searched for the requested information. "This must be what you're looking for. There was only one deposit in the month of May, and it was for two-hundred-and-fifty-thousand dollars."

Eric sat up. "That's the one. Where did it come from?"

"Let's see," Debra began. "It was wired from Chase, their Private Bank division, so it was a personal account."

"Whose account?" Eric leaned forward, anxious.

"The wiring instructions indicate the originating account was registered to an Abraham Armstrong."

Eric was certain he had misheard. "What?" he asked.

"Abraham Armstrong. I don't have an address listed, but you might be able to call Chase and get that information. Is that what you needed?"

Eric spoke softly. "Yeah, thanks Debra."

He hit the "End" button on his phone and dropped it in the seat next to him. Then he threw the car in gear and pressed hard on the accelerator, tires spinning on the wet pavement as the Crown Vic fishtailed down the street. He rolled down his window and placed the magnetic orb on the roof, activating its spinning red light.

Rain and wind buffeting the vehicle, Eric sped toward Still Pines Lake.

CHAPTER 37
October 11
5:05 P.M.

GRANT CLOSED THE DOOR to the study and walked behind the large teak desk. He pulled back the rolling leather chair and eased into its comfortable seat. There were no windows in the study, but the sounds of the tempest raging outside penetrated the dark wood walls. The storm was bad. As bad as he had ever seen.

Before leaving Julie's room, he had stood at her window in awe. The wind buffeted the trees with lightning illuminating the sky and thunder ripping through the air every few moments. He wondered if the electricity would last through the night.

Despite the raging storm, Julie had fallen asleep in his arms. Grant could not bring himself to wake her so he had gently slipped from under the covers, kissing her cheek before dressing and quietly closing the door behind him.

Now seated in the big leather chair, he opened one of the desk drawers and retrieved his grandfather's phone listings. Licking his thumb, he flipped to the page with the attorney's number. Grant picked up the phone and dialed Ronald Lister's office. A female voice answered.

"Swynnerton, Lister and Bailey. May I help you?" the voice asked.

Grant cleared his throat. "Yes. This is Grant Armstrong calling in place of Abraham Armstrong for Mr. Lister's five o'clock meeting. Is he available?"

"One moment, please," the voice responded.

Classical music drifted from the receiver as Grant waited close to three minutes, his fingers crossed. Finally, a man's voice came on the line.

"Ron Lister here. Is that really you, Grant?"

Grant exhaled a quiet sigh of relief. "It's me, Mr. Lister. How have you been?"

"Same as always." He paused. "Son, I'm very sorry about your grandfather. Abe was a good friend, and I'll miss him."

"Thank you, sir. I know Granddad felt the same about you," Grant said. "Listen, Mr. Lister, I was wondering if you could help me."

"Name it."

Grant's fingers uncrossed in his lap. "I've been trying to sort out some of Granddad's affairs. I noticed he had a meeting set up with you for right now. I was wondering if you could tell me what that meeting was going to be about..."

"Grant, I've already been through this with Phil and the rest of your family. I'm not at liberty to discuss the dispersal of Abe's estate until after the funeral."

"Hold on. That's not what I'm asking. I don't care about the dispersal of the estate. I don't care who's in the will. I don't care about the size of the holdings. I just want to know what the meeting was going to be about." Grant's voice tightened as he spoke, his frustration evident.

"Take it easy, son. I know how you must feel right now, what with you and Abe having that fallout earlier, but you have to know that he still loved you."

Grant's eyebrows furrowed. Fallout? "Hang on, Mr. Lister. What do you mean fallout?"

"I'm sorry, Grant. I don't mean to intrude. It's just that Abe was really concerned about you. He didn't hear from you for so long.

Frankly, it disappointed me as well. I know you were busy in Africa, but a letter or a phone call would have meant a lot to him. It's not my place to say, but he felt rather abandoned."

Grant was dumbfounded. "I—I don't know what you're talking about. I wrote Granddad once a week the whole time I was there. Same as always. I know he got the letters. He told me so at Christmas."

"It's a long time between Christmases, Grant," Lister interjected, his tone one of an elder gently chastising a youth. "You've got to realize that he was basically all alone at that house. You know how things are with your family. He could have used some contact from you."

Grant was shaking his head as he spoke. "This has to be some mistake."

"Please understand, Grant. I'm not judging you. I don't know what happened. I just wanted you to understand ahead of time."

The words barely registered. He changed gears abruptly. "Please just answer this, Mr. Lister. Did Granddad ever talk to you about changing his will?"

Another pause. "I told you. I can't disclose any details about the dispersal of the estate until..."

It was Grant's turn to interrupt. "I don't care about the details of the dispersal! Please listen, I need to know whether or not the meeting you had scheduled today with Granddad involved changing his will. That's all I want to know. Please, Mr. Lister, answer me that one question."

There was a long pause as Ronald Lister considered the request before answering. "Grant, the meeting today had nothing to do with the will. He changed the will two weeks ago. I came out to the house and had him sign the papers then."

Grant sat in silence. Overwhelmed. He needed details.

The phone clicked as a new voice came on the line.

"Excuse me, sir," the woman said. "This is the operator. I need a Mr. Grant Armstrong to pick up the line immediately. There is an emergency."

Grant clenched his fist. He had lost the call from Lister. What the hell kind of emergency could... "This is Grant Armstrong," he replied through clenched teeth.

"Yes sir. I have Detective Eric Johnson from the New York City Police Department about to be patched in. He asked that I interrupt the call. Here you are."

Another click and harsh static filled the receiver. Grant pulled the phone an inch away from his ear and spoke. "Eric?"

"Grant!" The garbled voice was barely discernible through the noise, and Grant couldn't understand the words that followed.

"Eric, speak up! I can't make out what you're saying."

Grant pressed his palm to his other ear and listened intently. He would call Lister again later.

CHAPTER 38
October 11
5:15 P.M.

THE OLD PINE had withstood storms for well over a hundred years. The tallest tree along the lake, it towered twenty feet over its closest neighbor. Tonight, it bent and swayed as the wind howled through its branches.

The tree stood by the entry to the covered bridge, an ancient sentry guarding the island's single access point. Its branches housed two bird nests. One was abandoned earlier in the fall. The other was home to two small birds who had yet to learn to fly. The mother bird protectively spread her wings over their heads, the rain washing over her dark feathers and into the nest.

A bolt of white lightning erupted into the trunk of the old pine. The force of the blast shook the needles from the tree's branches and upended the nest. The smaller birds, plummeting to the earth, mimicked their mother and took wing. Both discovered the talent for flight amidst the chaos of the storm.

The pine's trunk split at the hub of the strike, the turpentine in the sap igniting from the heat. Flames licked the fresh laceration despite the driving rain. The upper eighty feet of the tree creaked and began to topple. Slowly at first, then gaining speed as gravity finished what the lightning had started.

The falling tree impacted the roof of the covered bridge with tremendous force. The wood covering of the structure was weak, even more so than the railing which had split earlier in the day. The principal beam running down the middle of the roof cracked loudly as the pine struck its center, its weakest point. The tree bounced off the roof once, then slammed into the bridge again.

This time, the principal beam did not hold. The crack formed moments earlier expanded and then exploded outward as the beam fell in two halves. The tree crashed through the shingles of the unsupported roof and followed the shattered beam in a plunge to the floor of the bridge.

Although the load-bearing beams beneath the floor were stronger than those above, the weight of the tree combined with the sudden impact of the collapsing roof created a large fissure in one of them. The severed pine bounced against the floor and came to rest amid the debris of the obliterated roof.

For a brief while, the bridge sat still, silent save for the rush of the wind. Then, a slow series of pops emanated beneath the structure. The single cracked beam began to split. The fracture in the support grew to double in size, then double again. Finally, the beam broke with a loud pop.

With one of the principal girders destroyed, the weight of the bridge fell entirely on the other braces. Never designed to support the mass of the entire structure, the other beams cracked. Within minutes, the next girder gave way, followed by another.

The bridge collapsed under its own weight into the rushing water of the lake's main channel. The tree, now completely severed from its base, was caught in the rush of water and floated downstream before wedging onto the shore. The bulk of the bridge followed. Large chunks of flooring and shingles traveled down the channel toward the vastness of the lake beyond.

Unencumbered by the mass of the entire structure, a single board ran the length of the expanse between the mainland and the island. Smaller portions of the bridge remained attached to the anchoring beam and floated in the rising water a few feet below. These huddled piles of planks from the flooring strained against their moorings on the stout beam.

Running alongside both the mainland and the island, ripped from the roof of the decimated bridge, the severed phone line stretched out like two thin black snakes fighting the current.

CHAPTER 39
October 11
5:17 P.M.

"GRANT! I SAID Kane is coming to the island!" Eric was yelling into his phone to no avail. The call had been disconnected.

"Cellular fucking phones!" The storm was affecting what was already a weak signal along the stretch of highway. The Crown Vic was coming up on a rise, the signal would probably be stronger there. He would get another chance. He hit redial for the number to the main house just as the car crested the hill.

Driving with one hand and holding the phone to his ear with the other, Eric prayed that Grant would pick up. Through static, Eric could hear a distinct ring. Then another. The signal held, but there was no answer. Eric let the phone ring ten times before ending the call. Why wasn't he answering?

The grade on the highway moved downhill. Eric dropped the phone into the passenger seat and concentrated on the road. The signal wouldn't be good enough to attempt another call until he hit the next rise.

With both hands on the wheel, Eric peered through the windshield. He could only see for brief moments between the swipes of the wiper blades. On the plus side, the storm had diminished traffic to a state of near nonexistence.

At the base of the hill, the Crown Vic struck a large pool of water. Eric could feel the force of the spray on the car's underside against his feet as the tires separated the water. He eased his foot off the accelerator. Flooding out the engine or hydroplaning into a guard rail wouldn't help him, and it certainly wouldn't help protect his friend.

He forced himself to take deep breaths. Theoretically, he believed he might be able to beat Kane to Still Pines Lake. Stop him before he ever set foot on the island. After all, Eric had lived in the area his whole life. He knew which roads flooded during storms and which routes were fastest. Moreover, the island wasn't exactly easy to find for someone who had never been there. There were several backroads required to locate it.

Unfortunately, Kane had a healthy head start. Even assuming the killer had to take the time to steal a car, he could still be well ahead.

Eric clutched the wheel. He hoped that Grant had heard what he was trying to say before the call dropped. With any luck at all, the Armstrong family would have already fled the island.

CHAPTER 40
October 11
5:18 P.M.

G RANT LOOKED quizzically at the phone receiver. He plunged the disconnect button several times into the base of the phone before placing the handset back to his ear. Still nothing. No dial tone. No static. Nothing.

The storm must have knocked out the phone service in Still Pines. He returned the handset to the base of the phone and leaned back in his chair.

What had Eric been trying to tell him? The static had made his words indecipherable before the line had gone dead. He thought he heard the word 'Kane' but not in a way that made sense. And why would Eric have an operator break into a phone call just to update him on his case?

Grant's thoughts flashed back to the airport, remembering his friend cuffing him at the baggage claim. Maybe Eric was getting too comfortable in his role as the big city cop. Maybe he was having a little too much fun. The thought annoyed Grant. The call to Lister had been important, as critical as anything before it in his attempts to uncover his grandfather's killer. Another thirty seconds with the attorney would have given Grant a chance to learn more about the will, but his "friend" had cut him off.

Grant shook his head. "Dammit, Eric," he muttered.

He spun the chair to face away from the desk, and he stared at the dark wood of the wall. The sounds of the storm were still distinct. The booming sound of thunder mixed with the howling wind.

Grant contemplated his conversation with Lister. It was disturbing on so many levels. The will had been changed. Two weeks ago. And Grant and his grandfather had had a "falling out." Abe hadn't received any letters for months. And Phil and the family were hammering at the attorney regarding the estate.

None of it made sense and he couldn't decide which piece of the new information troubled him most.

The creak of the study door pulled Grant from his thoughts. He spun the chair toward the sound. The door was open a foot, and Julie's head poked through the space. Her hair was dry and hung loosely about her face. She had changed into a pink sweater, and she was smiling as she peered at Grant from the doorway.

"You snuck out on me."

"Sorry. Needed to make a phone call."

"May I come in?" she asked.

"Please," he responded and she entered the room.

"Am I interrupting or did you already make your call?"

Grant glanced down at the phone. "Oh, I already made it, but I won't be making any more. Not until after the storm at least. The phone went dead. Must have had a line knocked down somewhere."

"Sorry to hear that," she said as she walked around the desk and stood behind Grant. She reached over the back of the chair and began massaging his shoulders. Her grip was firm. Grant moaned.

"You sure are tense for a guy who just had some great sex." She stopped rubbing his shoulders and leaned close to his ear. "It was great, right? That wasn't just me?"

Grant laughed. "It was fantastic. Now don't stop."

Julie shifted her hands from his shoulders to the back of his neck. Her thumbs dug forcefully into the crease between his trapezius muscles and his back then moved toward his spine. He flinched.

"Okay, manly man here," he said. "But don't forget there's a cervical nerve between C3 and C4. That really smarts if you dig into it."

"Huh? Oh, sorry," she replied sheepishly as she loosened her grip. "I was never great at giving massages."

Grant dropped his chin to his neck as he tried to relax the muscles in his neck. She was right. Her massage technique was lousy. Maybe she had a poor teacher in the classes on physical therapy when getting her license. "We all have room for improvement," he said.

"What was that?" she asked.

"Nothing," he replied, knowing it would be better to endure the massage. It wasn't going to make his muscles any tenser. Besides, he needed to talk, and Julie remained his single biggest asset in understanding the mental state of his grandfather.

"Julie," he began, "when we were running earlier, you asked me if Granddad and I had a fight. What prompted that question?"

Julie moved her hands down Grant's back as he leaned forward in the chair. "I didn't mean to pry, Grant. I know Abe loved you. I was just curious."

"You're not prying. I just want to know what inspired the question."

"Well, it's just that for the first few months I was here, you used to write Abe all the time. He always had me read the letters to him. He hated having to use the magnifying glass to read things..." She trailed off, then resumed. "I'm embarrassed to admit this, but I kind of developed a crush on you. I got to know you through your letters. Reading about what you were doing in Africa, and the people you helped. It's silly, I know." She stopped massaging Grant's back. When he turned to look at her, her cheeks were blushing a shade to match her sweater.

"Anyway, after Christmas, the letters stopped coming so often. Instead of one letter a week, you sent one a month. Then the letters stopped coming entirely. I assumed you two had a fight. I mean, Abe never said anything, and your letters didn't imply it, but to just stop sending them... It worried Abe. I told him that you were probably super busy and didn't have time. I couldn't bear to think of the two of you upset at each other."

Grant nodded, trying to process what he'd just heard.

Julie stepped away from the back of the chair and stood by Grant, a questioning look on her face. "What was the fight about, Grant? Was it about money?"

"There was no fight, Julie. And money is never worth fighting over." His tone was gruff. He couldn't help it.

"I'm sorry. I didn't mean..."

"It's okay. Not your fault. Look, there's something else I need to know, something that may seem odd. Who collects the mail?"

"Huh?"

"The mail," Grant reiterated. "The postman has never been willing to drive all the way to the island. Who goes to the post office to pick up the mail?"

"I do sometimes," she said, "but usually it's Mona. On the days she comes out, she stops by town on the way to the island and brings it with her."

Grant nodded as he pushed the chair away from the desk. He walked past Julie toward the door. "Please excuse me. I need to have a chat with my aunt."

CHAPTER 41
October 11
5:57 P.M.

ERIC HELD THE PHONE close to his face for inspection. He was driving through a midsized town and the signal was as high as it had been since leaving the city. He knew this may be his last chance to help Grant before Kane got to the island.

He punched in the number and held it to his ear. Through lighter static, a familiar female voice greeted him. "Still Pines Sheriff's Office..."

Eric spoke loudly into the phone, unsure how clear the connection would be on the other end. "Laura, it's Eric. Is Mike at the station?"

"Hi, Eric. It's been a while. Mike's not here. He and Freddy are at Ralph's marina. The storm tore up his dock, and they're trying to save the boats."

"Look, Laura, this is important. I need you to get everyone over to the Armstrong—" a burst of static interrupted him. He flinched, pulling the phone away then returning it to his ear.

"I'm sorry, Eric, I missed that last part. What did you say about the Armstrongs?" Laura asked.

"I'm losing signal, listen carefully! Silas Kane has escaped. He's going to Armstrong Island. Their phone is dead. I need you to get Mike over there and get them off the island. Have him bring Freddy too. I'm on my way. We've got to stop Kane!" Eric was screaming into the phone as the town disappeared in his rearview mirror. "Did you get that, Laura?"

Static replied.

"Laura!"

The phone went silent as the signal dropped too much to maintain the call.

Eric set the phone in his lap and gripped the wheel with both hands, fighting the wind to keep his car on the road. He allowed his foot to press the accelerator a bit more. Kane was still ahead of him, somewhere.

A harsh jag of lightning leapt from the sky, striking the transformer on a power pole along the side of the road. The darkness erupted into a brilliant shower of white sparks, momentarily blinding him.

His foot eased off the gas, slowing the car as his vision returned to clarity. Navigating the harsh weather, Eric took a deep breath and uttered a prayer.

"God, he's taken my partner. Don't let him take my friend."

The prayer died on his lips without an Amen. Eric once more accelerated and dared his own death.

CHAPTER 42
October 11
6:05 P.M.

SHERIFF MIKE PUCKETT sat in the shelter of his cruiser and held the microphone of the two-way radio to his lips. "Come again, Laura. What did Eric want?"

"Hard to tell, the phone was breaking up," Laura's voice replied through the small speaker mounted under the dash in the Sheriff's vehicle. "But I did catch that he wants you to go to Armstrong Island."

"Cripes, Laura, that's on the other side of the lake. It'd take me forever to get over there, and I'm still helping Ralph," he responded. "I'm sure whatever problems the island aristocracy are having, they can wait a few hours."

"I don't know, Mike. He sounded pretty stressed."

"He lives in the city now, Laura, he's supposed to sound stressed," he chuckled. "Look, Freddy left a few minutes ago to check on his own place, give him a shout and send him over to check it out. The island isn't too far out of his way."

"Gotcha, Mike. Tell Ralph to be careful not to drown out there."

"Will do," Mike responded. He hung the microphone on the base of the unit and stepped out of the cruiser into the driving rain.

CHAPTER 43
October 11
6:19 P.M.

GRANT PUSHED OPEN the door to the lounge and scanned the room. The fireplace was roaring, though it could not compete with the howl of the wind outside the glass. Grant's eyes flicked to the large shotgun mounted above the red brick mantle then he noticed a small tuft of dark brown curls peaking over the top of the sofa.

"Mona, we need to talk," Grant said as he walked around the end table to confront his aunt.

Mona's eyes were closed. Her mouth agape. She was reclined on a series of pillows with her head bent forward, chin touching her chest. An empty glass rested in her loosened fingers, the edge lying against the cushion of the sofa with a dark stain still evident on the fabric.

Grant knelt and placed his hands on her shoulders. Her breathing was light but steady. Of any of his family members, he couldn't believe Mona could be responsible for Abe's death. True, she was the poster child for instability, she had always had problems—drugs, alcohol, her choice in men—and she fought with her father fiercely over all those issues, but Grant could imagine no argument so great that it would involve murder. Even over Brock.

The notion of his grandfather's death being nothing more than a tool to please Brock Rutland gripped his heart with a blackness. Brock had despised Abraham Armstrong, and Brock had made no bones about wanting the money. But could his aunt have possibly killed her own father out of desperation to keep such a scumbag? Grant shook the unconscious woman on the couch with more force than he had planned.

"Mona," he said loudly.

Her head bounced in rhythm to his shaking, and a small strand of saliva fell from her slack mouth, but her eyes failed to open.

Grant tried once more, shaking her harder. "Mona! Wake up!" The empty glass fell from her fingers and thudded onto the thick carpeting.

No reaction.

Grant reached down and retrieved the glass. Walking to the bar, he placed it on the silver tray by the liquor. The decanter had been left open. Grant held the crystal toward the light of the fireplace and swirled the contents. Less than an inch remained.

"Is she okay?" Julie was standing in the doorway.

"No, she's not," Grant replied. "She's an alcoholic, and she's had enough to drink in the past few hours to pass out completely."

"Can you blame her? I mean, after what Brock said...such an asshole," she muttered.

The emotions of the past two days, combined with the frustration at having Eric cut off his conversation with the attorney and Mona passing out before he could confront her overwhelmed him. Grant snapped.

"Forgive me, but I'm having a hard time giving a shit about Brock's less-than-winning personality." He paced the room, voice growing louder. "I give less of a shit about what Brock thinks about Mona's ass, and I sure as hell don't care about Eric's progress tracking down Silas-fucking-Kane!"

Julie whipped her head around as if she had been slapped. "What did you just say?" she asked.

Grant was still ranting. "I agreed with you. Spot on. Brock is an asshole. World class!"

Julie stepped in front of Grant, blocking his pacing steps. "Keep it down, he'll hear you. What did you say about—"

"Oh, I already heard him, sweet-cheeks," a deep voice interrupted. Brock stood outside the door. His face was red. Purple veins bulged from his forehead and neck. "What I want to know," he continued as he stepped in the room, "is whether or not the spoiled brat here has the stones to repeat it." His fists were balled into tight hammers.

Grant's rational side knew this was ridiculous. He knew the testosterone buildup in Brock's system from the steroids was amplifying his already aggressive tendencies. He knew that Brock outweighed him by at least fifty pounds and that a fight—besides being ludicrous for two grown men—would more than likely result in Grant being sent to the hospital.

And yet, he didn't care. Rational thinking gave way to rage, and Grant responded. "I said you're an asshole. A living rectum. Anus Maximus. And I wish Mona had never met you. You. Asshole." Grant's clenched his own fists.

Brock stepped forward. "Buckle up, buttercup—"

"STOP IT!" Julie screamed. She stepped between the two men, looking from one to the other. "You're adults! Stop acting like a couple of teenagers measuring your dicks!"

The words broke through Grant's rage. Hearing the expression "measuring your dicks" coming from Julie's mouth somehow made him realize how ridiculous the whole scene was. He only hoped Brock would calm down.

Brock seemed to be considering Julie's remarks when she turned and faced Grant. "Now what did you say about Silas Kane?" she asked.

"What?"

"You said something about Silas Kane, what was it?" She sounded fearful. Terrified. Grant first thought it was the result of the near-fight between him and Brock, but that incident now seemed frivolous to her.

"Uh, I just said that I didn't care about Eric and Kane. I was angry." Grant didn't like the thought of disparaging his friend, regardless of circumstances, and he was embarrassed at how severely he had lost his cool.

Julie was shaking. "What about Silas Kane? He's in prison."

"He escaped yesterday," Grant replied, his eyebrows furrowed at Julie's reaction. "It's been all over the news. Eric is running the operation to recapture him. Julie, are you okay?" Grant moved toward her but she backed away, stepping toward the fireplace.

"Yeah, I saw that on the television in the gym," Brock interjected. "Said he killed a cop when he escaped. Snapped his neck." His earlier anger with Grant seemed to have subsided as this new series of events unfolded.

"Where do they think he is?" Julie asked to neither man in particular.

"Who knows?" Brock asked. "Probably hot-footing it to the border."

"No. He's not," Julie muttered. She had backed directly in front of the fireplace now but shivered despite the heat.

Grant moved toward her. "Eric called me earlier. He interrupted the call I was trying to make and mentioned something about Kane. Julie, why are you acting like this? New York is a long way from Still Pines. It's not that big of deal. We're completely safe out here."

"You don't understand," she said. "Please tell me exactly what Eric said."

She was right. Grant didn't understand. All he knew was that the woman he had fallen in love with was terrified, and he wanted to help. He wasn't going to lie this time. "What he said didn't make any sense. There was a lot of static on the line and then the call dropped."

"Tell me," she whispered.

"I couldn't make much of it out, but he said something about Kane going to Rhode Island. That's on the opposite side of the city, so you really don't have to—"

"No," Julie moaned as her knees buckled. "No, no, no..."

She slumped to the floor, her back hitting the screen of the fireplace before Grant could catch her. The screen bent inwards, perilously close to the leaping flames.

Grant kneeled and pulled her away from the fire. Brock moved around the couch to help, his resentment toward Grant apparently forgotten.

"Grab her other arm," Grant directed as the two of them led an oblivious Julie to the chair next to the couch where Mona continued her drunken slumber.

Grant saw Brock's palm brush over Julie's breast as they helped her sit up, but he said nothing. Grant knelt in front of her and gently shook her shoulders. "Julie," he urged.

She regained coherence, blue eyes wide and looking directly into Grant's worried face. "Kane!" she exclaimed. She glanced about the room, as if expecting the escaped killer to be standing in the lounge.

"Julie, it's okay. It's me," Grant soothed. "I'm here. Tell me what's happening here."

Julie reached forward and hugged Grant fiercely. He returned the embrace with gentle assurance. Brock rolled his eyes.

Julie pulled away, breaking the embrace as she spoke. "We've got to get out of here," she said. "We've got to get off the island."

"What are you talking about?" Grant asked. "The storm is terrible. We can't leave."

"No, Grant, you don't understand," Julie seemed on the verge of panic, her words stilted and forced. "Kane isn't going to Rhode Island, he's coming to *this* island. Here..." she trailed off.

"Are you on your period or something?" Brock asked. "Because that would explain a lot. This is some crazy-chick talk."

"What *are* you talking about?" Grant asked.

"He's coming to the island. And if we're still here, then we're all going to die." Her eyes welled with tears.

The nightmare of the hooded creature underneath the bridge flashed into Grant's mind. "Tell me everything," he said. The fireplace roared behind him, but he suppressed a shiver anyway.

CHAPTER 44
October 11
6:41 P.M.

ERIC'S CROWN VICTORIA crested the hill overlooking Still Pines Lake. A powerful gust of wind forced him to pull the steering wheel hard to the left to prevent the car from sliding off the road. The storm had progressed from menacing to terrifying. The rain fell in thick sheets buffeted by the fierce wind. Black clouds and rain sealed the heavens from whatever diminishing rays the setting sun may have offered.

As Eric eased his car around the downhill curves, the thought struck him. *It's worse because he's here. Silas Kane* is *the storm.*

The island came into sight, and Eric shook off the notion. Mostly. Trapped in the driver's seat for the past eternity, speed limited by the weather, his emotions had begun to get the best of him. The fear for his friend, the guilt for his partner and the rage at the escaped killer had merged into a kind of a sick terror that what had occurred in the city might now be happening at the island.

But Kane was just a man. Eric reminded himself of the fact for the thousandth time. It had become a sort of mantra, warding off the sense of evil. He was a killer, but he was just a man, and he could be stopped.

He was close. He accelerated and guided the vehicle around the final bend of the road. As the wipers completed a deluge-parting sweep, he saw the other automobile. It was parked in the middle of the road with no lights.

Unable to react in time, he hit his brakes harder than was practical in the pouring rain. His tires locked and the rear of the Crown Vic swung around in a hydroplane. The passenger side of his vehicle struck the rear of the Ford Explorer and came to a crunching halt. The air bag exploded from the steering wheel at the moment of impact, catching Eric on the chin and nose— like being clubbed in the face with a heavy pillow swung by a tennis pro—and slammed his head back against the seat.

It took him a moment to recover from the jolt. His jaw ached. His face was hot. He ran his fingers along his cheek. The friction from the airbag material had burned his skin. He opened the car door and almost fell out when the seatbelt released.

Torrents of rain struck him and the stinging drops cooled his face. He was dazed from the airbag's impact but found his feet and held the door for support as he stood.

A gust of cold wind helped to clear his head. He assessed the Explorer. The back window had been shattered by the impact. Looking through the open space, the vehicle appeared empty. There was another car parked in front of the Explorer. It was parked facing the other way. Through the dark and the pouring rain, Eric couldn't make out anything except its glaring headlights.

As he surveyed the area, he realized how disoriented the crash had made him. What he saw didn't make sense. The road was supposed to round the bend and lead into the covered bridge accessing the island, but Eric couldn't make out the structure in the dark. There was no covered bridge. Moreover, he didn't understand why there would be two cars parked in the middle of the small road. He walked around his vehicle toward the other cars to figure out what was going on when he noticed the body on the ground beside the driver's door of the Explorer.

Kane.

The thought pierced the hazy fog of Eric's mind. His senses snapped back, and he drew his revolver from his shoulder holster, pointing it at the figure lying face down on the drenched asphalt. Two steps and he realized it couldn't be Kane. The man on the ground was far too small. He approached faster, crouching and scanning his surroundings as he moved.

Kneeling by the prone figure, Eric grabbed the shoulder of the man while still pointing the gun into the darkness, wary of any movement beyond the glare of the headlights. Eric pulled his shoulder and the dead body of Freddy Bowen rolled over. Blood oozed from the wound in his chest. Eric realized the dark puddles surrounding Freddy consisted of more than pooled rain water.

"Oh Freddy," he said. Peering into the darkness, Eric could now discern the front vehicle was, in fact, Freddy's cruiser.

He must have been sent after Eric's call to Laura at the sheriff's office. He had parked in front of the bridge which forced Kane to stop in the middle of the road as well. Freddy would have had no idea what Kane looked like, and Eric couldn't even be certain Laura had heard that part of his message anyway. Freddy may have just been coming out to check on the Armstrongs.

Eric again scanned the area as he pieced together the assault. Kane stops. Freddy gets out of his car to see who it is. Walks to the driver's window. It rolls down. Kane extends the barrel of his gun against Freddy's chest and pulls the trigger. A point-blank shot.

Freddy never knew what hit him.

Eric removed his NYPD jacket and laid it over the man's face. Freddy had been good friends with his father. Leaving him in the rain didn't seem right, but he had no choice.

Silas Kane.

Eric stood and approached the cruiser. Gun leveled at the darkness beyond. Kane had gotten past him, but he couldn't be too far ahead.

He's just a man.

A massive display of lightning ripped through the blackness as Eric reached Freddy's vehicle. For a brief moment, the entire area could be seen with perfect clarity.

The bridge was gone.

The shattering sound of thunder marked the return of darkness as Eric blinked the water from his eyes.

How could the bridge be gone?

He moved past the vehicle and reached the edge of the road. From the closer vantage point, Eric could see the damage from the storm.

The lake river separating Armstrong Island from the mainland whipped past in a whitewater current. The bridge was decimated. The last vestige of the structure was a single beam spanning the length of the channel from the mainland road to the island. The beam looked solid. It was six inches wide and about the same height. Several clumps of the demolished structure clung to the beam from the rush of water a few feet below. Eric noticed a black cable running from beside the road down into the stream.

That explained the phone.

Another flash of lightning illuminated the scene and Eric could see the road on the other side of the raging water. Although there was no sign of him, Eric knew that Kane was on that road. He had crossed the beam and was making his way across the island. To the main house. To his friend.

He's just a man.

Eric holstered his revolver and took a tentative step toward the beam. Toward the water. The memories came unbidden. He couldn't stop them.

The ride to Ellis Island on the ferry. The four year old Eric so happy to be on a spring day adventure with his parents. Standing on the back of the boat. Peering through the railing at the dark green water churning behind the powerful propellers. His mother and father turning to look at the Manhattan skyline. The boy seeing a teenager sitting on the railing, talking to his girlfriend as casual as could be. Little four year old hands grasping the latticed steel and climbing up. Turning and sitting his bottom on the top rail. Yelling for his mommy to look at him. Placing both small hands onto the rail for support. One hand landing in a wet pile of bird droppings. Jerking the hand away in disgust and losing his balance. Hearing his mother scream. Falling backward, his father's lunging hand missing him by only an inch. Falling. Falling forever. Wondering if he would be chopped up in the propellers. Hitting the water hard. Air knocked from his lungs. The freezing liquid filling his nose, invading his sinuses and his mouth. The helplessness as the powerful force of the propellers slammed him deeper under water and away from the ferry. Darkness everywhere. Water surrounding him. Drowning a certainty in his four year old mind. Death.

Eric gasped as he fought the wave of panic. He focused on the remains of the bridge. He had lived. His father had jumped from the ferry after him. His mother, cool under any circumstance, had grabbed a life-ring and thrown it over the side. Together, they had saved him. But the incident had scarred him. He would never go near the water again.

Playing on the bridge with Grant as a child was the bravest thing Eric had ever done in his life. He never told his friend that fact, and he suspected Grant never knew the depths of courage from which Eric was forced to draw in order to scale the roof of the bridge. He had been terrified and had hated every minute of it. But he had done it. He had to prove to himself that he could stand at least that. He hadn't wanted to be a coward in front of his friend. And he knew—*he knew*—that if he ever got in trouble, Grant would be there to save him.

Now it was time to repay the favor.

The thin beam extended over the water. The only access to the island.

The only way to save his friend's life.

Eric steeled himself.

He extended one foot onto the beam. The sole of his shoe covered the surface of the board. No room for error. He started to move his back foot onto the board but found it frozen in place. Locked to the ground as if encased by concrete.

That foot was his anchor, his last hold on solid earth. He looked at the water flowing beneath him. Black and churning in the strong current.

Eric took a deep breath and extended his arms out like a tightrope walker. This time, the foot moved.

He stepped out onto the beam.

Two feet from the safety of the mainland, Eric paused. Rain swept onto him from above and soaked his body. He inhaled the cool wetness. Once. Twice.

He took another cautious step. Balance.

Another step.

Another.

Eric kept his knees bent as he made slow progress across the board. He wanted to avoid looking down, to keep his focus on the opposite shore, but he had to look at the beam for his foot placement, and looking at the beam meant looking at the unfocused rush of water below.

Eric walked. He was a fourth of the way across and approaching the first of the pilings from the wreckage of the bridge's structure. A board was sticking up from the side of the beam, still nailed in place. The board was in turn attached to another support which tethered a sizable portion of planks and debris floating in the current below.

He reached the section and stepped over the board. The broken tip of the wood scraped against his crotch, prompting a sudden intake of breath. Another inch and the maneuver would have been much more difficult.

He resisted the temptation to reach down and grab the board for balance or rest. There was too great a possibility it would break off. And there was also the uncomfortable prospect that he would not be able to let go if he allowed himself a moment's rest.

Eric continued his progress for several steps. Almost to the halfway point. A strong gust of wind blew across the water and buffeted him.

His arms pinwheeled as he fought to maintain his balance. He was overcorrecting.

He fixed his eyes on the beam. The black swirling river. He wanted to throw up. He had to piss. He just wanted off this damn board.

Eric's balance returned as the wind died down. He lowered his arms to his sides as he caught his breath. He had to stay calm. There were people on the other side who needed his help.

He inhaled. The cold air felt good. His head still ached from the earlier blow from the airbag, but his senses were intact.

Eric again extended his arms and took another step toward the island.

A burst of lightning ripped through the air and the deafening crackle of thunder was instantaneous.

His foot slipped from the beam. He didn't have time to pinwheel his arms. No time to correct at all. He fell forward. His right arm hit the beam, smacking his bicep, and he bent his elbow hoping to hold on. The pain was immense. Eric's feet swung into the river and his body weight was being dragged, held only by his right arm.

Fighting against panic, Eric used his free hand to grasp the beam from its underside and pulled himself toward the support. With strength born of desperation, he lifted his legs from the water and flung one foot across the top of the board.

The balance of his weight removed from his right arm, he changed his grip to permit a better hold. Finally, he managed to swing his body onto the top of the beam, his arms and legs wrapped around the wood as if it were his lover.

He rested his cheek against the beam. He could hear himself breathing. Rapid and shallow.

He closed his eyes and forced himself to calm down.

His breathing slowed.

He opened his eyes and raised his head, focusing his vision along the board to the island.

He was only halfway across.

CHAPTER 45
October 11
6:47 P.M.

GRANT CLUTCHED Julie's shoulders in an attempt to still her shaking. "Julie—" he began.

"Grant, I love you," she interrupted. "Please, let's just go."

The words took Grant by surprise. She was the first woman to say she loved him since his junior year girlfriend in high school. Despite everything, it felt right.

"I love you too," he said. He meant it. "But we're not going anywhere with the storm. Now tell me what you meant by Kane coming here."

Julie's head dropped. Without looking him in the eye, she spoke. "I'm so sorry, Grant. Please forgive me. I didn't want to lie, but I had to."

"Will you stop with the blathering and spit it out?" Brock interjected. "Just say it. Rip it off like a fucking Band-Aid."

Grant shot him a stern look. Brock didn't seem to notice.

"It's Kane. I—Grant, I lied to you. Last night, when we were on the porch together, I told you that my father died when I was young."

"I remember," Grant said.

"I also told you that my sister ran away and I never saw her again. That was a lie. I saw her again at my mother's funeral. Before Mom died, she hired a private detective to track my sister down, and the hospital was able to contact her."

"Okay, but why would you lie about something like that?"

"You don't understand, Grant. My sister...wasn't well. It turned out she had been living in New York since she ran away. She...did things for money. Things I couldn't believe."

"Hooker?" Brock interjected.

"Yes, Brock. She was a prostitute," Julie sighed. "But that wasn't the worst. She was involved with a guy. A very bad guy. I met him once. He...scared me. Worse than I've ever been scared in my life. But Jenna said that she loved him. That he was different than all the other guys."

"Jenna," Grant said, repeating the sister's name. "The man she was seeing was Silas Kane, wasn't it?"

Julie nodded. "After we reconnected, I started driving to the city once a week to visit her. I thought I could help. I told her about my job. How she didn't have to be a—a prostitute. How there were a thousand things she could do with her life that were better than that. But after I saw Kane...I couldn't go back. Abe noticed I was upset, and he asked me what the problem was. I couldn't keep anything a secret from him—"

"No shit," Brock interrupted.

"Knock it off, Brock," Grant said. "This is important."

Brock snorted derisively but didn't say anything else. They both waited for Julie to continue.

"Anyway, Abe already knew about my sister—I explained everything when I got back from Mom's funeral—but he had promised not to tell anyone. When I told him about Kane, Abe said he knew of him. He had heard a news report that Kane was a suspect in several murders, but the police weren't able to catch him. Abe told me if the police couldn't do it, he would find someone who could. He hired a guy, a bounty hunter to track him down."

"And he caught him, right?" Brock asked.

"Yeah, he did," Julie continued. "But when I went to see my sister again, after Kane was arrested, her place was abandoned. I haven't heard from her since. I wanted to talk to the police, but then I read that they suspected Kane had an accomplice for some of the crimes he was accused of. I'm sure it wasn't Jenna. It couldn't have been. She wouldn't be capable of something like that. But I didn't want to risk the police thinking she was involved..." Her thought trailed into silence.

"I understand what you're saying, Julie, but why do you think Kane is coming here?" Grant asked.

"Super, my new brilliant doctor boyfriend is stupid," Julie said as she wiped her eyes with the backs of her hands. "Grant, if Kane escaped, he could have found out that Abe hired the bounty hunter, and he wouldn't know that Abe's dead. That means he could want to come after him. And if your friend Eric interrupted a phone call to warn you that Kane was coming to an island, then you can bet this is the island. He's coming. Kane is coming."

"Bitch," Brock said softly. "You led a fucking killer to this island?"

Grant stood and faced him. "It's not her fault, Brock. Now we've got a problem here, and we need to figure out a way to deal with it."

"We should leave," Julie said.

"No shit," Brock responded.

"I agree. Storm or no storm," Grant said. "Let's get Mona and load into the car."

Julie stood from the chair. Though still disheveled, she looked more composed than she had moments earlier.

"Hang on," Brock said as he walked to the fireplace. "If we run into this Kane guy, I'm going to be prepared."

Brock reached above the mantle and lifted the shotgun from the supporting mounts. He cracked open the barrel.

"What do you think you're doing?" Grant asked.

"Sweet," Brock muttered. "The old son of a bitch kept this thing loaded."

"Brock, that gun has been hanging there for twenty years. The shells in it have got to be at least that old."

Brock slammed the barrel back in place with a loud snap. "Better than nothing, doc. You just might thank me."

CHAPTER 46
October 11
7:10 P.M.

ERIC CRASHED through the low hanging branches of the trees along the makeshift trail. The wet pine needles slapped against his face and arms. His gun bounced against his side as the shoulder holster kept rhythm with his pace.

Traversing the bridge had been the single most terrifying experience the young cop had ever survived, but he knew it was only the beginning tonight.

His eyes had adjusted better to the dark once he got away from the headlights on the mainland side of the decimated bridge. He could now see a short distance ahead as he ran, at least when there was a break in the tree cover. He had had no choice but to cut through the woods if he was going to catch up with Kane. The island's road twisted and curved back on itself several times as it made its way along the island's north side. Having no familiarity with the island, Kane would have to stick to the road if he hoped to find the Armstrong house.

Eric, on the other hand, faced no such limitations. He and Grant had spent countless hours exploring every inch of the island during their childhood. And though it had been years since the two friends had chased each other through the pines, Eric felt at home.

He had selected a direct route which would take him through the woods and intersect with the road near the entrance to the guest house, about a quarter mile from the main house. He would beat Kane to the intersection. Set up an ambush.

Eric refused to believe Kane could beat him to the main house. He wouldn't allow the notion into his mind. He would intercept Kane. Stop him on the road. Before Grant and his family were ever in danger.

As his feet pounded through the needle-covered mud, Eric's thoughts returned to Abraham Armstrong. Why had the old man hired the bounty hunter? Did he know about Eric being on the case? Was he concerned for his safety?

Eric could think of no other connection, but the idea just didn't feel *right*. Why would Abe not tell Eric about it? Was he trying to do a secret good deed just as Eric had seen Abe's grandson do so many times?

Eric's foot landed in an unseen depression. His ankle flashed in pain. He swore and kept running. Though his vision had adjusted to the night, the forest was growing darker as the hour grew later. Somewhere over the stratospheric blanket of the storm, the sun had set and the moon had no hope of penetrating the black clouds. With the exception of the two houses, the island had no lights. The surrounding woods were now in a darkness only those who have spent the night in the remote countryside could understand.

Eric ducked under a large branch as he ran but pulled his head up too soon. A sharp needle grazed his eye as the branch slapped past his ear. Tears filled the wounded eye and Eric's vision blurred.

He had to find the road soon. If his memory was accurate, it was only another few yards.

He slowed to a fast walk, rubbing his eye.

Movement. Through the trees.

Eric crouched and unholstered his revolver in one smooth motion. He leveled the gun, arms extended toward the source of the disturbance. Was it an animal, or Kane?

The movement was lost in the rain.

He straightened and walked another five steps, shoulders hunched, right eye blinking the tears away.

Movement again.

A glimpse of metal.

Eric steadied the gun and fired. Sparks burst at the point of impact and he heard a startled grunt through the rain.

Kane.

Eric fired twice more.

No more movement.

Eric raced forward, gun held at the ready. He burst from the trees onto the road, shoes slapping against the asphalt.

Nothing.

He glanced down. A pistol lay at his feet. He crouched and picked up the weapon, holding it close to his face. The chamber of the gun had been obliterated. When he had fired, he must have hit the gun in Kane's hand causing the shower of sparks.

He scanned the darkness. No movement. No sign of Kane.

Eric inspected the ground. It was too dark and wet to assess any traces of blood. He couldn't know if his second and third shots had found their target.

Just as Eric started to turn, the back of his head exploded in pain from a powerful blow. He lurched forward from his crouch, his chest and hands smacking against the cold asphalt.

Acting on instinct, Eric rolled to one side as Kane's enormous black boot stomped onto the space of road his neck had just occupied.

Eric's mind was blurry, but his pistol was still in his hand. He raised it toward the killer. Before he could squeeze the trigger, Kane kicked the weapon from his grip, the revolver clattering onto the wet pavement six feet away.

Eric rolled the opposite direction and jumped to his feet, head still spinning from the concussive blow.

It wasn't supposed to happen this way.

Kane stepped forward and Eric threw a quick jab, the blow connecting solidly with the giant's jaw. Kane pulled back. Eric had hurt him.

He's just a man. He can be hurt.

Eric reset his feet and cocked his fist. Kane was faster. Massive hands grabbed Eric and twisted his shoulders, leaving his leg extended away from his body as Kane raised his knee and pistoned his foot downward, the thick sole of his boot striking Eric's shin. The bone snapped.

Eric cried out and dropped his hands to clasp his broken leg. He realized his mistake just as Kane brought both his hands, fingers laced to create a single rock-hard hammer, against the back of Eric's head.

Eric fell to the asphalt. His jaw struck the pavement and slammed his teeth shut against his lower lip, splitting it. The eruption of agony in Eric's head prevented him from moving. He couldn't see through the pain. Didn't know where Kane was. He managed to roll onto his back.

He could taste the blood from his lip, salty and hot in contrast to the cold puddle of water the back of his head was resting in.

He could hear the rain as if it were in some other world.

Eric tried to move his arms and legs. Nothing was responding.

He felt a foot against his side through the blackness. He redoubled his efforts and succeeded in focusing his vision. Silas Kane standing over him, Eric's own gun leveled at his chest.

He tried to roll to one side. To kick against Kane's legs. But his body refused him, the pain in his head distorting any attempt to command his limbs.

Eric's mind raced in his helplessness.

It wasn't supposed to be like this.

"That was a good punch."

Eric could hear the voice through the haze. He wanted to say something. Wanted to do something.

He heard the clacking sound of the revolver's hammer locking into place.

No. He had to save Grant.

"But this is where it ends."

The deafening sound of the pistol filled his head. His body jumped at the impact of the bullet. A dull throb in his chest accompanying the cacophony of pain.

Another retort of the gun.

A third.

A click as the hammer slammed onto a round already fired.

A metallic clink as the gun fell to the pavement next to Eric's ear.

Through the closing darkness, Eric could hear Kane's boots thumping the asphalt as he continued to the house.

To his friend.

As blackness descended over his consciousness, Eric focused on one thing. He couldn't speak it. Could only think it.

Grant. Get out.

Eric's eyes closed. Darkness fell.

CHAPTER 47
October 11
7:15 P.M.

"**D**ID YOU HEAR *THAT*, PHIL?!" Loraine screamed. "I told you it was gunfire!" Her eyes were wide and her fists were clenched.

"I heard it, *Loraine*," Phil said. "And you may be right, but it doesn't make any sense. Who the hell would be shooting a gun out here?"

Loraine moved to the front window of the guest house and peeked through the curtains. "How should I know? Just do something."

Phil sighed from his seat in front of the fireplace. It was a loud sigh. He tipped the glass of scotch to his lips and emptied the remainder with a long swallow.

Loraine glanced away from the curtain. "Now, Phil!"

"Of course. I'll get right on it." Phil set the glass on the table and took his time getting up. He stretched. He didn't need to look at his wife to know she would be infuriated. He repressed a smirk as he walked to the front door and unlocked it.

"Wait a minute, what are you doing?" Loraine asked.

"I'm going to the car to get my gun," he responded over his shoulder as he opened the door. Phil had once spoken to a hedge fund manager who mentioned always keeping a gun in his vehicle. That men of means needed to be able to protect themselves. And the guy was really successful. Phil had purchased a pistol at a sporting goods store the following day.

He stepped onto the small portico and began walking through the rain to the Mercedes. The drops were heavy and stung as they pelted his scalp. After a dozen steps, Loraine was by his side.

"There is no way I'm staying by myself. What's the matter with you?" she said, looking to her right and left.

They reached the car and Phil opened the passenger door. He leaned in and released the glove compartment. A shiny .38 special with a short barrel rested on top of the vehicle manual and insurance information. He grabbed it and held the pistol up to show Loraine.

"Okay, I've got my gun. Are you happy?"

"No, I'm not happy," she responded with a shiver. "I'm cold and wet and I want out of here."

Phil stepped aside to allow his wife entry to the vehicle. She stopped before she sat down.

"Wait," she said. "The shots sounded like they came from the road."

Phil rolled his eyes. "Don't be stupid. You have no idea where the shots came from. It's raining and thundering. We can't be sure they were gunshots at all!" he yelled.

"They were gunshots!" she screamed back. "You heard them too. Someone's out here, and they're shooting at people!"

"Fine. We'll go to the main house, would that make you happy?"

Despite his patronizing tone, Phil was nervous. Gunfire sounded different than thunder. And whatever they heard did sound like a gun. He didn't care for the idea of staying alone in the guest house either. At least there was safety in numbers at the main house. Maybe it was a thief. Or maybe it was a gang thing (not likely in the middle of nowhere in upstate New York, but you just never knew). Regardless of who was responsible for the gunfire, it was better to be safe than sorry.

"Yes, that would make me happy. Let's go to the main house," Loraine said, sounding almost satisfied.

Phil turned to walk around the car to the driver's side.

"Wait!" Loraine yelled, stopping Phil in his tracks. "If the shots came from the road, they might be carjackers. If they find us in the Mercedes, they'll kill us and take the car."

"Are you serious?" Phil exclaimed, exasperated. "What makes you think there are *carjackers* out here?"

"I heard shots, Phil! *Somebody* is on the road with a gun, and I don't want to die!" she screamed back.

Phil sighed another loud sigh. She was hysterical. She was panicked. But maybe she was right. "Fine. Do you want to walk to the main house? In the middle of a damned hurricane?"

Loraine stared past him, at the pouring rain and darkness and the path that led to the main house. She seemed to be reconsidering her options. That was enough motivation for Phil to accept it.

"Great, let's go!" he said and began striding toward the path in the trees.

Loraine looked inside the Mercedes, checking the ignition. The bastard had taken the keys with him.

She grunted in frustration at Phil as he disappeared into the tree line. Not waiting for her. Not even looking back to see if she was coming.

Loraine stepped out of the car and slammed the door with all the force she could muster. Part of her hoped the window of his precious Mercedes would implode at the force, but it held firm.

The rain soaked through her sweater as she marched toward the figure of her husband fading into the darkness of the trees. He was going to pay for this.

CHAPTER 48
October 11
7:16 P.M.

"**D**ID YOU HEAR THAT?" Brock asked as he stared out the open garage. The floodlights surrounding the house illuminated an area about thirty yards around the structure, but there was only blackness beyond that.

Grant checked to make certain Mona's unconscious body was completely inside the car and closed the back door. "Yeah," he said. "Sounded like gunfire."

"We need to get out of here," Julie whispered into Grant's ear as she shifted her weight from one foot to another, like a child needing to pee.

"Come on, Brock," Grant agreed. "Let's get moving."

Brock remained at the entrance of the garage, the old shotgun clasped in both hands.

"Hang on a second," he said.

He appeared to be deep in thought. Grant hoped he didn't hurt himself from the strain.

Brock finally spoke. "If those shots came from the road, then that means Kane is here."

"Likely," Grant nodded, "but if we're hearing shots, then it's possible that Eric and the police already confronted him."

"I'm not gonna bet my life on *possible*, doc. One way or another, we know Kane is on that road. If we get in this car and drive down that road, then it's more than possible that we'll run into him. Sounds like a trap to me."

"What if he's right, Grant?" Julie murmured.

Brock seemed to take the comment as a sign of encouragement. "Damn right I'm right. Kane set a trap for us. Those first shots were probably Phil and Loraine getting whacked."

The image was powerful and stunned Grant for a moment. "No...if we think the shots were from the road and not the guest house, then that doesn't make sense." Grant didn't want to consider the alternative, but it remained a valid possibility.

"No," Grant repeated. "No, Phil and Loraine wouldn't be on the road. Why would they try to leave the island? The phones are down. There's no way they could know about Kane. But you're right. They could be in danger. We need to get them out, too."

Brock looked at Grant with wide eyes. "Are you serious? Fuck Phil and Loraine! It's too late for them anyway. We've got to focus on ourselves, and I'm telling you, there is no way I'm getting out on the road in that moving target." He pointed the shotgun at the car to emphasize his point.

Grant couldn't believe his ears. "Look, we've got to warn them somehow. The phones are down so we don't have a whole lot of options here."

Julie moved next to Grant and took his arm. She peered out of the garage into the blackness of the storm.

Grant turned toward her. "I have to warn them, Julie. You understand that."

"No, Grant. Don't leave. Please don't leave me here," she said.

"I'm sorry, Julie. They're my family. I have to help."

"Take me with you." It wasn't a question.

Grant nodded and turned to Brock. "Okay. You stay here. Julie and I are going to the guest house. We'll cut through the woods on foot. I know the way."

"Screw that, doc. Kane's after your girl, and he'll come *here* trying to find her. I don't plan on ending up dead because of some skirt. I'm going to the guest house, too."

Grant sighed. "No, somebody needs to stay here with Mona to protect her in case Kane does show up."

"I disagree," Brock said. He stood in front of the car then squatted so his eyes were level with the windshield. "She's laying down in the backseat. You can't even tell she's in there. She's probably safer than all of us."

Really, Grant thought, why don't you offer to lay down in the back seat with her? But he held his tongue if for no other reason than Brock was probably right.

"Fine," Grant said. "Let's get moving."

"All right. And if we do run into big-bad-Kane," Brock's eyes narrowed as he caressed the shotgun, "This baby better work."

CHAPTER 49
October 11
7:26 P.M.

GRANT MOVED through the pines at a quick pace with Julie and Brock right behind him. He had been away from the island for a long time, but Grant knew this trail like the back of his hand. The night was dark and the rain further dimmed their vision. Once the glow of the main house's flood lights was behind them, the group had to rely entirely on Grant's sense of direction.

Julie kept pace behind Grant, sometimes so close that her toes would step onto the back of his heel, but Grant said nothing. He would just adjust his shoe with a hop-step and continue. Grant could tell Julie was scared. Terrified. He didn't blame her, and it somehow intensified his feelings for her. Protective instinct drove him now. He hadn't even known her a week ago, but he knew he would defend her, with his life, if it came to that. *Nobility or stupidity?* Grant wondered. He hoped the former.

A small branch went unnoticed and grazed Grant's cheek as he passed. It cut a fresh trail through the water droplets clinging to his face but failed to do more than scratch him. Fortunately, the trees seemed to be blocking the worst of the driving storm. Water still poured in from the pine canopy above, but the drops didn't sting from the driving wind as they did in the open.

A muffled grunt came from behind Julie, and Grant knew that Brock had encountered the same branch. He smiled. Brock's presence concerned Grant. He didn't like the notion of Brock carrying a shotgun. He had seen too much of the man's erratic swings in behavior to trust him with a weapon. No matter what Brock chose to believe, performance enhancing drugs played havoc with the testosterone levels if used long enough. If a guy was already a bit unstable, it wouldn't take much to push him over the edge, and Brock wasn't the picture of stability to begin with.

The thought stopped Grant in his tracks. Julie bumped into him from behind.

The steroids.

Grant's mind flashed back to the gym. Brock guiding the needle into his vein like a pro. And Mona? Knowing she picked up the mail at the post office. Grant's letters that had never reached his grandfather. It didn't seem possible. Not Mona.

But Brock. The needle.

"What the—" Brock exclaimed as he bumped into Julie in the dark, knocking her forward a second time into Grant.

Following Brock's exclamation, Grant heard another sound in front of them. In the trees. He saw movement.

It all happened in an instant.

Brock stepped to the side of the path, leveled the shotgun at the disturbance and fired both barrels even as Grant screamed for him to wait.

Two flashes in the dark were accompanied by the cracks of returning gunfire.

Grant dove to the ground, pulling Julie with him and shielding her body with his own. He saw Brock fall backwards.

The screaming continued even as the noise of the gunfire diminished, echoing off the surrounding pines. Grant realized it was him. He closed his mouth.

He raised his head and scanned the area. Pine needles were stuck to his cheek. Brock's legs were twitching.

Phil stood on the trail, ten yards in front of Grant, his pistol still pointed their direction. His eyes were wide. His mouth agape.

Grant looked past Phil and could make out the bare soles of Loraine's feet. The blast from Brock's shotgun had knocked her out of her shoes.

Julie remained pressed against the ground, her hands covering the back of her head.

"Phil," Grant spoke softly.

Phil's head jerked at the sound. His eyes narrowed at Grant. His mouth still hung open. His head tilted as he looked at Brock's body, then turned to his wife, lying on her back behind him.

Phil knelt and put his hand on Loraine's shoulder, then pulled his hand away as if she was hot to the touch.

He turned back to Grant. The look on his face suggested comprehension. And horror.

"Phil," Grant started again as he got to his feet.

"No," Phil whispered. "No!" He turned and bolted back into the night toward the guest house.

"Phil, wait!" Grant called after his uncle, but he had already faded into the darkness.

Julie sat up as Grant moved to Brock and knelt, checking for a pulse. He was no longer twitching. Blood was seeping from his stomach and—much worse—from his chest. Grant assumed the worst and as he pressed his fingers against Brock's neck. His assumption proved correct.

Grant stood and ran to Loraine. Her eyes were open and her chest was a bloody cavity. He dropped to his knees but didn't check her pulse, only used his fingertips to close her eyes.

He felt dizzy.

"What the hell?" he uttered and fell backward onto his ass, his legs in front of him.

Julie rushed to his side and put her arms around him. She gasped when she glimpsed Loraine.

"Oh, Grant," she whispered as they held each other in the rain.

A swath of lightning swept through the sky and a deafening crash of thunder followed. The noise pulled Grant back to his senses and seemed to do the same for Julie.

Together, they stood, not letting each other go.

"We've got to get back to the house," Grant said.

Somewhere in the storm, Silas Kane still walked.

CHAPTER 50
October 11
7:39 P.M.

G RANT AND JULIE maintained a quick pace on their return trip, tempting fate at slipping on the wet ground. When the glow from the floodlights of the main house came into view through the trees, the pair broke into a full-fledged sprint.

They ran into the garage and spun to face the storm outside, peering into the darkness as if expecting a fanged monster to be in hot pursuit. Grant's thoughts flashed to his dream of the hooded creature beneath the bridge, and he realized he very much *was* expecting a monster. He wondered where Eric was, or the rest of the damned police force for that matter.

He looked at Julie. She was leaning forward, hands resting on her knees as she caught her breath, staring into the night.

Grant was trying to come to grips with what had happened in the woods. Brock and Loraine. Dead. Killed while the maniac they were fleeing was nowhere in sight.

Grant turned and walked to the car, opening the back door to reveal Mona's still unconscious body. If they survived the night, her world was never going to be the same. Her husband dead. Shot by her own brother.

Maybe that wasn't so bad. The first part, at least.

Grant chastised himself for the thought. Brock was an ass, but he didn't deserve to die. And Grant was a doctor. He considered life sacred. And yet, the image of Brock with the needle in the gym earlier that day plagued him. There was a strong possibility Brock was responsible for the murder of his grandfather. Now, he might never know.

Brock may not have deserved to die but Grant wasn't planning to go into mourning.

Mona shifted in the backseat and moaned. Grant shook his head and banished thoughts of Brock for the moment.

"What are you doing?" Julie asked.

"I'm getting Mona inside. She's coming with us," Grant replied, feeling guilty for ever allowing himself to be talked into leaving her in the car. Too many people had died this night, he was going to protect Julie and Mona no matter what.

Brock had carried his wife out to the car, but Grant now had no options except to accomplish the task of moving her back into the house on his own.

He reached into the back seat and maneuvered his arms around his aunt, pulling her upright. He adjusted her body so that her arm was around his shoulders and lifted her out of the car. The pressure sent waves of pain through Grant's tender wrist, but he maintained his grip.

Julie opened the door leading to the kitchen, still looking over her shoulder into the darkness outside as Grant walked through the entryway with Mona cradled in his arms. Julie followed him into the house, closing the door behind her and locking it.

"What now?" she asked.

"We go to the study," Grant replied as he walked that direction. "No windows and we can slide the desk in front of the door. No one will be able to get in."

Julie skipped in front of him as they proceeded down the hall to the study. She opened the door and held it for Grant to go through before closing and leaning against it from the inside.

Grant walked behind the teak desk and gently lay Mona on the floor. He stood and assessed the heavy wooden beast. Placing one hand on each side, he shoved with all his might.

White hot tendrils of pain engulfed his right arm as the sprain in his wrist erupted in agony. He released his grip and clutched his wrist against his stomach.

"Shit!" he exclaimed. The desk hadn't moved an inch.

"Let me help," Julie said as she moved over to Grant, placing both hands on the desk next to him.

"Don't bother," Grant sighed. "That thing must weigh four or five hundred pounds. Even both of us together wouldn't be able to move it. Damned old world craftsmanship."

He left the desk and snatched one of the chairs from along the wall using his uninjured hand. He wedged it beneath the doorknob, leaving a solid angle for the legs of the chair to dig into the carpet.

"It'll have to do," Grant said as he examined his handiwork.

"Will it be enough?" Julie asked, staring at the chair with suspicion in her eyes.

Grant eased himself onto the floor beside the desk, keeping the door in plain view. "Hopefully, we won't have to find out. Eric should be here soon."

Julie sat on the carpeting opposite Grant. "I hope you're right."

The two sat in silence. The storm outside could still be heard through the thick paneling of the walls. After several minutes, Julie broke her gaze from the door and turned to Grant.

"I'm scared," she said.

"Same here," Grant agreed. "But it's going to be okay. We're going to get through this. I promise." He tried to think whether he'd ever offered a more empty assurance, but he had to believe it, and he wanted Julie to believe it, too. All he wanted was to protect her. To make all of this go away.

"I know it's probably wrong to think this after what happened out there, but I wish we still had a gun," Julie said as her eyes returned to the door.

Grant sat on the floor in silence. His mind was racing. A gun. His grandfather hadn't been much of a sportsman. To Grant's knowledge, he had never even been hunting. The shotgun above the mantle had been a gift from a business associate, and to Grant's recollection, had never been fired before this night.

Now, Grant wished Abraham Armstrong had been an avid hunter and had kept a whole arsenal of weapons in the house.

Hell, he would be happy with a simple pistol.

A thought hit him with ferocious clarity. Why didn't he think of it before? Abraham wasn't the only Armstrong to have lived in this house.

"I've got to go," he told Julie as he got to his feet.

"What?" she asked. "What do you mean, you've got to go?"

"I know where I can get a gun," he said. "You stay here with Mona. It's the safest place in the house. When you close the door behind me, lock that chair back in place."

Julie leapt to her feet in front of him. "No-no-no. Please don't leave me here."

Grant put his hands on her shoulders and kissed her. "Only for a minute. I'll be right back," he said. "I promise."

He pulled the chair away from the door, opened it, and stepped into the hall.

CHAPTER 51
October 11
7:41 P.M.

PHIL DASHED through the woods toward the guest house. Branches slapped at his chest and face. His foot encountered a smooth flat rock and jerked forward on the slippery surface. His knee straightened, his momentum forcing his bodyweight onto the hyperextended leg.

He fell sideways, his knee aflame in agony. He thrust his hand out to break his fall, the pistol still tight in his grip. His wrist bent backward when the gun struck the earth. Phil landed on his side, his wrist and knee screaming in pain.

He held the revolver close to his face, peering at it through the darkness like it was a mystery object.

The sight of it sickened him.

Loraine. Dead.

Brock. Killed by the gun he was holding.

Killed by him. He was a murderer.

Phil regarded the pistol as if it were a tarantula in his hand. He hurled the gun into the trees in disgust. The revolver bounced once and was lost in the undergrowth.

He got to his feet.

He had to keep running. He wasn't sure why. His thoughts were no longer coherent. He was vaguely aware that he was acting out of panic. Shock.

So much had happened so fast. But it wasn't his fault. That much he was sure of.

He said it out loud. "Not my fault."

He limped at a fast pace toward the safety of the guest house. If they had only stayed in the house, none of this would have happened. But *Loraine* wanted to go to the main house.

"Not my fault."

Loraine wanted to walk through the woods.

"Not my fault."

And killing Brock...it was self-defense. Brock fired the first shot. Brock killed Loraine.

"Not my fault."

Loraine was dead. Murdered. He didn't feel real grief. Not now. Maybe later. Definitely if he was confronted with a murder trial. His wife had been killed right in front of him. He pulled the trigger in self-defense. He had no choice.

"Right...not my fault."

The lights of the guest house were ahead. Phil quickened his pace, even as each step brought a fresh wave of pain through his sprained knee.

He was almost safe.

As he approached, he could make out a large man standing by the front door of the house, looking the structure up and down.

His thoughts were jumbled. Why was the man here? Didn't matter. Phil could use him. Relief washed over him.

He called to the figure standing in the rain, "Hey, hey!"

The man turned as Phil broke through the trees and onto the driveway, his body hunched from the agony in his leg as he ran.

"Hey," he said as he approached the figure. "You've got to help me. There's been an accident. It wasn't my fault."

He slowed his pace. The man was wearing a black jacket. He was huge. Seven feet? The lights of the house were behind him. Phil couldn't make out his face in the shadows, but he thought he saw the white teeth of a smile.

"Of course, I'll help," the man said in a deep voice. "Why don't you tell me what happened?"

The tone of the man's voice stopped Phil in his tracks. A cat offering to assist a field mouse. It felt wrong, but still...Loraine. Brock. He needed this man to trust him. To perhaps back him up later.

"I—I was going to the main house. *Loraine* and I were going. And there was a gunshot—"

"Yes, I thought I heard gunfire," the man's voice was soothing.

"Loraine was shot. And Brock. They're both dead. But it wasn't my fault." Phil's mind raced. He had to convince this stranger of his innocence. It was imperative.

"Someone yelled. It was Grant. It startled me. And Brock shot first. It wasn't my fault. Grant shouldn't have yelled." Phil hadn't planned on blaming his nephew, but once it sprung from his lips, it made sense to go with it. Everything would click into place.

"I fired in self-defense," he said. "I never would have shot if Grant hadn't yelled and Brock hadn't fired his gun."

Spin it just right.

"I understand," the stranger's gravelly voice assuaged. "Do you still have the gun? Show it to me."

"No. No, I threw it away."

"That's a shame."

Was it working? The stranger seemed to be on his side.

"You see that it wasn't my fault, right?"

"Obviously. Grant shouldn't have yelled. Where is Grant now?"

Phil just had to stay on his toes. Make it happen. Work the angle.

"Down the trail toward the main house," he said, pointing toward the trees.

"Got it. Is Abraham Armstrong at the main house?"

The question halted Phil's racing thoughts. It made no sense. Abraham Armstrong? Why would the stranger ask about his father? The query led to another series of questions, each returning Phil closer to a rational state of mind. Who was the man he was speaking to, anyway? Why was he here? What on earth did his father have to do with anything?

He took a step back as he stared up at the giant's darkened face, trying to make out any of his features through the blackness of the storm.

"You didn't answer my question," the man said.

"Who are you?" Phil asked, retreating another step from the man in black.

"Who are *you*?" the stranger enquired in response.

"Phil Armstrong," he responded, unable to imagine doing otherwise.

"You're Abraham Armstrong's son?" the stranger asked, taking a step forward, closing the distance between them.

Phil nodded.

"And where is your father?"

Phil fought to form the words. "He—he's dead. He died three days ago," he stammered. He wanted to turn and run—race back to the main house—but the pain in his knee made that unrealistic. His only option was to answer the stranger's questions and hope to please him. Then maybe he would leave him alone.

He wished he hadn't thrown the gun away.

"That's too bad about your father. Really. One more question, Phil," the man asked, continuing to advance. "Who's Grant?"

An easy question. Phil was relieved. "My nephew."

"Oh," the man replied. "Abraham's grandson, then?"

Phil nodded. He just wanted this night to end.

"Then that'll have to do," the stranger's deep voice said.

Splintering fingers of lightning erupted into the clouds overhead, and for a moment, the entire island was awash in brilliant white light.

The face which Phil had been trying so hard to make out was bathed in ghostly illumination. The man was indeed smiling, his eyes narrowed to feral slits.

He was going to kill him.

The thought barreled through Phil's consciousness with certainty. The stranger was going to kill him.

Sprained knee or no sprained knee, Phil decided to make a run for it. He spun and launched himself toward the trees. He had taken two steps when he felt his shirt tighten around him as powerful fingers grabbed the material from behind. Phil was suddenly airborne, his feet in front of him as he was propelled backwards into the marble chest of the giant behind him.

Phil saw the stranger's huge palm pass in front of his face and grip the side of his head. He felt the other hand find a similar position on the opposite side of his skull. Before he had the chance to scream, a tremendous force jerked his head to the right.

Phil heard a loud crack and realized he was looking at the man's chest instead of the tree line. But that was impossible.

The man released his grip and stepped to the side. Phil could see the guest house. He dropped to his knees. It was the wrong way. His knees were wrong.

Darkness encroached as he fell to the wet earth. It was cool against his cheek. The house lights grew dim then were gone.

He heard the footsteps of the stranger walking toward the trees.

CHAPTER 52
October 11
7:50 P.M.

GRANT RACED up the stairs. Not bothering to turn on the lights, he jogged down the dark hallway. He passed the entrance to Julie's room and his own, coming to a stop at the closed door of his father's old room.

He opened the door, reached into the darkness, flipped the switch on the wall, and stepped into Jack Armstrong's former quarters.

Grant glanced around the room for the second time since he'd been home, paying closer attention to detail this night. The space was sparsely furnished, just as it had been when its occupant was still alive. Only a bed, a dresser and the roll top desk. Grant's father had always been something of a minimalist.

He walked to the desk and pulled the chair back. Unlike the time his father lived here, the surface of the desk was a mess. The only items on it which were familiar were the antique lamp and the wood-framed picture of the Armstrong boys. Grant, Jack and Abraham. Three generations. The same picture that rested beside Grant's bed.

Grant shuffled the papers scattered across the desk. Basic anatomy sheets. A clinical nutrition study guide. A course assessment with "Julie Russell" printed at the top. She had made a B. Grant was glad the room was being used. Especially by her. Besides, this desk was about to save their lives.

He knelt and pulled on the bottom desk drawer. It didn't budge. Locked.

Grant opened the top drawer, hoping what he sought would still be there. The silver dish was in the drawer, as it had always been. A few paperclips, some old coins and the small gold key. Not exactly Pentagon-level security, but just what he needed. He breathed a sigh of relief.

"Thanks, Dad," Grant whispered as he snatched the key and slid it into the lock in the bottom drawer. It turned easily.

Grant knelt and opened the drawer. It rolled out smoothly, still gliding perfectly on its wooden runners. A set of old insurance papers rested on top.

He removed the papers, and there it was. The polished wooden box containing the gun. General George Patton's revolver purchased by Jack Armstrong at a charity auction so many years ago. Locked away in the drawer for so long, never leaving the box. It was going to now.

Grant removed the box from the drawer, placed it on top of the desk and flipped open the lid.

He cocked his head. Confused. The pistol should have been sitting in the cloth-lined confines of the handcrafted box. Instead, there was a stack of papers bound by a large red ribbon,

No. Not papers.

Envelopes. Blue envelopes.

Puzzle pieces assembled in Grant's mind. Everything from the past thirty-six hours fell into place.

No.

He could see it now. All of it. He felt as if he had been slugged in the stomach with a sledge hammer.

Reaching into the box, Grant removed the bundle of blue envelopes, the red ribbon falling away as he began to flip through them. Six months of correspondence to his grandfather rested in his hands. Six months of Grant's life, never seen by the eyes of the intended recipient.

Every envelope was open.

"Oh Grant," the words came from the doorway behind him. Her voice was soft. Sad.

Grant didn't turn around, his back remained to the door and the woman who stood there. His eyes left the envelopes and turned to the picture of his grandfather, his father and himself. His mind flashed to the other picture he had noted the previous day. The one on Julie's nightstand.

His head pounded as the world came down around him.

"Why did you have to come up here, Grant? Why?"

He still did not turn around. Tears welled in his eyes as he asked a simple question, the only question that really mattered.

"When did Julie die?" His voice sounded funny to him. Like someone else was speaking.

The woman in the doorway drew in a deep breath. When she spoke, her tone was one of resignation. "Back in March. It was a Thursday."

Grant nodded. There was a lump in his throat. His father and grandfather stared back at him from the photograph. The other picture in Grant's mind. The one of the somber family, with two blonde-haired girls who looked so very much alike...

"How?" he asked softly.

"I didn't kill her. You have to believe that. *So much* of what I told you earlier is true. About my family. My father was a bad man. A rapist. He deserved to die."

The statement carried venom.

"But he didn't commit suicide, did he?" Grant made the connection easily. Everything was, after all, becoming perfectly clear.

"No. I shot the bastard. And that's when I ran away. He deserved to die, the fucking prick..." The words trailed into silence for several moments. "But what I said about my mother was true. She did hire a private detective to find me. But she was already in 'the facility', and I didn't feel the need to see her again. I was making a living, doing fine for myself—"

"You were a hooker," Grant said with a matter-of-fact tone, his eyes still on the desk.

"Yeah, I was, Grant. I was a hooker. Jenna the hooker."

Jenna. Her name is Jenna.

"But let me tell you something. I was doing it on *my* terms. No pimp. No lousy *man* making decisions or telling me what to do!" She stopped and took a deep breath.

"I'm sorry, Grant. It's just that sometimes I get upset. Anyway, the hospital contacted me, like I said, for my mother's funeral. I went. I'm not sure why. But Julie saw me. She went all sweet-sister ballistic on me. She wanted to become the best of friends after that. She started to come see me in the city. Every week. Tell me all about what she was doing out here, on the Island of Make Believe. She told me about the trees. The lake. She told me about reading letters out loud to Abe, letters from his grandson. She told me about the physical therapy. She even tried to teach me the nursing stuff. Give me a head-start to go back to school. Make me just like her since she was so perfect. But she wasn't perfect. She was clueless."

"So that's how you were able to pull it off. Granddad's physical therapy would have been simple. He wasn't on any medication and didn't have any serious problems, nothing that would require significant medical training," Grant was speaking almost to himself as he filled in that part of the story.

"Right, all I needed to do was help him exercise his hip. Julie had shown me how. It wasn't rocket science," the woman paused. "Anyway, I had started seeing this guy, Silas."

The hair on the back of Grant's neck stood as she mentioned the monster's first name so casually.

"We had some fun," she continued. "But then one day Silas and I knocked over this Korean convenience store. I drove the car. Silas killed the guy. He didn't tell me he was going to kill him ahead of time. We got back to my place, and Silas said he wanted to grab more booze.

He liked to get wasted after a big day like that. He was pretty far gone already, so I told him I'd go out for the liquor. When I got back from the store, I saw Julie's car parked in front of my apartment. It was Thursday. When I went inside..." There was a long pause. "Julie was on the floor. She was dead. Silas was gone. I guess he thought she was me. Lucky for me. Not so much for her."

A tear rolled down Grant's cheek. He had fallen in love with a woman who didn't exist.

"I got scared," the woman at the door said. "So I ran. I didn't go back to the apartment for a long time. Hours. Anyway, once I calmed down enough to figure out what was what, I went back. Opportunity doesn't knock twice, you know? I couldn't let this go to waste. I mean, we were sisters. She wouldn't have wanted me to waste my life in the city when there was this...place. This island. And a bazillion dollars and a lonely old man. This is what she would have wanted."

"Her body?" Grant asked, uncertain he wanted to hear the answer.

"I'm not a monster, Grant. But I couldn't let anyone find the body. They would have identified her fingerprints and that would have royally fucked up the rest of my plan. So I put her where I thought she would be happiest. I weighted her down and laid her to rest right here in the lake. I did it right. I said a prayer and everything."

Grant felt sick. The vivid image from his second dream filled his mind. Julie taking his grandfather's place, chained and drowning in the depths off the shore by the big oak tree.

"So I came out here. Your grandfather's eyes were terrible and he was half-deaf anyway so I doubted he could tell a difference. When he asked me why I was acting strange, I told him about Silas Kane and my 'sister'. That worked out better than I expected. After all, I didn't like the thought of Kane running loose. It only took a little prodding to get Abe to bypass the police and hire a bounty hunter. He turned out to be really cooperative after spending some time with the new Julie."

The words hit home with a vengeance. "So you were sleeping with him."

"Not at first," she said. "He wouldn't even think of such a thing. It took a long time and a lot of subtle encouragement to get him interested. Shit, you've never seen such a goody-two-shoes."

Grant looked at the picture on the desk. Three generations of Armstrong men. She had no idea.

"And of course, your family didn't help. I can't tell you how much I hate your fucking family, Grant. Ugh. I was so glad when you told me that you hated them too."

Grant's eyebrows furrowed at the remark, but he kept his back to the door, unable to face the woman speaking.

"But once I got rid of them, once Abe finally told them to leave us alone, things became easier. The old man started loosening up a little. Started enjoying the special massages I was giving him."

Special massages were not an image Grant wanted to picture. His mind flashed to the wince-inducing "not-special" massage she had given him earlier. Not the technique of a legitimate physical therapist. Why didn't he see it before?

"I would swim topless when Abe thought I didn't know he was there. Eventually, he gave in. He is, after all, a man. And men are all interested in just one thing. Learned that from my father. My *father*. That's why you can't let them get to you. That's why you've got to be the one in control. I was in control with Abe. He thought I loved him." She paused. "Okay, I know he was your grandfather so you probably don't want to hear this, but can I tell you how messed up it was trying to do it with a fucking octogenarian? He couldn't get it up, Grant, so he liked to watch me. I used to take showers in his bathroom so he could sit in his wheelchair and watch me lather up. Do you know how disgusting that is?"

Grant's sadness burned away into a growing anger. The memory of the raspberry bath gel and shower pouf from his grandfather's shower seared his consciousness. Why couldn't he see it before?

"I bet it was disgusting. I feel for you. The trauma you endured," he said through clenched teeth. "But it sounds like you got what you needed. The will was changed."

"It wasn't just changing the will, Grant. Abe and I had a long discussion about what he should do. He really seemed to value my opinion. After all, I was the only one who cared about him. And I was his wittle tushy muffin. He transferred all his assets into a living trust with me as the sole beneficiary. No time wasted in probate that way. His attorney was against the idea, but Abe was of sound mind. You should have heard your grandfather lay into him. It was something else. Anyway, my plan was for Abe to die, and I could transfer the funds to an offshore bank account and be in Bermuda before your relatives could do anything about it."

"Impressive. You know a lot about finance for a prostitute," he said.

"Just because I was a hooker doesn't mean I'm an idiot, Grant," she scolded him. "I had to do something while I pretended to be carrying on goody-Julie's pursuit of her degree. I really did go to the library twice a week, but I wasn't studying nursing. There are a lot of very informative resources on the subject of wealth management, Grant. You just need to know where to look and take a patient approach."

"Speaking of patience. Why kill him? Granddad was an old man. Why not let him live? Wait it out?" Grant asked.

"Because I'm patient but I'm not fucking Job," she spat back before stopping herself. "I'm sorry, Grant. I didn't mean that. It's just that— well, after Abe kicked them out, Phil threatened to hire a detective to dig up information on me. That was too much of a risk. When Abe invited everyone to the house to try to make peace, I decided not to make a fuss. He was lonely and he wanted to get everything off his chest. He thought if he told them the truth, told them that the money was ruining their lives so he had removed the possibility of an inheritance, they would understand. He thought they would accept it and forget the money and learn to be a family. Part of me would have *loved* to have seen the reaction of your aunts and uncles when they got that news—that would have been something else—but I couldn't let it happen. It was too risky. Phil would have hired the detective. So I had to do something. And like I said, opportunity only knocks once. The timing was perfect."

"So you killed him. You used him and you killed him. And then you used me."

"No," her voice sounded hurt. "That's not it at all. Don't you see, Grant? I've spent my entire life hating men. All men. I thought they were all alike. Even Abe was nice at first, until a little prompting proved he was just like all the rest. But when I started reading your letters out loud to Abe—just like Julie told me she used to do—I couldn't believe them. You were so sweet. And the stories you told. You were helping people and getting nothing in return. And you seemed to actually be happy doing it. You're different, somehow you're different from all the others...I love you, Grant."

He couldn't believe his ears. For the first time, Grant turned to face Jenna Russell. She was standing just inside the door with her hands behind her back, her posture that of a shy schoolgirl.

"You what?" he asked incredulously.

"I love you, Grant. Truly, madly, deeply. I want you to come away with me. Jenna is my past. I'm Julie now, and I'm rich. Really rich. We can run away and move to an island or a beach, just like we talked about this afternoon. And we'll never have to worry about the rest of your family again." Her voice was sweet, her face smiling. She was utterly insane.

"And the fact that so many people have died here tonight? What about Mona? What about Kane?" It was the first time he'd thought about the killer since he discovered the envelopes.

"Don't worry about Mona. She's still downstairs. She's asleep. But she's just as bad as the rest of them, Grant. We don't need her. She's a loose end. We can make it completely painless. No one will ever know. You're a doctor, I'm sure you know how to do stuff like that."

Grant could not believe his ears.

"As for Kane," she continued, "our little walk in the woods gave me time to calm down and think. If your friend really thought Kane was coming here, then half the state's police force is stationed somewhere outside on the road to meet him. Those gunshots we heard earlier were probably Silas Kane's last stand, you know? And if not, then I've got this just in case." She brought her hands from behind her back, holding General Patton's .357 revolver purchased by Grant's father so long ago. "I started keeping this under my mattress as soon as I found it. A girl can't be too careful, you know."

Grant remained in place, standing at the desk. Torrential rain battered the window. He was stunned.

"Jenna, I—" he began.

"No, Grant. Call me Julie," she interrupted. "I like it when you call me Julie."

The only thing Grant could think about was his grandfather. An old man, lying in his bed, blindly trusting his nurse, his lover, as she inserted a needle into his arm.

"*Jenna*," he said in a stronger voice. "I've never hated anyone in my life as much as I hate you right now."

From the expression on Jenna's face, it appeared Grant had just slapped her. "You don't mean that," she said quietly, her voice breaking.

"You turned my grandfather against his own family. You lied to him. You took everything he had."

"You don't mean that, Grant," she repeated forcefully. "Why did you have to find those fucking letters?!"

"You killed the man who raised me after my own father died," Grant continued, tears in his eyes. "And my grandfather died thinking I had forgotten him. I hate you, you fucking bitch."

Jenna raised the gun and pulled the hammer back on the revolver. It clicked loudly into place. "You don't mean that, Grant!" she yelled. "Now tell me you love me. Call me Julie and tell me you love me!"

A deep voice resonated from the darkness of the hallway. "Julie... Jenna...either way, you look good for a dead woman."

CHAPTER 53
October 11
8:00 P.M.

J ENNA SPUN and retreated three quick steps into the room. Away from the emerging figure of Silas Kane. She pressed her back against the wall, her gun leveled at the giant. He ducked his head as he passed through the doorway, filling the frame with his mass.

Grant remained still, standing at the desk. The sight of Kane in his black jacket conjured a terrible sense of recognition. The creature in the dream. Face shrouded in black except for its demonic eyes and fanged grin. The man in the doorway replicated the monstrosity. Goosebumps broke out over Grant's body as a wave of fear crashed over him.

Kane was ignoring Grant, staring at the woman holding the shaking gun. "Now why don't you tell me what the hell is going on here, Jenna," his gravelly voice rumbled.

For all her bravado about controlling men and being able to handle Kane, Grant watched the woman huddled against the wall seem to lose all her resolve as she was stared down by the killer in the doorway.

"Hey—hey baby," she stammered. "I did it for us. I came out here and got all the money. For us. You and me."

Kane took a step toward the woman, ignoring the gun pointed at his chest. "What are you talking about? And why aren't you dead? I killed you."

"No. Julie. You killed the old Julie. So I came out here and got the money. For you." Her words stuttered.

Kane seemed to consider this. "How much money?" he asked, moving a step closer to her.

"M—millions. More than millions," she responded, a hopeful smile on her face.

Grant observed the exchange in breathless terror. Silas Kane was standing before him. Unarmed and staring down the psychotic bitch who murdered his grandfather. His vision clouded with the images from his nightmares. Kane. Julie. Abe.

What are you going to do now, boy?

The words, spoken by his grandfather in the dream while he was struggling for his life in the coldness of Still Pines Lake reverberated through Grant's head. He could no longer hear the conversation between Kane and Jenna.

What are you going to do now, boy?

The question was no longer a threat. No longer a menacing intonation from a monster beneath the surface of the water. The words Grant now heard were spoken in the gentle tones of his grandfather, Abraham Armstrong, the man he had loved so dearly.

What are you going to do now, boy?

No longer a question at all, it was his answer. His salvation. The world snapped back into clarity as the threads of a plan formed in Grant's mind. He may die, but not without a fight.

"You've got to be kidding me." Grant spoke. Strong and loud.

The pair swung their heads towards the source of the statement. Grant was looking directly at Kane.

"C'mon, Kane. Eric told me you were supposed to be smart," Grant said, speaking to Kane as if the giant was a slow child. "You can't possibly believe what she's shoveling on your head right now. You're like a big, dumb puppet and she's got your strings."

Kane's expression transformed from surprise to anger. No one had ever spoken to him in such a manner.

"You're playing right into her hands," Grant continued. "She gets the money. You kill everyone on the island so there's no one left to question her identity. Then she kills you. It's the perfect crime. And poor 'Julie' there gets to live out her life sipping umbrella drinks on a beach. I can't believe you could be so blind. There's got to be a brain up there somewhere, isn't there?"

Kane's face had turned a deep shade of crimson. He took a step toward the skinny guy about to die, then stopped. It made sense. He glanced toward the blonde girl. The barrel of the pistol was no longer shaking.

The game was up, and Jenna apparently knew it. Kane lashed out with his fist just as her finger squeezed the trigger. His blow hit the gun in the same instant the hammer struck the cartridge, the bullet missing Kane and burrowing into the wall beside the door. The weapon flew from Jenna's hands and landed in the hallway as Kane's other fist flew at her face between her outstretched arms.

The lightning-quick blow struck her in the nose and sent her flying backward, the back of her head smacking the wall with a gut-wrenching crunch before she crumpled to the floor.

Grant's sprang into action, bolting toward the bedroom window. He drove himself forward with his arms shielding his face, smashing through the glass and into the chaos of the storm. Shards of glass imbedded into his forearms. His shoulder landed on the roof of the porch, and Grant rolled until he fell once more—unwilling to pause for even a moment with Kane behind him.

He thudded onto the wet ground, landing on his side. Pain flared in his ribs and hip, but as he scrambled to his feet, he could tell no bones were broken. He spun to get his bearings—swimming pool and tennis court to his right, garage and driveway to his left—then bolted toward the tree line, running at a dead sprint for the safety of the woods.

Kane raced to the broken window in time to see the skinny man who must have been Abraham Armstrong's grandson roll off the roof of the porch. Grant Armstrong. The driving rain from the furious storm poured through the open window. Kane considered going into the hallway for the gun, but there was no time. Besides, after the way Grant had spoken to him, Kane relished the thought of killing him with his bare hands.

He kicked out the remaining shards of broken glass and squeezed his mass through the window frame. Stepping onto the slick porch roof, he saw Grant racing toward the trees.

"Oh, no you don't," Kane said.

Kane leapt from the porch, landing on both feet, knees bending as he hit the grassy earth. He stood in time to see the fading back of Grant Armstrong disappear into the darkness of the trees.

"You are so fucking dead," Kane murmured as he bolted after the fleeing man.

Grant ran like a man possessed, stinging rain biting into his skin. He ducked and weaved through the branches as they whipped past his face. The trail was overgrown, and he wished that he had paid more attention to its details the previous day.

Still, he knew the island better than anyone else. He may have been away for a while, but this was his home. And these were his woods. And he was going to make this work.

All he needed was for the rain to continue. And for the darkness to do its part.

Once out of the range of the floodlights, Grant couldn't see five feet in front of him through the driving storm.

It was perfect.

Kane crashed through the trees as wet branches slapped his cheeks and shoulders. A steady stream of curses poured from his mouth as he sprinted through the underbrush.

He couldn't see a fucking thing, but he knew that Grant Armstrong was ahead. And he was going to kill him. If he couldn't get the old man who hired the bounty hunter, then he sure as hell was going to make his grandson suffer for his deeds.

A large branch smacked Kane in the forehead and the sharp needles punctured his skin. Pouring rain washed the blood from the wound as he ran.

Oh, he was going to make this guy bleed until he begged to die.

"Run all you want, Armstrong. You're a dead man!" Kane screamed.

Grant burst from the trees into the clearing. Through the darkness and rain, he could barely see his hand in front of his face. He was purely dependent upon his familiarity with his surroundings.

Amidst the pounding sounds of the storm, he heard Kane's murderous yell. He was close.

Grant had been sprinting as fast as he could, but he knew that Kane's height gave the monster a longer stride. And he was faster than Grant had expected.

Please God, he thought, *let this work.*

Kane increased his pace, pushing his legs as hard as he could, reveling in the thrill of the chase. He was an animal now. A predator. And he could smell the kill.

They had entered a clearing. And without the trees acting as annoying obstacles, he knew he was gaining on his prey.

Movement.

Armstrong was just ahead of him. Another few steps and it would all be over.

Grant pounded his feet against the grass, thighs screaming in exhaustion even as compensating adrenaline burst through his veins.

Another few steps and it would all be over.

He prayed once more. No lightning. Just wait five seconds. Don't let him see.

Grant took another five steps.

He could hear Kane's heavy breathing.

Five more steps.

He was certain he could feel Kane's hot breath as the killer was reaching out to grab him by the back of the shirt and drag him into the grass for the kill.

Five more steps.

A flash of recognition of his surroundings.

Two more steps.

Fingertips scraped against Grant's shirt between his shoulder blades.

One more step.

JUMP!

Kane reached out his hand. Almost there. Another inch and it would all be over.

His fingers brushed against his prey's back.

Armstrong leaped into the air.

Kane uttered a confused grunt as, unable to stop his forward momentum, he stepped into nothingness.

The figure in front of him seemed to be flying away even as Kane fell forward, arms reaching for purchase, just missing the back of the shirt clinging to Grant's floating body.

The icy cold water startled Kane as he broke the surface of the lake and submerged into the frigid depths. His senses exploded in shock as he fought for the surface.

The rope hanging from the old oak tree held fast as Grant swung suspended above the lake, hearing the splash of Kane's entry into the churning water a few feet below just as he reached the pinnacle of the pendulum's swing.

As the rope returned toward the land, Grant risked a look down and saw Kane struggling in the freezing water. The rope was almost over the shore when Grant leapt away and landed roughly on the ground beside the tree.

Kane broke the surface of the lake and took a deep breath, gagging against the water he had taken in through his nose and into his sinuses.

He treaded water as he got his bearings in the darkness. The large drops of rain splashed into the choppy lake all around him, causing smaller drops of backsplash to strike his face.

He discerned the shore through the gloom and swam toward it. Armstrong was going to suffer. Oh, the bounty hunter had it easy compared to what Kane planned for Armstrong.

The thought made Kane smile as he reached the steep shore line. The three foot bank rose from the lake at a ninety degree angle. Unable to get a foothold, Kane reached one hand up to search for some form of purchase.

He grasped a thick root protruding from the dark embankment. That would do.

He pulled himself up with one arm and swung his other hand onto the shore, gripping a solid clump of grass. The pained smile remained on his lips, etched into place as a glorious reminder of the agony he was going to submit Grant Armstrong to once he got out of the lake.

He released the root and swung his other hand to the edge of the bank, finding a similar purchase. Kane hoisted himself up onto the grass, his legs dangling beneath him as his upper torso straightened, supported by his powerful arms.

A wave of brilliant white pain exploded in his head. He couldn't see through the blinding light brought forth by the blow. Willing himself not to fall back into the lake, Kane forced his vision to clear through the pain and locate the cause.

Grant's wrist erupted in agony. Tendrils of flaming pain sprang up his arm from the pressure on his injury.

Fighting through the fiery ache, he grasped the handle of the hickory baseball bat and brought it over his shoulder once more.

After leaping from the rope, he had retrieved the old bat from the wooden box beside the oak tree—the bat he had swung thousands of times in his childhood as Eric pitched the ball—but his first swing had only glanced off the side of Kane's head.

Grant's sprained wrist had buckled at the impact, decreasing the effectiveness of the swing.

It wouldn't happen again.

The rage, the loss, the terror of the past thirty-six hours filled Grant as he steadied the bat next to his ear. This would be the last swing even if it meant breaking his wrist.

Lightning illuminated the sky, revealing Kane's face and his insane grin. The same grin as the creature from Grant's nightmare.

What are you going to do now, boy?

The bat sliced through the air as Grant powered the swing with all his strength. The blunt end of the hickory smashed into Kane's skull with a sickening thud as bone caved into brain.

Grant's wrist flared in searing agony and he released his grip on the bat. It fell to the earth and landed between the giant's outstretched hands.

Kane remained in place for a moment, his head now oddly shaped as the left side of his skull had become concave. His expression was one of confusion.

Then, the killer's legs began to slide into the water as his elbows buckled, no longer supporting the weight of the dead man.

Grant stood on the shore in the raging storm and watched Silas Kane slip into the icy waters of Still Pines Lake, a deep rumble of thunder punctuating his departure from the living.

CHAPTER 54

October 11
8:22 P.M.

GRANT WALKED back through the woods at a slow pace. His legs weighed a thousand pounds each. His right arm was a vessel of throbbing agony.

When he was halfway up the trail toward the house, the rain slowed and the wind died down. The terrible storm was finally ending.

By the time the white glow of the main house's floodlights was visible through the trees, the rain had ceased altogether.

Grant stepped from the tree line in a state of exhaustion. His mind and body were spent. The events of the past hour were still unreal, like strands of some gossamer nightmare.

As he approached the house, a woman's figure appeared from the open garage door. She weaved as she walked.

Mona, Grant thought, and he breathed a sigh of relief.

Then he noticed the pistol clutched in the woman's hand.

Jenna stepped into the illumination of the floodlights and faced Grant. She stopped a few feet away from him. Her once beautiful face was marred by a broken and swollen nose. Blood seeped from one of the nostrils and ran into her mouth. Grant could hear her stifled breathing.

He stayed where he was, too tired to move, ambivalent about what was to happen next.

"Say you didn't mean it, Grant," she spoke in a wet, nasally voice. Her eyes pleading with him.

"No," he responded simply.

She raised the gun and leveled it at his chest. There was no shaking now. She was in complete control.

"Say it, or I swear I'll kill you," she ordered.

"Go ahead. You killed my grandfather. Your actions killed Loraine and Brock. I meant every word."

"No!" she screamed and fresh blood poured from her crushed nasal cavity. "Say you love me, or I'll fucking kill you!" Her eyes were bright with rage. She was going to do it.

Grant dropped to his knees. He was done.

"Then do it. You're not getting anything from me," he replied. He lowered his head and closed his eyes.

He was ready.

The snap of gunfire echoed across the island. Grant flinched. He felt no pain. He opened his eyes and checked his chest. No entry wound.

He looked up at Jenna. Her gun was still pointed at Grant. A black and hollow cavity had replaced her left eye.

She fell forward, her face thudding against the asphalt, the gun clattering to the driveway.

Grant spun to his right. Just inside the tree line, Eric Johnson lay on his stomach. Habanero Pete, the snub-nosed .357, had been removed from his ankle holster and was gripped in his outstretched hand. His legs were stretched behind him, one of them at a terribly unnatural angle. He was covered in mud. His face was scraped and bleeding. Pine needles protruded from his hair.

Grant got to his feet and ran to him, suddenly glad to be alive. He knelt next to Eric as his friend set the gun on the ground and spoke.

"Please tell me I had a good reason for shooting the pretty healthcare worker," he said through clenched teeth.

"You did," Grant said as he assessed his friend, "saving my life."

"I'm going to need something a lot better than that," Eric said and started to laugh. He rolled to his side and clutched his arms to his chest as the laughter turned into a fit of gurgling coughs.

"Take it easy," Grant said as he returned his friend onto his back. "What happened?"

"Kane." Eric's eyes grew wide and his hand moved to retrieve his gun. "Where's Kane?"

"He's really, really dead." Grant replied. "Just lie back." Eric's shirt was caked in mud. Grant ripped it open, buttons popping into the darkness, to reveal the thick black vest. Three silver slugs lay deeply embedded in the Kevlar.

"You wore a vest," Grant muttered. "Not as dumb as you look."

"Told everyone on my team to wear them," Eric stated through labored breaths. "Said that everyone had to wear a vest if we were going... after..." The words trailed off as Eric sank into unconsciousness.

Grant removed the vest and scanned his friend's bruised torso. The bullets hadn't penetrated the skin but had done their damage nonetheless. A quick check with his hands confirmed at least two broken ribs, and from the wet sounds of Eric's breathing, one of them had punctured a lung.

Grant glanced at his friend's mud-smeared pants and obviously broken leg. Compound fracture. Severe by the angle. His shirt sleeves were torn, his forearms bloody and muddy. How far had his friend crawled to get to the house? What kind of hell had Eric gone through to save his life?

It was Grant's turn now. A cough racked Eric's body. It was accompanied by a fine red mist. A thin trail of blood seeped from the corner of his mouth.

In the cool breeze of the storm's aftermath, Doctor Grant Armstrong went to work saving his friend's life.

EPILOGUE
October 13

THE AUDITORIUM of the church was packed. Mourners stood in the aisles and behind the pews at the back of the building. Some waited respectfully in the foyer as the service honoring Abraham Armstrong was conducted.

When the minister concluded his remarks, he asked if any members of the assembly would like to approach the lectern to say a few words about the deceased.

One at a time, the population of Still Pines made the journey to the microphone. They each told of a particular instance when Abe had helped them out in some way. For some, it was making a mortgage payment when the bank was about to foreclose on their home. For others, it was medical bills paid after the insurance had run out. For more, it was new winter coats for their children when their own limited finances wouldn't allow it. All were tied together by the same theme, the old man had politely requested the incident never be mentioned. "Sometimes bad things happened to good people," he would say. He didn't want a spotlight just for doing the right thing.

Tears filled the eyes of many speakers as they related how meaningful the assistance had been. That they weren't sure how things may have turned out if Abe Armstrong hadn't been there to lend a helpful, silent hand.

Grant and Mona sat on the first pew in front of the podium. They held hands and nodded to the mourners as they stepped down from the microphone, their tale of nobility spoken, and their gratitude expressed. Grant tried to smile at each of them as they passed but the tears made it difficult.

The service lasted more than three hours. There had never been another like it in the history of Still Pines.

◇ ◇ ◇

Grant pushed open the door of the hospital room and stepped inside. Eric looked up from his book and smiled.

"Whatcha reading there?" Grant enquired. "*Horton Hears a Who?*"

"Nothing that deep," Eric replied as he closed the book and set it on the table beside the bed. The large text made the book thick, appearing much longer than Hemmingway's actual tale had been. "I appreciate the loaner. I've never read it before. It's good." He paused. "So how did it go?"

Grant walked in front of the bed and draped his coat over the back of a nearby chair. He was still wearing his suit and tie. "It went well. Incredible, really. The whole town turned out. I had no idea."

"Sounds about right," Eric said, nodding. "Abe was a great man, Grant. You should be proud."

"I am," he replied softly. "So how about you? Feeling any better?"

"Good as new. I went for a crutch-assisted walk down the hall today. Set a speed record for this wing. The nurses want me. It's hard to rest when they keep sneaking into my room."

"Uh-huh, I thought you were supposed to stay in bed at least another couple of days."

Eric grinned. "That's what the chart indicated, but I told them my doctor was a quack. They seemed to agree."

Grant smiled back.

"So what's going to happen with your grandfather's estate?"

"Sheesh, what a mess," Grant began. "I met with Granddad's attorney yesterday. Since he basically established a living trust with an already deceased woman as the primary beneficiary, the assets will revert to the structure Granddad assigned for the secondary beneficiaries."

"I assume the name 'Grant Armstrong' is written on one of those lines. Does that mean my best friend is now a man of wealth, despite his grumblings about hating money?"

"Afraid so. The way things stand now, I'll inherit seventy percent of the estate with Mona getting the rest."

Eric raised his eyebrows. "I don't want to pry, so tell me if it's none of my business, but just how rich are you?"

"Didn't make billionaire status...but pretty close."

Eric let out his breath in a long, slow whistle. "Damn. That's a lot of money. You know that means you're buying dinner from now on. I mean, like, every time. Forever."

Grant smiled. "Deal. No lobster though."

"So what now?" Eric asked. "Back to Africa?"

Grant shook his head. "I don't think so. There's a lot of good I can do right here. I've got the resources to set up a great children's clinic. I guess I need some time to think about it. But I do know this, out on the island, I'm home." He paused. "I don't want to leave again."

A nurse knocked on the door and peeked her head inside. "Mr. Johnson? There's a young woman out here to see you. Patricia O'Brien. She said you asked her to come."

Eric inhaled deeply. "Please tell her I'll see her in just a second."

The nurse nodded and retreated into the hallway, the door closing behind her.

"What's that about?" Grant asked.

"A tough conversation." Eric picked up a small box from the bedside table and clasped it between both hands.

"I'll take off then. You stay in bed. No more showing off. I'll come by tomorrow after Phil and Loraine's funeral." The words sounded odd to Grant. It was an odd time.

Eric was staring at the box. "Okay. Sounds good," he said, sounding as if he were in another world altogether.

Grant grabbed his coat and started to open the door when Eric looked up, returning from whatever place he had been.

"Grant," Eric said as his friend turned to face him. "Good to have you home, buddy."

"Good to be here, buddy." Grant opened the door and walked out, passing a lovely red-haired young woman in the hallway.

◇   ◇   ◇

Eric swallowed hard as he extended his hand, offering the box to the girl.

"He would have wanted you to have this."

Trish O'Brien accepted the box and held it for a moment before opening it. She looked older than Eric remembered. He didn't know if the change was a natural progression into adulthood or if her father's murder had forced maturity upon her.

She lifted the necklace from the box and held it up. The gold cross dangled in front of her face. It shone in the afternoon sunlight that spilled into the windows of the hospital room. Eric had cleaned and polished it himself. No trace of his partner's blood remained.

"Thank you," she said. Her eyes were red but only a single tear escaped as she unclasped the necklace and put it around her neck. She wiped the wetness from her cheek, lifted the cross and rubbed it between her thumb and forefinger before dropping it inside her shirt so it rested against her skin. She couldn't have mirrored her father more exactly if she had been trying.

"So what now?" Eric asked.

"Now? I don't know. Get through it," she sniffed. "I'm a senior. I'm going to finish out my year and leave for college. Somewhere far, far away from here."

"Listen to me carefully, Trish. I owe your father my life. And more. I wouldn't be here right now if it wasn't for him. That makes you my family. Wherever you go. Anytime. Anywhere. If you need me, I'll be there."

It was Eric's turn to wipe his eyes.

"I believe you," Trish replied. "And I'll remember."

She surprised him by sitting on the edge of the bed and leaning into him for a hug. The unexpected embrace hurt his broken ribs. He didn't care. Her face was buried into the pillow over his shoulder, sobs muffled.

He held her for a long time.

◇ ◇ ◇

The barrel-chested man leaned forward over the counter, his sizable mass perched atop the lab stool. The *New York Times* was spread in front of him. He could have read the same thing on the computer to his left, but some things were better the old-fashioned way.

Hiram Kane finished the article and crumpled the newsprint into his fists. You couldn't do that with a computer screen.

The death of his second son had made front page headlines for the third day in a row. It seemed people couldn't get enough of the story as "new and shocking" details emerged daily.

Sheep. All of them.

He turned from the counter and assessed the thin young man standing in front of the whiteboard on the other side of the room. Jonas Kane was nothing like his brothers.

His hand moved quickly, the marker etching a new iteration of the formula onto the board. Jonas stepped back and cocked his head, then used the sleeve of his lab coat to erase the latter part of the equation as he recognized a discrepancy and corrected the ratios.

"We need to restock our Methacrolein supply before we can distill the new batch," Jonas said, his eyes never leaving the whiteboard.

"Of course," Hiram replied. He watched his youngest son work. His personality was so different when they were down here. When Jonas stepped behind the lectern of the church above the basement laboratory—when he became the preacher, the leader of the masses—it was a transformation more impressive than any chemical reaction.

And that was exactly what the plan required. More so now than ever.

The death of Marcus Kane at the desert testing facility in New Mexico had shaken Hiram's plans but not stopped them. The murder of his second son, however, had erased his only insurance. There was no more time to lose. Implementation would be accelerated.

Vengeance wasn't reserved only for those who had killed his offspring. It was imminent for everyone.

Hell was coming. Soon.

Hiram Kane smiled.

◇   ◇   ◇

Grant walked to the water's edge and leaned against the big oak tree. The rope was almost perfectly still, hanging straight down over the water. The lack of breeze on a fall afternoon was a surprise. With the sun shining, it was almost warm. Grant loosened his tie and shed his jacket.

The world had changed, and he wondered how much he had changed with it.

His grandfather. Phil. Loraine. Brock.

Julie.

Authorities had discovered the body of Silas Kane washed ashore at the far side of the lake. The swift current created by the storm had carried him a long way. The demon under the bridge from Grant's nightmare was quite dead, and the bridge itself was gone too for that matter, but they still haunted his dreams.

He knew it would get better in time.

The old bridge had been replaced with a basic structure that allowed access to the island, but Grant's first plan for his home was to build a new covered bridge. Something his grandfather would be proud of.

He glanced at the water below the old oak tree. It was smooth. Barely a ripple.

The nightmares still lingered. His grandfather under the water, later replaced by Julie. Dreamscape coincidence or something else? Something greater? One way or another, the dreams had saved his life, and now they wouldn't leave him.

But he would give it time.

A search for Julie's body had been undertaken with no success. Given the months that had passed since her sister had deposited her into the water combined with the horrific storms, Grant was not given much hope by those responsible for the search.

He took a deep breath and looked above the horizon. The sun would set soon but for now it was brilliant. He closed his eyes and his vision remained white from the brightness.

He lowered his head and opened his eyes. The reflection in the water was barely affected by ripples. Grant saw himself. He saw his father. He saw his grandfather.

What are you going to do now, boy?

He sat on the grass and leaned back against the oak, allowing one dress shoe to dangle above the water.

I'm going to watch the sunset, he thought.

It was the most beautiful he had ever seen.

THE BOOK THAT STARTED IT ALL…

ALSO AVAILABLE FROM DEREK BLOUNT

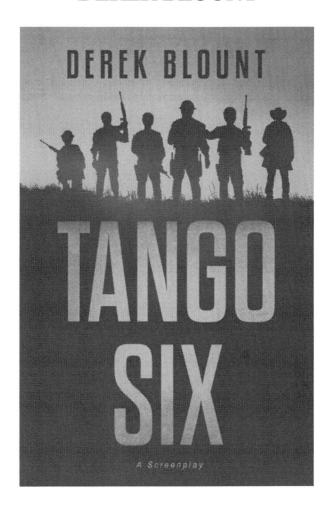

An advancing war. An impossible rescue mission. One chance to save the world.

Brimming with unforgettable characters and imbued with the same brand of adventurous fun as the Indiana Jones film series, *Tango Six* will rivet you with suspense, laughter and fist-pumping action.

A Note from Derek Blount

Thank you for reading *Second Son*. If you haven't yet read *Hostile Takeover*, please give it a try. I think you'll like it. Also, please join our email list at derekblount.com for notifications about future work (such as the gripping conclusion of the *Hostile Takeover Trilogy*...coming soon).

In other "thank you" news...

Thank you to my wife, Bethany, for whom words cannot adequately express my appreciation, my admiration and my love.

Thank you to my boys for filling my heart with an ever-present joy by virtue of their very existence.

Thank you to my parents, whose examples taught me to be a husband, a dad and a man.

Thank you to my sister, Jessica, who means as much to me today as when we were young...and even more.

Thank YOU, dear reader, for investing your time with me. I hope our journeys together are always worth your while. May there be many more.

Made in the USA
Middletown, DE
07 April 2020

88408490R00201